OUT OF THE GEMMIC SEA

BETHANY P SIU

This book is a work of fiction. Names, characters, places, and incidents are a product of the author's imagination or are used fictitiously. Any resemblance to any persons or locales, living or dead, is entirely coincidental.

www.pixelandpen.studio
ISBN 978-1-948807-73-9
Cover Design by Moriah Huang.
Editing by Dani J. Caile

For more information, email www.linebylionpublications.com

LINE BY LION
PUBLICATIONS

For my husband, Elliott. I'm so glad you're not a lizard.

TEMNOBRE
CASTLE
VODASTAD
THE
MOLVAN
SEA
COMMISSION
CRASH SITE
THE KHIRIAN ARCHIPELAGO

VODANIYA, MOLVA
SOSNA VILLAGE
MIROSTAD
MIRONIYA, MOLVA
TOSCA
THE TOSCAN MOUNTAINS
THE GEMMIC SEA
GEM CITY
AGAPETOS
FARI
THE GEMMIC COMMONWEALTH
DRAKIPEIROS

TABLE OF CONTENTS

OUT OF THE GEMMIC SEA

BETHANY P SIU

Chapter One

LUNGS AND HEART

Kaeda

I walked along the rows of lungs. Each pair floated in its own glass box, suspended in a matrix of sustaining magic. In the brilliant white of the lab, they inhaled and exhaled like a row of quiet pink butterflies, waiting to take flight.

Most of them anyway. These lungs had all been grown based on the anatomy of patients with SOWSS, Sudden Onset Weather Sensitivity Syndrome, and they behaved as such. The extra panel at the top of each box allowed my colleagues and I to control what kind of air the lungs breathed. Warm or cold, dry or damp, vacant or infused with magic. The lungs that breathed both magic and weather reacted, filling themselves with fog or rain, or growing ice crystals. In fact, lungs fourteen through seventeen were almost too frozen to function.

I rolled my high-backed healer's chair over to the boxes that housed the frozen lungs. If these lungs belonged to a patient, they would be coughing up ice and blood. I had seen it, and remembering I sat and thought through treatment options, yet again. If I thought long enough, it would come to me. I knew it.

Time passed, marked by farewells from the other healers. "Goodnight, Healer Straton." And "See you on Monday, Kaeda."

I waved in response. They wouldn't be offended that I said nothing. That was the nice thing about working in the lab. When a researcher was focused, no one minded if she didn't pause, smile or wish everyone a good weekend.

It wouldn't be a good weekend for these lungs. Not if I couldn't find a solution.

We're missing something, I said to myself. I'll go over all the research again.

I poured over data and diagrams, hoping for the pieces to somehow fall together and show me the solution, but no epiphany came. I found myself again looking at the lungs, struggling to breathe through the night.

These are patients, I pretended, as I looked down the row. What do they need? They don't need you to unravel the mystery of SOWSS. They just need a treatment that will keep their lungs from…

Doing magic.

This thought hit my mind like a strong breeze, kicking up a storm of questions. How? Why? Could other organs work magic without the instruction of a brain, of a person? Were they already?

But I shook the questions away. If I was right, I didn't need to know the answers. I only needed to make it stop.

I ran to the door and nearly collided with the lab's nighttime security guard, dressed in skirted Gemmic armor, who had doubtless come to tell me how late it was.

"I need a magical restraint. I need to take it apart. I need to make the enchantment accessible to the lung tissue," I said, dashing around the guard to the nearest supply closet. I found a box of single-use magical restraints made of enchanted wire with an adhesive backing. I ran back.

"Healer Straton, it is nearly midnight," the guard's usual line. "The lab will still be here tomorrow."

"Lung seventeen won't last until tomorrow."

In the lab I stripped the enchantment from one of the magical restraints. Now I needed to break it down, attach it to an aerosol that would settle into the lungs, and hopefully restrict the lungs' ability to do whatever they were doing.

I lost track of the time working out how to fragment what was usually a solid enchantment of interlocking magical constellations, but finally had it, a fine mist of enchanted particles, each carrying the restraining instructions. I added these to the air breathed by lungs sixteen and seventeen.

Nothing happened immediately. The lungs had been breathing magic-rich air that simulated a chilly winter's day. Even if the restraint worked, it might take a long time for them to recover. The question was, could I safely heal them using magic? So far, we hadn't been able to. The lungs would sabotage the magic we used, making their condition worse.

I waited a few minutes, letting the aerosol settle, then wove a new tangle of magic, a fine web of bright lines and points, like a cat's cradle decorated by stars. I added this enchantment to the matrix around the lungs to promote warming, healing, and revascularization. As I watched, the lungs breathed a little deeper and some of the deadened patches began to pink up again.

Tears sprang to my eyes. You'll live, I thought, as I looked at lung seventeen. You're going to make it.

I went back to work. Created another version of the aerosol. Made notes on the progress of the lungs I had given it to. Drafted a quick proposal for a clinical trial as well as instructions for creating the aerosol. When I had finished it was late, too late to catch a ferry home, but that was fine. The ascleppa attached to the university had rooms with bunks for the healers on call, and the beds were as comfortable as my bed at home. Maybe even more so.

I hung up my protective lab cape and then headed for the locker room, pausing in the cleansing chamber that sealed off the magical pathology wing from the rest of the research center at the Healer's School of Agapetos. When I stepped out into the locker room the warm tingle of ambient magic rushed around me. I breathed in the magic, happy that my lungs didn't turn it into anything malicious. Then I traded my lab boots for a pair of sandals and wrapped my woolen palla around my shoulders before heading downstairs.

As I walked down the brilliant lights and stark white of the lab gave way to the more usual arching architecture of the Gemmic Commonwealth, the walls decorated by frescoes of fruits and flowers. A brisk coastal breeze blew through the darkness of the columned walkway as I crossed from the research center to the ascleppa, where softer lights were always on. It was quiet tonight, though. The healers in their white togas, the nurses in their tan tunics, and the students in blue, all walked softly and seemed in less of a hurry than usual. No one stopped me to ask for a consultation as I made my way through the pastel halls with their neat coffered ceilings to my favorite on-call room. There I found a bunk and lay in the peaceful darkness, full of the triumph, the relief, the joyful exhaustion of a job well done, and fell happily asleep.

A few hours later a surgeon's call to take a look at an appendix woke me up. The clock said it was still early, not yet dawn. I stared up at the bunk above me and thought over what to do.

I could stay, have breakfast in the ascleppa cafeteria, find someone who needed help with something, or go back to the lab and run more tests.

But my cousin, Aline, would worry. She didn't like it when I stayed at the lab all night, but she would worry if I didn't come home on the weekend.

I should go home. I had some yogurt and a cup of tea in the cafeteria, made sure my mess of curly hair wasn't too wild, and made my way back outside.

Early morning birdsong trilled in the air as I walked across campus. Blue shadows pooled behind the stone columns and relief-decorated porticos as the sun began to rise, bright and blazing. The brilliance pierced my mind with immediate regret. No hazy marine layer clouded the horizon today and that meant...

I stepped out the front gate of the Healer's School. From the height of the university, I could see across the rambling whitewashed walls, blue domes, and tiled steps of Agapetos, all the way to the glimmer of the Gemmic Sea, just beginning to catch the first light of dawn, and across the ocean, my island.

I should be used to it by now, the island's reconstructed shape. It had been what? Five years? But still, my mind recalled the way the island of Fari used to look, the single gentle rise, so different from these contours that looked jagged even at a distance.

My heart felt as jagged as that silhouette. No matter how many magical puzzles I solved, no matter how many lives I saved, I couldn't smooth those edges. I couldn't change what had happened. I couldn't put the island back how it was. I didn't want to go home and face the reminder.

Then I had an idea. I hurried back to the research center locker room to put on my extra wetsuit.

Aline said that I carried my wetsuits around obsessively. I said I liked to be prepared. Prepared for moments such as these when I really needed a swim. When I had made my way down to the harbor I didn't head for the ferry, but instead walked to the fish market. Most of the Farian fishing boats had already unloaded, and the enchanted cases and boxes of ice displayed a dazzling array of silver and orange fishes, glossy squids and lobsters, and heaps of oysters. In a few places grills had been set up, preparing skewers of squids, whole fish, and clams and mussels. Soon the rest of the city would wake up, and Gemmic humans and Cats would begin to stop by, picking up breakfast or lunch, but for now the market was completely Farian, full of wiry, brown-skinned fishermen, their dark hair held back with colorful headbands.

As soon as I walked into the market the fishermen began shouting greetings. They all knew me. I had delivered their babies, set their bones, stayed up all night with their feverish children.

"Good morning, Healer!"

"Hi Kaeda!"

I did my best to figure out who was speaking and to smile and say hello back, though my mind was still full of the broken island, and smiles didn't feel like the appropriate expression. When the exchange of good mornings had calmed down, I said, "Is anyone sailing back to the island soon?"

"I am," answered Skipper Celso. "You need a ride? Have you had breakfast yet? The bonito is just coming off the grill."

Chapter Two

PEARLS

Kaeda

THE Gemmic ferry drivers didn't like it if I jumped off mid-trip. To be fair, it probably wasn't safe with the speed the ferries traveled. But the Farian fishermen? Well, they expressed concern, maybe even disapproval, but most of the island was used by now to me swimming in the ocean alone. And so, about an hour later, I wove a water breathing tangle of magic for my face and stretched some magical flippers out from my toes and leapt off the fishing boat and into the dazzling blue waters.

It wasn't far from the ship's path to my favorite of Fari's reef ranges: Star Bed Reef.

You would never guess, swimming through this paradise, that a few years ago the Gemmic Council had authorized use of experimental submersible explosives. The corals, rebuilt with help from Magisophic Genesis Specialists, looked much the same as they had before, layers of pink shelves billowing out like flattened clouds. Between them, glittering silver hemispheres made up of carnivorous polyps flashed with bursts of light to attract fish. It was these twinkling lights that gave the reef its name, but most of the fish seemed to ignore them. Vibrant blue wrasses and rust-colored blennies darted between golden-fingered anemones, spiky purple urchins, and rusty-orange sea stars, giving the starburst corals wide berth.

The corals would have to wait for a passing school of foreigners to really feast.

None of them, the fish, the corals, the sea stars, knew that they were replacements for the sea life blown to pieces in the war. Looking at them, even I couldn't tell the difference. I could pretend, for a while, that nothing had changed.

I breathed deeply into the mask of water breathing magic I had woven over my face as I soaked up the beauty around me. I would do some pearl hunting, I decided. Farian pearl divers usually worked on the oyster beds, where ink oysters and crusty oysters delivered perfect, round, shiny pearls. Lace clams built larger, oddly shaped pearls, with only the faintest hint of iridescent nacre. Economically, they were worthless. But I thought they were fascinating. I had a collection at home, knotted into strands of macramé hanging on my bedroom wall. I sometimes let my eyes run along those strands, pausing to admire each satiny lump. It was like looking at a big tangle of complex magic, the kind of magic I really liked.

I found a few clams. Small ones. Not notable enough for today's achievement of successfully treating SOWSS. Then, as a small cloud of angelfish flicked away in front of me, I spotted it: a massive lace clam, nestled in a narrow rift of the reef. At thirteen inches across, it was the largest of its kind I had ever seen. It held its fluted shell slightly open as it filtered the water around it, showing its velvety insides. Delighted, I sent a wad of magic down to search for pearls and found three, two of moderate size, and one almost two inches long.

Now I was faced with a dilemma: because of the projections of coral growing into the rift, I could only reach the clam by swimming straight down towards it, leaving my legs extending above me. So far, I had encountered nothing more dangerous than a barbed eel, which had retreated into its hole as soon as I glimpsed it. Head down in the rift I would be blind and vulnerable to approaching danger, and furthermore the clam was so large that I wouldn't be able to pull it up out of the rift. I would have to cut the pearls out of it while wedged, upside down, between the reef faces.

The longer I looked down at the ruffled edges of the huge bivalve the more irresistible the challenge became. I untied my mesh pouch from my belt, tied it around a nearby piece of coral, extended both arms into the rift, lifted my feet above my head, and began to pull myself down.

The rift was about five feet deep, deep enough that I would have to inch most of my body into the crack between the reef faces. A wiry Farian diver might have fit more easily, but I had inherited my father's Gemmic physique – tall and athletic, and with a swimmer's muscles.

Crabs dashed into hiding, a small octopus jetted away, and another barbed eel eyed me suspiciously from its hole. The mask of magic over my nose and mouth shimmered as I breathed more heavily. Finally, the clam was within reach. I crafted a tangle of magic that would cause the clam's adductor muscles to relax, and it drifted open a bit further. Then, with one hand and both thighs holding me steady in the rift, I slipped my other hand into the clam and felt along the creature's mantle for lumps.

There. The massive pearl.

I crafted another sliver of magic, the most precise blade I could manage, incised an opening, extracted the pearl, and healed the wound, all within seconds. I was rewarded by the sight of a pink-orange pearl with the slightest golden sheen, shaped like a warped cross between a starfish and a swimming squid.

On the swim home I thought about what I might do with this pearl. The woven tapestry on my wall really had enough pieces. I had enough pearls sitting on my desk to toy with when my mind needed a break too. I would have liked to weave it into a piece of jewelry but… only Farian women with children wore pearls. Perfect, round pearls of course. Maybe this pearl – but no, people would ask questions.

I made for Fari's largest remaining beach, where there was still a stretch of sand extending into the water. As soon as I had climbed high enough for my head to leave the water, I smelled lunch. Even the Gemmic Peninsula could probably smell it, the aroma of garlic and frying milkfish. I had planned to visit the clinic first, change out of my wetsuit, shower, and then head home, but knowing that my cousin Aline would be frying milkfish with the rest of the island, I headed straight into town.

I answered a fresh barrage of greetings as I made my way up the dirt path lined with grassy date palms, tall willowy coconut palms, and ruffly clumps of ferns. Here and there the path branched off toward a wooden house, most with window boxes full of flowers and yards full of herbs and vegetables. Everywhere someone was coming home with groceries or picking a green onion from their garden or just looking out the kitchen window to see who they could say good afternoon to, in this case, me.

It wasn't as easy as watching the fish, but now at least I had endorphins to buoy me. I said hello to old Mr. Lim, out picking a few loquats. He had lost his wife. She had been one of many that had fallen into the crack on the east side of the island.

Through a kitchen window Lea Tamayo waved at me. She had fallen in the quake, and though she had survived, her unborn child hadn't. In another yard the Leto children played, while their mother hollered for them to come inside and eat. Most ran in, but not Pietra. She had had terrible nightmares since the war, partially about the Khirian invaders and partially about her house collapsing into the sea. Her family used to live in Cova Coroa, where I grew up. Now Cova Coroa was gone, and so were my mother, Pietra's older brother Arjo, and so many others.

The fish, the coral, those the Gemmic Magisophs could fix or replace. But not the people.

I waved and called a hello as Pietra's mother came out of the house to fetch her, then I kept walking.

When I reached Aline's house, I heard the spatter of my cousin's vinegary marinade in the cooking oil and above that, the lively voices of her three sons. Opening the door, I saw them all already sitting down for lunch.

"Not today, the Wizard Archavie cried, and suddenly his Magic, Turus, rose behind him, in the shape of a giant dragon!"

Paco and Bento shrieked with delight as their older brother, Marco, turned the comic book he was reading to show them the picture of the pirate-hunting wizards: Archavie, colorful robes whipping about him, flame-red hair standing in peaks, and Harol, strands of gold glinting in his long ropes of hair, broad white smile brilliant against his dark skin. The ghostly blue shape of a dragon rose behind them.

Aline glanced up from the stove. "At the lab all night again?"

I could hear the tiny sand grain of disapproval in her voice, but I decided to ignore it. "Yes," I answered.

"Swim home again?"

"Yes."

"Well, wash your hands and put a towel on your chair. Better eat something before you go get some rest."

I sat down at the table, taking my place across from ten-year-old Marco who kept reading. "The dragon's fiery breath swept across the deck, sending the pirates leaping into the water! But then, "look," Wizard Harol called out. "the captain has Sheilani!" Sure enough, Captain Kane held the duchess in front of him, his dagger at her throat."

"Use your mind control!" Paco urged the illustrated wizard. "Mind control him!"

"Alright, that's enough violence for one morning," Aline said. "Their father brought home the latest Wizards at Sea book last night," she told me as she set plates of fried milkfish and crisp spinach pastries on the table. "Apparently Qawahn traders have been visiting Gem City and Wizard Archavie is with them, so the stories are very popular right now."

"Archie and Harry are going to rescue Duchess Sheilani!" Bento exclaimed.

"She's Harol's true love," Paco added.

"Her Magic is the counterpart of Harol's Magic." This from older, wiser Marco. He closed the book and tossed it behind him onto the living room sofa.

"Sounds like you've been brushing up on your magical theory," I said, serving spinach pastries onto my plate while Aline cut up fish for the younger boys.

"We're learning about the life cycle of Magics at school. Most Magics have a counterpart, a partner from the dawn of time."

"And how did your magical proficiency exam go?" I asked.

Marco's face fell. I saw him glance wistfully at my forearm where an enchanted ink design displayed the seal of the university, proof of my education. Meanwhile Paco and Bento both burst into fresh chatter. "We can do magic! Look Cousin Kaeda!"

Both twins frowned and I could sense the ambient magic gathering in front of each of them. There was quite a bit of ambient magic on the island today, and it seemed fresher than usual. The magical current from Gem City shifted this way and that from day to day, flowing toward the equator, and usually the bulk of what reached Fari was magical waste, frils and blus. Just like any pollution, frils and blus could cause health problems, especially for sensitive persons, and many families had shielding tents they could put up around their kids' beds on a bad day. Today though we seemed to be right in the middle of the runoff, getting the freshest of the magic that the mainland hadn't used. I should remind Aline to store some. You couldn't work magic without magic to work, and even though I regularly brought magic back with me from the mainland, it didn't hurt to have extra for emergencies.

The magic in front of the twins began tangling itself into knots as they concentrated. I focused too, seeing if I could determine the function of the knots.

"No magic unless it's homework!" Aline exclaimed, and the magic over the table tumbled back into peaceful stillness again. "Now eat! All of you." She fetched a pot of hazelwrack tea as the boys began to eat, and her tone remained sharp as she asked me, "So, did staying out all night solve it?"

Her tone said that I should have been home, participating in family life, eating dinner, and going to sleep at a reasonable hour like everyone else, not hiding in the lab. I wouldn't tell her that I had slept a bit at the hospital.

"Not completely," I answered, "but I did come up with a new treatment that I think will help a lot."

"Are they going to give you another award?" Bento asked.

"Probably not this time, but the treatment will save lives."

The little boy made a face as if they really ought to give me awards for everything, but he said, "I guess that's good."

I helped clean up after breakfast, while Aline sent the boys out to play. "Don't forget to look through your mail," she called to me, as I began to head down the hall to my bedroom. "There's another scroll with the seal of the Gemmic Council."

I'll burn it, I thought, but I said. "I'll take care of it."

"It looked important. Don't forget about it."

"Don't forget to store some magic."

"If you had been home last night, you would know I already have. The cells are full."

When she left, I looked through the pile of mail on the bench by the door and took out the scroll. A heavy parchment, tied with a ribbon, sealed with the owl in a laurel wreath seal of the Gemmic Council. It looked just as official and important as the other two I had received, which were still sitting on the desk in my room. I added this third one to the pile before drawing the magically darkening curtains in my room and curling up in my bed.

But whenever I began to drift to sleep, I remembered the tremors beneath my feet as I stood, a student in a blue tunic, safe and separate from the war, in the garden at the Healer's School. I had felt only ripples of the blasts that had made my island crumble. But those ripples seemed endless. Tears started in my eyes, and my chest tightened. The emotion built… but then crumbled, like a wave that should have crashed but didn't. It remained, a deep, cold, unresolvable swell that left a nauseous feeling in my stomach.

Determined to think about something else, I reached over to my bedside table and felt around for the warped pearl. I held it, feeling its smooth strangeness. It would be the perfect centerpiece of a necklace. So what if only mothers wore pearls? I had a Magisophic degree. I had won three Thavma awards. I had probably saved hundreds of lives and had helped bring many into the world. Wasn't that enough?

Finally, holding the pearl, I fell asleep.

Chapter Three

WAVES

Reef

REEF'S shoal swam around him, a perfectly spaced pattern of pearlescent white bodies against the deep blue of the water. They filled the surrounding ocean with their chorus of heartbeats. The vibrations wove together, a web of safety in the water, with Reef in the center, as they swam back from a successful hunt. Reef let them take their time. Every one of them had a belly full of mackerel, from the highest ranking pointswimmers to the most recent recruits, and they were towing several large tuna back to the archipelago to share with the females watching eggs. The largest tuna was nearly fifteen feet long, as long as the smallest Khirians in Reef's shoal, nose to tail. Quite a catch. The other shoals would be impressed, and Reef was glad. He didn't have any eggs waiting to hatch. He had let another summer pass without fighting for a mate and that meant a lot of puzzled looks from other Khirians, wondering why a shoal leader would not participate in mating season. But, kill by kill, catch by catch, he would shore up his reputation, as he did every year.

It wasn't too difficult. He had an impressive shoal, and for whatever reason, it continued to follow him. And his pointswimmers, in Reef's opinion, were of as high quality as the navarchs. Beach Cliffs, the largest Khirian on the island, Redwater, the most ruthless, Even Keel who never panicked, and Breaking Wave, who put up with Reef and turned his orders into action. Reef knew each of their heartbeats, each of their swimming patterns, and sensing them out in their positions in the shoal's swimming formation, he thought the autumn would be just fine, even without a clutch of eggs.

At last Reef felt the shift in the water as the ocean currents branched to skirt around the Khirian islands. The pull of the tides on the sandy shores promised rest, and sun, and though he hadn't signaled an increase in speed the tails of the swimmers in Reef's shoal swished a little faster.

As they neared home, Reef sensed the swimming pattern of another Khirian coming toward them. The messenger chirped the short command to surface. Reef repeated it and swam upward and the shoal broke the surface together, a flotilla of gleaming white scales beneath the bright morning sun.

"The navarch calls for a meeting in Echo Cove," the messenger said in a grumbly roar.

Reef coughed an acknowledgement. "We will swim there now."

The messenger nodded and dove back into the sea.

"What do you think that's about?" Even Keel asked, drifting up from the back. Redwater and Beach Cliffs bobbled up beside them too, Beach Cliffs smooth and iridescent, Redwater marked all over with brown scars.

"Probably wants to show off his new eggs," Breaking Wave commented, from ahead, the ridge on the top of his sharp nose flashing in the sun. "Come on, we shouldn't keep him waiting."

Most of the Khirian shoals had already gathered in the stone bowl of Echo Cove on the north side of the biggest island.

The males of the shoals at least. Most females were guarding eggs or waiting to lay them. In Reef's shoal Beach Cliffs was the only female in attendance.

Reef's shoal surfaced near their usual spot on the western shore and found places to sit on the rock.

The navarch's shoal covered much of the central island of the cove, turning it to a mountain of brilliant white scales and swishing tails. The navarch, Silent Strike, sat at the top, with his pointswimmers around him. Others circled the island, drifting in the clear blue waters. When Reef's shoal had all left the water, Voice of Thunder, the navarch's left-flank pointswimmer, spoke.

"The navarch has heard news that the humans are gathering in Gem City. They are planning to send a group to Molva."

No reaction from the gathered Khirians. A group of Gems going to Molva? So what?

"The navarch wishes to send a Khirian representative to Molva with them."

Scattered grumbles and exclamations, but Reef sat silently and his shoal took his cue and did the same. He wouldn't want the navarch to think that anyone disagreed with him, shocking as the statement might be.

"The navarch will not change his mind," Voice of Thunder boomed. "The navarch will take four shoals with him to the Gemmic Commonwealth. Shoal leaders who wish to present their shoals for consideration may speak to the navarch's pointswimmers. You all may go."

"What do you think of that?" Wave asked Reef, as the other shoals began to disperse.

Reef rumbled. He didn't know what to think.

"I can tell the navarch that we want to stay on the archipelago. Someone will need to guard this season's clutches."

Reef thought he just barely glanced at Beach Cliffs. She was so huge that it was hard to tell when she was gravid, but at this time of year she probably was. Reef also knew that Wave and Redwater each had a clutch waiting to hatch. But if what the navarch said was true… eggs came every year, but this had never happened before.

"No," Reef said, "tell him we want to go. Take your section with you. We'll meet you back at Mossrush."

Wave rumbled, polite, but uncertain. "You're the leader," he said, and he and his group of Khirians walked off to speak to the navarch's pointswimmers.

The rest of Reef's shoal traipsed across the island, doing their best to avoid the nests where protective females curled around mounds of sand and palm fronds covering eggs. They returned to Mossrush, a clearing surrounding a waterfall where cascades of water and cascades of moss tumbled down into a small pool.

The shoal spread out, relaxing in the familiarity of their usual home base, taking turns laying in the sun. Reef was drowsing and basking when Wave returned.

"We're in," he said to Reef, sitting down on the moss at the pool's edge.

"That easy?" Reef asked.

"You have a reputation for not losing your temper. The navarch doesn't want to start a fight. At least, not without meaning to."

Reef shut his eyes, enjoying the noon sunbeams and also basking in Wave's report of the navarch's good opinion. But Wave did not stretch out to bask, nor walk off to swim. Instead, he sat, frowning, until Reef opened his eyes again. "You have something else to say?"

"I don't think it's a good idea," the pointswimmer said, in a voice too low for the others to hear.

"What?"

"Going to the humans. It could start another war."

Reef rumbled his agreement. It could.

Wave looked over at him. "I know you. You don't want to fight another war."

No. Reef didn't. The war was like a bad dream. Sometimes it *was* a bad dream, lurking in the shadows of the islands, creeping up on him when he slept. The marches across Molva, leaving trails of corpses. The bloody rivers and the gore-strewn meadows. The taste and smell and sound of mammals everywhere, most of them suffering in one way or another. And most of all, the rage.

"You don't just want the honor of accompanying the navarch," Wave guessed, disbelief raising his voice, "you actually want to go to Molva."

Reef whispered in response, "The Khirian who goes with the humans, he will start a war if he doesn't keep his temper."

Wave thoughts about this, rumbled again, and lay down onto the moss. "If someone must go, you should go. You're probably the only one who could put up with them."

"Even Keel could."

"Even Keel would forget himself and eat their pets."

They both laughed, and when they stopped laughing Wave said, "We'll make it happen. Or maybe the navarch will change his mind and it will come to nothing."

Reef thought Wave probably dozed off after that, sleeping in the sun, full from their hunt. Reef didn't sleep. He watched the clouds pass and the birds fly overhead through the gap in the trees above. When he thought of Molva, he felt a tiny dread in the pit of his stomach. But when he thought of his people, here on the island…

Already rival shoals and vengeful past mates had stolen and broken many eggs, leaving trails of slime through the forest before they hurled whatever had begun to grow in the eggs into the Chasm. Fights followed. Sometimes Khirians died. And it didn't end when the remaining eggs hatched. Wanted hatchlings had to be guarded until they could fight for themselves, and unwanted hatchlings would be culled, either quickly slain, or thrown alive into the Chasm to die, broken, in the pit.

When Reef considered fighting for a mate, he only had to remember this, and his resolve returned. Not only that, but this season five males had died fighting over females and one female had strained so long trying to lay her first clutch that her mate, afraid the eggs wouldn't make it out, had simply cut her open and pulled them out himself, while she bled to death.

Reef wouldn't have let it happen. If they had been in his shoal, he would have stopped it. But they weren't, and picking a fight was too dangerous.

But Reef had seen human healers bring their patients back from what Reef thought were mortal injuries, and he had seen humans die to protect their offspring, men die to protect their pregnant women, and the strong die to protect the weak.

He didn't understand why they did it, or why humans respected that behavior, but part of Reef wanted that for his people too.

He watched the clouds and the birds until the sun was too high overhead to look at the sky any longer. Then, brimming with warmth, he finally shut his eyes.

Chapter Four

THE WIZARD ARCHAVIE

Kaeda

ALINE woke me with her insistent knocking. "Kaeda. Kaeda, wake up," she whisper-shouted through my door.

"Coming." I closed my fist, making sure I hadn't lost the pearl, then set it on my bedside table again before staggering to my door and pulling it open. "Is someone hurt? Is Mirikit having her baby?"

"Wizard Archavie and Speaker Matapang are here."

Visitors? This did not seem like a legitimate reason to wake me. "If there's not a medical emergency—"

My cousin spoke sternly and deliberately. "Wizard Archavie Johnsbee and Speaker Diwata Matapang are here to see you."

"Archavie from the book?"

"Yes." She stepped into my room, mostly closed the door behind her and whispered, "When I came back from the market, I found a pirate hunting wizard, and the Farian representative from the Gemmic Council waiting on my front step. Would you like to tell me why?"

I brushed back the curls that had fallen into my face and glanced over at my desk where the council's scrolls sat, still sealed.

"Kaeda! You didn't open them?!"

"The Gemmic Council—" I began, but Aline interrupted.

"You hate them, I know, but you're a citizen of the Commonwealth. You can't just ignore official correspondence from the government!" Aline brought the scrolls over and thrust them into my hands, and then said. "I'm going to go and offer our guests some refreshment. Wash your face and come out there and act like an adult."

And then she left.

I looked down at the scrolls, rage swelling in my chest. Not because of her comment. I knew that on Fari no one would see me as an adult until I had babies. But because the Gemmic Council dared to send me mail. What letter from the council had ordered the navy to pull back and leave Fari to the Khirians? What official correspondence had said, yes, experimental explosives seem like a good way to end the war?

I broke the seal and tore open the scroll.

To: Healer Kaeda Callista Straton, Magisoph, MThx

On the recommendation of Diwata Matapang, Speaker for the Island of Fari, The Gemmic Council would like to invite you to join the Molvan Magical Crisis Commission.

I almost quit reading there, but something in the next couple of lines caught my eye:

At the request of the Duchess of Temnobre, this specialized group will travel to the Vodaniya region of Molva to determine the cause of Molva's magical drought and other Unknown Magical Phenomena.

Magical drought. Unknown Magical Phenomena. The words tickled my mind like the smell of backlava in the oven or the sparkle of sunlight on the sea. Suddenly I felt hungry, but in my heart rather than my stomach.

"I'm sure Kaeda will be out any minute," I heard Aline say.

But the Gemmic Council? I wouldn't do a thing for them.

I felt a mental scoffing, as clearly as if it had been audible, and I jumped. The scoff had not been my own, and I noticed now a tiny magical presence hovering in my mind.

Turus, I told you to leave the healer alone! A psychic voice exclaimed. The voice addressed me next. *My apologies. My Magic is a terrible eavesdropper.*

In a rush I remembered that according to Marco's books, the Wizard Archavie could read minds.

I washed my face as quickly as I could, pulled on a fresh tunic and stola, and stormed out of my room and down the hall. The Wizard rose from the sofa as I walked into the room. He was as tall and colorfully dressed as his published persona. The massive invisible presence of his magical companion, Turus, filled the room.

"If you're going to spy on my mind, then get out." I demanded.

"Kaeda!" Aline exclaimed.

Beside the wizard sat Diwata Matapang, a petite, brown-skinned lady with blunt salt-and-pepper bangs, wrapped in a white stola with a silver clasp on each shoulder, the crest of the Gemmic Council on one, and the pre-war shape of our island on the other.

I put a hand on my chest and dipped my head to her. "I'm sorry Speaker. I read the letter, but I won't have anything to do with the Gemmic Council."

Matapang glanced up at Archavie and said, "I suppose we'll just tell the council to find someone else to study the curse of ursinthropy."

"Yes," the wizard agreed, a smile making his blue eyes extra sparkly and his beard extra pointy as he sank back onto the sofa and crossed one leg over the other. "Healer Straton probably isn't interested in a magical affliction that turns people into bears."

"Tales of shape-changing creatures are just legends," I said.

It was a standard piece of magical knowledge. Only archons, whose physical bodies had fully fused with magic, could change shape at will. But as usual, Aline shook her head. "Farians used to swim in the sea in the shape of sea lions," she said, depositing a plate of coconut cookies on the coffee table in front of her guests.

"Ah yes, the Otariidae," Archavie replied.

I rolled my eyes, both because I knew he must have snatched this word from one of our minds, and because it was ridiculous. "Legends," I reiterated.

"Kaeda has been to university, and thinks she knows everything," Aline commented, this time adding a pot of tea to the table.

"I suppose we shouldn't even bring up the disappearing magic then," Matapang said, accepting a cup of tea and taking a slow sip.

I couldn't help myself. "Magic doesn't disappear. It's one of the foundational principles of magical theory."

"Maybe you can tell Lady Georgina Batbayar where the magic has gone then," Archavie added. His eyes caught mine. They weren't real, I thought. No human being had eyes naturally that vivid. As he stared at me with those too-blue eyes he added, "The Crisis Commission is her request, not just a plan of the council."

He emphasized the last phrase, and my curiosity was so piqued that I couldn't even feel angry that I knew he was reading my mind.

I sat down on one of the wicker chairs opposite the sofa. "Fine," I said. "Tell me what's going on."

Archavie and Matapang refreshed me on recent Molvan history. Some thirty years ago Molva had experienced a magical cascade of unknown cause. Prior to that, the Molvan Archon, Bogdan, had gone missing. Without the archon, of course, the supply of magic decreased, but after the cascade the magic began vanishing.

"Then the Khirians invaded, and since the war Molva has been experiencing what the duchess describes as magic-destroying storms, amongst other things," Archavie concluded. "Not to mention increasing trouble with werecreatures."

"Trouble?" Aline asked. "Farians think of the ability to change shape as a gift, a gift that Fari somehow lost."

"Molva used to think of ursinthropes that way too," Archavie said, "as a special creation of the archon. But now that special creation is attacking people."

I sat, chin in my hand, deep in thought. Of course, I would have no real idea of what was going on in Molva until I was able to study it.

But would I study it? The last time I had left home to study magic I had come back to find that home shaken to pieces. The skills I had intended to use for healing were turned to the identification of crushed bodies.

But before I could say anything Aline came over to pick up the empty teacups and said, "She'll go."

"That's my decision," I said.

"You've made it. I can see it in your eyes. I'm just saying it before you talk yourself out of it. If you don't go, you'll just walk around in a haze of frustrated obsession."

Her voice had taken on a snappish tone towards the end, and I looked up. Was that how I appeared to her? A person in a haze of frustrated obsession?

Aline added more gently, "You think the Gemmic Commonwealth should have gotten involved in the war sooner, stopped it from spreading, protected Fari. What if this magical drought spreads? What if you could have stopped it? Do you want to be like them, ignoring the plight of strangers?"

While my fists clenched and my stomach tied itself in knots of sadness Aline repeated, "She'll go."

"Who else is on this Commission?" I asked.

Archavie's foot had been bouncing jauntily in its shiny leather boot as if he were unaware of the emotional weight of our conversation. Now it bounced a little more vigorously as he glanced at Speaker Matapang. She glanced back.

"I assume if I've been ignoring my mail that the rest of the commission has already been selected," I said.

"Yes, well, there's me of course," Archavie said, with the tone of one clearly putting off bad news. "And Miss… what was it?"

"Gamalielle Aisop," Matapang said, "a Cat and an expert in stealth magic."

"Since whatever the problem is, it seems to be invisible," Archavie added with an extra dash of smile.

I nodded and waited. An "and" lingered in the air waiting to be said and clearly the two of them didn't want me to know what was on the other side of it.

"And a Gemmic weapons expert," Matapang said suddenly, as if she'd found the perfect words to cover whatever was so hard to say.

But my mouth had gone dry. I had to know, was it bad, or was it worse? "Who?"

Speaker Matapang took a deep breath and looked genuinely apologetic as she said, "General Lysander Straton."

Chapter Five
FAMILY
Kaeda

"NO, no, no."

"He's your father Kaeda."

"Exactly."

This exchange between Aline and I took place in my room, where I had been pacing since Speaker Matapang made her announcement. Matapang had graciously offered to give Archavie a tour of the island, and the two of them had left. A relief I'm sure to Aline, since she couldn't stop me from behaving in what she considered a very childish manner.

"You can't avoid him forever," she said from my desk chair, where she sat calmly, watching my pacing.

"I can."

"Well, you shouldn't."

"He abandoned us!"

"Your family lost a child. I can't imagine the pain."

My brother Gil's death was at the top of the list of things I didn't think about, closely followed by the time right after it, when my parents had started fighting, and then stopped fighting, and then stopped talking altogether.

"A child, and then a father." My voice shook with rage, and yet my brain already seemed to have moved on. There was no point being angry. Whatever I felt, I had to make a decision.

"He was not Farian. There was no comfort for him here," Aline said. The gentleness in her voice invited me to cry, but I was done feeling, and done pacing. I stopped, hands on my hips, and thought. It was a simple choice: would I let my father's presence keep me from doing the good I could do?

When Matapang and Archavie returned from their tour, I told them I would join the Commission.

"Splendid!" Archavie flourished the bouquet of picked flowers he was holding, nearly smacking the blooms against the front door. He laughed at his near miss and then added, "There is a bright side to all of this. The Gemmic Council has a cursed body in their morgue. Any magic that comes near it vanishes. It's been thoroughly autopsied, and no one can figure out why. That's something to look forward to, isn't it?"

I kept the promise of the cursed corpse in mind while I packed. Most of the Commission, I gathered, had read their mail and was already at the council building, preparing to leave in a week or so. I was late. Very late.

Wizard Archavie meanwhile, disrupted the peace of the house by entertaining Aline's sons. He turned their comic books into colorful birds. Soon the books were zooming around the house, and the boys zooming around after them, whooping with delight.

I did my best to ignore it all. I already felt embarrassed that Archavie had witnessed so much tension, anger, and internal drama, not to mention my judgment of him in his gold-trimmed red and purple robes as a rather silly pirate-hunting celebrity.

"Archavie says he'll stay for the party," Bento cried out as he opened the door to my room without knocking.

"Party?" I asked, but Bento had already run off to play with Archavie, leaving my door slowly drifting open. I walked over to close it but first called down the hall "There's a party?"

"You made a medical advancement," Aline answered from the kitchen, where I could see her punching down risen dough. "And the Gemmic Council has recruited you for an important mission. Of course there's a party."

Mysterious cursed corpse, I reminded myself. Fancy lab. Hours of study. Worth a party.

"Speaking of the party," Archavie said, while the comics fluttered back to him and settled into his hands in the shape of books. "I think your mother would like you to do some homework before it begins."

A chorus of groans.

"And wash up," Aline added.

Reluctantly the boys traipsed off to their rooms. Marco was the last to leave. As he went to collect his comic books from Archavie, the wizard motioned him closer and whispered something in his ear. A relieved smile, the biggest smile I had seen him wear in a long time, spread across the boy's face. He glanced up at Archavie, who winked at him, and then trotted off after his brothers.

Watching them go, Archavie caught my eye. "I think my fair hostess would appreciate some help taking things to the square for the festivities. If you don't mind showing me the way."

"It's just down the street," I said. To myself I added, and I know you've already had a tour. Of course, the wizard probably heard that as well.

"Kaeda, help me out and show our guest around," Aline ordered. "There's a basket of pears and a basket of figs. You can each carry one."

Archavie picked up the pears and I begrudgingly gathered up the figs, and the two of us stepped out the door and into the breezy coastal evening. The palm trees formed a rustling mélange of golden highlights and navy shadows as the sun set, and the wind carried the scent of the ocean.

Afraid the wizard would offer some comment on my recurring swells of angst, I tried to think of a way to take control of the conversation. Archavie beat me to it. "Look, I think we got off on the wrong foot, what with Turus spying on your mind and all."

"Yes," I agreed.

"I just want to explain that it's awfully difficult to not hear people's thoughts, especially when they're near me, and especially if they have anything to do with me."

To me it sounded like an excuse.

"Maybe, but can you imagine always hearing voices or smelling smells and going through your whole life pretending you don't just so other people won't be put off?"

"That would be frustrating," I acknowledged, "but what's the alternative? Let you read my mind and give up my privacy?" He had probably seen my plans to pick up a piece of protective headwear from the university on our way to Gem City.

The wizard took a deep breath and slowed his pace. I followed suit, guessing he wanted to talk more. The dirt of the path scuffed beneath our feet as he went on. "If I didn't want you to know that I was reading your mind, you wouldn't. Or you would forget as soon as you thought of it, or you would find yourself surprisingly unbothered by it."

Well now I felt bothered. And disturbed. And threatened.

"I'm sorry." The wizard stopped and turned toward me. I stopped to face him too. Archavie held the basket of pears before himself like an earnest offering, and his probably artificial blue eyes shone as he looked at me. "I don't mean to come across that way, I'm just trying to explain how it is."

"Is that what you're doing to all of them?" I asked, gesturing about to the ferns and palms, behind which other stretches of neighborhood extended. Was he dampening the concern of my community? Just so they would welcome him instead of being afraid of him?

"I can see that I've gone about this the wrong way," Archavie said quickly, "but your altruistic concern for the wellbeing and respectful treatment of others is exactly the reason I want to be your friend. I apologize for being so bad at it. I don't have very many friends to practice with and I'm sure you can imagine why."

Of course I could, once he pointed me in that direction. Suddenly, I felt sorry for him, and understood the almost childlike way he was asking me to be his friend, as if friendship was something we could just decide on. That, of course, made me want to be his friend. But another rational part of me recognized the feeling of wanting to help and told me to take a step back.

"I'll have to think about it," I said.

"Think all you want," Archavie replied, cheerful once more as he hugged the pears to himself.

As we resumed our walk I asked the question that had been growing in my mind. "Why does the council want you?"

I realized too late that my phrasing was as tactless as Archavie's request for friendship, but the wizard didn't seem to mind. In fact, he burst into laughter so boisterous that he had to brush tears from his eyes before answering. "They don't want me! I invited myself! Turus and I want to go to Molva. We have been traveling the Sphere of Verrum looking for Turus's counterpart. He won't let me marry anyone but his counterpart's wizard, you see. We've searched Marklund, which is my homeland; the Queendom of Qawah, which is Harol's homeland; and now the Gemmic Commonwealth with no success. Molva is next on the list!"

He really is lonely, I thought, and Archavie did not contradict me.

We had reached the village square where several of my neighbors busied themselves setting out tables and filling them with flatbreads, fruitcakes, whole roasted fishes, dishes of hummus, bowls of olives, trays of grilled oysters, and baskets piled high with kumquats, grapes, pomegranates, tangerines, and persimmons.

Before we added our pears to the feast, I had one more question. "What did you say to Marco? He seemed very happy about it."

"Ah," the wizard paused, whether to think or just to add drama I couldn't be sure. "That depends."

"Depends? On what?"

"On whether we're going to be friends."

By the next morning I had decided I might as well give friendship with the wizard a try. I had glanced through Marco's library of Wizards at Sea comics and determined Archavie to be flamboyant and conceited, but harmless. That, combined with the way he made a fool of himself trying to play ukulele for the children at the party, and then delighted everyone by filling the trees with glowing butterflies, inclined me to give him a chance.

The shiny Gemmic schooner that had brought Archavie and Speaker Matapang to the island was waiting for us at the northern harbor. The three of us boarded the vessel and then waved goodbye to the Farians gathered to send us off as the ship set sail. When the island had become a distant tuft of green and Matapang had taken a seat out of the wind, I moved a little closer to Archavie and said, "Okay."

"Okay?"

"Okay, I accept your overture of friendship."

The wizard clapped his hands and leapt with excitement. I felt my cheeks turning pink and almost changed my mind. I couldn't decide whether to think of him as manipulatively endearing or honestly ridiculous.

"A bit of both," he confessed.

"However, I have terms," I said.

"Name them."

"Turus is quite a large Magic. I'm guessing he could control a mind if he wanted to, or search through it for memories."

"Oh yes. He's quite good at those things."

"Well then, I understand if you can't help but hear my thoughts, but don't allow Turus to search my mind or manipulate my thoughts, and don't share my thoughts with anyone else."

The wizard held out a hand. I regarded it with confusion.

"Oh, you shake it," he explained. "It's something Marks do when we're sealing a deal. Of course, the wildmen may also spit in their palms or cut their hands first, but we're civilized townies, you and I, not blue-painted savages."

He continued to proffer the hand as I processed this. When, at last, I extended my own hand in return Archavie wrapped it in a chilly grip and pumped it up and down a few times. "I'm thrilled," he told me. "Does this mean I can reply to your thoughts now?"

"You might as well reply to my thoughts, but if you do it often, I will become annoyed."

The wizard nodded his understanding, and I thought it might be nice for someone to know what was on my mind, and perhaps even to understand, without me having to go to great lengths to explain things to them.

"Speaking of that," Archavie said, "just let me know if you want to talk about your father."

"I don't."

"In my experience people manage situations better if they've processed their feelings ahead of time. Believe me, when Harol was pining for a lady or stewing vengeance his judgment was never as sound."

I've lived with the grief for a long time, I thought back, knowing he would observe the memory that came to mind. The last time I had seen my father had been at the mass funeral on Fari. He had cried then, and I had been furious, feeling that he shouldn't have been allowed to cry for my mother or for the island when he hadn't lived with either of them for twelve years. But as usual the anger had fizzled out and not interfered with my life. When I told him I didn't want to talk to him, I didn't even feel angry anymore, just sure. I didn't need him, so what was the point in subjecting myself to the emotional upheaval of interacting with him?

Perhaps it had been long enough now that when I saw my father the associated feelings would be mere froth on the shoreline. I had climbed the cliffs. I had a steady perch. I could stay dry. It would be fine.

I realized that the trail of my thought had stretched longer than I anticipated and that Archavie was watching me with wide eyes.

"What?"

"I've just never encountered someone with quite that… method of emotional management," the wizard said, blinking. "It's quite fascinating."

I don't want to be fascinating, I thought. I want to make complete sense. "Let's talk about something else," I said.

"Of course, of course. But if you don't mind me asking, how did a Gemmic general and a Farian healer end up together?"

A reasonable query. "He was just a soldier when they met. He ended up at the healer's school at Agapetos after a skirmish with the Toscan Cats. My mother had recently graduated and was working there."

Archavie waited like there should be more. There was more, but I didn't want to think about how they had once loved each other. How he had changed his career path so he could remain stationed at Agapetos. How she had married him even though everyone on the island told her it might break the bloodline that kept her family's souls tied to the island. They accepted him in the end, but they didn't seem surprised when he left.

Archavie and I watched the waves for a little while, while I put the memories behind me. Then I remembered that having agreed to terms of friendship, I could repeat my question from the previous day. "Oh, what did you say to Marco?"

I felt a surge of anxiety that did not belong to me. "I was hoping you would forget about that," the wizard said.

"Per our terms of friendship, you can't," I said wryly. I had to admit to myself that I felt pleased to have made him feel something uncomfortable in turn, but I also had a reason for my question. "Normally I'd respect your privacy, but Marco is my little cousin. If you offered to take him on a pirate hunting adventure or something—"

"No, no, nothing like that," Archavie turned and leaned against the rail of the ship with pretended nonchalance. "I told Marco that I can't work a shred of magic either. I could see that he felt sad about having no magical talent."

"You can't craft ambient magic?"

"Nope. Not without Turus. I'm not a magician."

I couldn't quite believe it. I had never met a wizard who was not a magician.

"Marklund doesn't have much free-floating magic, and I know from your current analysis that exposure to fresh ambient magic in the womb helps one develop the aptitude to work it. But I must ask you not to tell anyone."

"Of course," I said. "But if something were to happen to Turus—"

Archavie laughed. "Nothing is going to happen to Turus. Nothing ever does."

Chapter Six

VANISHING

Kaeda

WE said nothing more on the topic. While we sailed up the western coast of the Gemmic Peninsula I worked on knotting my giant pearl into a necklace of tea-stained cotton twine. From time to time, I glanced up at the dusty golden beaches and cliffs of olive groves, towering palms, and landscaped parks that blanketed the coast in green all the way back to the distant Toscan mountains. Between the lush foliage, the coastal cities gleamed white and terra-cotta orange, with stairs, walls, and domes rising in tiers. Occasional golden domes marked structures belonging to the Gemmic Myalo, the order devoted to knowledge and teaching, and the Kyrillan Dunamis, the order specializing in physical and magical martial arts.

I had brought along a button in white mother of pearl, and when the knots of off-white and tea brown fibers had stretched long enough to comfortably sit around my neck I made a loop at one end, attached the button to the other, and fastened the necklace so the huge pearl sat just beneath the nook between my collarbones. I might as well wear it. No one in the Gemmic Commonwealth would assume it meant I was a mother, and the solid lump of the pearl was comforting, a reminder of the beauty and calm always waiting in the ocean.

Towards evening we sailed into the vast crescent-shaped harbor of Ismelinos, the coastal gateway to Gem City, the capitol city-state of the Gemmic Commonwealth. The harbor and city streets streamed with chariots and tall fair-skinned pedestrians, statuesque and swathed in bolts of pastel fabric, with bits of gilded flora twisted into their curly hair. The smaller figures of Gemmic Cats wove their way between or at times floated through the air.

A chariot and driver were waiting for us and expertly navigated the crowded city streets while the locals paused in their errands to look at us. I was used to people's eyes snagging on me when I visited my father's family in Gem City as a child. Besides the Speaker for Fari, my mother, my little brother, and I would be the only Farians for miles. But today they weren't looking at me, or Speaker Matapang. Archavie had stood up in the chariot so that he could more easily wave to passersby.

"I always count it as a compliment when people stare," he said to me, as the men and women on the sidewalks waved back.

We dropped off Speaker Matapang at her villa, then rode higher and higher above sea level up towards the plateau of the forum crowning Gem City until at last we reached the summit and pulled into the oval drive. The Gemmic Council's ocean-view terraces stretched to the north and west, and the Council building complex to the east, fronted the portico holding the public entrance. I had toured the terraces and complex once as a child. Even though I was grown-up now the buildings still looked intimidatingly tall and vast, all soaring columns and intricate mosaics of multicolored marble. A set of stairs, tall and wide enough to hold a sizeable choir, rose from the drive toward the portico, and down these stairs ambient magic flowed, slow like fog, but robust and powerful as a waterfall.

Three figures emerged from the huge bronze doors, crossed the portico and began to descend these broad marble steps as we exited our chariot. The foremost of the three wore a white toga with a laurel leaf clasp on his left shoulder. A Gemmic Councilor, quite a young one, with brown curls continually falling into his eyes. Two servants accompanied him, and beside them…

He looked much the same as I remembered, though his curly hair was perhaps more thoroughly grey. Helmet under his arm, broad, armor-clad shoulders wearing the crimson cloak of the Dunamis, tall nasal bridge, strong chin, and bowed lips. He looked so impeccably Gemmic that when I was a child, I thought the idealized face on Gemmic coins belonged to him and thought that meant he was important. Now I just regretted that I had inherited so many of those features. Still, I was relieved to find that whatever I felt — and I was far from sure that I knew what feeling it was — remained small, a manageable knot in the pit of my stomach.

The young councilor reached us first, and my father remained silent as the young man greeted us. "Healer Straton." He touched his hand to his chest but before he could nod to me, Archavie leapt forward.

"Theo," he exclaimed, "I'm glad it's you coming to welcome us!" The wizard extended his hand and Theo's face flushed red. Apparently, the councilor didn't remember how handshaking worked. When the young man did not shake his hand Archavie gave up and moved on to my father. "General Straton, good to see you again."

My father stepped forward and shook the wizard's hand. "You as well, Wizard Johnsbee. And Kaeda," he nodded to me. "It is good to see you."

I nodded back. "General Straton," I said. There, that would let him know to expect formal interactions, not familial ones.

Archavie meanwhile continued his introductions. "Kaeda this is councilor Theo, Theodolus Astinasious. Theo this is Kaeda. She's every bit as smart as her reputation implies."

"I heard that there's a cursed corpse for me to study," I said bluntly.

Councilor Theo seemed taken aback and Archavie chuckled. "Isn't that why you all invited her here?"

"Of course," Councilor Theo agreed. "Follow me."

We walked together across the portico and through the public rotunda mostly devoted to a mosaic of the Archon Gemma, seated on a throne, golden curls framing her face as she gazed into the distance, beautiful but silent as she was currently, sleeping in her temple and making magic, but offering no guidance.

Archavie decided to be infuriating and walk ahead with Councilor Theo, talking, as far as I could tell, about menus. This gave my father space to walk beside me, which he did.

Lay your ground rules, I told myself. Let him know where you're coming from, and set your boundaries.

"When I heard you were on the Commission, I almost didn't join," I said. "But I think I can be helpful."

"I agree."

"While we are working together, I am going to pretend that you are not my father. You are a Gemmic hero. I am a Farian healer. The fact that we share a last name is an incredible coincidence."

Silence. We walked on. Archavie said something about scallops, and how they were better than just about anything else. My father's coin-stamp visage remained still and unreadable as the currency itself. At last, he said, "I cannot pretend you are not my daughter; however, I will not bother you."

The knot in my stomach surged up, like a flame given oxygen, and for a moment I was afraid I might scream, but just as quickly as it had swelled, it dampened again. "Fine," I said calmly. "That will be fine."

We descended one flight of stairs, and then another, finally arriving at an underground doorway guarded by a quartet of Dunami soldiers. Even from outside I could sense the intensity of the containing constellations. Whatever was in there, the Gemmic Council must have thought it was very dangerous.

"Healer Straton from the Commission," Councilor Theo explained. "She's here to see the body."

"Are you wearing any magic?" a guard asked.

"No," I answered.

"Then you can go in. The barrier will remove any residue."

As a guard opened the door, Archavie spoke up. "This is where Turus and I stop. He's not comfortable in magically contained spaces."

I nodded and stepped through a thick straining barrier and into the room. The white walls crawled with magic that illuminated the space, but in the room itself… no magic at all. Not even within the corpse, laying on a table, elevated on a body block, neatly cut open. And yet…

As I stepped towards it my skin prickled with goosebumps. The dead man's skin was a healthy warm tan color, and the open and empty body cavity remained brilliant red. The organs too. I glanced at the second table where they sat, neatly separated into stainless steel dishes. They had been disconnected from a blood supply for days. Without magic how could they have been preserved? And yet the lungs were pink, the heart so red that I expected it to start beating.

"May I have some magic to use for study," I asked.

"The supply cabinet in the wall," one of the guards called in.

I found the cabinet, pulled on a pair of gloves and slid one of the enchanted cuffs up my arm. Then I turned back toward the corpse, ready to begin my study. I was about three feet from the body when I felt the magic I had brought with me begin to disappear. I took a step back. It was just as they had said. The magic seemed to vanish completely.

But that wasn't possible. It had to be here somewhere.

Chapter Seven

MOLVANS, DEAD AND ALIVE

Kaeda

A week later I still hadn't found the disappeared magic, and I still couldn't say for sure that the body was dead.

Lady Georgina Batbayar said the man hadn't had a pulse in over a fortnight, and the council's staff healers had tried every trick in the book to revive him before beginning the autopsy. Councilor Theo told me that Gamalielle Aisop, a Gemmic Cat and an expert on stealth magic, had inspected the body, and hadn't found anything either. I had not seen Gamalielle at work. In fact, I hadn't seen her at all yet, but perhaps that meant she really knew her craft.

General Straton had searched for magical effects in the body too, and he repeated his examination alongside me, just in case together one of us would catch something the other missed. But no, nothing. At least the experience proved to me that we could successfully work together. As he and I went over the body together, I felt nothing. At least, not much. At least, not so much that I couldn't stuff it down and get on with my work.

Archavie had things to say about that. Things like "You know, if you don't acknowledge and deal with your feelings, they'll keep getting bigger."

I didn't agree. Unlike magic, feelings seemed to be things that could really fade away.

Suit yourself, he said. *But don't say I didn't warn you.*

I spent as much time as I could in the morgue, poring over every inch of the corpse again and again. Somehow the vessels remained full of blood, even though the blood didn't move. The skin didn't bleed when cut, but it remained warm to the touch. I had to be missing something. Something preventing the usual deathly pallor and chill. Something that would make any magic within a yard vanish. The only thing I had noticed was that at times the corpse's blood vessels looked shiny, almost silvery. But when I looked harder the effect was gone.

It was probably nothing, nothing but a sign that I had been staring at the body for too long. I leaned back against the high, supportive cushions of my healer's chair, and shut my eyes. When I opened them again, I saw Archavie's flame-red hair peeking around the door.

"Any progress?" he asked without stepping into the room.

"Not a bit," I answered.

"Well, the council will feed you anyway. I've come to tell you that lunch is ready."

I sighed as I lifted myself from the seat. I felt stiff from sitting still, fatigued from focusing on one thing, and my eyes hurt, probably from spending all day in this magic-lit cell with no windows.

"Maybe this will brighten your day." As I made my way to the door Archavie held out a scroll and a pamphlet. "Your work is all over Neos Mageia and Anakalypsi Magazine."

I untied my hair and shook out my curls, breathing deeply as I left the magic-free room and returned to the thick ambient magic. "Let me see."

"Healer's New Puff Snuffs Ice-Lung Disease," and "University of Agapetos Researcher Discovers Cure for SOWSS," the headlines read.

"It's not a cure. It's a treatment," I said in critique as I glanced over the articles, "but I'm glad the university will have support for clinical trials." I handed the publications back to Archavie. "I'll ask for lunch to be brought to my room."

"I expected a little more excitement," the wizard said as he fell into step beside me walking down the hall. He held out his elbow to offer an escort. It was a custom that he had picked up from the visiting Molvans, and he had done it so many times by now that I put my arm through his automatically.

"I didn't cure anything. I'm glad my treatment is saving lives, but there's more work to do."

"That doesn't mean we can't celebrate."

"I am celebrating. Deep down inside."

"Is that how you feel everything? So deep down even you can barely see it?"

"Not everything. Currently I'm feeling a little annoyed but also happy to have your company right on the surface."

"I'm flattered that your feelings about me are worth acknowledging."

"You're welcome."

We made our way back above ground, but as I attempted to turn off toward my room, Archavie kept his grip on my arm, pulling me to a stop. "You won't want to miss this lunch," he said. "Trust me."

"I have nothing to report," I said, thinking of facing Lady Batbayar across the table again. I liked her. She was probably some twenty or thirty years older than I and reminded me of a barracuda, but vertical instead of horizontal, a straight-up-and-down woman in a charcoal grey gown with rays of glimmering silver in her perfectly twisted dark brown hair. Our Molvan guests had all been distinctly shorter and lighter in build than the Gemmic population, but that didn't stop Lady Batbayar from having a strong presence in a room. She didn't make small talk and didn't mind when I didn't offer her a Molvan curtsey. I could imagine the flicker of disappointment in her eyes if I told her again that I had found nothing.

"Oh, don't worry, her ladyship has plenty of other things to think about right now," Archavie said, lifting an eyebrow.

"Like what?"

"Come and see."

We walked across a columned arcade bordering a garden, past mosaics of the Architects of Creation, the great Magics of the past who had helped create the world. Being Magics they had no true physical form, but here Gemmic artists depicted them in humanoid form. Asteri, the Architect of Stars, resembled a dark silhouette of a man but colored by points and glows in white, blue, and purple. Fyta, Architect of Plants, was a green lady made of vines. Fauna, Architect of Animals, stood with her back to the viewer. Besides her fur cloak and long brown tresses, only one hand could be seen, human, but clawed, holding the edge of her cloak.

Gemma and Kyrillos were included too, though as far as I knew neither of them had played a role in shaping the world. Both looked like Gemmic humans, tall and fair, Kyrillos in gleaming armor, all bits of silvery stone, and Gemma draped in flowing white. They faced one another, holding hands. The title beneath Gemma said, Architect of Civilization, and the title beneath Kyrillos said Architect of Peace.

Every time I passed it, I rolled my eyes a little bit, but those feelings were included in the too-deep-down-to-bother-with category.

We passed them all, walking toward one of the smaller dining rooms. It was almost a columned arcade, open to the garden on one side. Archavie and I could clearly see through the columns to the dining table, where the number of visiting Molvans had doubled, divided neatly into two groups, clearly at odds with one another.

On one side stood Lady Batbayar, perfectly poised as usual, though the chair behind her said she had risen suddenly and the beaded strands hanging from her silver circlet swayed and sparkled as she spoke, as if they'd like to fly loose and give expression to her anger.

"When I see my land, my people, in danger, it is my responsibility as a person of rank to do what I can to help."

She spoke to a person several seats down the table and when I saw him my thoughts skidded to a halt. He did not match the other Molvans at all. He was too tall, as tall as the Gemmic councilors at the head of the table, and his clothing was not the same. Lady Batbayar and her attendants wore tailored, close-fitting clothing in shiny fabrics made shinier by embroidery with metallic threads. Archavie told me this was the fashion in the Vodaniyan region. Gowns. Frock coats. Waistcoats. It all looked terribly uncomfortable to me, but this man, if a man he was, wore none of those things. Instead, a heavy black robe hung about him, the deep hood drawn up and completely black inside, hiding his face. The shadow within it had to be enchanted to be so dark.

He's also wearing robust anti-mindreading protection, Archavie complained as we approached, *I can't even get an emotional vibe off him! It's infuriating.*

One of the mystery man's voluminous sleeves extended toward the table and a single gloved fingertip tapped on the table as if he thought this conversation was a massive waste of time. "This is not your concern," he said, a whispery impatient voice floating out from his hood.

"Since the dov, I assume, cares about the wellbeing of the Molvan people, as do I, I'm not sure why there should be such a conflict," Lady Batbayar argued back.

Another newcomer spoke. He looked so ordinary beside the stranger in the robe that I had hardly noticed him. This stranger wore the standard Molvan brocaded grey, a slim figure with dark serious eyebrows and a dark, serious beard. "What Magiologist Svevolod means, your ladyship, is that it is not your decision to make. And I'm sure he says that with the deepest respect."

Archavie and I reached the table during this exchange. Archcouncilor Gallo, standing at the head of the table with Councilor Theo and a couple of other councilors on either side, cast a wistful glance at the serving dishes that had already been placed before turning to Archavie and I.

"Healer Straton, Wizard Johnsbee, allow me to introduce Magiologist Svevolod, advisor to Dov Voda, and Viktor Essen, the dov's Secretary. Secretary, Magiologist, this is Healer Kaeda Straton, and Wizard Archavie Johnsbee."

While I politely nodded, Archavie stretched over the table to offer a handshake, exclaiming. "So pleased to meet you!" Svevolod merely turned his hood to regard the hand, but Secretary Essen reached across and gave it a shake. "Well, don't let me stop you arguing!" Archavie said, with the air of one truly not wishing to be a bother. "I'll just pop some risotto!"

He dropped into his usual chair, which was next to mine, pulled over a dish of risotto, and snapped his fingers. The little bits of rice steamed and puffed, increasing in volume until the bowl appeared to be filled with an herby cloud.

In Marklund we will often pop corn for entertainment, he explained to me. *This will do I suppose.* He picked up a few pieces and tossed them into his mouth.

You think this is entertaining? I thought back as I sank into my chair. I wasn't entertained. I felt concerned for Lady Batbayar. She had taken a few deep, calming breaths during our introduction. I also felt concerned for my research. I had seen higher-ups shut down a project before, and my gut told me that's where this was going.

I glanced around the dining room again. I didn't see Gamalielle, but she was probably hiding nearby. My father, however, was also conspicuously absent.

Where's General Straton? I mentally queried. Surely, he should be a part of this.

Oh, he went down to the harbor to look over our transportation and was delayed. I imagine he's going to regret not being here.

Then the conversation drowned out Archavie's thoughts.

Archcouncilor Gallo spoke first, "Correct me if I misunderstand, your ladyship, but it sounds as if the dov was not aware of your request to involve the Gemmic Commonwealth in Molvan affairs."

"That is correct, Archcouncilor," Secretary Essen replied.

"The dov," Lady Batbayar said in a biting tone. "The dov is preoccupied with grasping for control of the rest of the continent. If he wishes to focus on conquest, perhaps he should allow his local lords and ladies to manage their own affairs."

"The dov has given me the responsibility of managing Molva's magic," Magiologist Svevolod's whispery voice broke in.

"And a fine job you've done." The crystals hanging to either side of the lady's face flashed. I glanced toward Svevolod and Essen, but neither of them seemed in the least offended or taken aback. Lady Georgina, a slight flush in her cheeks, collected herself and said more calmly. "The dead man was found on my estate. In life he was my groundskeeper. I view the wellbeing of my staff as my responsibility, and this death as my failure to protect those who rely on me."

"The dov would wish for nothing less from his nobles," Secretary Essen replied politely, "but your request for Gemmic aid—"

"The Commission may stay at my home in Temnobre forest. The dov need not be involved."

"*If* the Commission visits Molva at all they will stay in Vodastad, in the palace. Nothing else will happen and no one else will approach the so-called cursed body until it has been safely moved to Vodastad."

Silence. Lady Batbayar's expression was fixed on Magiologist Svevolod, an expression so sharp and icy I wouldn't have been surprised if he took some magical damage from it. But she didn't argue.

There it was. Sudden death to my studies.

I was shaken from my dire thoughts by the sight of Archavie's puffed risotto drifting up from the dish in front of us and rising toward the ceiling. Essen noticed it. Then Lady Batbayar. For a moment we all watched the risotto levitate upward.

"Don't mind me," a yowly feline voice called down from above, "Just enjoying the spectacle."

Lady Batbayar shut her eyes, and when she opened them again her expression was bright with realization. "No one will approach the body. That includes you Svevolod. The remains belong to one of my servants and were found on my estate. His body was brought here by the Trade Corridor's Transportation Guild, and I think you'll find that according to the paperwork, the remains now legally belong to the Gemmic Council."

She went on to say some very complicated things about next of kin and magical dangers and getting the Trade Corridor's Legal Guild involved. I saw the muscles in Secretary Essen's jaw working, and Magiologist Svevolod's fingertip stabbing down at the table as if he would pierce the wood with it.

Clearly, they wanted to fight back, but neither produced an argument. Essen requested to see the paperwork and Archavie said, "Now, I don't want to rush anyone, but the kitchen has the most amazing shawarma prepared and they're not going to bring it in without permission, so perhaps the debate could continue over lunch?"

He glanced at Archcouncilor Gallo. In fact, we all did, and I noticed for the first time the map of Molva on the wall behind him, traced with a sailing route.

Gallo sank into his seat with a sigh. "Roll up the map, Theo. I will need to discuss the travel plans with the Commission Formation Committee. For now, the morgue will be off limits to everyone."

Chapter Eight

TALES AND VISIONS

Kaeda

AT first, I was furious. Then I told myself I wouldn't have gotten any more done today anyway. My brain was too tired. Hopefully the ban would be temporary, and the temporary ban would give me a chance to rest.

I had observed some magnificent windows in the council's library and after lunch, a lunch in which Archavie badgered the Molvans with witty questions and Svevolod sat like a specter of doom and didn't eat a bite, I decided to see what I could find out about Molvan magical history and sit in the sun and read until I had digested enough to go for a swim in the council's pool.

In the library, shelves rose like the trunks of massive trees toward the lofty ceiling. Pillars of knowledge, or at least of ideas, beautifully lit by the soaring south-facing windows. A librarian helped me find the appropriate shelf, mostly books rather than scrolls, thankfully, and left me to explore. I gathered a few likely tomes, picking out those translated into Gemmic, and found a window seat.

I did my best to read through some of the legends but sitting in the cozy warmth of the window seat, with the fragrance of jasmine blossoms drifting from the cascades of vines hanging on either side, my mind began to wander. I looked up from the pages and gazed at the reliefs in white marble decorating the library walls. They depicted the Gemmic archon, Gemma as a young shepherd girl, wizard of an enormous Magic. It surrounded her like a cloud, indicated by a shimmer on the surface of the marble. The mergence with that Magic was shown in a scene where teenage Gemma floated in the air, curls spread like a halo around her. We dated our calendar from that moment, from the birth of our archon, the start of a new age. The next scene showed Gemma sitting on a rock, reciting Gemmic Law to a crowd. The next, Gemma holding the plans for the city, while workers toiled behind her.

That was not-so-distant history, several hundred years ago. I decided to think back further, seeking any time, any reason, that magic would disappear.

Thousands of years ago, so the legends went, there had been no ambient magic, only whole magical beings which we now called Magics. Then the Architect of Stars rebelled. He didn't want biological beings to take charge of the sphere he had made. He didn't want them to mine it and build on it. He recruited many of the first Magics to help wipe out humanity.

That had been the first war, and the Creator put a stop to it by shattering the Architects and the other first Magics. All of them. Even the ones who had supported humanity. She sentenced them to begin their lives again as helpless dust, the ambient magic that drifted about the sphere, until they gathered enough of themselves to search out a wizard. They would live their new lives always attached to a mortal, forced to work together, and hopefully learning to respect biological life.

If I thought about it too long, it felt weird, the idea that some of the ambient magic I used for enchantments might belong to ancient magical beings of great power. So, mostly I didn't think about it. In the Gemmic Commonwealth most of the ambient magic radiated from Gemma. We weren't sure what this meant in terms of magical theory. Was it the end of the life cycle of magic? Would Gemma eventually disperse again? Or was it more like magical reproduction? Would the magic from Gemma eventually form new Magics, Magics who had not existed at the dawn of time?

These were matters of great debate amongst Gemmic magisophs, but as far as we could tell, archons were a complete fusion of Magic and wizard, an interlocking of magic and matter that rendered the wizard immortal and anchored the Magic to them permanently. There were four archons on the sphere of Verrum: our archon, Gemma; her counterpart, Kyrillos; OmaOma in Qawah; and Zhiyov in Molva. Each of them was formed of a human wizard, and a fully grown Magic. And none of their history included the destruction of magic or Magics.

Alright, a dead end there. I turned my attention to Bogdan. He was the archon who seemed to have gone missing, and stories about him shed little light on why, though they did convince me he was unusual.

To begin with, Bogdan was sometimes called Boginya, a feminine name, and had been reported to be both a man, and a woman. Because of this it was hypothesized that the archon, most safely simply called Bog, was a fusion of a male wizard and a female Magic, which was highly anomalous. Usually, the gender of a wizard and their Magic matched, like Archavie and Turus. And then Bog was reclusive, which did not follow the typical pattern of an archon. OmaOma ruled the Queendom of Qawah. Gemma stayed in her temple to provide magic for us. When Kyrillos returned to visit her, we all celebrated the Gemmic holiday of Homecoming.

Bog, however, went out of his way to avoid civilization. The chronicle of archon sightings in the tome I had found consisted almost entirely of people who got lost in the wilderness, many of whom almost died and were rescued by the archon.

Perhaps nothing had happened to Bog, I thought, closing the dusty book, and closing my eyes as well. Perhaps he simply left. Perhaps he was merely tired, tired of rescuing pilgrims trekking through the woods. I could relate to that.

I was considering this and considering whether I might want to take a nap before having a swim, when I heard voices.

"Why would he stand in your way? Surely you and the dov want the same thing."

I recognized my father's deep, steady voice. Lady Batbayar answered him, sounding as brisk and barracuda-like as usual. "It is not for me to say what the dov wants."

"I am sorry I was not there. I will talk to the Archcouncilor."

I opened my eyes again. If I leaned forward, I could catch glimpses of them through the latticed scroll sections of the stacks. My father looked even taller and more powerful than usual beside the slight figure of the duchess, and she especially delicate, hands clasped lightly in front of her, now and then glancing up at the stacks as if she wished General Straton would go away and leave her in peace.

"How kind of you, to offer your support," she said, "But please leave Molvan political matters to me. I don't wish to make them any more complicated."

I blinked, suddenly fully awake as I took in Lady Batbayar's ironic tone. Where had the irony come from? What had I missed? I listened intently, hoping my father's reply would give me a clue but for some moments he said nothing. When at last he spoke he only said, "My lady," and I heard his footsteps retreat.

I sat back against the cushions of the window seat, running through the things they had said. His, "I am sorry I was not there," sounded softer than my father's standard public tone, and the duchess's "how kind of you," unusually bitter. Had they met before?

Of course, it wasn't surprising that I didn't know. I didn't know most of what my father had been up to in the last fifteen years, and I told myself that I didn't care. He was General Straton, teammate, and who he talked to hardly mattered to me. Lady Batbayar seemed to be keeping him at arm's length anyway, which I thought showed good judgment.

I decided I would go for a swim to clear my head. I gave my father a few minutes head start and then began to make my way back towards the main doors, but as I passed a corridor between two rows of shelves, I stopped. Between the shelves sat a large, round armchair, carved of stone, decorated with gold, and lined with cushions. In it sat Lady Batbayar, book in her lap, head and shoulders bent just enough that I could tell something was weighing on her. I found myself pausing when perhaps I should have kept walking, and she noticed me and looked up.

Well, then, I should say something, shouldn't I? "Are you alright your ladyship?"

A wry and weary smile creased her face and she spoke with the same trace of irony. "Yes. I am so at peace that I am reading children's fearytales."

She held up the book, its green leather cover embossed with a golden figure, human-shaped except for its arms which were flung back, fingers lengthened and webbed into bat-like wings. The title was written in Molvan, the alphabet deceptively similar to Gemmic, yet incomprehensible. I had seen it in the Molvan section, but without a Gemmic translation.

"I'm not familiar with fearytales," I said, peering a little more closely at the figure on the cover, taking in its sharp features, pointed ears, and the horns hidden in its fanciful swoop of hair.

"Tales of the creatures of Bogdan. Some, like the fearies, haven't been seen in hundreds of years, but the werebears remain." She held the book, running her fingertips across the embossed cover. "When I was young, I used to run out into the woods, hoping one of those bears would find me, deliver a message from the archon, tell me... What to do..." her voice trailed away, and she shook her head, sending the crystals of her headdress sparkling.

"Is that the werebears' role?" I asked, "Messengers of the archon?"

"It used to be. At least that's how the stories go. Now, well, they've attacked smaller settlements, infected people with ursinthropy against their will. No words, only violence." She settled her hand over the cover of the book with a wistful look, as if willing the past to return.

By now so many people had referenced Molva's shape-changing creatures that I could not easily deny their existence. Still, I wouldn't quite believe it until I saw it. Shape changing was not easily done. As far as we knew only archons could change their shape at will, a side effect of the complete mergence of matter and magic.

Again, my eyes were drawn to the figure on the front of the book. "And what about those? The winged people?"

"The fearies," the lady supplied. "The stories say that as time passed Bogdan grew sad, watching his creatures surrender to death. So he made the fearies, deathless creatures, to keep him company. But as they lived longer and longer they became cruel, haughty, despising mortals. Tales tell of them drinking the blood of humans, as if hungry for life. Others tell of them dealing death after death, as if they longed for death themselves. That was in the time of the khans," she met my eyes, looking sharp and ironic again. "When our people were united and viewed the werebears as warrior oracles, not ravenous monsters."

I frowned, wondering how much historical weight to give to her fearytales. In my silence, the duchess straightened, settled her shoulders into their usual, confidently back position, and said formally. "I am sorry your research has been interrupted."

"I hope to pick it back up in Molva," I said, my thoughts still elsewhere.

"I will do my best to see you can," the duchess said. "Please, don't let me keep you." She gestured in the direction I had been walking and I took this to mean I was dismissed.

I went and changed into my wetsuit and made my way to the council's swimming pool. It was massive, and due to the ornate blue tile and the border of potted plants, I had assumed at first that the pool was merely decorative. Councilor Theo however, assured me that guests were welcome to swim, and that the councilors in residence often used the pool for exercise. He said that, but I had yet to see anyone else use it.

Until now. This time when I went down to swim, I saw another figure in the water, in a silver wetsuit. My father. Ugh. Of all the people I didn't want to swim beside.

I turned right around. I would make my way out of the council complex and down the steps to the sea instead. Swimming in the ocean wouldn't be as easy, not a simple back and forth of mindless exercise that would let me think and build up some endorphins, but maybe that was for the best. The ocean would demand all my attention. It would distract me.

I didn't know that what waited for me in the ocean would be far more than distracting.

I swam out to a safe distance from the beach and began to swim south. Garibaldi, bat rays, and leopard sharks joined me on my swim, quiet and welcome companions. I was watching them and enjoying the mild tidal pull of the Gemmic Sea, when I thought I caught sight of a white glimmer in the distance. I stopped in midwater, narrowing my eyes and peering through the blue. The water was not as clear here as it was around the Farian reefs, and I wondered if it had merely been sunlight flashing off a dolphin. But no, as I watched I saw no pod of cetaceans, just a curl of brightness, nearly out of sight.

My heart, already working hard due to the swim, now raced frantically. Too still for a shark. Too long for a sea lion. Too small for any of the local whales, unless a baby. Maybe it could be that, a baby whale.

But my experience watching whales and the terror in my gut told me it wasn't. That bright curl was what Farian fishermen always looked out for, what woke Farian children in nightmares, a creature I had never seen alive. The word rang through my mind like an alarm: Khirian.

Chapter Nine

THE KHIRIANS

Kaeda

I pulled magic to myself quickly, tying it into a knot that should knock anything unconscious. But I knew that if it was what I thought it was, the magic would be no use. Khirians were terrifying specifically because of their magical resistance.

As if it knew I had seen it, the white shape flicked into motion. While I held my useless knot ready, the creature swam away. When I could no longer see it I spun in the water and, heart still racing, sped toward shore.

Memories of the distant war beat at my mind like the beat of my heart. Soldiers hurried into the ascleppa with limbs torn off. Rooms full of the reek of festering wounds full of unfamiliar bacteria. The never-ending race to synthesize enough magical blood substitute to keep up with the demands of the battles. The most of a Khirian I had ever seen was a hacked-up head and torso the navy had dragged into the healer's school. They brought it in so we could study the pathogens that were killing the soldiers who lived long enough to have their wounds closed.

I remembered the gaping, sharp-toothed maw and muscled, white-scaled form of the dead creature, big enough to grasp a human head in its jaws, strong enough to tear the head from the body. It wouldn't be so terrifying if they responded to magic like any other creature. But they didn't. Magical attacks simply didn't work unless they were strictly elemental, and Gemmic schools didn't teach much of that. Gems tended to view fire and lightning as too primitive to be worth study.

I reached the sandy stretch of shore near the acropolis and stopped, panting into my water breathing magic. I would run up the steps to the council complex, I thought. I would tell the first Dunamis guard I saw.

But I sensed a familiar magical presence at the edge of my mind. *Don't do that,* Turus remonstrated, *you'll start a panic.*

There are Khirians in the Gemmic Sea. People need to know.

Perhaps, but if you start shouting it out to every idiot in armor, they may launch ships and start a war. You don't want another war, do you?

Khirians are war beasts. If they're here, then war is here too.

Yes, yes, Khirians are war beasts, and your father is a heartless bomber.

That's not a fair comparison. I'm trying to protect people.

Just like you're trying to protect yourself by not letting your father near you.

"Stop!" I said aloud, stomping across the shore toward the steps. "You're not supposed to be searching and messing with my thoughts."

Mortals, Turus griped. *I could tell you that the Khirians come in peace, but you won't believe me. Fine. If you must tell someone, tell someone with a level head. Someone with some authority and experience.*

You want me to talk to my father.

He's learned his lesson about hasty interventions and collateral damage.

Has he now?

You might know if you talked to him.

Thanks, but I'll just take the news to Archavie.

No, no, the council trusts your boring stoic father far more than my very fabulous wizard. You take the news to him.

"Fine," I said aloud. "I'll talk to General Straton? Happy?"

As a clam you haven't cut up for pearls.

I ran back to the council's pool and found my father toweling off. He saw my concern and met me halfway across the stone of the courtyard.

"What is it?" he asked.

"I think I saw a Khirian in the water," I began, and I explained the whole thing, ending with, "but Turus claims they're here peacefully."

An ambassadorial delegation of sorts, Turus said.

My father considered all this, brow furrowed, towel still in his hands. "I will speak to the Archcouncilor. I will suggest we prepare to receive them."

"You think it's possible they're not here to fight?"

"They are people. Interrogations proved that much. We should allow them the chance to make peace and if a conflict should arise… better to lure them out of the water. It's much easier to fight a Khirian on land. Thank you for your report, Healer Straton," he concluded in an official manner. "I will take care of it." Then he strode off.

I watched him go but felt the presence of Turus linger.

You can leave me alone now, I told him. I've done as you asked. I haven't started a panic.

Yes, well, unfortunately my considerate wizard wants to remind you about the Molvan Magical Crisis Commission Inaugural banquet tonight. He is sure you'll forget.

I don't think they'll be throwing a banquet, I thought. Not after the dov has said he doesn't want us, not with the Khirians supposedly coming for peace talks.

Oh, believe me, they will. The council's not going to relinquish an excuse to feast, and the presence of a Duchess is the perfect excuse, even if she is reminiscent of a predatory fish. The councilors will hope to placate the Khirians and then bury their worries in food and drink.

Olives. Oysters. Baklava. Now that I had turned over the responsibility for the Khirian sighting I felt my appetite again. But first I would send a message to Aline, ask if anything unusual had happened, make sure they were okay. Then I would run back to the library, see if that fearytale book was back on the shelves. I'm sure the council had a translating stetsalog somewhere that could read it to me. That would distract me from persistent war memories, from that dead heap of Khirian and the endless reek of rotting flesh.

Just make sure you give yourself time to get dressed.

How long could getting dressed take?

Clearly, I had never dressed for a council event. When I returned to my room, book in hand, I found that the maid assigned to me had laid out a bunch of clothing options that weren't even mine, stolas in a rainbow of colors, and jewels and bangles to match. My heart turned away from them. No, I wouldn't pretend to be Gemmic. Not today. Today I would remind everyone that I was from Fari, and that while the

Gemmic peninsula had been safe and whole, my home had been invaded, attacked, and shattered.

"I'll wear this," I said, and I pulled from my wardrobe my best Farian gown, an ankle-length sheath in ivory linen with a wealth of tiny shells and beads sewn around the high neck and the hem.

"But this plum purple would suit you so well." The maid, a young lady with curly blond hair and a curvy figure swathed in drapes and tucks of pink, spoke with diplomatic flattery, but I answered her frankly.

"Those are Gemmic clothes, and I am Farian."

The young woman's politeness did not waver. "Yes miss." She fetched an olivewood box from my bed and brought it over to me. "I am sure something will match."

The box held a collection of earrings, necklaces, cuffs, and hairpieces.

No, I wasn't going to wear any of that meaningless shiny nonsense. Instead, I picked up my woven pearl necklace, which I had left on my bedside table during my swim. "I'll wear this."

The maid took a step closer, and her fair brow furrowed as she looked at the necklace. "What is that?"

"It's a pearl," I answered, holding the necklace it out so she could see.

"It's huge!" she exclaimed. "How did you make it like that?"

"Like what?"

"That shape."

"Not all pearls are round," I said. "In fact, most aren't."

"Really? I've never seen one like this. Where did you get it?"

"I found it," I answered, then added, "in a clam."

The maid's eyes widened, and I barely held back a laugh. I didn't have the heart to tell her all natural pearls were found inside clams and oysters.

"Anyway, I can get myself dressed," I said.

"Perhaps I could at least style your hair," she suggested.

Oh, sure, why not? A bit of magic would at least keep my curls tamed.

An hour and a half later, after a bath and what felt like an age of hairstyling, I remembered why I didn't like wearing my hair in a Gemmic style. The tower of sculpted hair felt tall and heavy on my head, and my scalp itched a little from the tickle of pins holding dozens of pearls. Perfect, round pearls in white and pink and peach. They kept my worry alive, reminding me of Fari, and of all the people I knew there.

Finally, however, toward the end of the hairstyling I received a message from Aline, saying that Adao and the other fishermen had sighted unfamiliar ships, and decided to stick to an eastern route further from the Gemmic Sea today, and that everyone was okay. Next came a message from my father, saying that he had spoken to the council, and everything was under control.

For the time being there was no war, no crisis.

At last, a knock sounded at my door and when I detached myself from the maid, insisting I had enough pearls in my hair, I found Archavie waiting in the hall. He had managed to find something even more colorful and ostentatious to wear than his usual vivid robes. He wore a voluminous midnight blue cape with a flaring collar, decorated on the inside with stars and planets that flashed with enchanted light.

"Yes, I do enjoy a good stare," the wizard said, and as usual he held out an elbow in my direction. "But of course, everyone will be distracted by something else."

"What do you mean?" I said as I put my arm through his and let him lead me out into the hall.

"Ah, here it comes." The wizard gestured toward a folded bit of paper, zipping towards us in a swallow-like fashion. He plucked it from the air, unfolded it and read, "Archie, get your bum in here. Council can't deal with these frilsing lizards. Where are you? Signed, G. and with an ugly kitty face." He lifted his eyebrows and held out the paper so I could see the scrawled note, complete with a cat face sticking out its tongue. "Must be from Gamalielle. Guess we should hurry then."

But I stood frozen. Behind me, the maid gasped. "Lizards? Khirians?"

"I thought it was all under control," I said. "Turus said they're not here to fight."

"That's true, but they are here to make a demand. Very sorry to alarm you miss," the wizard said, looking back through my door where the maid remained, eyes round as sand dollars. "Would you prefer I remove that information from your mind? No, she wouldn't, she wants to go tell everyone. Well, I suppose the cat's out of the bag anyway. Enjoy your evening."

He shut the door and made to walk down the hall, but I kept my grip on his arm, and pulled him to a stop. "If you know what this is about, tell me."

"The Khirians want a spot on the Commission."

"What?!" No, it felt like a bad dream. "The council can't be considering it."

"Well, according to Turus it's mostly pandemonium right now." Archavie rested his hand over mine, his blue eyes bright and earnest. "Turus and I are going to do our best to keep things civil, but as I'm sure you can imagine, it wouldn't hurt to have an extra healer around, just in case."

Yes. I remembered again the bite wounds, crush injuries, punctures, broken bones, all in a jumble. Yes, of course, I would go. If there was a catastrophe, I was determined to be in the thick of it. I was determined to help.

Picking up my skirt, I hurried through the council complex with Archavie. At the passageway connecting the guest wing to the central section of the council complex we ran into a pair of Dunamis guards, who began to utter an objection about how it wasn't safe for me to be here.

"Oh tosh," Archavie said. "Who do you want to be around if the Khirians start tearing bits off people? The best healer in the peninsula? I think so. Find her a spot with a view."

The guards accepted this, and while Archavie ran off toward the doors that would take him to the floor of the chamber, I climbed the marble steps that would take me to the upper balcony. As I did, I began to hear them: harsh inhuman voices, low growls, and shrieking cries, punctuated by the pounding of weapons on stone.

I emerged from the staircase into the vast white space of the council chamber where a row of archers stood ready along the expanse of the wide curving balcony. A few of them took notice of me as I stepped out of the doorway, before training their eyes downward again. I crept toward the balustrade, and the council room came into view, lit by sparkling magical light from huge, draped chandeliers. A magical barrier several feet thick cut the oval room in half, and to the left of the barrier, for the first time, I saw live Khirians.

Even from my distant vantage point, they looked huge, taller than even the tallest councilors by at least a couple of feet. I looked down on thick necks, broad shoulders, deep ribcages, muscled arms, all covered by white scales. Their tails doubled their length, making some probably eighteen feet long.

But despite the size and the scales, it was the Khirians' faces I found most alien. Lizard-like, but with a taller skull than most lizards I had seen, head and arched neck almost horse-like. Elliptical-pupiled eyes sat on the sides of their heads, and those sharp teeth that I remembered so well lined their powerful jaws.

On the other side of the wall of magic, behind a row of soldiers, most of the council and attending representatives stood in their tiered seats, tense, looking ready to fight or flee at any moment. I scanned the seats and spotted Lady Batbayar's steel grey and sparkling headdress on the balcony on the opposite side of the room and Speaker Matapang's blunt bangs and white stola on the ground level, sitting in the back row. Many of the other councilors had their hands raised towards the barrier, reinforcing it as best they could, but it wouldn't matter. Khirians could tear through such magic as if it wasn't there. What we really needed was—

A wall of fire roared to life along the barrier as Archavie strode out onto the floor to stand beside Archcouncilor Gallo and General Straton. "Welcome!" his voice boomed, magically amplified. "I gather you would like to join the commission."

Standing at the front of the gathered troops, the Khirian leader coughed out an answer. The room seemed to take it as a yes.

"We will consider your request," Gallo told them. "We will have a decision for you tomorrow morning."

But the Khirian leader would not be put off. "Now!" he bellowed. He needed no magic to enhance his voice; the room seemed to shake as all the mammals jumped. "We will not leave until you send a Khirian to Molva."

Gallo turned to my father. Archavie leaned in too and the three quickly conferred. When they broke apart again Archcouncilor Gallo announced, "Very well. We will conduct our deliberation now."

He waved a hand and the shifting and tail-swishing sounds of the Khirian troops faded. I understood that the magical barrier surrounding them had become soundproof, and the gathered councilors understood it as well. They erupted into arguments.

"It would jeopardize everyone's safety."

"The Molvans would never hear of it."

"The Khirians' reputation."

"They eat people."

"Animals!"

"Monsters!"

The archcouncilor held up his hands for silence. "You all agree on what we shouldn't do. Does anyone have an idea of what we should do?"

"Tell them no," Lady Batbayar's voice rang out. She had come down from the balcony and now she, Magiologist Svevolod, and Secretary Essen had joined Archavie and the others in the center of the floor. "They devastated my homeland. They have no right to demand an invitation."

"On this the duchess and I agree," Essen said.

"Disband the Commission," Svevolod's voice rasped, "and the complication will disappear."

"No," Lady Batbayar objected. "Haven't we agreed on a compromise?"

Archavie raised his hands to quell the argument. "Even if we tell them no, then what? I can tell you, their navarch won't want to lose face by giving in to us, even if we tell them the trip is cancelled."

"We can defend ourselves," a councilor spoke up. "They've only brought a small group ashore. The Dunami can handle them."

"So, you'll kill them because they asked to be included?" Archavie clarified.

"As far as we know they didn't even exist until Molva's first magical cascade. That was, what, twenty years ago? Thirty? And since the second cascade, they've done nothing but kill, destroy, and terrify."

"But you would consider them people?" Archavie asked.

Confused muttering broke out, and I found myself thinking of the werebears, viewed now as monsters, but not always. My father had said they were people, hadn't he? People didn't have to be monsters.

Another councilor spoke above the noise. "Sentient they may be, but we can hardly consider them on equal terms with humanity."

"Oh, with *humanity,*" Archavie glanced around the room. There were many Cats on the council. Covered in fur and rarely more than four feet tall, the *felis loqui* didn't look much more human than Khirians did. They were basically cat-shaped, though they'd taken to walking about on two legs rather than four, and usually wore clothes. "The Cats have only been sentient for what? A couple of hundred years?"

"Yeah, but we never ate people," Gamalielle's voice argued from somewhere in the crowd.

Before the room could begin a philosophical debate about personhood, history, and moral responsibility, my father spoke up. "This is all beside the point. I am sure neither the council, nor Molva," he glanced at Lady Batbayar, Secretary Essen, and Magiologist Svevolod, "would wish to endanger lives unnecessarily. One Khirian will be easier to control and subdue than an army. I suggest we accede to the navarch's demand and add a Khirian to the Commission."

A rash of muttering broke out across the councilors, and I saw Lady Batbayar and Secretary Essen confer quietly with Gallo and my father. When they had reached a consensus Essen quelled the debates, calling out, "We agree. Better one Khirian than a hoard. We will allow one of their number to join the Commission."

Gasps and mutters filled the room again. I cast my eyes across the rows of giant white lizards. Now that I saw them alive, I felt something more complicated than fear. I remembered the white flicker in the water. I remembered my father, and now this assembly, declaring that they were people. People at home in the water, which was intriguing and gave me an odd stomach-twisting feeling of jealousy. Also, people who had eaten other people.

That was the puzzle, wasn't it? The puzzle of everything in war. How did people do what they did? Why? If these lizards were people, and if one of them were to join the commission, perhaps I could have an answer to that question. Remembering the distant white shape, I wanted one.

But as I looked back toward Archavie and the councilors all wondering fled my mind and I shrieked out a warning. A figure had walked into the room from one of the ground level doors. It shouldn't have been walking at all. The last time I had seen it, it had been lying on a table, dead.

Chapter Ten
BOOM
Kaeda

SOMEONE gave the order to fire. The archers on either side of me took aim and loosed their arrows. Screams and gasps filled the council chamber as the councilors scrambled away from the ambulating corpse.

It had gathered its organs, stuffed its brain back in its head and its entrails back inside its neatly dissected trunk. Now it held one arm wrapped across its body, keeping the incisions shut and its guts inside. As dozens of arrows continued to pierce its skin the corpse let go of its torso, allowing the arrows to hold it together.

It didn't seem to mind the arrows. In fact, its dead lips began to twist up in a smile. I noticed that, though many of the arrows glowed with enchantments, the enchantments vanished when they came within three feet of the corpse. Now four feet. The range of the empty magical space increased with each moment.

To me this seemed like a bad sign.

My father had worked up a plate of magic, probably a shield. Other Dunamis guards had rushed in from the opposite door on the council's side of the room and begun to do likewise, preparing to form a second magical barrier between the dead thing and the fleeing councilors.

Then a voice shook the air. The corpse had opened its mouth, but there were no words to the voice, only sounds rattling out from the dead throat. The dead glassy eyes swept across the room, taking in the baffled and horrified audience.

The magicless space rushed suddenly inward toward the corpse. I heard my father shout, "Get down!" saw him pull Lady Batbayar to the floor. In the next moment, the body exploded.

I dropped to the floor but still felt bits of flesh landing in my hair and on my arms. A strange pain followed, as if my arms had been bruised. Looking at my skin I saw dead grey patches spreading from the splashes of gore. Screams erupted in the council chamber.

I grabbed the nearest bit of free-floating magic and wove it into two filtering disks. I slipped one onto each of my shoulders and slid them down my arms, tearing out whatever was harming me.

Whatever it was continued to destroy, or at least render invisible, any magic it touched it. I did manage to strain the curse out, but only by pouring more and more magic into the filtering disks. Finally, I drew the last of it out through my fingertips. The ends of my fingers turned grey and lost their sensation, but they could be repaired later.

I turned to my left, where the nearest archer lay on the ground, shrieking. The spray of gore had hit him in the face. His eyes had already turned a greyish white, but as I moved the straining discs towards him, I felt a hand on my arm.

"The councilors." One of the other archers pulled me to my feet. "Help them. We'll do the best we can."

The councilors could die for all I cared, but then I remembered that Matapang and Archavie and Lady Batbayar were also on the lower level. Nodding, I thrust the magical discs towards the woman who had helped me up. "Use these to strain out the curse. You'll have to add more magic to them as you go."

I ran a few steps past her, in the direction of the east staircase, but found myself facing an obstacle course of bodies. Other Dunami archers stumbled blindly or clutched wounds where shards of flying bone had bitten into their skin. I turned and headed in the other direction, where the path was clearer. I had turned onto the west staircase and run halfway down before I realized I was descending into the Khirian half of the room.

The Khirians all had their backs to me, watching the horror unfold. The thick magical barrier, now a mere film full of holes, seemed to have protected them from the explosion.

They're on a peaceful mission, I reminded myself, and going around them will take too long. "Let me through," I shouted. "I'm a healer. Let me through."

I wasn't sure whether they understood me, or whether they were simply too confused to do anything but make way, but the troops parted, and I ran through a forest of scales, teeth, claws, and drawn weapons. Here and there elliptical-pupiled eyes, golden, green, grey, watched me in surprise. At last, I felt a magical presence in front of me. Turus made a rift in the magical barrier, and I dashed through it and into the chaos on the other side.

"Here! Here!" I recognized the voice as the one that had spoken from the ceiling during lunch and dropped to my knees beside a tawny-furred cat I assumed must be Gamalielle Aisop. She bent over a female councilor whose stola was soaked with blood. An extra rib stuck out of her chest like an arrow. I wove another disk of magic, but as I slipped the disk into the councilor's body, I felt her heart go still. Even if I strained out the invisible magic, I didn't think I would be able to start her heart again, not after the damage done by the unseen curse.

"There's nothing I can do," I murmured to Gamalielle, then I stood again and scanned the room. Matapang, safe, standing in one of the upper rows. Archavie and Gallo, safe. Lady Batbayar, safe, standing beside my father who shouted, "We need to work a piece of purging magic for the whole room. Healer Straton, Councilor Panousias. Aeschylus and Aura Xarhakos."

Then Gamalielle's voice screeched again. I looked down to see the cat gaping at the dead councilor. The woman's face had gone grey, and the grey had begun spreading out of her body, up into the air in smoke-like tendrils.

No, not into the air, I realized, into her Magic. This woman was a wizard and her Magic hovered around and above her, hugging her corpse.

"It's infecting her Magic!" someone shouted.

"What will happen?"

"Someone, stop it!"

Archavie and Straton rushed over to us. I tried to find a way to put a barrier between the councilor and her Magic, but it was impossible. The Magic was attached to the woman, it behaved irrationally, swirling and shifting, likely beside itself with grief.

"Tell her magic to break away," a whispery voice spoke. Magiologist Svevolod stood opposite me, still and inscrutable in his dark robe.

"If it takes the curse with it—" I began, but the magiologist interrupted.

"It will not. The curse will remain behind."

He sounded very sure of himself, and I couldn't think of a better idea. I glanced up to Archavie.

"What is the Magic's name?" Archavie asked the others.

"Raysent," Straton answered. "The wizard is Irene Skarlatos."

"Raysent," Archavie pleaded, looking into the smoke swirling mass of Magic. "Raysent, you must leave her."

The other councilors joined in.

"Raysent, you must leave her."

"You're in danger."

"Please, Raysent!"

Magic shifted in the room. The councilors might not be much good at healing, but they knew how to use magic for the purpose of persuasion. I wondered if it would work. When a wizard died, his or her Magic usually lingered with the body for a few days mourning the loss, then drifted away as its connection to the wizard's body faded. It would be painful for the Magic to abandon its wizard now.

"She's dead, Raysent."

"Don't let this curse take you."

"For her sake, Raysent. She wouldn't want you to stay."

I heard their voices trembling, then I felt Raysent tremble as well. As they pleaded with the magic, Magiologist Svevolod knelt beside the body, and extended an arm. His sleeve was so huge and shadowed that I could just barely see the edges of his gloved fingers grip the extra rib sticking out of the councilor. Meanwhile the cursed grey of the councilor's skin pinked back to its natural color. Frils, would she become the next not-quite-dead corpse for us to study?

"Please, Raysent," Archavie whispered, "before it's too late."

The smoke stretched like thousands of grey threads. Then a cry cut through the air and the smoky filaments collapsed back onto Irene as the Magic tore away. At the same moment, the magiologist pulled the rib from Skarlatos's body. All the greyness seemed to come out with it and vanish.

Around the council meeting chamber, other wizard councilors choked back sobs. I glanced up at Archavie and saw tears streaming down his face. Then Gamalielle said. "So, should we expect this one to blow up too?"

Svevolod shook his head. In the moment I had looked away, he had set the rib back down on the councilor's chest and risen to his feet, returning to an unfathomable pillar of darkness.

"What did you do?" I asked.

"Nothing."

I got nothing more useful or specific out of him as we cleaned up the mess. Two other councilors, a few visiting Molvans, and several Dunamis guards, died before Straton and I and the others managed to work up a giant sheet of magic to rid the room of the invisible curse, though by that time it seemed to have stopped spreading. We took the barrier that had separated us from the Khirians, adjusted it, and swept it across everyone, collecting a pile of grey bits and pieces. Thankfully whatever the curse was, it seemed to have burned out. No more magic disappeared. No one else exploded.

"Just to be safe, this should be stored carefully," I instructed as we neared the end. "No contact with living matter, and no contact with magic."

I looked up and took a deep breath. Most mammals had already left the room and now, as Archcouncilor Gallo finished speaking with them, the Khirians began to disperse as well. The Commission gathered, minus Gamalielle who had disappeared, and Gallo strode over to address us next.

"I have done as we discussed, wizard," the Archcouncilor said to Archavie. "And requested that the Khirians present three candidates tomorrow morning so that we can choose one."

"We were scheduled to depart tomorrow morning," I reminded him.

"Yes," Gallo said with a sigh. "I don't want to delay the departure. If we delay a day… it may turn into a week."

"The departure is not necessary," Secretary Essen said. "As you can see, Vodastad is capable of handling matters in Molva."

"How did Magiologist Svevolod handle it?" I asked. "And where is he?"

"Magiologist Svevolod's comings and goings are none of your concern," the secretary said cooly, and Gamalielle snorted with laughter.

"Hiding something much?" the cat heckled.

Archcouncilor Gallo raised his hands, as if he couldn't bear to hear one more moment of social bickering. "This crisis has now spread beyond Molva and has killed some of our own. The Commission *will* travel to Molva, and I hope the dov will support them as they seek a solution to this unknown danger. Now, see a genesis specialist about any parts you've lost and then go get something to eat. We've cancelled the banquet and sent the guests home but there's still a feast of food in the banquet hall."

With that the Archcouncilor departed, and our group dispersed. Archavie and I made our way toward dinner. I gazed down at my hands. The straining magic had removed the cursed flesh from my fingertips. Though I had treated many patients who had lost body parts, this was the first time I had experienced it and I felt dazed, looking at hands that were mine and yet not familiar. "Did you lose anything?" I asked Archavie.

"No," the wizard answered. "Turus made a bit of a wind, blew the nastiness away from Gallo and me. General Straton was so focused on protecting the duchess that I don't think he noticed I'd done anything."

He said "protecting the duchess" like it was something I should ask about. I shook my head. "If there's drama, real or imagined, I don't need to know. I have more important things to think about."

"Healery things I presume."

Yes, in fact. I was thinking about Irene and Raysent and worrying about Archavie and Turus. Archavie had said nothing ever happened to Turus, but nothing like this had ever happened to anyone, and now it *was* happening.

You worry too much, the wizard's voice sounded in my mind. Once again, he extended an elbow.

"You should at least let me do a physical and make a body print for you." I said as I laced my arm through his.

He patted my hand. "I am perfectly healthy and do not need a doctor. Trust me. Just eat a little something and get yourself ready for the afterparty."

"Afterparty? It's still on?"

"Of course! The explosion was here, not at the harbor. The Qawahns aren't going to change their plans. Besides, what better way to banish thoughts of walking dead than a raucous celebration?"

"Reading a book until I fall asleep?" I wondered if there were any fearytales about animated dead.

"On no, no. That will not help you sleep. Besides, you did promise to come."

I did promise, but that was before all of this.

Still, fearytales were just tales, and this was my opportunity to meet the Qawahn merchants. Archavie had told me that they would be sailing to Drakipeiros next. Another unbelievable announcement. That continent had been magically sealed for centuries, but Archavie claimed that Harol had reestablished trade. Negotiations were at a tenuous point, which was why Harol would not be accompanying his friend to Molva.

"Alright, alright," I agreed.

"I'll meet you out front in half an hour?"

"Sure."

"And bring your tools."

"My tools?"

"You know, your… healer's kit or whatever you might need." At my look of surprise he added, "You never know what's going to happen at one of these shindigs."

"Now I'm wishing I could read your mind."

"See you later."

A genesis specialist regrew my fingertips and some patches on my arms, and then I did as Gallo suggested and ate a quick plate from the banquet hall. A wail like the howling of wind gusted through the council complex as I walked back to my room, rising and falling as Raysent roamed the halls and courtyards. Her inconsolable voice sounded all too familiar, like the endless grief lurking at the corners of my mind. Now that I had left the crisis, I felt an emotional crash looming. It threatened to overtake me if I wasn't careful, if I didn't find something else to pay attention to.

Maybe going to the party would be for the best.

I slipped through my door and shut it behind me, ready to quickly change clothes, and stopped short.

Gamelielle sat on my couch in front of my fireplace. The firelight flashed on her brassy fur and sparkled on the scales of the huge fish she held in each hand. Two more fish lay, half eaten, on the floor. They looked like the ornamental carp from the fountain in the courtyard.

The Cat turned her huge, unfocused eyes toward me, and I immediately thought something was wrong with her.

"I've decided," she said, her words slurring together "we're gon' be friens."

Yes, an enchantment sparkled in her blood. It had come from the fish, which had been drugged to remain lazy and docile in the council fountain.

"You're so brave," the cat rambled. "And so… smart… and beautiful. I wanna be you whenIgrowup."

I sighed. "I'll help you get back to your room," I said. The cat was probably light enough that I could steer her down the hall without trouble.

"Hadta make sure you're okay," Gamalielle added with a hiccup, as I nudged her off the couch. "Hadta make sure you weren' gonna loose your mind. Gonna do annnathing selfistructive."

She was talking about herself, I realized. Frils. I couldn't just leave her alone. I would have to find someone to keep an eye on her.

"You still want to go?" Gamalielle asked. She turned her face up towards mine, chewing in slow motion. At such a small distance, I saw myself reflected in the Cat's massive pupils, saw my haggard expression and disheveled curls.

"Go where?"

"Molva o'course."

"Yes. I don't fully understand what is going on and I want to study it."

"Witha frilsin'Khirian? Witha blood-snacking, big'n'bad Khirian?"

I had forgotten about the Khirians. "Yes, even with a Khirian."

"I was in the navy, you know. Not a sailor, just a magical consultant. Stationed me on *The Alacrity*, off Ismelinos. You think that boom-body made a mess? You should see what Khirians do to a ship's crew." She swayed on her feet. "Like soup in the water. Like soup with chunks. Big chunks."

No, no, I was not going to be dragged back to the war again. I was not going to collapse into a sobbing heap of unbearable memory. Not tonight, even if it meant an unempathetic dismissal of her story.

"I'll find a servant to help you get in bed," I told her. "I can't stay. I've promised Archavie I'll go to the Qawahn's afterparty."

"You're invited to the party on the *Hanohano*?" The cat exclaimed. She rose sharply into the air to be at my eye level and seemed suddenly much more clear-minded. "Why wasn't I invited? Bliv'n'blus, Archie really knows how to leave a person out. I'll be ready in five."

Some forty-five minutes later the three of us had arrived at Harol's flagship, the *Hanohano,* which formed the centerpiece of a multi-ship party. We had seen it from the acropolis, a trio of lit decks, with fireworks frequently bursting over the dark water. Now as we piled out of our chariot the buoyant music of the steel drums, the crackling explosions of the fireworks, and the rise and fall of waves of laughter, were almost deafening.

Harol bounded down the gangplank to meet us and I found myself impressed by the accuracy of my cousins' comic books. Harol matched the illustrations perfectly. Energetic, muscular, skin nearly as dark as his black hair, the pirate-hunter embraced his tall, freckled Markish friend. Their clothes coordinated, I noticed. Harol's vest and baggy pants the same hues as Archavie's usual red and purple robes.

"And you brought a date!" Harol exclaimed. "Two dates!"

"Don't say that," Archavie warned as Harol kissed my hand and then Gamalielle's. "Or Turus might feel jealous and kill them."

Harol didn't seem worried about that. "A doctor," he exclaimed, with a glance at my satchel. "Good, good. We just started bungee jumping from the rigging. Someone might get hurt. Come."

"Bungee jumping!" Gamalielle squealed. "I love bungee jumping!"

Chapter Eleven

HELP

Reef

WHEN the Khirians had returned from the Gemmic Council building the navarch had marked three circles in a sandy stretch of beach. Each circle represented one of the candidates who would stand before the Gemmic Council offering themselves as potential members of the party. When the sun rose, whoever had managed to claim one of these circles would be included.

Reef sat on a rough shelf of coastal rock and watched the fighting, dramatically illuminated by brilliant cool moonlight on one side and the light of dozens of tall, flickering torches and several bonfires on the other. The excitement in the air, the distant colorful blasts of fireworks from the harbor, and the wealth of fire kept most of them awake and eager, despite the chill of the autumn night. It was a scale and claw contest. No weapons allowed. In the firelight streaks of shed blood marked gleaming white scales with splashes of brilliant red.

Looking at the red on white, Reef remembered the blood of humans spilled across the marble floor of the council meeting chamber.

The Khirian troops' discussion of the exploding body had mostly consisted of graphic retellings of the event to those who hadn't been lucky enough to witness it. Few expressed curiosity about why the body had exploded, or whether it had anything to do with the mission to Molva. It had been a magical event, after all, and Khirians couldn't work magic.

Normally that would have been enough for Reef, but the knot of dread that he had begun to feel when the navarch mentioned Molva had twisted a little tighter when the dead body walked into the room. Reef didn't know why, and not knowing the reason for the feeling bothered him more than the feeling itself.

Because he couldn't make sense of it, he pushed the feeling away. His primary concern now was getting as many of his shoal swimmers as possible into the lineup and making sure he won a place himself.

As he watched the current battles Reef saw Breaking Wave crossing the sand towards him and knew from his quick stride that he had news. Sure enough, when Wave was still several yards away, he jerked his head in the direction of the ocean surf and the brilliant moon. He wanted to talk without being overheard.

Even Keel lounged nearby, laid back as always. "I'm going to speak with Wave," Reef said to the swimmer. "Keep an eye on things until I get back."

Keel coughed an agreement. He glanced out toward the ocean but asked no questions. In a few minutes Reef had joined Breaking Wave at the edge of the beach where the waters of the Gemmic sea splashed and curled around their feet and tails. As soon as Reef was close enough to hear, the pointswimmer spoke in a grating whisper. "Leader, I can't find Beach Cliffs."

Reef held himself still, refusing to let his tail whip and betray his worry. He guessed Breaking Wave was doing the same. "When did you last see her?" Reef asked.

Wave shrugged. "She was at the other end of the beach with us, watching the fighting. She said she was going to go for a swim. I told her to come right back, but she didn't."

Frustration and worry rumbled up in Reef's chest. If he guessed correctly, Beach Cliffs was in more danger than his swimmers currently doing battle. "I told her to stay behind on the archipelago."

"Seems like she doesn't listen to you either," Wave remarked.

"We have to find her."

Wave nodded and coughed a respectful yes. "She must have gone up the coast. She would have wanted to get away as quickly as possible. I will go with you."

For a moment Reef considered going alone, but with the Khirian shoals currently involved in such fierce competition, it wouldn't be safe. He nodded. "Tell Keel and Redwater you and I are going for a swim. Ask them to keep an eye out for a good fight for me. I'll meet you at the other end of the beach."

Breaking Wave caught up to Reef before he had reached the other end of the camp and the two of them walked out into the dark water together, flaring their backfins open as they went. "She will have gone north," Reef said, "to the caves to hide. If you sense her underwater, signal me."

In a rush, the vibrations, currents, and fields of energy making up the tapestry of the ocean's life began flooding in through Reef's fins. The reverberations of the tide tore against the shore's boulders and hit Reef as the gentlest of thunders. Tiny hums from anemones mingled with the click and shiver of feeding crabs. Occasional flicks and wrigglings, wrapped around rapid heartbeats, told Reef there were some small fish about. Sculpins, most likely. Reef even felt the strong swish of other Khirians hunting in the water, but none of them were large enough to be Beach Cliffs.

Wave must not have sensed her either. The two of them swam out and north until they had left all the other swimming Khirians behind, then Reef screeched out the short command to surface. He and Wave bobbed up and looked across the waves. There were no ships in sight, and no one, mammal or reptile, on the moonlit beach. "We can walk from here," Reef said.

They returned to the beach, which at this location was no longer sandy, but covered with rocks of all shapes and sizes, from pebbles to great rough slabs of stone, and kept heading north.

She would have come this way, Reef thought. He knew Beach Cliffs probably better than she thought. He knew what she would do… but what if they couldn't find her in time? Then he heard a cry, the long creaking cry of a Khirian in pain. Wave kept pace with him as Reef ran, leaping across tide pools and sliding along algae-coated rocks. He saw a jagged hole in the face of the beach bluffs, a cave, the perfect place to hide. He also saw the beginnings of a trail of blood.

"Wait here," Reef commanded as he reached the entrance, then he ducked inside.

The creaking had stopped. Beach Cliffs had probably heard them approach. Only a meager patch of moonlight filtered into the cave.

"Beach Cliffs?" he barked into the darkness.

"Go away," the answer sounded from the shadows, a hoarse and shaking voice, but unmistakably Beach Cliffs. Then pain overwhelmed her, and she shrieked again, a terrible sound that made Reef pull his fins in tighter.

"Your eggs have come?" Reef asked. Even as he asked it, he knew it was a pointless question. Of course, her eggs had come. Nothing else could defeat Beach Cliffs like this. This was her third year without a mate but for some reason her eggs always grew, and when they tried to force their way out of her they made her bleed. Reef asked a marginally less stupid question: "What can I do?"

"Come in here and kill me," Beach Cliffs answered. Reef's eyes had begun to adjust to the deeper darkness of the cave. He could make out her white-scaled bulk, curled against the left wall a short way inside. Mostly white-scaled. Her legs and tail were streaked with blood.

"I will not kill you," Reef said.

"Then I will die—" the female Khirian began, but another screech of pain interrupted her words. She curled inward in agony, and Reef's mind began racing.

He knew on the archipelago, the other female Khirians had some way of breaking the eggs so their contents could be expelled in liquid form and the soft shells deflated and pushed out. That was why Reef had told Beach Cliffs to stay behind. Refusing to be left out of the journey to the Gemmic Coast, Beach Cliffs had disobeyed him. What could Reef do now? He considered trying to break the eggs himself, but how? By putting some sharp object into his soldier's cloaca? Would she let him? Would he kill her by accident? Would he even have the nerve to try it?

Beach Cliffs screamed again and the sound made Reef feel sick with grief and anger. She was one of his best, strongest, toughest, most reliable swimmers. She shouldn't have to die like this. "Stay calm," he ordered her. "Try to hold them back. I will do something. I will not let you die."

Breaking Wave was waiting for him when Reef exited the cave.

"What are you going to do?" Wave asked.

"Keep watch," Reef said. "Do not move from this spot. I need to find a healer." He started back south, looking for a way up the bluffs.

"A healer?" Wave exclaimed. "You mean a human healer? Reef, you can't do that."

"Don't tell me what I can't do, pointswimmer."

Wave followed, rebuffing Reef's order with his usual fierce candor. "If anyone finds out, they'll take the shoal from you. I don't want to deal with Knotweed or Shorecrust as shoal leader."

"Then make sure they don't find out."

"You think a human will help?! They're stupid and cowards. We eat them. They fear us. They won't help, or if they do, they'll bring an army with them. Everyone will know."

He was probably right. It was an impossible situation, impossible that a human would help, and impossible that Reef should stay and allow Beach Cliffs to die.

Then a memory pushed itself into Reef's mind. He remembered the tall, brown-skinned woman weaving her way through the Khirian ranks shouting that she was a healer. Reef had been just a few feet from her, close enough to see the shells stitched across the eggshell-colored fabric of her dress, strangely comforting and recognizable, like a piece of coastline detached from the water. But then his eyes settled on her brown skin. He hadn't seen human skin that color, or eyes that deep brown, in many years, and the memory it brought to his mind made him hope to never see her again.

He did his best to brush all those feelings aside, the comfort, the confusion, the fear. Healer, she had said, and as he remembered her now, he thought she had looked remarkably unafraid. Perhaps if he could find her, or a healer like her, he could convince them to help.

"I have to try. Guard the cave until I get back. If something happens, Redwater will help you keep the shoal."

Breaking Wave gave a growl of disapproval, but Reef knew that Wave would follow orders. He always did in the end. "All right," Wave called after him. "I'll be here."

Reef continued north, in the direction of the Council Building, looking for a place where he could begin to climb the beach bluffs. There was another obstacle he would have to face, Reef realized: with the Khirians nearby the Kyrillan Dunami would vigilantly guard the coast. This thought made Reef pause and look up at the edge of the cliffs over a dozen stories up. He couldn't see anyone, but they had probably spotted him already. Would they let a Khirian advance, or rain arrows down on him from above?

The helplessness and humiliation of defeat began to creep into his mind. Reef fought it back. There had to be something he could do.

My, my, you have a lot of feelings for a cold-blooded creature.

The voice made Reef jump. He spun, tail scattering pebbles, and pulled his maul from his back, ready to attack the source of the voice, but there was no one there.

The voice chuckled, not aloud, but in Reef's mind. *Poor, ignorant reptile,* it said in amused lament.

It had to be magic. But magic couldn't affect Khirians.

Not magic, a Magic. And I'm special, the voice added.

It was reading his mind!

Don't worry about it. Just be glad I'm on your side.

A shiver ran down Reef's fins. "I don't want trouble," he said, hoping the unseen person would be able to understand Khirian.

I know. You want a healer.

Yes.

Lucky for you I know where you can find one, and you won't even have to venture inland. She's on a boat.

Reef turned as a fresh volley of golden fireworks rocketed up from the harbor.

Look, I've even lit it up for you, the Magic commented.

No, this couldn't be happening. It had to be a trap.

Well, that's your gamble then, isn't it? Will you trust me and let me lead you to your piece-of-coastline healer, or make for the council building by yourself and try to explain to the Dunamis that you need a midwife?

Reef looked from the ocean to the cliffs and then back again. She's out there, he asked?

She's out there.

Reef took a deep breath. Alright, he agreed, and he hurried back out to the water.

Reef swam south again, past the Khirian camp, down to the harbor, the knot of dread tightening in his belly. This time at least Reef could make sense of it. Human boats, he didn't like to swim around them. Most of his experience of human boats involved violence and death. But he had a mission, and he wouldn't let his trepidation derail it.

In the harbor the surface of the water was choppy, not just with waves and ships, but something else Reef didn't recognize.

It's a water show of sorts. There are a lot of spectators, so don't surface until you're right near the hull.

Reef did as he said and saw, some yards from the ships, two giant shapes made of water, like enormous cat lizards with wings. They seemed to catch the moonlight and glow with it, silvery white and shimmering. As he watched they lunged toward one another and clashed together.

Dragons. You must have been too far inland in Molva to see them. I'm rather fond of dragons myself, but these are merely displays created by Archavie and Harol, not the real thing. Now, if you move a little further to stern and climb up, you should find her.

Reef did as he recommended and found an anchor rope to climb.

Watch out, the Magic warned.

Reef heard a retching sound and swung to the side just in time to dodge a spatter of vomit.

"I could put an anti-nausea knot in your brain," a calm female voice suggested.

"Nah, too much magic in me already," a higher-pitched voice replied. It sounded strained, and shortly retched again.

Ready this time, Reef pulled himself further left as the vomit cascaded down.

"Besides, I'm making room for another round of shrimp."

"I told you not to jump so soon after eating."

Go now, the Magic told Reef. *This is your best chance to stay undetected.*

As Reef hauled himself up the rope he heard the spectators of the magical water-dragon match shouting, stomping, and applauding. Overhead the calmer voice cried out

"Gamalielle!" Then it took on a scolding tone. "Turus, you can't just knock people unconscious!"

Reef pulled himself up the last few feet of rope and over the railing of the deck, landing as lightly as he could on the other side. He had arrived in a relatively private corner of the ship, between crates of supplies, a good place to go throw up. The brown-skinned healer crouched on the ground, holding the limp form of a tawny-furred cat who had vomit on her whiskers. The healer wore Gemmic clothes now, a cascade of deep purple fabric, with a shawl on top, and she pulled the cat a little closer as she looked up at him, her dark eyes wide, clearly terrified. If she were in the water, Reef guessed he would feel the racing of her heart. Maybe she wasn't as fearless as he thought.

Oh, give her a medical emergency and she'll forget fear exists.

Reef hoped so. "Healer," he said, finding the word much harder to pronounce than to recognize. "Need healer."

The healer looked around at the air and said in a shaking voice. "I take it this is your scheme?"

She was speaking to the Magic, Reef realized, and it answered so both she and Reef could hear. *What gives you that idea?*

"Because you're here and you're not raining down fire on…"

Him.

"On him."

You are correct.

The healer fixed her eyes on Reef again. The Magic was right, the bright blaze of bravery had already come into her eyes, but Reef couldn't bear to look at them long. He started to feel other boards beneath his feet and hear shrieks of terror between the musical pings of the Qawahn's drums.

"You're not injured," the healer said. "Why do you need a healer?"

Reef's throat was closing up. The healer. The mock battle. The knowledge that with every passing moment Beach Cliffs might die. Get it together Reef, he told himself, but speaking human words was difficult at the best of times.

Use your own words then, Turus said. *I'll translate.*

"One of my shoal," Reef explained in Khirian. "She is gravid, and her eggs will kill her. They can't come out. She is bleeding. She will die if you do not help."

The healer considered this. "I do have my healer's tools with me, at Archavie's insistence." She spoke to the unseen Magic again. "Does this mean you're going to take care of Gamalielle?"

Just leave her here.

The healer groaned.

Fine, I'll send someone to get her after you're gone.

"Promise?"

I swear on my wizard's life. Just help this desperate reptile. I'll even fly you there. Now let's get going before it's all for naught.

Chapter Twelve

PROVEN

Reef

THEY made their way back to the cave, Reef below the water and the healer soaring above it. Every time Reef surfaced, she was there, holding tightly to her satchel while the ocean winds whipped her cloak about her and sent her curly hair flying about her face. Finally, Reef returned to shore and Turus deposited the healer on the rocks just beyond the tide.

The shoreline here from waves to cliffs was all slabs of stone, pitted with tide pools, layered upon one another in slick uneven steps. At least they were lit by the moon, the shine on the rocks and the algae like a warning saying tread carefully, you may fall. With his huge, clawed feet and tail for balance, Reef could run across them evenly, but the healer stumbled and wavered, even after she had taken off her sandals.

"Turus," she called, over the roar and crash of the waves.

Do you expect me to do everything? The Magic answered irritably.

"Don't be difficult, not right now."

I'm not the only person here who can help you. Mortals. Always wanting a handout.

Fine. Reef would rather not have the Magic interfere any more than it needed to anyway. He didn't trust it. He quickly closed the distance between himself and the healer and held out his hands. She regarded them, and Reef saw the fear flicker back into the shadowed depths of her eyes. What had she seen Khirian hands do? Whatever it was, he hoped she could put it aside.

"We must hurry," he told her. "I will not hurt you." He hoped it would be true, as she reached out determinedly and took his hands, he thought hers were so small and so soft. He told himself not to hold them too tightly. He knew he could break human bones. He had never tried not to before.

But she did not seem to be in any pain as she gripped his hands and together, they picked their way across the loose rocks and slabs of stone broken up by tidepools. Breaking Wave came to meet them some yards from the cave entrance. Without asking, he grabbed one of the healer's elbows. "Hurry," he also said. The tone in his voice drove the healer's comfort out of Reef's mind. He took hold of her other arm, and he and Wave carried her the rest of the distance to the cave.

Reef understood then, why Wave hadn't made any brash comments about his surprise at Reef's success: Beach Cliffs had stopped screaming. From the cave Reef heard only a guttural crackle and thin whine.

The healer stumbled past him and into the cave. "Turus," she called. "I know you're there. Stop being a jerk and make me some light."

A beam of light shot down from the ceiling of the cave and fell upon Beach Cliffs where she lay on the cave floor. She had lost a lot of blood. Reef could see it in the pale color of her backfin, which hung weakly, half unfolded from her back.

"My name is Kaeda," the healer said, as she approached Beach Cliffs. "I'm a healer. I'm here to help."

Unsurprisingly, Beach Cliffs used what was left of her strength to level a clawed swipe in the healer's direction.

"Stop," Reef stepped forward to growl at her.

"Leave me alone. Let me die." Beach Cliffs creaked out.

"I won't let you die."

"You should."

Reef's tail slapped the cave floor in a thunderous crack. "Don't argue with me, swimmer!" he roared. "My shoal would be weaker without you. You will let the healer help you, you will live, and you will swim with my shoal again."

Reef could see in Beach Cliff's expression that she had given up. She was ashamed of her present situation, but if Reef would take responsibility for her life, then she would obey him. "She will do whatever you say," he told the healer.

"Do Khirians have blood types?" The healer asked him.

Reef shrugged. Different types of blood? Wasn't all blood the same?

"No transfusions then," the healer sighed. "And my magical blood substitute wouldn't work." She knelt and addressed Beach Cliffs. "I'm trying to heal the tears in your birth canal, or, that is, your cloaca, but your resistance to magic is making it nearly impossible. As far as I can tell your eggs have decided it's time to come out, but your cloaca won't let them. It's not stretching as it should, so the eggs are tearing you apart. Please try not to push. I'll try to come up with another solution."

Beach Cliffs cast an exhausted look up at Reef as if to say he could make her cooperate, but he couldn't make her talk to this stupid woman. Reef waited in trepidation while the healer shut her eyes and sat in silence. When she looked up at him again, Reef asked, "She will not die?"

The healer sighed, climbed to her feet, and motioned for Reef to follow her to the other side of the cave. "Try not to push," she reminded Beach Cliffs as they moved away. When they were out of easy earshot, she faced Reef and answered his question. "I've stopped the bleeding, but I can't heal her properly and I can't stop her labor. Honestly, the safest thing to do would be to get her to an ascleppa where I could work with a team."

"No," Reef interrupted.

"She's terrified and exhausted," the healer argued. "An ascleppa would have the non-magical equipment necessary to safely remove the eggs by cesarean section, and to collect her own blood so there would be less danger of her dying from exsanguination."

Turus's translation didn't make much more sense to Reef than the healer's Gemmic words, but he knew getting more humans involved would cause more problems than it would solve. Beach Cliffs shrieked, and the healer reminded her not to push.

"I don't know anything about the Khirian nervous system," the healer went on. "Without help, I won't be able to do surgery. I don't know if I'll even be able to slow her contractions. The only option will be to try to get the eggs out through her cloaca, but I can't tell for sure if that will be possible. I don't know how much of the situation is brought on by her extreme fear and the rapidly progressing labor, or whether she has an issue with the hormones or hormone receptors in her reproductive system. I don't know enough about Khirians to make an accurate assessment."

Again, Reef had no idea what she was talking about, but he didn't think it had to be so complicated. "Usually, other females will break the eggs for her," he informed her. "Can you do that?"

"Break them?" The healer exclaimed. She glanced back toward Beach Cliffs, then looked up at Reef again. Reef tried to read the expression on her face but couldn't tell if she was sad, worried, shocked, or something else entirely. "How many times has this happened?" she asked.

"This is the fourth year," Reef told her.

The healer's mouth hung open for a moment, then she set her jaw in determination. "What's your name?" she asked.

Reef swished his tail, not sure he wanted to tell her. "You're her commanding officer?" the healer asked instead.

"Yes."

"And does she trust you?"

"Yes."

"Good, because she doesn't seem to trust me, and this is going to be uncomfortable for all of us."

The two of them rejoined Beach Cliffs, and the healer explained what she wanted to do. She would attempt to relax her patient's cloaca and increase its elasticity with a combination of massage and non-magic medicine Reef didn't bother trying to translate. She would hopefully be able to ease Beach Cliff's pain and minimize loss of blood until all the eggs had been pushed out safely.

"I'll need you to roll onto your back," the healer instructed, as Beach Cliffs screeched in response to another contraction. The woman looked through her satchel of healer's supplies and finally pulled out a jar full of a transparent jiggly substance, along with several other small bottles, a syringe, and a towel. "And keep doing your best not to push."

Beach Cliffs turned a wide eye up toward Reef. Her expression said she would rather die than let a human healer massage her cloaca.

"You are Beach Cliffs," Reef said, "and you will live." That would be enough, he thought, to remind her of her own strength. He was right. Beach Cliffs took a deep breath and shifted away from the wall and onto her back. Then she gave Reef a sharper look.

"Turn around."

Reef obediently turned his back and took a few steps away to make room for his tail behind him. "Ready?" the healer's voice asked. "This gel already contains both a magical and nonmagical analgesic– that is, a pain reliever – I'll give you something a bit stronger as well. It should be safe, though I don't know how well it will work on a Khirian. I want you to take a deep breath. Inhale. Now exhale. Another. Inhale. Now exhale. Here we go."

Beach Cliffs growled, but since the healer didn't scream, Reef assumed Beach Cliffs had not attacked her.

The healer's work took a long time. Eventually Breaking Wave looked in on them and received an ear-splitting rebuke from Beach Cliffs in response.

"It's not like it's mating season or anything," Wave grumbled as he and Reef left the females in the cave.

Reef shrugged. He didn't understand it either, but he didn't want to make Beach Cliffs more uncomfortable. He could tell from the tone of Beach Cliff's voice that she had calmed down and was in a lot less pain.

"How long will it take?" Breaking Wave asked. They had walked out toward the surf where the ocean breeze blew cool air inland over the moonlit waves. Now Reef's pointswimmer glanced up at the bright disk of the moon. "If you want to fight for a circle, you should go back soon."

Reef shook his head. "Not until the healer has left."

"Is Beach Cliffs still in danger?"

Reef wasn't sure, but he didn't want to leave the healer here without protection. "I want to make sure she doesn't hurt the healer."

"The healer is just a human," Breaking Wave said in a dismissive tone.

"Just a human who saved one of your shoal mates," Reef growled back.

Breaking Wave grumbled, and Reef heard his tail scattering pebbles behind them. "Fine. I promise Beach and I won't hurt her. You should go back."

Reef shook his head. If he went back now, he would be too preoccupied to fight well. He had hoped to be able to accompany the Gem's party, but he told himself saving Beach Cliffs would have to be worth the sacrifice.

Wave grumbled again. "I don't understand you."

That was fine, Reef thought. His swimmers didn't have to understand him; they just had to respect him and obey him.

He stood outside for a few minutes longer and then left Wave to keep watch as he returned to the cave. The healer's work seemed to go on forever, and she kept talking the whole time. Her chatter was probably driving Beach Cliffs crazy. Finally, the healer said, "All right, push." A few moments later she cried out with relief and joy. "That's the first one! Good job!"

Reef resisted the urge to turn around. Praise followed praise as egg after egg made it into the cave whole and unbroken. "Five," the healer announced. "That's the last one. You did so well."

Silence followed this proclamation, and a shiver of trepidation scuttled across Reef's fins. Without waiting for permission, he turned, ran the few steps to the healer, caught hold of her with both hands, and pulled her back away from Beach Cliffs, just as Beach Cliff's shrieked again.

"What's going on?" the healer cried.

Reef continued to drag the human away as Beach Cliffs turned onto her side and used her tail to sweep the pile of leathery eggs toward herself. She curled around them and began to cry more violently than she had yet that night.

"What's going on?" This time the question came from Breaking Wave as he met them at the mouth of the cave. The healer automatically shrank away from the less familiar Khirian and towards Reef, which made it all the easier for him to pull her outside.

"She's fine," Reef said. Wave was willing to accept this explanation, but the healer wasn't.

"Please tell me. Did I do something? What is it?"

Reef pushed her away from him more forcefully than he meant to, and she stumbled on the rocky shore and fell. He should have been gentler, he thought, to a human who had saved one of his shoal, but it was difficult to remember. "Your job is done," he said. "You can go."

The healer pulled herself to her feet. "I'm not leaving until I know my patient is alright," she said. "And my satchel is still in the cave."

This human had proved to be determined enough that Reef didn't doubt her words. "Fetch the healer's tools," he ordered Wave. As his pointswimmer's footfalls faded into the cave, Reef spoke softly to the healer. "I told you all of her eggs were broken."

"Yes but…" The healer looked toward the cave, her brow furrowed. "These eggs were not fertilized. Were the others?"

"Fertilized?"

"They had baby Khirians inside?"

Reef nodded. "Only the first clutch. All died."

The healer looked up sharply. Now, lit by the moon, he could see the clarity of her eyes, rich in color like pebbles after rain. No, more like those lakes in northern Molva where the water sparkled coppery brown instead of blue. Tears welled over the brown, then overflowed and ran down the sides of her face in two long streaks.

Reef didn't understand. He knew humans cried this way, with tears, when distressed or in pain, but why should she cry now? He was sure he hadn't hurt her, and she did not seem frightened.

For a long moment, Reef held her gaze. She could not be crying for Beach Cliffs, he thought at last. A human would not cry for a Khirian's loss. Would she?

Then Breaking Wave returned. The healer brushed away her tears, and took the satchel without further protest.

"I will make sure you get back safely," Reef said, but the healer shook her head.

"You should stay here with her. Turus will take care of me."

Reef didn't argue. He could smell the coming dawn. There might still be time for him to win a space in the lineup, but only if he hurried. "If you tell anyone what has happened," he said, "I will find you, and I will kill you."

The healer smiled a little as if she didn't believe a word of it. "Don't worry, I won't tell anyone. If our species ever become friends, I would be happy to help your swimmer lay another clutch." When neither Reef nor Wave answered, the woman said, "Well, goodnight." She turned and began to pick her way across the rocky beach.

The two Khirians watched her for a moment or two, then Wave said, "Run. If you go now, you can still make it."

"You will make sure Beach Cliffs is all right?" Reef asked. "And you will not kill the healer?"

Wave scoffed. "How long have I been in your shoal? How many of your strange orders have I followed? Go. Go!"

Reef turned and took off running back toward the Khirian camp. The black of the sky had begun to fade into blue grey, but the fighting wasn't over yet. As Reef came into view of the Khirian camp, Even Keel and Sea Star ran to meet him.

"Where have you been?" Keel asked.

"Have you lined up a fight for me?"

"Yes," Keel answered, "but not a good one. It's almost dawn."

The watching Khirians gathered around the circles had grown much calmer since Reef had left. As Reef, Keel, and Sea Star approached, Voice of Thunder spotted them. He and the navarch sat atop a tumbled row of boulders, watching the proceedings. The Voice of Thunder gave a beach-shaking roar. Reef skidded to a halt so when the crowd turned to look at him, he wouldn't appear to be so hurried.

"Unseen Reef, will you fight?"

Reef coughed a yes, then listened as Keel whispered in his ear. "Stonefish has the second circle. He's your best choice for a win without making any enemies or fighting one of your own."

Reef grumbled an acknowledgement before walking forward. The crowd parted and made space for Reef to pace along the row of circles so he could pick his fight. Reef did, taking time to note that Lightning, one of Reef's quickest, hardest-hitting swimmers, held the third circle, and Urchin Sting, one of Reef's newest recruits, the first.

Urchin Sting would be an easy fight, and was young enough that he probably wouldn't mind if Reef beat him. But Reef didn't want to. He liked Sting. Everyone liked Sting. But no one liked Stonefish. Reef stopped in front of Stonefish's circle. "Unseen Reef will challenge Stonefish," Voice of Thunder called out.

Stonefish glared at Reef, his eyes gleaming sharply between the many rugged ridges on his face. He was a fierce opponent, and unfortunately Reef knew little about his fighting style.

The Khirian spectators shifted around them, forming a ring around Stonefish's patch of blood-soaked sand as Reef and Stonefish both flared open their fins. The defending Khirian threw back his head and roared. Reef did the same. The members of their respective shoals joined in as well, bombarding the coastal bluffs with noise.

As usual, the opponents exchanged three breaths of roars, then Stonefish pulled in his fins and lunged towards Reef.

Reef expected him to attack first, and to attack fast. Stonefish probably wanted the fight to be over quickly before Reef could do anything impressive. As the crowd of Khirians continued to lend their vocal encouragement, Stonefish slashed with both sets of claws.

Reef ducked beneath the sweeping strikes and pushed forward, grabbing hold of Stonefish's shins pushing so the Khirian's momentum carried him over Reef's shoulder and sent him crashing into the sand and pebbles of the beach. Reef leapt onto his back before the other Khirian could rise and wrapped both arms around his throat, hoping to cut off his air supply.

No such luck. Reef felt a wave of muscular energy roll down his opponent's body, and then Stonefish's tail whipped around to slap Reef's side. At the same time, the downed Khirian had reared up off the ground. It was an impressive display of both strength and tail flexibility. Reef couldn't keep him down, but he dug his claws into Stonefish's neck so as the other Khirian rose Reef's claws would rake across his throat. He realized too late that Stonefish was turning sharply as he rose, driving his right elbow toward Reef. The elbow struck Reef in the face, knocking his head back and giving Stonefish an unobstructed target. Two sets of claws tore across Reef's stomach and Reef felt sharp flashes of pain as four of the claws bit into his front fin.

Reef staggered back with a roar of pain and anger, and quickly glanced down at the slashes. The cuts were straight and not deep. They would heal easily, but in the meantime, the nerves in his fin spread a terrible stinging pain up and down the centerline of his body.

Stonefish was on his feet and squaring off to face Reef again. Again, Reef saw the fierce, merciless look in his eyes. Again, Reef thought Stonefish didn't want the fight to go on for too long. He knew Reef had a reputation of waiting until late in a fight to really show his skill. Usually, Reef liked to drag a fight out, put on a show for whoever was watching, but right now Reef only wanted to win. It had been a long night already; he wanted to get this over with. Before Stonefish could attack again, Reef charged at him.

He landed one hit, barely scratching Stonefish across the nose with his right claws, but Stonefish caught Reef's left hand in his right, and with his left leveled a punch at Reef's face. Reef dodged, and the punch glanced off the side of his neck. Stonefish tried to grab his neck instead, but Reef brought his right arm up and broke the hold easily.

Then Stonefish did something else Reef had not expected. Taking advantage of his grip on Reef's left hand, he pulled Reef down, leaned back on his tail, and kicked out with both legs. His feet hit Reef's chest and left shoulder, tearing deeper gashes into his torso and Reef felt a pop and a wave of pain as the jolt dislocated his arm.

Reef couldn't believe it. He must have been more distracted and exhausted by Beach Cliff's situation than he thought, and now he would have to fight with one arm.

Impressed murmurs rose from the crowd as Reef was pushed backward. Falling back toward his feet, Stonefish continued forward, in a headlong lunge at his now severely injured opponent. Again, Reef sought to land him on the ground. He leapt to the side and spun so his tail smacked against Stonefish's back. Already overbalanced, the strike sent Stonefish back down into the blood clumped sand. Again, Reef jumped on his back, driving his knees down hard into Stonefish's shoulders. With his good hand he found the claw-gashes he had already made on Stonefish's throat and gave a grating growl as he dug his claws deeper. Stonefish would know that if Reef cut his throat too deeply, he could kill him. At the same time, Reef hoped Stonefish would realize he was showing him respect. The ventral fin did not continue across a Khirian's throat. Reef could have raked his claws down Stonefish's backfin in revenge for his own cut fin, but he hadn't.

If Stonefish was conscious of Reef's courtesy, he didn't show it. He grabbed hold of Reef's good hand, turned his head, and sank his teeth into his opponent's forearm.

Those who saw the bite fell silent. A bite meant a challenge to the death, and for Reef, it was the last straw. Fueled by adrenaline and rage, Reef tore his arm out of Stonefish's mouth. He hardly felt the pain, though he saw a weeping red valley where a chunk of his arm used to be.

With a roar Reef drove the elbow of the same arm down into Stonefish's head again and again as the Khirian twisted beneath him, until he could see Stonefish's eyes were drifting out of focus. Then, still ignoring the damage to his right arm, Reef grabbed the top of Stonefish's snout, anchored a foot inside of his adversary's mouth, and stood up, tearing off the other Khirian's jaw. He recognized Redwater's voice first, then Teeth of Shark's and Keel's voices, as the Khirian spectators erupted in a riot of cheers.

Reef threw the body down with disgust and stalked to the center of the circle he had won. He fanned out his fins, lifted his head, and roared again. His shoal roared with him. Keel and Redwater came to help Reef push his dislocated shoulder back into place, and the light of dawn spilled over the cliffs from the east. Reef would stand before the council.

Chapter Thirteen

THE KHIRIAN IN THE PARTY

Kaeda

I did not go back to the party ship but found the coastal path up to the council complex and headed straight for my room where I cleaned up and changed out of my bloodstained clothes as quickly as I could. Then I scrambled to find paper and graphite and write everything down. Sketches, notes, observations— the details slipped from my fatigued mind before I could get them all onto paper. I sketched what I could remember of the chambers and connections of the female Khirian reproductive system, some notes about Khirian bone marrow, which seemed able to produce red blood cells at a much quicker rate than human bone marrow and did my best to roughly draw a Khirian skeleton.

A few hours ago, Khirians had seemed terrifying and alien. In some ways I guess they still were. But I had met a male Khirian desperate to help one of his soldiers, and a female Khirian in desperate need of medical intervention. Both of their predicaments were so relatable. How many times had a family or neighbor come to me to request help for someone in dire need? How many mothers had I coached through difficult labors? Suddenly they had become people to me. And one of those people would shortly join my team. It would probably be the officer who had come to find me, since Turus already seemed to have picked him out.

You never know, Turus said in my mind. *Reef might be dead by morning.*

I looked up sharply.

I'm just kidding. He'll be fine. More or less.

I reminded myself not to take Turus too seriously and got back to scribbling. I didn't want to waste an ounce of the knowledge I had gained. I wrote until I found myself yawning and struggling to keep my eyes open, but I kept myself going long enough to vaguely sketch out a couple of Khirian visages, noting the patterns of ridges on their faces. The female Khirian had only a few, Reef had many, and the other male had one extra ridge down the center of his nose, an unusual feature I had not seen on any other Khirian. Then I paused. I was missing something, I thought. Something important. As I took a deep breath and my mind stilled, an image rose to the surface. Hands. Reef's hands, reaching out to help me across the rocky beach.

I picked up a fresh piece of paper but waited and took a moment to remember. Compared to an oviduct and cloaca, how familiar were four fingers and an opposable thumb? And yet how intimidating they had seemed at that moment.

I began another sketch, trying to get the details right. The finger closest to the thumb was longest, the pads of the palm substantial. The hand did not have the bony boxyness of some human hands, not as much of an obvious skeletal distinction at the wrist. Many anatomical features of a Khirian, I reflected, were smooth, aerodynamic, ideal for swimming.

I paused again and closed my eyes, letting my thoughts drift back so I could make a note on scales, but instead found myself dwelling on another memory. When Reef told me about the female Khirian's first clutch of eggs I had been struck by the sadness of her losing all her children. As I began to cry, I saw him watching me.

I wouldn't have been able to capture his look in graphite. I would need green. Many shades of green, dimmed to a mossy darkness in the night. Despite the shadows there was something bright. Something bright and deep, like one of the pearls I liked to find, hidden but catching a ray of sunlight. It called me to swim closer, to figure out what it was, why it was there.

Those eyes… but those teeth. The concern for his swimmers now… but what violent history five years ago?

A puzzle for another time. Now I could barely pull back the covers before I collapsed in my bed and fell asleep, exhausted.

I must have slept through the delivery of my breakfast tray, because when I finally woke it was to Corinna exclaiming that the council was about to meet. I barely had time to wash my face and grab a pita stuffed with goat cheese and dates before rushing off to the council meeting chamber.

They could choose the Khirian representative without you, Turus remarked.

Not a chance, I thought back.

You can't wait to see Reef again.

I laughed out loud. There's enough drama happening already without you making some up, I told him, though my heart gave a sudden thud as I nearly lost my footing on the perfectly smooth floor.

It was the sandals, I told myself. They were probably damaged by my coastal hike yesterday. I chose my steps more carefully and made it to the doors to the meeting chamber. The tiers of marble seats were already filling up with councilors from the incorporated city states, and speakers from some others.

Gamalielle bounded up as I walked into the room. "Come on. I got seats in the front row." As I followed her across the wide-open space of the chamber floor to the seats on the other side the cat rambled on. "I can't believe I passed out before the water dragon battle ended. Archie told me our team won though. Did I miss anything else?"

I remembered Reef vaulting over the rail of the ship, white scales glistening with seawater in the moonlight. "Not really. Just more of the same."

Gamalielle sighed. "I wish Turus had woken me up. It's probably going to be all seriousness from here on out."

"It's probably best that you got some rest."

We found the seats where Gamalielle had strewn a cloak topped with assorted pastries to claim our space. "Did you have breakfast? Here! Eat up."

As we picked up the snacks and brushed away the crumbs a moderator's amplified voice cut through the chatter. "Attention. Will all attendees please find their seats?"

As the other spectators settled into their places, I saw Archavie, Gallo, and General Straton come to stand in the center of the floor. When the commotion of the room had stilled, the Archcouncilor gave the signal for the doors to be opened.

The council chamber must have been soundproofed, for the Khirians were waiting just outside. Now the harsh rumble of voices, the brushing of tails, filled the room as the Khirians filed in, filling the western half of the floor.

Their leader stepped out in front. "Three swimmers, as you asked."

Three Khirians emerged from the group. And… was that him? I recognized the pattern of ridges on his face… but those gashes? Brown stripes of clotted blood ran across his chest and stomach. The wounds looked recent enough that I would still be able to stitch them shut effectively, but I didn't think that was the worst of it. He held himself differently, stiffly, as if in pain, and one arm had been wrapped in seaweed from the elbow down.

Archavie, I have to help him, I thought.

Don't worry, the wizard answered. Then he stepped forward, his voice echoing off the high walls. "The Molvan Magical Crisis Commission is serious business," he began, with exaggerated solemnity. "As such, the Archcouncilor has invited me to read these recruits' minds to determine which will be the best fit for our party. With a flourish he pushed back his long, flowing sleeves. "If any of you object to having your minds read, please rejoin your comrades."

Two of the Khirians shifted uncertainly but Reef didn't move at all. He was probably already used to Turus's interruptions, I thought.

"Very well," Archavie said. "I suggest you close your eyes. This can be rather jarring."

He lifted his hands. As one, the Khirian candidates stumbled, and laughter rippled across the tiered seats. I saw the other two Khirians hold out their arms for balance, but Reef only widened his stance.

So, both arms injured so badly that he didn't want to move them, and me forced to rely on physical means of healing. I would need to ask Gallo to delay our departure.

If you don't choose him, I still want to help, I thought to Archavie.

I felt the wizard's amusement like a happy pink sparkling in my mind. *This is all for show really. I can barely get into their heads. I'll start eliminating them now.*

One of the Khirians came to its senses. It shook its head, turned, and walked back to the group. The other did the same. Finally, only Reef remained standing before Archavie.

A smile broke across the wizard's face. "Reef," he said, "welcome to the Commission."

I lifted my hands to clap. It seemed like the right thing to do. But seeing no one else preparing to applaud, I let them fall back into my lap.

"Were you just going to clap for scale-face?" Gamalielle asked, crumbs falling from her whiskers.

I shrugged.

"I can't believe this." The cat rose to her feet and shouted. "Hey, Archie, did you ask him if he's eaten people? If you really can read his mind, then tell us what you saw?"

"It's my policy to maintain confidentiality when I've done a mind search," the wizard replied.

"Which means yes! If he hadn't, you would tell us."

"We agreed this was the best course of action," General Straton reminded her, while the rest of the room began muttering again.

This might be a good moment for an interruption, Archavie thought to me.

I leapt to my feet. "Excuse me Archcouncilor, Reef is badly injured, and there's not much time until our scheduled departure. I should take him to the clinic right away."

Gallo nodded. "Please follow Healer Straton," Gallo said to Reef. "She will get you patched up."

Meanwhile Gamalielle shouted. "If anything happens, I just want everyone to remember that the Council decided to send a bloodthirsty, man-eating monster on this mission."

Councilors began to speak up, many reconsidering the decision to send a Khirian with the party.

Don't worry, we'll sort it out. Archavie told me. *Just keep walking. No one will stop you.*

I did keep walking, and Reef followed close behind, out of the disorganized arguing of the council chamber, and into the quiet of the hall outside. No one got in our way, though some half a dozen guards fell into step around us. I kept wanting to glance back, to ask Reef how he was doing, and then wondering if that would seem strange. Besides Archavie and Turus, no one knew that I had already met Reef, and that that meeting gave me a reasonable level of confidence that he would not kill me. If I didn't want to give it away, how wary did I need to pretend to be?

Calm down, Kaeda, I told myself. He's your patient. If they can't deal with you taking care of a patient, that's their problem. I slowed down a little to walk beside Reef and saw the guards adjusting their grips on their weapons.

"How are you feeling?" I asked.

Reef only rumbled a little in response.

"There's a clinic just off the combat practice yard," I said. "I've packed most of my own things by now, but the clinic should have everything we need." When we arrived at the door of the clinic room where I had done physical exams for the party I looked around at the guards. "Please wait outside while I take care of my patient."

"Healer Straton, Khirians are dangerous."

"So are *impentum tardigradum,* invisible exploding curses, and plenty of other things I deal with on a daily basis. I will see my patient alone."

Apparently, they couldn't think of anything to say to that; when I opened the door and ushered Reef through, the Dunamis soldiers remained outside.

I had done a bit of diagnosis already. I could tell that his right hand was very swollen and walking beside him I could smell the infection, even over the smell of seaweed. The glassiness of his eyes suggested to me that he probably felt sick, though being a reptile, his body couldn't produce a fever.

"I want to take your vital signs," I told him. "I have a stetsalog that could do it on a non-Khirian. I doubt it will work on you but… we might as well try."

The stetsalog hung on the wall, a panel of magic between two steel handles. It began looking for a subject immediately when I took it from the wall. I pointed it at Reef until it had anchored its attention on him, and then let it go. It hovered in the air beside him, and to my surprise it began to display heart rate, blood pressure, temperature, and respiration.

"Well, alright," I said in surprise, "I don't know what your pulse and your temperature should be, but at least now we'll have a record."

A couple of padded benches flanked the door. I pulled one over and set it beside the reclining chair where the patient would usually lay. The chair would be too small for Reef and wouldn't accommodate his tail, but the bench would be an adequate substitute. Then I opened a drawer, found a blue square of magic-coated fabric, and spread it out like a tablecloth on the reclining chair. The sanitary sheet would trap and kill any viruses, bacteria, or harmful bits of magic that touched it.

"Go ahead and sit on the bench and rest your arm on this, and we'll work on getting this… bandage off."

While Reef settled himself, I wrapped a protective enchantment around my hands and up to my elbows and spread another over my face. Reef, meanwhile, remained still, as if moving hurt, and avoided looking at the seaweed-wrapped wound.

"It hurts, doesn't it?"

Reef barely nodded.

I wove a pain-blocking knot and settled it at the top of Reef's spine. I saw his eyes widen. He blinked.

"Did it work?"

Another nod.

I felt goosebumps prickle across my skin. The vitals monitor and now the pain-blocking knot too? This wasn't supposed to happen. Even the most powerful magicians in the Gemmic Commonwealth couldn't affect Khirians with magic like this. I had to conclude that it was something unique about Reef.

It occurred to me that Turus had somehow chosen for us a Khirian who lacked the normal Khirian magic resistance. A Khirian who would be susceptible to magical attacks. Instead of feeling relieved, I felt worried for Reef's sake.

"Does magic normally affect you like this?"

A vigorous shake of the head.

"When you've been in combat or… anything. Has magic been able to harm you or do anything to you?"

"No," Reef answered emphatically. "Only… fire, lightning."

"Elemental magic. Yes, that's what I would expect. Well, since it's working, I'm going to continue to treat you with magic. It will be the most efficient and most effective. Is that alright with you?"

A nod.

"Alright. I'm going to use a magical scalpel, which I should be able to calibrate to cut through the seaweed without harming you."

I crafted a precise blade of magic and showed it to Reef before beginning to cut the seaweed away. Reef's hand and arm had swollen so much that the scales were separating, the skin between them glowing the colors of a rotten sunset. The sight of it didn't bother me, but the smell. What was it? Some combination of rotting flesh, sulfur, and the fishy reek of warm seaweed. I adjusted the enchantment over my face to filter it out because it was making my stomach turn.

Fortunately, the seaweed on Reef's arm had retained enough moisture that it was not glued to the wound. Clearly, he had been bitten by another Khirian. My wartime experience told me that. The bite had torn through his tough scales and thick skin and ripped a piece of flesh from his arm, and the gap had been filled with…

I bent closer to look at the yellow mush packed into the wound. It reminded me of something. "Is that a sea urchin?" I exclaimed.

Reef glanced down, then looked away again and nodded. "Ahk-ahk," he said.

"Is this typical treatment for a bite wound?"

The Khirian blinked at me.

"Turus?" I called.

Yes, your highness?

"Don't be sarcastic; just translate for me. Reef, is this how you would usually treat a Khirian bite?"

While Reef rasped out a Khirian explanation, Turus filled in the meaning. *Yes, they call it the Protector Shell Urchin. The flesh of it helps to keep wounds from going bad, and it will build a hard outer shell. A temporary bandage until a wound begins to heal.*

"What it's doing, as far as I can tell, is emitting some kind of sulfurous substance that is acting as an antibiotic. It's a great idea, and I think it has helped slow the infection. I'm going to clean the urchin out, then I'll make an antibiotic healing field and see if that works as well as the pain blocking knot."

Having never strained sea urchin out of a wound, it took me a few minutes to craft the appropriate constellations. Finally, I lifted some sixteen ounces of urchin from Reef's arm, placed it in a dish, and got back to the magic that I knew.

My antibiotic field was hissing and sizzling across the bite wound when Archavie looked in at the door. "The council is all sorted out," he told us. "I thought I might be helpful as a more friendly translator than my uncivil Magic."

"It's up to Reef," I said.

"Yes," Reef said.

A few minutes later all that remained of the infection was a wealth of white blood cells. I began to work another enchantment that would promote revascularization and healing and caught Reef up on the treatment. "The urchin helped to protect your arm, but some tissue has been damaged beyond repair, and as you can see, a piece of your arm is completely missing. If we bring in a genesis specialist, they should be able to grow it back, using your left arm as a model."

I heard a "tsk" of disagreement and Archavie said, "Turus and I agree that it would be best not to tell anyone else that magic works on Reef."

"Do you know why healing magic can affect him?"

"Not a clue," the wizard answered cheerfully. "Handy though, isn't it?"

Is that why you chose him, I asked, letting Archavie see my worry that this would put Reef in danger.

No, the wizard replied. *Though it has been helpful that Turus can read his mind. But no, I chose him because despite a desire to win, and despite fear and danger, Reef did what he thought was right. I anticipate any Khirian accompanying us will face a great deal of emotional stress and will need a great deal of conviction to counter it.*

That was a deeper analysis than I expected, and of course predisposed me to think even better of Reef than I already did.

"It's up to you, Reef," I said aloud, turning my mind back to the missing piece of his arm. "We can bring in a genspec and your arm will be good as new. Or I can do my best, but you'll have a big scar and reduced strength and range of motion in your hand."

Reef considered this before saying, "No one else."

I got to work, ignoring knocks on the door and calls from one person or another saying we were all late to board the ship.

"Take your time," Archavie said. "They're not going to leave without us."

The scar tissue I helped Reef's body make was more durable and flexible than what a body would make on its own, but no substitute for the muscle, skin, and scales that had been bitten out of Reef's arm. When I tested his hands against each other the right could not close all the way, nor hold its grip as well.

Reef performed his own test, pulling his maul from his back. He fumbled for a moment, then adjusted his grip.

"He thinks it will be fine," Archavie reported, as Reef stowed the weapon again.

"Alright. In my limited experience with Khirians it seems that you rely on the natural armor of your scales. Since I can't grow your scales back, I would recommend we find some additional protection for your right forearm. A... gauntlet or something."

"Vambrace I think is the word you're looking for," Archavie supplied.

"Sure. I suggest we visit the armorers and see if they can fit you with a vambrace for this arm."

I wore out the council and the Commission's patience, insisting on preparations for taking Reef along. He was cold-blooded, and I had been told about the Molvan winter. He would need a magical means of staying warm. And since I could use magic on him as well, I wanted to make a body print, lest he lose more than a little bit of his arm during our journey. This I did not explain to anyone but Archavie, but I gathered up the supplies I would need to make the print while we sailed to Molva.

By the time I had gotten everything together and created a warming field that I could anchor to Reef's single vambrace, it was nearly noon, and the council was discussing whether to postpone the departure until after lunch.

"Oh, and we should make sure the ship is stocked with food appropriate for a Khirian," I added.

"You mean like the crew?" Gamalielle quipped.

It was going to be a long trip.

Chapter Fourteen

THE SKY AND THE SEA

Reef

MAYBE it was the absence of Khirian heartbeats in the vast empty blue around him. Maybe it was the constant presence of the ship, looming always on the surface of the water like a dark cloud. Maybe it was simply his own exhaustion, swimming for so long without other Khirians in formation, where he could take a break in another swimmer's slipstream.

Whatever the reason, Reef felt a knot of dread in his stomach. He knew he would have to return to the ship sooner or later, if only to avoid exhaustion, but he didn't want to.

And remember, Kaeda wants to finish your body print before we land, Archavie reminded him.

Ugh, Kaeda. Reef respected her skills, but he couldn't make her go away. She watched him. Well, they all watched him, but Kaeda watched him differently, not in a wary manner, as if she knew what to expect, and knew it was danger, but in a piercing manner, as if she were searching him.

It was terrible. When he looked at her, he tasted blood, felt living flesh struggle against his jaws. He felt that he was going to fall into the deep brown of her eyes and never find his way out. He reminded himself repeatedly that Kaeda could not read his mind as Archavie could.

Correct, the wizard agreed. *But remember that I have read your mind and I'm still here talking to you, and I picked you out for the Commission.*

Reef didn't understand that, but he did know that some of his emotional upheaval was the wizard's fault. At the selection, Archavie and Turus had rifled through Reef's memory, tearing up layers of justification like a hatchling turning over rocks to look for crabs, letting all the safely buried thoughts and feelings go scurrying wildly about. Reef had done his best to catch them and put them back, but with the stress of joining the commission and the separation from his shoal, it was no easy feat. The persistent knot of dread especially refused to listen. It remained, irritating him with its inscrutability, worst when he looked toward the Molvan's ship, sailing ahead of them.

Reef waited, hoping Archavie would give him an explanation that would finally let him extinguish the feeling of looming doom.

Sorry, I don't know why you're feeling that. It could just be because you're doing something new, and you have lots of painful memories related to boats. You know, you could try sharing your concerns. I'm sure Kaeda or General Straton would both listen.

No, absolutely not, Reef thought.

In that case, Archavie interrupted, *why don't you get some sunbathing in before you visit the medbay?*

Yes, good idea. Basking was the best rest he could get these days, since he could barely sleep if he was belowdecks at night. General Straton had hung a knotted rope from the outcurling stern of the vessel. The rope allowed him to come and go, and the stern made a decent place for sunbathing. Now Reef found the rope trailing in the water and began to haul himself up.

The weight of his weariness pulled him down along with the weight of his body, but he kept climbing. Up, past the spikes that ringed the rest of the hull of the battleship, spikes meant to keep a Khirian from climbing aboard. But then, of course, they had added the decorative prow and stern, perfect anchors for grappling hooks. It might have made Reef laugh if he wasn't so tired. He reached the curl of the stern and did his best to keep from looking at the deck. If he started paying attention to sailors, he wouldn't be able to sleep at all. Instead, he settled down onto the smooth, carved wood, letting his limbs hang over the sides. This is just a huge log, he told himself, worn smooth by the weather. The tree is partially submerged. You feel the waves. You are at home, by the water at Mossrush. Your shoal surrounds you.

It wasn't so hard to believe once the sun began to warm him. The midday rays struck his scales like the pressure of water turned into light, like the mesmerizing song of whales, but felt instead of heard. Reef wondered if sensing magic felt like that. In seconds he was asleep and dreaming.

A warm, shallow stretch of ocean beneath a starry night sky. A floor of white sand and thin strands of weeds, traversed by velvet rays and silver blennies with leafy fins. Reef swam at a leisurely pace. He had been here before. He was looking for the chasm, the place where the floor dipped away into cool darkness. There were always more fish there, with more colors than Reef ever saw when he was awake. They gathered in the coolness and swam in a broad spiral, and whispered to each other, but never to Reef. He could hear their words, but never understand them. Sometimes he wondered if he could fan out his fins while he slept, would he be able to understand them? If he could call on all his senses, would their words make sense?

He wondered but could never find out. If one of his fins snapped open, even for a second, it woke him up.

Still, somehow, in his dreams, he managed to swim well, even with his fins closed. He swam into the middle of the swirling, whispering fishes and did what he always did in this dream. He swam down until the light of the moon was a faint wavering disk, and then he turned around, racing towards the surface. Fragments of color and fragments of sound blurred all around him and then suddenly stopped. The last few feet before the surface, the water was always clear, empty, silent. Then Reef broke through the wavering silver of the water and arced into the air.

Only in his dreams could he leap so high. In waking life, he was too heavy to propel himself so far out of the water, but he could remember jumping like this when he was younger and smaller, and it felt the same now, brief but exhilarating.

And then, as sometimes happened, Reef found himself hanging in the air, looking up at the stars. They seemed much closer in his dreams than they did when he was awake. Their light bled into the clouds, making them sparkle and glow red and purple. Reef loved the feeling of weightlessness and height and was prepared to linger and watch the sky until the dream ended, but he was not prepared for the sky to move. The clouds and stars swiveled. To Reef it seemed like the rotation of a giant eye, moving to focus on him.

Reef wriggled in the air, hoping to shake himself loose from the grip of his leap. He was done. He was ready to be in the water again.

But the air wouldn't release him, and Reef knew that he had to acknowledge the gaze of the sky before it would let him go. "I see you," Reef said at last. "I see you."

The sky looked at him a moment longer. Then the stars and glowing clouds swiveled again, directing their attention to the distant shore of Molva. Reef felt a terrible dread wash over him, as if the clouds had opened and rained down fear.

"What do you want?" Reef asked. "What are you afraid of?"

The sky had no answer. It continued to gaze toward the shore, then jerked, flicking back and forth as if looking for something else in the water. Reef didn't know if it found it or not, but the stars suddenly flattened, turning back to the inanimate sky, and Reef found himself falling, falling, falling.

He woke with a start, afraid that he had rolled off the stern. But no, he felt the glossy wood beneath his stomach. He clung to it, asking himself what had just happened, and why. It took several seconds for him to calm himself. Archavie had not spoken to him, he realized. He had offered no commentary.

I don't usually bother reading your mind when you're asleep, the wizard thought. He paused, reviewing Reef's memory, and then added, *People have nightmares.*

True. Even Reef had nightmares, but never one like that, where he was sure someone was watching him.

Have you ever sailed to Molva as part of a team of humans? Have you ever had a psychic wizard talking to you at all hours of the day?

That was a good point.

You're returning to a place where you fought in a war. No wonder your brain can't relax.

Most of the dread that had rained down on Reef remained, despite his return to consciousness, and now disappointment joined it. Usually basking in the sun gave him a sense of invincibility and wellbeing. Instead, he felt wary and on guard as he rose from the stern and saw General Straton waiting for him on the deck.

General Straton seemed to be assigned to watch him, and Reef could understand why. Archavie, despite his power, was not a trusted member of the Gemmic community. He was like a colorful blenny or wrasse: fun to watch swimming around the reef, but not a member of any school.

Straton, on the other hand, was one of the senior schooling fishes, not to mention one of the biggest. No wonder the other humans deferred to him. Reef had heard that he had held the port city of Ismelinos against the Khirian forces. No easy feat. When Reef climbed back onto the deck he stopped and gave Straton the grumbly cough of greeting that he would have given a Khirian commander.

"Are you heading belowdecks for an appointment with Healer Straton?" the general asked with his usual stiff civility.

Archavie had explained that Kaeda and the General shared a name because she was the General's offspring. This also helped Reef to understand the man's reputation. He had produced a very healthy, brave, and highly magically adept descendant, who had also been selected for the Commission.

"Yes," Reef answered.

The general gestured for Reef to walk and fell into step beside him.

Reef didn't mind the escort. The rest of the crew didn't look quite so hostile when Straton was with him, as if the general's safety negated Reef's danger. Reef had noticed that Straton and the ship's captain, Avranas, seemed to know each other, as if they were old allies.

All of that made sense to Reef. Military rank. Social hierarchy. And Straton had made it very clear that if Reef followed orders and cooperated, he wouldn't let the crew harass him, so walking with him was almost a relief, until the General surprised him by saying, "You seem uneasy."

It caught Reef off guard. How could he know? He couldn't read Reef's mind either.

Yes, but what empathy Kaeda has she has inherited from him.

Empathy?

It means feeling what another person is feeling. No, not like that. Emotions. General Straton is good at reading people.

"If something has happened, I would like for you to tell me," The general said.

It was a strangely Khirian way of asking without asking.

What should I say? Reef queried Archavie, while he and Straton continued across the deck.

Tell him the truth.

But Reef would never tell a Khirian commander "I am unsettled by a bad dream." In fact, if he had been surrounded by Khirians he would have made sure his unease didn't show. He hadn't realized Straton would notice and comment.

Trust me, it's a fine response for a human setting. Go ahead and try it.

Reef put on his human-talking voice, a gentler, more rumbly voice than the one he used to talk to Khirians, and said, "I had a dream."

Straton turned towards him as they were walking. He was one of the taller Gems Reef had seen, but still at least a foot shorter than Reef's eyelevel. Now the man glanced up and his eyebrows lifted just enough that Reef could tell he had not expected this answer. "You're under a lot of stress," the general said. "It is not surprising that you should have uncomfortable dreams. I'm sure Healer Straton could give you something to help you sleep peacefully."

"Yes, sir," Reef said.

"Though I can understand if you don't want to sleep surrounded by enemies."

"Yes, sir."

"But I need you to be at your best. I don't want exhaustion to compromise your judgment."

He didn't want Reef to start attacking people like a snappy overtired hatchling. Reef could understand that. Straton didn't know how accustomed Reef was to managing weariness.

"Yes, sir," he said again.

Archavie and Kaeda were both waiting for him in the medbay when General Straton dropped him off. The wizard paused in whatever he was chatting about to look up and smile, while Kaeda began to unroll a rug for Reef to lay on.

"Have a good nap?" she asked.

There it was, the familiar remembered scream that always rose when he looked at her, but he could push the memory away more easily after sunbathing. He gave a polite grumble.

"Archavie told me you were basking. Do Khirians bask on a regular basis?" she asked.

And so, the questions began.

What would she find to gush about this time, Reef wondered? She had already enthused over his increased lung capacity and three sets of eyelids, questioned him about his collection of scars, asking if he would like any of them erased. She had been fascinated when Archavie explained that the scars were trophies and identifiers, and further fascinated when he told her that what she thought was a sliver of shrapnel buried in the back of his right shoulder was actually the remnant of a shark bite. What the shark had had stuck in its teeth, Reef didn't know, but he had lost so much blood from the wound that Wave hadn't wanted to dig around in it trying to get the metal out. The shoal had simply wrapped it up with sea urchin and guarded Reef while he slept off the sickness that followed.

That was a particularly big scar though, and Reef did let the healer work on it, softening the scar tissue to increase his range of motion.

This appointment proceeded quietly at first. The healer settled into her chair, Reef's bodyprint open on the table beside her, a ghostly blue replica of Reef, but lacking some details. Reef stretched out on the floor and let himself relax. Then after a while he heard a sharp intake of breath. There it was, the introduction to whatever the healer would carry on about this time.

Believe me, she is trying so hard to maintain professional calm in the face of something so interesting.

"You can sense heartbeats in the water?" the healer asked.

Reef was so tired of trying to communicate with humans. You can answer, he told Archavie.

"Yes. Heartbeats, currents, things like that," the wizard said.

"The network of nerves connecting to your fins is just – it's incredible. I've never seen anything like it. The electrosensory pores on either side are very similar to those of sharks."

"Reef has those on his face too, I think." The wizard said.

"Yes. Reef, would you open your fins? I should get an idea of how the joints work."

No, Reef thought immediately. Tension swept across his body and his fins automatically closed a little tighter. No, that was too far.

"Are you alright?" the healer asked. "Did I do something?"

Is this… what was it again?

Empathy? Yes, Kaeda has her empathy turned on right now. Sometimes she's quite oblivious, but right now, she knows you're feeling something uncomfortable. Besides which, she's monitoring your heart rate. You could try talking to her.

Not a chance.

Doesn't it feel nice, knowing that I know what's going on in your mind? Doesn't it feel nice for Straton to look out for you?

Straton is trying to protect everyone from me, Reef clarified.

Well, aren't you glad I'm *your friend? This is an opportunity to make another one.*

Reef still didn't understand the human concept of friendship and tended to consider Archavie's mental interference an acceptable tradeoff for the wizard teaching him Gemmic and helping him navigate social situations. But as he considered it again, he thought that he did appreciate the wizard's companionship. Without it he would feel quite a bit lonelier.

One friend is enough, Reef decided.

Archavie sent a mental groan his way in response.

Reef observed the healer looking from Archavie, to Reef, and back again as she waited for them to finish their telepathic conversation. At last Reef decided that he should allow the healer to study his fins. Wasn't he doing this so the healer would have an accurate map to work from if he were injured? And if he were injured, what would he especially want healed properly? His fins. Sure, it was terrifying to give the healer that knowledge of him, but if he started making decisions based on fear, he would make mistakes.

"If you're uncomfortable…" the healer began at last, but Reef interrupted, rolling over and rising to his feet.

"I am fine," he said.

He stood up straight so he could fan out both fins at the same time, feeling a little disappointed that his fins wore their dusty brown winter hue rather than the brilliant purple red of summer. Not that this human would know the difference.

The healer made a thoughtful noise. "Okay, I want to make sure I map each joint and all the nerve bundles properly. I've never done this before, so it may take a while. Let's start with the dorsal fin."

It did take a while. Quite a while. Reef wasn't used to opening and closing his fins repeatedly. The small muscles got tired, and he wished he had napped longer beforehand.

After a lengthy stretch of time the healer spoke again, "So how are you doing? I can't imagine it's easy to be traveling on a Gemmic battleship."

Don't, Reef thought to Archavie. Don't tell me to talk to her.

Suit yourself.

Reef remained still and silent but couldn't stop the thoughts and feelings from swelling in his chest. His loneliness in the water, the sharp looks from the crew whenever he set foot on deck, their muttered words, "monster" and "man-eater."

One of the best ways to avoid talking about something in human conversation is changing the subject, Archavie prompted.

Reef watched Kaeda, as she glanced from his back to the bodyprint, networks of lines appearing in the blue map at her instruction. Then his eyes settled on something else he had noticed.

"Pearl," he said, looking at her necklace, and he struggled to put together the appropriate sentence.

"Reef says that's a very interesting pearl, and is wondering where you found it," Archavie supplied.

"Oh, thank you," Kaeda replied brightly. "I found it in a lace clam on Star Bed reef."

She went on to tell him a story about jumping off a boat in the middle of the ocean and pearl hunting alone. Reef found himself astonished, and curious. Could it have been her lone human heartbeat he sensed off the coast when his shoal swam ahead to scout out the Gemmic Sea?

"You swim alone?" he asked.

Kaeda shrugged. "Sometimes I'll go out with the pearl divers, or swim with the children in the cove, but I like being alone. It gives me space to think."

Reef understood that, but he was still surprised. "You are not afraid?" Perhaps that shouldn't have surprised him. If she would follow a strange Khirian to an unknown cave in the middle of the night, what else could possibly scare her? He also remembered vaguely a lone human heartbeat off the coast of the Gemmic peninsula when he and a few others had scouted the Gemmic Sea. Could it have been her, he wondered?

Meanwhile the healer went on. "I do feel afraid sometimes, swimming in deep water where I can't see the bottom. But the reefs near Fari are usually pretty safe and I always bring magic with me for self-defense."

Reef blinked at her and did his best not to imagine all the ways she could die in the water. Why? Why should I be concerned about her? She's just a human. She means nothing to me.

She's on your team. You usually look out for team members. That's a good thing.

"Where do you like to swim?" the healer asked, but Reef had had enough human conversation for one day. He didn't answer, and when Archavie told the healer this she nodded and didn't press him for information. She was still working when the dinner bell rang. She rose from her chair with a sigh. "Nearly done. Will you join us for dinner?"

Reef had tried eating with the Commission. Once. And endured the watching eyes of a ship full of mammals who were probably imagining him eating their friends. "No," he rumbled.

"I know it's awkward," the healer said. "But we'll have to eat together eventually."

When I have to I will, Reef thought.

That's a short sentence. You could go ahead and say that out loud, Archavie reminded him.

"When I have to, I will," Reef said slowly.

"Alright, well, I think we could fit one more session in before bedtime if you're up for it."

"I can toss some fish overboard for you if you'd like," Archavie suggested.

As the sun set the uneasiness that Reef felt increased. He felt that something was wrong, but he tried not to give the feeling too much credence. He swam and ate the fish Archavie threw down for him, so at least he didn't have to hunt.

Eventually Archavie reminded Reef that he had one more appointment with Kaeda. Reef was wondering whether he could manage to sleep on the rug in the medbay, when he felt something strange in the water.

No, not exactly in the water, but on top of it like a boat, except that it did not drift in the waves. In fact, it didn't move at all, just sat there, pressing on the sea to the northwest, between the *Deterrance* and the Molvan vessel. It felt almost like a wind on the sea, but like no wind Reef had ever encountered.

I'm going to swim out a little to investigate, Reef told Archavie.

Suit yourself. Just don't go so far that you lose us.

Reef sped up, passed the ship, and struck out west towards the unknown thing. He had not gone far when, for the first time, he felt it move, heading in his direction.

What is it? Reef wondered. He stopped, feeling the water drift around him, focusing all his attention on the thing.

No flash of recognition came, but as he felt it blow towards him the knot of dread in his stomach seemed to whirl and shrill, becoming a complete certainty of danger. He turned and sped back toward the ship.

Turus will take a loo– oh no – it has him – this doesn't – it can't – I don't –go warn

The wizard's mental voice vanished.

Chapter Fifteen

AN ATTACK AT SEA

Kaeda

I was belowdecks when the ship's lookout spotted it, and I might have missed all the action if Gamalielle hadn't come zooming into the medbay with a grin on her face singing, "Unknown Magical Phenomena, what could it be? Something fun for you to see! No, no, no, bring your stuff! Remember the last UMP!"

The emergency alert began to chime a piercing bell call as Gamalielle and I ran to the stairs and up to the top deck where lantern light cast swaying shadows down on the deck. We arrived just as a lookout was calling, "Khirian aboard!"

"Shields!" Captain Avranas's voice rang out, and a shell of shimmering magic sprang to life around *The Deterrance,* obscuring the clouds and stars. "Fire harpoons and siege blasters!"

Weapons fire shook the ship.

"What are we firing at?" I called.

Reef pulled himself onto the stern, leapt down to the deck, and ran over to join the rest of us on the quarterdeck with Captain Avranas, Chief engineer Thea Sideris, my father and a huddle of violet and scarlet fabric.

"Archavie?" I asked.

The person curled up on the planks of the deck wore Archavie's colorful robes, but the hands held over his head were bony, skin nearly transparent where it wasn't freckled, and the hair poking between his fingers was thin and rusty orange rather than brilliant red. I crouched beside him. This was not the Archavie I was used to seeing.

"Cannons will be ready in twenty seconds," Sideris reported from her station at the ship's stetsalog. The magical construction stood in glowing humanoid form, the ship's statistics displayed on a panel of magic held between its arms.

"No magic," Reef barked. "Turus is with it."

We all looked down at Archavie. "Can you help him, healer?" General Straton asked.

"I'll try. What's out there?"

"We don't know," my father answered. "The lookout noticed a disturbance in the water."

"Turus went out," Reef added. "Archavie said 'it has him.'"

I turned my attention to Archavie. There didn't seem to be anything wrong with him. Not medically. But of course, he had never let me examine him. I realized now that he had probably been wearing a glamour, a sort of magical disguise the whole time. I had no Archavie baseline to compare the current one to, but I could tell that he was conscious, heart racing, trembling, making small whimpering sounds that didn't reach up to the rest of the group. "I think he's having a panic attack. I can try to calm him."

"Impact from the Unidentified Magical Phenomenon in ten, nine," the engineer called.

"Forward thrusters," the captain ordered. "Current and magic."

The deck shuddered as the thrusters kicked in. "No effect on the UMP." The engineer reported.

"Frils we're gonna get 'sploded on again!" Gamalielle yelped.

"Impact in five," stated Engineer Sideris.

"All hands, brace for impact!" Captain Avranas shouted.

"Reef, get Archavie!" ordered General Straton.

I had dropped a calming knot in Archavie's brain. Now I let Reef haul the wizard off the ground and over to the banister of the quarterdeck where we held on.

"Two, one."

A sound rang out across the deck. It reminded me of the steel drums I had heard playing on Qawahn ships, and it made my heart dance, not knowing whether to be fascinated or terrified. Everyone stood silent as the ship rocked from the impact. Across the deck, off the port bow, the shield wavered and flashed. I could see, now, how huge the invisible thing was. It pressed against a third of the portside shields, but not solidly. If Turus was out there, perhaps he had become tangled in the phenomena, disrupting its form. As the two of them wrestled and swirled against the shield it pinged with musical tones.

"Captain," Sideris cried, "It's draining the magic from our shields." Avranas stepped back to view the information held by the stetsalog. "I'm pouring magical reserves into the shield to maintain the enchantment," the engineer continued. "But it's just… going."

"Turus! Turus!" Archavie's sudden scream made us all jump. My knot seemed to have calmed him enough that he could stand and talk. Reef let go of the wizard and Archavie reached out towards the flashing shield, hands grasping the air, shouting in a language I didn't recognize.

The pattern of the UMP changed. Then another steel-drum impact sounded at the back of the ship.

"Let me in!" Turus called aloud, bold and indignant.

"Lower aft shields. Let the Magic aboard," the captain said.

The invisible mass of Turus swept across the deck and crashed into Archavie. The wizard dropped to the deck again, unconscious this time, even as a healthy wash of color swept across him.

"Turus! Will you stop knocking people out?" I scolded as I hurried to check the wizard's vital signs.

"How long until the cannons are ready?" the captain asked.

"Twenty seconds for the cannons," the engineer reported, "but we'll run out of magic to sustain full shields before then."

The captain amplified his voice and spoke to the crew. "All hands, retreat behind the foremast immediately!" Then he turned to the engineer. "Prepare to rotate the shields to close off the rear of the ship." His eyes swept across the party. "Do you have any other insight? Ideas? Anyone?"

A form took shape on the deck, the massive ghostly cat-lizard shape of a dragon, but with eyes that had no pupils or irises, only starry sparkles. It spoke with Turus's voice. "This is what you'll do: abandon ship, tell the lifeboats to scatter. I'll fly out to keep an eye on them and get in the UMP's way if it tries to chase anyone, but I don't think it will. It seemed to want to eat me. Once the shields are down, I suspect it will be drawn toward the ship's kentro, which is a denser piece of magic than I am. He's fine," The magic added, glancing down at his wizard.

"Port bow shield is going down!" Sideris called.

"Rotate starboard bow shield to close off the ship aft from the fore-mast."

"Yes sir."

Over the ship the air wavered as the wall of magic shifted. The port bow shield looked as if it was being burned away, a hole forming, edges darkening where the UMP pressed against it. Then it began to crumble. As the unknown mass contacted the ship the planks split and splintered. The mounted siege blasters seemed to explode, reduced to sawdust and fragments of metal.

"What's happening?" Gamalielle asked.

"I think it's… I think it's tearing the enchantments out of the ship," the engineer stammered.

Goosebumps prickled across my arms. The cursed Molvan body had absorbed magic. Now this phenomenon was pursuing Turus, tearing the magic from our ship. I remembered Svevolod taking the rib from the dead councilor's chest. But Svevolod wasn't here now to guide us, and this phenomenon seemed to have arrived without a physical vessel.

"Captain! Hull integrity – we're taking on water. The hull is supposed to be protected against magical attacks!"

"Can you keep us afloat long enough to evacuate?"

"With the hull this fragile I could probably send a magical pulse through the shield and cut off the front third of the ship. If we have the magic to sustain it the shield could keep the rest of the ship from taking on water while we get everyone off."

"Wait," I said, feeling numb as I struggled to comprehend her suggestion. "Did you just say you're going to cut off the front of the ship?"

They all turned toward me as if my question made the idea more real. "I think it's the only thing we can do," Sideris said. "But even if we get everyone off the ship, the lifeboats are enchanted too. It will annihilate them."

"I don't think it will," Turus said. "If it was drawn to me, then reasonably it should be drawn to the ship's magical core. If the lifeboats distance themselves before the kentro is destroyed, they may escape."

"We'll do as Turus suggests," the captain said. "Go," he said to the Magic. "Try to draw it west."

"Take care of my wizard," Turus said. Then he vanished.

"All hands, this is the captain. We are abandoning the ship. In order to stay afloat long enough to evacuate we will be severing the forward section of the *Deterrance.* I repeat, we will be severing the forward section of the ship. Prepare for turbulence." He turned to the engineer. "Go ahead."

Sideris made some adjustments, arranging bits of magic on the ship's stetsalog. Waves of magic pulsed along the shield that separated the party from the front of the ship. A series of cracks rang across the deck, like a toppling forest, and then the forward section of the ship began to sink away into the sea.

"Commission," my father called. "Follow me."

I ran back down to the medbay to grab the rest of my gear and the party's medical records, then joined the crew piling into lifeboats. Reef still held the unconscious Archavie and seemed unsure what to do with him.

"Just lay him on the floor of the boat," I said. "I'll try to revive him."

"Looks like we've got our own current thruster and emergency shielding," Gamalielle commented as she settled into the driver's seat at the front of the boat. "Of course, both of those will be useless if that thing comes after us." Then she shut her eyes and said, "Creator, remember me. I've been frilsing interesting. Too interesting to forget. Don't bliv me out if I die."

The main deck of the *Deterrence* held an enchantment providing a gentle magical heat and protection from the wind, but this lifeboat was only enchanted to stay dry on the inside and as we descended towards the water the night wind tore at us cold and fierce, threatening to rip my palla from my shoulders. Even that didn't wake Archavie.

The lifeboat settled onto the water with a light splash, and Reefand my father used oars to maneuver it out into the water.

"Hunker down," Gamalielle instructed. "On a boat this small the thrusters have some kick."

We all gripped the side of the lifeboat, and a moment later it lurched forward and began to speed across the waves.

"I'm taking us northeast… I think." Gamalielle called over the wind. "Yeah, there, see the other lifeboats?"

In the eerie light of the cloudy night, I could see the lanterns of the other lifeboats bouncing across the water. Then I heard a crackle. I turned back toward the Deterrence and saw the shields flashing, darkening, crumbling. The lights of the ship went out. A minute passed. The waves near the ship flattened.

"It's coming." Reef said, and I heard that same note in his voice that I had heard when he came to ask for a healer. It sounded like fear.

"It should remain near the ship's magical core," my father reminded them.

"Look at the water," Reef said.

My father looked. "It's chasing the lifeboats. They're starting to scatter. Now it will have to choose a direction."

"I'll take us a little further north," Gamalielle said, hand on the tiller.

"Coast of Molva, rocky. Dangerous," Reef cautioned.

"Don't get too close to land," my father agreed.

Don't get too distracted, I told myself. Get Archavie to wake up.

"It appears to be following us," my father said, sounding puzzled.

"Frils, what does it want?" Gamalielle snapped. She angled the boat even further north.

I looked up. I had spent a lot of time underwater and knew that even rocks you couldn't see from above could be dangerous for a boat.

My father was apparently thinking the same thing. "Careful Miss Aisop," he said. "We're not trying to land. We want to go back to the commonwealth and regroup."

But panic seemed to have overwhelmed the Cat. "Frils, I don't understand! Why is it chasing us?" Gamalielle screeched as she steered us this way and that. "We have a frilsing Khirian, a couple of magicians, what does it want?"

A break in the water. Something ahead. "Slow down," Reef said. "Slow down."

But Gamalielle wasn't paying attention.

"Miss Aisop," my father broke in. "Give me the controls."

Another break. A barrier. "Turn!" Reef and I shouted at the same time.

My father took hold of the wheel and tried to turn the boat, but it was too late. The lifeboat struck rock hard enough to send all of us flying.

I sucked in a breath, gathering what magic I could into my hands, expecting to be suddenly swallowed by dark water. Instead, I felt arms around me, steel plates against my back and across my chest. A magical shield sprang up around my father and I, much better than the shield I could have made myself.

For a moment time seemed to stand still. I was small, a child, sobbing in his arms while the body of my little brother lay nearby, pajamas stained with blood. A chaos of voices surged around us, but the only one I heard clearly was his, telling me it wasn't my fault while he held me tightly, keeping the chaos at bay.

Then we hit the water. The Molvan surf hurled our eggshell of protective magic from side to side. My father kept his grip on me, and I came to my senses and began knotting magic as quickly as I could. "Water breathing magic," I explained as I fixed a tangle across my face, then reached over my shoulder to spread one across his.

The slam of another wave, then a jarring impact as the waves threw us against a stone. I heard Gamalielle shrieking somewhere, but up and down and all directions seemed lost as the surf tumbled us.

"I'll try to anchor us to a rock," my father said. "Hold on—"

But another crush of water lifted and dropped us. The shell broke and my father's grip with it. I thought I heard him shout my name, while I grasped at his armor, but the tide pulled me away, his gauntleted fingers slipped through mine, and soon I was lost in the dark chaos.

Chapter Sixteen

FRIGHT, FLOATING

Reef

REEF let muscle memory adjust his body to the shifting waves. That was easy. Navigating the rocks in the dark, less easy. He found a safe place, deep enough to avoid the pummeling surf, and focused, trying to find the rest of the Commission.

He couldn't see much of anything, but he could sense them. Two heartbeats, not far from him. Close together, but quickly drifting apart.

Reef braced his feet against a rock. The smaller person hurtled toward him, dragged by the current. As she flew by in a rush of limbs and fabric, Reef pushed out and caught her around the waist.

He recognized the rhythm of her heart, the way it sped up and slowed down, the pulse of her breath in the magic that shivered across her face. Yes, it had been her swimming alone in the Gemmic Sea that day. He felt something about that, a flash of awareness he didn't fully understand, as if something deep inside him recognized something deep inside of her.

It was a strange feeling, but Reef had no time to dwell on it. The heavier figure with the slower heartbeat, the one that must have been General Straton, had passed to the other side of the nearest stand of rocks. Reef wouldn't be able to navigate them with the healer in tow. He would need to take her to safety first.

He swam hard, paying attention to the currents, keeping the healer as close against him as he could. When he found calmer water, he swam up and rolled over, pulling the healer above the waves.

"Kaeda!" Gamalielle screeched. She had been watching, apparently. In the clouded starlight Reef saw her levitating a few yards over the water.

Then he sensed something else, also over the waves, flattening the surface of the water. Oh no. "It is near," he called, as magic pulled the healer from his arms and up into the air.

"General Straton!" the healer cried as she flew up toward Gamalielle.

"I gotta get her to shore," the cat shrilled. "If that thing catches me, we'll both crash."

"I will look for him," Reef shouted back. Gamalielle had already flown several yards toward shore, dragging the healer with him, but Reef saw that the healer's eyes were trained back toward the rocks. If he had seen her afraid before, well, it was nothing to the wide-eyed desperation on her face now.

He dove down again, and just in time. The waves over him flattened and he felt something, something that must be magic, reaching down into the water. The alarm inside him, the dread-turned-to-terror he had felt when he first sensed the UMP, had reached a new level of shrillness. Reef tried to calm it, telling himself again and again, it can't affect you, it can't affect you. Magical attacks will not harm you. The thing tears out magic, but there is no magic in you.

Ignoring the fear, he swam a little deeper and began to skirt the rocks, searching for any sign of the general. The first thing he noticed was blood on the water. A heartbeat, but faint, no waterbreathing respiration. Hopefully that meant his head was out of the water. He was near the surface at least. But that meant that in order to reach him Reef would have to swim right into the UMP.

It had descended several feet into the water now, slowly, like slowly sinking sand. As Reef observed it something inside him shivered and said no, no, no.

Fear is just a feeling, Reef told himself. It doesn't control you. How many things have you feared and done anyway. You can do this. On three. One, two –

When he was younger, Reef had once swum into a fright floater, one of the few jellyfish capable of stinging a Khirian. The disorienting bite, the sickening ache, it felt like certain death. He felt something similar now as he swam into the UMP. Colors and shadows assaulted his vision. Buzzing and tingling bombarded his senses. He couldn't feel. Couldn't see. The waves struck him, and he didn't know how to move. He could barely tell where the water ended, and the air began. He wanted to scream and didn't know if it was safe to breathe.

Two things he managed to discern: which direction was up, and the pull of the waves towards the beach. He couldn't save the general now. He didn't even know if he could save himself. He could only try to make it back to the shore and hope that his magic-wielding allies would be able to help.

He followed the waves, relieved every time he took a breath and found that it was air, not water. At last, he heard shouting through the chaos, then felt a resistance beneath his feet. Sand and pebbles. Soon he was digging his hands into the sand too.

"You're almost there! Keep going." Kaeda's voice pierced the endless shrilling and buzzing in his ears.

"The UMP doesn't come past the water's edge," Gamalielle said.

Reef dragged himself onward, expecting, any minute, to reach out and find that his arms were no longer attached, that he had been shaken apart by the magical something.

"Almost, almost."

"He's cleared the water," Gamalielle said.

A shriek from the healer. "It's like a piece of the UMP came with him. It tore the magic right out of my palms."

Reef turned toward her voice, but couldn't see much, just a human-shaped shadow in the darkness. Then someone cast a magical light.

Blood. Blood on her hands. Brown skin. Dark eyes. Thick ropes. Bright water. Wooden boards. Blinding sun. Reef felt a scream in his throat. Everything hurt. Were his bones breaking? His organs exploding? What was the magic doing to him?

The healer shouted something else, and then there was nothing.

Chapter Seventeen

THE STRANGE SHORE

Kaeda

GAMALIELLE managed to levitate Reef a few yards further inland. The cloud of magic that had followed him onto the beach slowly shrank as if absorbing into him, until it was gone.

It didn't make sense, but whatever. I didn't need sense right now, I just needed not a crisis. I was shaking, from the cold and from feelings that seemed to have spread through my body like an untreatable virus. I was about to lose it, but first I checked Reef's vital signs, made sure he wasn't dying, and tied a new warming enchantment onto his vambrace so the cold wouldn't kill him. Then I left him to recover and shuffled back to Gamalielle, still-unconscious Archavie, and the campfire Gamalielle had made.

She had made a real fire because our supply of magic was so small. Our supply of everything was small. I had my satchel, but it had been battered and soaked by seawater. Until I did a thorough inspection, I couldn't be sure how many of the first aid supplies inside were still functional. Besides that, I had only the magic I had been wearing, which included the party's bodyprints and a set of cuffs on my upper arms with a small supply of magic tied to them for general use.

Gamalielle had been industriously running back and forth across our stretch of beach looking for anything that had washed up. Bits of lifeboat. Bits of gear. Bits of sail. She had a small heap of things in front of her, and she was glaring at them, swearing. Whatever she was hoping to find, she didn't seem to have found it.

At least her heap didn't include my father's body.

In some ways it was a relief. In some ways it merely prolonged the suspense. He was probably dead. But until I saw his body, I couldn't be sure. I would hope. I would wish. I would strain toward any conclusion that at least allowed me to *know*.

"Would you check again?" I asked.

The Cat looked up, nodded, and trotted off across the beach. I waited, arms around my knees, muscles twitching with unwanted adrenaline.

"No corpses," Gamalielle reported when she returned. Then she said more gently, "he's a tough guy. I'm sure he's fine."

I pressed my hands over my mouth and shut my eyes. It was like trying not to throw up, holding back those emotions.

I felt Gamalielle's little clawed hand on my arm. "He's probably on another stretch of beach, doing a much better job setting up camp than we are."

I shook my head. I remembered the waves, the rocks, the cold. And he was wearing armor. If the UMP tore the buoyancy enchantments out of it, he would sink like a stone. He would either be battered to death or drown or both.

A wave of grief rose from my stomach. I was ready to scream it out. Vomit it out if need be. But as so often happened, the feeling faded, burned out before bursting, like a damp firework.

I drew in a deep, shuddering breath, like the tide rattling back over the rocky shore, and gathered myself. "I'm fine," I said to the Cat.

"You sure? I don't even like my family but I'd sure as blivs wail about 'em if they were lost at sea."

"I'm sure."

Gamalielle hesitated and then said, "Well, okay then, I'm going to look for more sail bits. Maybe I can at least make a windscreen or something."

I watched her traipse back out across the beach. The sadness had sunk into my stomach with all the other sadness stored up there. Memories of my father flickered out from the recesses of my mind and flashed across my consciousness. When he had carried me around on his shoulders so I could pick lemons from the higher branches. When my mother showed me red blood cells under a microscope, and he pretended not to know what they were so I could explain how blood worked. When Gil and I would sit, one on either side of him, at bedtime, and he would read us stories about sentient trees and Gemmic heroes and hidden treasures.

My mother rarely had time for things like that. She was always taking someone's blood pressure or giving vaccinations or offering consultations, and if she wasn't treating someone's diseases she was cooking. She would give us cooking lessons, science lessons, magic lessons, but if it wasn't a teaching moment, and if we were healthy and well, she was too busy.

But then Gil had died from a magic-induced hemorrhagic fever. He hadn't been the only one. That year the rush of magic from the Gemmic Homecoming holiday had been too strong for many young Farians not used to so much magic all at one time. When Gil died, my mother didn't stop. She kept hurrying from patient to patient. I knew she was trying to save lives, but… well, it had been my father who held me while I sat beside Gil's body and cried. He had been there then, but within a year he was gone.

In many ways, it would have been easier if my mother had left. Without my father, and with no little brother to keep me company, my mother and I had stopped being a family. We were just a healer and her kid assistant.

Now we would never be a family again. And of course, I hadn't wanted to. Until this moment when I wondered "What if?"

"What if nothing," I said to myself. "It will do no good to dwell on it now."

I pulled up the hood of my Molvan traveling cloak and wrapped the fabric more tightly around me. Gamalielle had set our fire in a sandy place between some rocks. Now I scooted over to one of the boulders and settled myself against it to sort through what was in my satchel. Quite a bit would still be useful, though my notes on Khirian anatomy were soaked. I spotted more paper and pulled out the Molvan book of fearytales. I had forgotten that I packed it, intending to ask Lady Batbayar more about Molvan history if I had the time. I set the waterlogged book and the limp pages of notes as close to the fire as I dared, and then took a breath and looked out at the sea.

The edges of the clouds shone with moonlight and starlight, and as the tide went out stretches of damp sand shimmered with seawater left behind. It would have been so beautiful, if not for the ominous presence of the UMP, moving back and forth along the waterline, interrupting the waves.

I heard a rustle and shifting in the sand and when I turned, I saw Archavie finally stirring. He sat up and leaned against the nearest rocks, glanced at me, and then surveyed the beach with his eyes hanging open, the corners of his mouth turned down, appropriately horrified by all that had happened.

I remembered him collapsing on the ship, the drastic change in his appearance and demeanor.

"I don't want to talk about it," the wizard murmured, "any more than you want to talk about your father's probable death."

"You're on my team, and I'm your healer. If you collapse, that's something we need to talk about."

"I'm not sick. I didn't have a… heart attack or anything."

"No, I'd guess you had a panic attack."

"Turus and I have worked together for so long that I just don't know how to get on by myself."

Well, that was one of the grossest underestimations I had ever heard. "You were like a different person. I can tell now that you're wearing a glamor to change your appearance. I'm not even looking at the real you. In an emergency, how am I supposed to treat you?"

I had pushed too hard. Archavie sat up a little straighter, a stiff expression on his face as if he had been insulted. "This is the real me. I appreciate your concern, I really do, but you don't need to worry. Turus won't leave me again. I talked to him about it."

"It's extremely rare for a Magic to leave its wizard completely while the wizard is still alive. Usually the kentro – the concentrated center of the Magic—will remain. The fact that it happened once makes me concerned that it may happen again."

Archavie nodded along with my lecture, listening politely as if humoring me. "Like I said, I talked to him about it. Definitely a one-time thing."

"As a medical professional I still recommend you allow me to do a physical exam, take a medical history, and make a bodyprint. As a member of the Commission, I recommend we exchange some phrases so that we can have some level of communication just in case you lose Turus again."

I had begun to sound angry. I felt the grief well in my throat again, and tears sting my eyes. Archavie scooted closer to me and held out his hand. I wasn't sure what that was about, but I took it, and held his gaze while he said, "I'm not going to die. I'm not going to leave you. I swear."

The color of his eyes, I knew, was fake, but the earnest intention seemed real. Still, it was a promise I didn't think he could make. "You don't have control over that," I said more calmly. "All you can do is plan for the worst."

"I respect your evaluation and your fear, but you'll just have to trust me on this." He squeezed my hand, then let it go as Gamalielle dashed back to our camp.

"I found it! I found it!" She dropped down to her knees with a small round canister in her hands.

"What is it?" I asked, hoping for some kind of communication or navigational device.

"Nip!" the Cat unscrewed the lid to reveal an assortment of small paper packets, dried mushrooms, and whole rolled leaves. "Still dry! Thank the creator!"

"You've been combing the beach for drugs?" I stammered.

"Frils yeah! Now listen, I saved ya'll's lives, not unlike how I saved a lot of sailor's lives during the war, and on account of those memories and this frilsing awful night, I'm about to lose my mind, so I'm going to take some initiative and lose it peacefully in a pinch of nip."

As she spoke, she took out one of the twisted paper packets, turned her traveling cloak around backward so the hood was in front, and dumped the dried leaf contents of the packet into the hood. Now she pulled the hood over her face and flopped down onto the sand.

"As a healer I should caution you about the use of… whatever is in that box." I let my sentence trail away with a groan.

"She's not listening to you anyway," Archavie said, "but she knows what she's doing."

"I should check on Reef."

"Great idea. Yes, I think he's waking up. He's a much better patient than either of us."

As I approached, Reef pushed himself up on his elbows, blinking and gazing across the rocks and sand.

"How are you feeling?" I asked.

"Fine," he said, as he climbed unsteadily to his feet.

I searched his face for signs of pain or fear. None. But I did notice a trace of confusion in the forward tilt of the ridges above his eyes.

"Your vital signs look normal now. The magic that came onto the beach with you seems to have vanished. Do you have any idea what happened?"

"Attack," he said, stumbling through the Gemmic words. "Not ever something like this."

"Since both my magic, and the magic of the UMP have been able to affect you, I think we should be cautious about exposing you to magic in the future."

Reef nodded. His eyes scanned the coast, as if he couldn't quite believe this was happening. "General Straton?" he asked.

My heart leapt up to clog my throat again, but to my relief with each surge the emotions faded more quickly and I was able to speak again in a moment. "We haven't seen any sign of him. It isn't your fault. The UMP's attack ultimately rendered you unconscious. If you had passed out in the water, you both might have drowned."

Reef rumbled and I got the impression that he agreed.

"It must be scary," I said. "You're used to having resistance to magical attacks."

Reef rumbled again. The ridges above his eyes tilted forward a little more. I guessed that he was thinking. If he had been human, his brow might have been furrowed in thought. "I… felt it," he said slowly.

"Felt it?"

"The UMP."

I nodded. "Yes, I can tell it affected you strongly."

"No," Reef corrected, "I felt where it was."

"Your fins picked up its location as it disrupted the water," I guessed, but Reef shook his head.

"At first, but then, later, I knew where, how close. I couldn't… see it," Reef's already stumbling explanation ceased. He sounded as confused as I felt trying to comprehend him.

"You sensed the magic?"

Reef shook his head again. "It was a feeling."

"Like a hunch?"

"Hunch?"

"We'd call it a gut feeling. An instinct. Something like that."

Reef rumbled his agreement. "Hunch."

"Where is it now?"

"Off the shore, further out. I think." Reef frowned again.

"And have you felt this… hunch before?"

Reef's eyes widened as if he had only realized it now. "At the Gemmic Council building."

I took a deep breath. So, Reef had some ability to detect these magic destroying… things. I had no idea what to make of this and decided that now was not the time to try. "Well, maybe eventually I'll be able to figure out why this is happening, but for now I'm just glad the UMP has backed off. Gamalielle's probably strung out on nip by now so we might as well try to get some rest before morning and decide what to do when everyone is awake and sober."

Reef looked up. "Nip?"

"Catnip. It's like… well, I don't know if Khirians use recreational drugs."

Now Reef growled. To my surprise he climbed out of the tent, rose to his feet, and stalked across the beach toward the campfire. I ran after him.

"What are you doing?" I asked, but before anything could happen, Archavie waved a hand in our direction, and Reef halted.

"I'm going to save you a lot of energy and just tell you, if you try to lecture Gamalielle about using mind-altering substances when we all need to be on alert it won't do any good. She'll just argue semi-coherently and hit you with tickling magic."

Reef's tail swished, kicking up sand and rocks. "Who is in charge?" he asked.

Archavie glanced at Gamalielle, and then his eyes settled pointedly on me.

"I – no, I can't lead the Commission!"

"You're easily the most sensible person here," Archavie commented. "Besides Reef, but he's a Khirian so no one is going to listen to him."

"No," I lifted my hands to fend off this obligation. "We're stuck here together, and we're going to share responsibility and make decisions as a group."

The wizard shrugged, "Yes ma'am," he said, and I couldn't help but feel that I had somehow lost the argument.

Reef spoke next, a calmer rumble. "You have not slept yet?"

"No," I admitted.

"Then rest. I will keep watch next."

Chapter Eighteen

THE SHAPE OF THINGS

Kaeda

WHEN I woke up again, I heard jovial voices. Gamalielle, Reef, and Archavie all sat around the fire. Above it, crabs and other shellfish simmered suspended in a sphere of water.

"Kaeda!" Gamalielle and Archavie called together as I sat up.

I saw the wizard elbow Gamalielle, and the cat groaned. "Alright, alright!" she cleared her throat. "I solemnly swear not to do nip while we're on the road." Then she muttered, "I was in a dark place."

"Aren't we all!" Archavie exclaimed. Then he added, "Have some seafood soup!" He waved a hand and a smaller sphere of water detached from the whole and floated toward me.

I caught it by magic and carried it with me as I scooted closer to the fire. As the heat seeped through my leggings, warming my shins, I told myself things would be alright. We were a group of capable people, chosen by the Gemmic council. We would find a way out of this. We wouldn't be stuck here.

But the dreams of the past night clung to the edges of my mind, dreams where the ground shook and the people I loved fell into chasms. Usually these dreams included my mother, with her round face and quick eyes, and Gil, looking so similar but with a curly mop of hair, and sometimes Aline or other cousins, aunts, and uncles. Now my father had joined them. It made anger tighten my chest. I didn't want to mourn him too. I was determined not to, even if he had saved my life.

As I settled myself beside the small blaze Gamalielle asked, "How are you doing?"

"Fine."

The Cat accepted the lie with a nod and went on talking, "Here's what I think. We wait here, keep a low profile. They know we went this way. They'll send someone to look for us."

"We won't be able to get out this way," Archavie said. "Not if the UMP stands guard. The Gems would have to disenchant a ship to send for us, and even then, we know it will attack Reef and Turus. Besides, Reef thinks it would be too dangerous to send a ship here."

"Rocks," Reef rumbled, as he glared at the fire.

"Well, so much for that." Gamalielle tossed a bit of crab shell into the flames. "We'll have to find a way to a friendlier piece of coastline. Any idea where we are?"

"According to Turus's scouting we've landed in the Mironian Wilderness."

"The what?" I asked.

"What's left of the Miro Dovniya," Archavie explained. He waved a hand and an illuminated map appeared in the air. "Between war with Dov Voda, war with the Khirians, and the magical drought, this southern part of Molva is mostly ghost towns, abandoned farms, and rambling forest."

"Glad somebody was paying attention during Theo's presentation," Gamalielle commented.

"Miro, dangerous." Reef put in.

"Reef says Miro is more than usually vicious and unpredictable," Archavie supplied. "He's heard from the Khirians stationed here."

I studied the map. "Where are we?"

A bright, blinking spot appeared on the southern coast. "Turus's best guess," Archavie said.

"And what's this?" I pointed to a blue fissure down the center of the continent. It was too wide to be a river. Some distance north of us it veered east and emptied into the Gemmic Sea.

"Torgovyy Channel," Reef answered, then he nodded to Archavie.

"The Trade Corridor. It's well-defended and hard to get into, but it connects most regions of Molva."

"Then why didn't we just go that way to begin with?" Gamalielle asked as she broke open a new crab. "It connects to the Gemmic Sea, and it looks like it goes all the way up north. Seems obvious."

"Politics," Archavie answered neatly. "Lady Batbayar sent the cursed body down that way, but to bring us up through the channel might have seemed secretive. And of course, once Dov Voda was involved, he wanted us to sail straight to his capital city. The Trade Corridor is independent. They're run by guilds, not a monarch.

I looked over at Reef. "You're the only one of us who has been to Molva before. What do you think we should do?"

"You're asking the Khirian?" Gamalielle quipped. "You planning to invade the continent?"

"Reef is uncertain," Archavie answered, ignoring the Cat, "but he is hesitant to go near the ocean until we can throw off the UMP. I can tell you from Harol's experience that if we can get to the Torgo and prove that we're an official Commission of the Gemmic Council, we can probably get safe passage anywhere."

"Even Reef?" I asked.

"Okay, wait, why are we worrying about scale-face?" Gamalielle cut in. "He's only in the Commission because the council didn't want to fight the hoard. Honestly, whatever happens—"

"He saved my life," I said.

"Yeah, but—"

"But what? He could have swum to safety, but he rescued me, and he went back for my father, at great risk."

"Yeah, but… he's a Khirian." The Cat said it as if that was the only fact that mattered. "He's a Khirian so let's just say, you know, thanks, but this is over now, go back to your clan of cold-blooded killers."

When I shook my head Gamalielle went on, "You know what I kept thinking about last night? Being on the *Alacrity* when the ship started going down. Everyone running and screaming and the Khirians started coming up over the sides. Anyone who knew how to levitate went up in the air like a kite in autumn, and I looked down and I thought… who am I supposed to save? I can levitate like, two at best." Her voice shook as she looked at Reef. "Two! You got the rest of them. Frils, I want some nip!"

I couldn't think about the war right now. I refused to. Instead, I said in the calmest voice I could manage, "We're going to do our best to be a team, at least until we get to safety. Reef is part of that team, and we may need his help."

As I filled her in on Reef's surprising ability to sense the location of the UMP Gamalielle's eyes grew round, but she at least calmed down. When I had finished, she blew a breath out through her whiskers. "So, you're saying this lizard is like… an UMP-o-meter?"

"Something like that."

"Archons."

"So can we agree to consider Reef's safety?"

When Gamalielle nodded I said, "Okay, so would Reef be able to travel through the Trade Corridor?"

Archavie answered. "According to Harol, traveling in the Torgo is mostly a matter of paperwork and permissions. They'll transport almost anything, providing it's done according to procedure and the appropriate guilds get paid. Reef says he'd rather take his chances with the Torgo than with the UMP."

"Then I think it makes sense to travel north and look for an entrance to this Torgovyy Channel. Judging by the map we could travel the channel either back to the Gemmic Commonwealth or northwest to Voda. We can decide when we get there."

I glanced around at the group, at Reef's scaly bulk and Archavie's colorful apparel. The channel might transport us, but if the local ruler was as vicious and unpredictable as Reef said…

As if reading my mind Gamalielle cut in, "Yeah, we're going to need a disguise."

While we finished up breakfast Gamalielle and Archavie began to work on disguises. Gamalielle easily changed her appearance to that of a skinny little Molvan girl. The illusion held as long as you didn't look too closely. Archavie turned his hair and beard grey and collected his freckles into age spots. His clothes similarly faded in color.

"If I say or do anything that doesn't make sense, or if I space out because Turus is talking to me, just pretend I'm senile," he said.

I required the least change. As far as I could tell Turus just pushed around the melanin in my body, so that my skin lightened a little and my hair darkened.

"There are quite a range of Molvan features," he told me. "You don't look typical, but if we get up close with anyone, that's the least of our problems. I don't want to layer on heavy magic we can't sustain."

Now only Reef remained. We all stood, surveying him.

"Well, the way I see it," Archavie said, "I can disguise Reef as an exceptionally large, burly human, or I can turn him into a horse."

"But can you?" Gamalielle asked. "What about Khirian magic resistance? Not that that stopped the UMP."

I don't think it's safe for Gamalielle to know about Reef's weakness, I thought to Archavie.

I agree, but it's also not safe for Reef to walk around looking like a giant lizard. "I think Turus can manage," the wizard said. "As I'm sure I've said before, he's special. So, Reef, human or horse?"

"Horse," Reef said, but I shook my head.

"Human," I countered. "If Reef is going to give us any more local insight, he'll need to speak, and if somehow we end up in a physical fight…" My eyes went to the maul still strapped to Reef's back.

Reef looked at Archavie. Archavie looked back. The wizard raised his eyebrows. Reef's tail swept the pebbled beach. The wizard raised his eyebrows yet further.

At last, their mental discussion came to an end. "Fine," Reef grumbled.

Archavie gleefully clapped his hands. "Brilliant! Alright, everyone stand back, and get ready to be impressed!"

Gamalielle and I settled down across the fire from Reef and Archavie as the two of them found a patch of beach with more sand than pebbles and the wizard rolled up his sleeves. He lifted his hands, and a wind began to whip across the beach. Since weather effects and specific posture were not necessary for working magic, I assumed these must be for effect. When Reef began to rise into the air, as if lifted by the wind, Gamalielle muttered, "Wizardy showoff," and then shouted, "Hey Archie, make him glow!"

The corners of Archavie's lips twitched up. Light began to shine from between Reef's scales, as if some radiance within him was about to burst out.

I rolled my eyes and Gamalielle chortled. Meanwhile, Reef rotated slowly in the air. His tail began to shrink, his muzzle shortened. The scales smoothed together, the glow pushing itself dramatically out of his fingers and toes. Gamalielle and I watched until a ragged shape – the tent – blew over our heads and wrapped itself around Reef.

"Aw, come on Archie!" Gamalielle heckled. "Khirians don't wear clothes!"

Archavie didn't respond to her, he was busy flipping through my mind, checking various details of anatomy to make sure Reef would be a reasonable human facsimile. As the thoughts, memories, studies, and images, raced through my thoughts I saw a human face taking shape, and the tent forming itself into clothing around a magnificently muscled human form.

A magnificently muscled and obviously *Gemmic* human form. He had skin nearly as fair as his white scales, a tall nasal bridge, bowed lips, strong chin, and curly blond hair, in addition to being well over 6 feet tall.

Gamaielle gave a whoop. "From carnivore to candy! Archie you've got skills."

Archavie bowed, but as Reef settled slowly back down to the ground, I felt a flutter in my stomach. Why? What was that? Why should I feel disturbed by his human appearance?

As Reef's feet, now wearing boots, took his full weight he staggered and promptly fell on his backside. I saw him glance behind himself, as if looking for a tail and I found myself blushing in vicarious embarrassment.

I did my best to push this strange reaction to the back of my mind. "It would be better if he looked Molvan," I said.

"Yeah, as much as I love the look, she's right," Gamalielle agreed.

"Turus defends himself by saying that he was borrowing Kaeda's mental models, and that, on average, Gems are larger and taller than Molvans, which makes it easier to pack Reef's mass into a Gemmic shape. However…" He snapped his fingers. Reef's skin turned from porcelain to warm beige, his hair darkened, and his nose melted a little into his face. "Better?"

No, in fact the flapping, fluttering, winged things in my stomach feeling intensified. I was glad that I had eaten already. I certainly wouldn't be able to eat now.

"He's still too gorgeous," Gamalielle appraised, as Reef climbed awkwardly to his feet again. "And too young. He's gotta be like seventeen."

Archavie gave an exaggerated groan. "How about, 'thank you, Archavie?'"

"Thank you," I said. Then I turned to Gamalielle. "Reef's disguise will suffice. Especially if we can keep our distance from other people."

"No one's gonna want to keep their distance from *that,* if you know what I mean." Then the cat's eyes narrowed. "You okay Kay? You look a little freaked."

"Being undercover is not my favorite thing."

"Being sober isn't mine. Too bad!"

It took maybe an hour of travel through the landscape of overgrown brush, shaggy-barked eucalyptus trees, and fallen pines, for me to make sense of my feelings. Every time Reef turned toward me my heart beat a little faster. When he spoke to me it took extra time to gather my thoughts and make words. I kept watching him, watching him, watching him, and when I wasn't watching him, I was remembering the particulars of his face, his grey-green eyes and always-frowning mouth.

When I viewed the situation objectively, I could easily diagnose myself. I was attracted to Reef, or at least to the stupidly beautiful and yet perpetually grumpy human disguise Archavie had given him.

Since this was Archavie's fault, I decided to address it with him.

What do you want me to do? The wizard replied, his mental voice a veritable bouquet of amusement. *Give him a pretend skin disease? Make his nose disappear? Tell the group, sorry, Kaeda can't take her eyes off Reef so, in the best interest of the party, I need to make him as hideous as possible?*

Why did you make him so attractive to begin with? I asked.

Did I? I don't see Gamalielle swooning over him.

I didn't have this problem until you made him into a… moving piece of Gemmic statuary.

I beg to differ.

Memories flickered through my mind, like pages of a flipped book. Reef's bright, deep look on the beach. Sketching out his hands on a piece of paper. Watching him swim alongside the *Deterrance,* a long white shape flickering like a flame hidden in the waves. And every conversation, where I nudged, pushed, wanting to know just a little bit more about him.

Don't dig through my mind, I reminded the wizard. Besides, all that was different. That was just curiosity. I might feel the same way about any unknown person or creature. I doubted my own analysis, even as I gave it.

Yep, Archavie agreed.

Regardless, my prior feelings have been either transformed or exacerbated by Reef's metamorphosis, and since that is your responsibility, and is temporary, I would like you to suppress my psychological symptoms so I can get on with this quest.

Archavie laughed aloud.

"What are you two brain-whispering about?" Gamalielle asked.

"We're talking about how your fur fluffs out in the humidity!" Archavie replied.

The cat swore under her breath.

I'm sorry, Archavie thought to me, *but in my experience things like that tend to grow back, often worse than before. It's like any other deep feeling: if you ignore it, it will only plague you.*

If that's true, then I'll deal with it later, but right now, we're traipsing through Molva. I don't want to be distracted.

Suit yourself.

I didn't feel Turus's magic, but when Reef looked back toward me again, I found, to my relief, that all I felt was a tiny ping in my chest, probably residual anxiety from the whole experience. I looked around with greater clarity, and at once began to analyze the Molvan landscape. I could tell at a glance which plants had relied on magic for their health. The pines, a wavy-trunked variety I had never seen in the Gemmic commonwealth, had all lost their needles, and many had collapsed, as if torn down by a wind that had ignored the other trees. In many places I could see new growth struggling to push through dense tangles of something that resembled a fern, but with much stiffer woody spirals that remained intact even though the plants were clearly dead.

I wanted to take a sample, moreso when we came upon the remains of a family of what resembled armadillos. Their armor, intricately overlapping plates, was still intact, though much of the flesh had rotted away. We found more and more of these armor skeletons as we went on, suggesting that they too had died for lack of magic. I wished I had the appropriate tools to take a sample for later study, but no.

As we travelled further inland, we saw crumbling fences, abandoned towns, and an occasional well. Gamalielle had brought along a couple of canteens she had found washed up on the beach, and we were able to fill these, so at least we had water. In addition to the man-made buildings, we began to encounter rocks naturally sculpted into towers and arches. They looked as if they could be ruins of more ancient buildings, the largest pillars five or six feet in diameter.

"Worms," Archavie supplied, as we walked beneath a giant arch, double Reef's height, of matte gold and brown rock. "Reef's seen them further north, but he says they aren't usually dangerous as long as you don't disturb them."

I glanced up at the stone, trying to imagine a worm that large, and walked a little faster.

The worms caused us no trouble, and as we traveled, we saw nothing else threatening. A squirrel dashing across a maze of fallen pine logs, a quail rustling in the undergrowth, a man in the distance with a herd of goats. And, I noted, no magic. No magic anywhere.

Chapter Nineteen

FEET AND CLAWS

Reef

PRAGMATICALLY, appearing to be human seemed like a good idea. And Reef was hardly going to tell the humans that he couldn't handle what they experienced every day. But… it was terrible.

The moment his feet had touched the ground in human shape Reef had wanted to scream. But wanting to scream was not an unfamiliar state of being for Reef, and staying calm was second nature. So, he did not scream, but carried on, glaring as he braced himself against each breath of wind, each brush of fabric, each footfall.

It was as if, he thought, the wizard had spread the skin of his fins across his entire body. Normally, if a wind blew, he felt it in his eyes, in his mouth if his mouth was open, but not across the rest of his face. Normally he felt the ground as a surface, but all dulled by his layer of scales. Normally the sling of his maul, and any other equipment he might wear, were merely weight, hardly even something he felt. He had not realized just how protective his scales were.

Now the air seemed to assault him. Every touch, every texture, *everything* came right up to him with no barrier. Close, intense, inescapable.

I apologize, the wizard said. *I wanted you to be realistically human enough to stand up to at least a little scrutiny. Perhaps I got carried away. It's skin deep though. Your organs are still more or less Khirian, if that's any comfort.*

It wasn't, but there was nothing Reef could do about it now. Nothing but try not to be carried away by the feeling of everything, carried away on a tide of sensation into a sea of exhaustion and madness.

I think that might be overstating the situation a little.

Reef wasn't sure.

When they finally stopped for the evening, when they escaped from the increasingly cold and violent wind into a decrepit old barn, Reef found a corner, sank onto the moldering remains of hay, prickly and crunchy, leaned against the boards, rough and uneven, and closed his eyes, shutting out the dryness and the human construction. He listened to the wind outside and imagined it was blowing off of the ocean.

The ocean was still there. He had walked away from it, but he knew it still beat at the Molvan coast. The breeze still blew over it. He imagined that the ocean had blown the wind here to check on him, to see that he was still alive. He was, and as long as he lived, he could return to the ocean. It would still be there, waiting for him.

But there was a rustle some few feet to his right and when he opened one eye, he saw Kaeda also easing herself down onto the musty ground. She groaned as she stretched out her legs. Reef remembered that she was also from an island, and wondered if she missed the water as much as he did.

"I don't like walking," Kaeda said.

Reef grumbled an agreement. Traipsing across Molva in Khirian form during the war had been bad enough, but this? Without a tail to balance him he felt constantly in danger of pitching forward or falling back, and with his eyes in the front of his head he couldn't watch for threats on either side. Besides that, he was simply out of practice. On the archipelago he only walked from one body of water to another and got off his feet as soon as possible.

"If we could have swum some of that distance," the healer added wistfully. She groaned again and Reef saw that she had bent one leg up and was pulling off her boots.

"Yes," Reef agreed, feeling a little comforted to have someone echo his thoughts. Kaeda had started to rub her feet. She knew about human bodies, didn't she? Perhaps this was a good thing to do. Reef also pulled off a boot, looking with dream-like confusion at the lumpy human foot that belonged to him. He watched how Kaeda rubbed her thumbs along the arch of her foot and began to do the same to his own.

It felt awful. And then it felt better. He copied what she did and found his strained muscles relaxing one by one.

"You know, you could let me levitate you a little bit," Gamalielle said, drifting over.

"We should save our magic," Kaeda replied.

"Maybe you should save your feet," the cat shrugged. "But whatever you say."

That night they slept out of the wind and were able to pull up a little water from the old well on the property, but the next day they found themselves wandering across a plain turned into a maze by a host of stone arches, boulders, and pillars of all shapes and sizes. The wind of the previous night had blown in clouds, making even midday colorless, dim, and grey.

A cloudy day always put Reef on edge. Khirians loved the sun. Sunny days were for doing things. Cloudy days, for sleeping. So walking on and on beneath the heavy sky felt strange.

Still, his gut told him there was something worse in the atmosphere than sunlessness.

Turus feels it too, Archavie thought to him. *The worms create a sort of magical interference. Something in their natural armor. He doesn't like it.*

Magical interference shouldn't bother him though, Reef thought. There was something else. A feeling that someone or something was watching them.

Ah, yes, that.

"I don't want to alarm anyone," The wizard said aloud, "but a couple of werebear scouts have noticed us. Or, not *us* exactly, but they've noticed that there is magic in our vicinity. They seem to be able to smell it. Turus has convinced them that there's nothing, and told them to go home, but we will want to keep a low profile."

"Lady Batbayar said werebears have been viewed in the past as messengers of the archon," Kaeda said, as they wove their way between the worms. "Maybe it wouldn't be so bad if they found us."

"Maybe, but these seem rather desperate to find magic. I don't want to take any chances."

A couple of hours later, they were all glad of Turus's interference. They found a road leading through the worms, and since no one was nearby they decided to travel on it for a while, since twisting their way between the worm trunks became as tedious as picking a path through a thick forest. On the road, they found evidence that the bears were not as benign as Kaeda might have hoped: a heap in the packed dirt, which, as they drew closer became the remains of a caravan.

"Frils, what happened," Gamalielle whispered, as they slowly skirted along the opposite side of the road, covering their faces against the reek of death.

A few years ago, Reef would have said Khirians. The claw marks on the wood of the broken wagons and on what remained of the mangled bodies were of similar enough composition. But Khirians would probably have eaten the bodies, or at least have dismembered them for fun. These were more or less in one piece, save where scavenging animals had grazed on the decaying flesh.

"Survivors?" Kaeda asked.

"No," Archavie said. "Not here anyway."

"Do we wanna um… loot what's left? What?" Gamalielle added, as Kaeda shot her a sharp look. "We don't exactly have a lot of resources right now. Maybe the bears missed something."

Reef wouldn't have minded picking through the remains, but the humans had more scruples. After deciding that it would be too dangerous to try burying the bodies, what with worms all around, they walked on along the road.

The invisible sun slipped away toward the horizon and dim light turned to thick shadow, and still the plain of worms stretched on.

"If we find a comfy spot, Turus can make us a fire." In the aftermath of their discovery, and in the muffled twilight, the cheer in his voice fell flat.

"And I can catch us some food," Gamalielle added, in a more appropriately grim tone.

"Is it safe?" Kaeda asked.

"As far as bears go, yes, Turus is turning their attention away. As for the worms…"

They looked at Reef, who surveyed the stones for a moment. Yes, his mind said, but something deeper said no, keep walking. "If we are quiet, the worms will be safe. But… a feeling," he paused, looking around at the deepening gloom which, without sunlight, was a collage of greys.

"A magic-consuming UMP?" Kaeda asked.

"I don't know." As Reef tried to pay attention, he felt confused. It reminded him of swimming around a shipwreck, unfamiliar shapes marring the water, making a mess of his senses.

"I was telling Reef earlier that the worms create some kind of magical interference," Archavie said. "To Turus they feel strangely impenetrable."

The healer frowned and placed her palm against one of the stone columns. "Fascinating. And you can feel that Reef?"

Reef shrugged and rumbled.

"While Kaeda is being fascinated, I'm going to go hunting," Gamalielle said, and she leapt away into the darkness.

"We should not stay," Reef said more firmly to Archavie, but the wizard was gathering dry brush and clearing a space for a campfire, and Kaeda had sat down already to pull her boots off again.

"I agree," Archavie said, as he lit a blaze. "Turus doesn't like the wormhenge either, but we do need to eat, and make some plans. If we keep traveling northeast, we're going to run into a forest, and Turus thinks that might be where the bears live, so we need to consider—"

He was interrupted by Gamalielle sprinting back into the camp. On her feet. Reef couldn't remember ever seeing her actually run before.

"Frils! Frills! Frils!" the cat yelped as she dashed into the clearing.

"What is it?" Kaeda asked. While the healer tugged her boots back on, Reef and Archavie both turned to scan the darkness swiftly descending around them.

"There was an eyeball!" Gamalielle, screamed. Her own eyes and pupils were round as marbles as she pulled a pair of daggers from her belt, staring back the way she had come.

"An eyeball?" Kaeda said, sounding disbelieving.

"I'm not on the nip, okay?! I was hunting, I nearly got this hare, but it scampered into a bush, so I pounced, and in the bush, there was an eyeball, just an eyeball, on a silvery stalk, like a – like a mushroom or something. Like a frilsing wire-and-eyeball mushroom. And I screamed, and then I saw this pillar of darkness, and I was going to zip away, but I fell. My levitating enchantment had just poofed out! So, I ran, and I'm telling you, there's something out there!"

"Silver wire," the healer breathed. "Sweet magic."

Reef didn't know what that meant to her, but the feeling deep in his gut rocked like a boat between "I told you so," and "get out of there."

"Reef, do you feel anything?" Kaeda asked.

Nothing. And something. Tremors in the air. Interrupted echoes of fear. "We should—" he was about to say "run" but it was too late. Something like a star flickered overhead, even as Reef's feet shifted, preparing him to move. The something fell, straight down into the campfire.

Chapter Twenty

SHAKEN AND WORMED

Kaeda

A flash of light. A thunderous boom. The blast threw me back against the nearest worm, and for a moment I could see nothing, just shimmers and darkness.

"Kay! Kay!"

My arms wouldn't move. My eyelids wouldn't lift.

"Kay! Get some magic in your head! Frils!"

I heard a groaning, felt a shaking in the earth.

"What do you mean they don't have brains?" Archavie shouted, "How can something that big not have a brain?

"Okay, this is the most basic first aid, it's the only thing I know," Gamalielle's voice said much closer. A warm rush of magic and I regained enough consciousness to feel the pain in my head.

"You're alive!"

The campfire seemed to be all around me now, scattered into the brush where it multiplied into crackling clusters. Smoke and dust filled the air, and shapes rose up through it. Worms, their matte surfaces golden in the firelight, shed showers of sand and soil as they stretched upward.

"Never fear," Archavie called from the other side of the camp, "Turus and I have fought bigger sea monsters than this. How about a little lightning to turn this stone to glass?"

The wizard raised his hands. Crackles of lightning arched between the half-dozen worm pillars, now arching high into the sky, and chunks of worm armor cracked and fell.

"Kay, you with us?" Gamalielle was bending over me. I looked up toward her just in time to see a four-foot whorl of yellow teeth and purple gums, rushing towards us. Before I could so much as scream or cover my face, Reef was there. He caught the edges of the creature's mouth in his hands with a roar, and held it, worm teeth cutting into his hands, blood running down his forearms as he wrestled with the creature. When the worm gave up biting anyone and lifted its head, Reef held on. As the worm pulled him up, he climbed onto its back.

Even in the midst of the chaos I felt a swell of awe, like a wave lifting my heart. Magic I could do, but grappling a worm? Scaling a living boulder? With torn bloody hands? Within moments Reef had his legs wrapped around it and his maul in his hands to strike the creature.

"I'm okay," I answered Gamalielle. "I'll borrow your magic." She had set a very basic piece of healing in my brain. I began to adjust it to more quickly resolve what I guessed was a concussion.

"Go for it," the Cat said. Another worm lunged down and Gamalielle tossed something at it, shouting curses as the magic sparkled across the worm's face and set it twitching.

Finally, I had the strength and stability to push myself up. I would take this knot of magic, I thought, and craft it into something that could hopefully knock one of these worms out.

I began to adjust the tangle as Archavie loosed another volley of lightning, but then, in the flash of illumination, I saw something else. Beyond Archavie, between the stone shapes just outside our camp, a dark figure stood wearing a familiar black robe. The hood was raised, and a magical shadow beneath hid his face.

"Archavie!" I shouted.

The wizard glanced towards me, and that was the last thing I saw before another explosive blast tore through our camp.

The wave of force hurled me into the darkness, tumbling across dirt and brush, bruising my ribs and knocking the wind out of me, but at least I stayed conscious. When I struggled to my feet again the camp was a blaze several yards away, the campfire multiplied to a brush fire in a living city of waving rocks. Some had fallen now, sprawled in ruins on the earth, leaking purple blood, but many still arced overhead, and it seemed that the thunder of the blasts had woken more.

I staggered forward, struggling to gasp in air, and shaping the bit of knockout magic as I went. I didn't see Reef or Gamalielle as I neared the fire, but I did see Svevolod. He had moved in and stood in the center of the camp now. Wind, or I suppose invisible magic, seemed to rush out from him constantly, blowing the fire away, and whipping the red and purple robes of Archavie, who lay at his feet. Svevolod had one sleeve raised in the air, one sharp black finger pointed at Archavie. His whispery voice came to me indistinctly as if through water, "You are mine."

I didn't know what he was doing, but it seemed to hurt Archavie a great deal. The wizard screamed and jerked and curled on the ground as if his own lightning had been turned back on him.

Fury surged in my chest. I changed my magical constellation to one meant to disassemble any magical constructs and changed its shape, a spike, not a knot, meant to pierce through a troubling magical effect. Of course, if Svevolod had one of the magic-eating things with him, my magic wouldn't last long, but I only had to distract him long enough for Archavie and Turus to escape.

I ran between the patches of blazing brush and threw my spike. Svevolod must have heard my footsteps. He glanced my way. But he wasn't quick enough to stop the disassembling spike. It plunged into the invisible magic surrounding him and vanished to my senses, but it must have had an effect. He turned his attention away from Archavie and seemed to be trying to sweep my magic out of his.

I no longer felt my bruised ribs or the lingering pain in my head. My heart beat so fiercely, the adrenaline hitting me so intensely, that I knew I had to keep moving or I would collapse. I dashed in, dropped to my knees by Archavie, and hauled him off the ground.

Go! Turus shouted. *Go! Hide him! Keep him safe!*

The wizard's legs didn't seem to be working, but at least his feet were beneath him now. With his arm over my shoulder, his shuddery whimpers in my ear, we staggered toward the darkness.

"No!"

I glanced back to see Svevolod reach towards us. Fingers whipped towards us, stretching out on a mesh of silver. The glove fabric and flesh and blood all fragmented, decorating the wires like beads. For a bizarre, dreamlike moment I took in this sight, then the surrounding worms, deciding apparently that this magician was the greatest threat to their territory, began plunging toward him, one after another.

I didn't wait to see what his fate would be but kept dragging Archavie onward. I saw no sign of Reef or Gamalielle.

Even if they had been mere feet away, I don't know if I could have found them. More worms woke every moment, constantly changing the landscape, the spreading fire sent smoke and shadows and crackles of sound spinning through the night air.

I thought only of getting Archavie as far from Svevolod as possible, and this kept my feet moving even as we left the smoke and rumbles behind, even as the adrenaline faded and left my legs shaking, my teeth chattering in the magicless cold.

"Reef?" I called. "Gamalielle?"

But that was not who found me.

Chapter Twenty-One

TEAM MAELSTROM

Reef

THE worms seemed to have forgotten Reef was there. Maybe they assumed him dead. Reef held still as he could, pinned to the ground by the worm that had fallen on top of him, watching the living pillars looming overhead as they swarmed by in a shushing and scraping and shaking of the earth.

He kept hoping that the worm on top of him would regain consciousness, but the longer it lay there, the more he was sure it was dead.

At least the ground was uneven due to the slithering excavation of the worms. The dip in the earth beneath him was probably the only reason he hadn't been crushed to death, and the only reason he had a little breath left in his lungs. He was afraid to breathe out though, afraid he wouldn't be able to inhale again. He could hold his breath for quite a long time. If he was calm.

He wasn't calm. He was trapped. He felt the thrashing terror that told him an UMP was nearby, and a weird conviction that it was attached to the robed figure who had attacked them. At least the magician seemed to be leading the worms away.

When the thick of the woken worms had passed him, Reef tried to dig his elbows into the dirt and brace his palms against the body of the worm to push it up, but it was too heavy. Then he heard a different swishing and scraping. He looked straight over his head and saw on the upside-down ground, Gamalielle, limping towards him, one arm tied up in a sling made of a scarf. She stopped, the golden-orange light of nearby fires flickering in her eyes as she looked down at him.

"I could leave you here, and let you die," she muttered. "Magic knows I'd like to. But I can't find Kaeda, and I can't find Archavie, and if I find them later and they find out I left you trapped under a worm," she shook her head and grumbled. "Idealistic twits will be beside themselves." She heaved a great sigh and grimaced, her whiskers twitching. "You better thank me," she growled.

The weight pressing on Reef began to lift. Reef rolled and scrambled out and the worm crashed back down behind him. "Thank you," he said.

"Yeah. That was the last of my magic, and I'm pretty sure my arm is broken, and I don't even know what happened to my ankle and I was gonna use that magic to try to heal myself but lucky for you I decided to chew a heap of nip instead and that's keeping the pain at a happy distance. For now. Better hope we find our better halves before it wears off and I get really mad that I chose to save you."

"I will carry you," Reef said.

"Frils no! How are you even on your feet? You got worm-smushed but you're fine! Frils, I hate Khirians." With that the cat hobbled off.

"What are you doing?" Reef asked.

"Heading for the forest where we'll have some cover. If Archie and Kay have any sense, that's what they're doing too."

"Bears," Reef reminded her.

"At least Archavie can mind-bend the bears! Worms don't have brains apparently. Come on we gotta flee this frils-fest while the worms are swarming Mr. Evilpants."

Reef glanced back past the worm that had nearly crushed him. He could barely see, through the smoke and waving worm trunks, that most of them had converged on a single location, drifting slowly west. An occasional burst of light or crack of sound broke through the mass of stone-armored bodies, testifying that Mr. Evilpants, as Gamalielle called him, still lived.

"What if they are behind?" Reef asked.

"If they're out in that mess, we're not going to be able to find them. Turus has probably got them out of trouble already anyway. Let's get moving before Svevvy blows his way to freedom and starts up his 'kill the Commission' party again."

He couldn't deny her logic, but as Reef walked alongside the limping Cat, he thought that at her pace it would take them days to reach the trees. "Let me carry you," he said.

"No."

"You are very slow."

"Yeah, 'cause I'm injured, and you're gonna be injured if you come any closer!"

This was in response to Reef stepping nearer, intending to pick her up, but she had a dagger in her free hand, and looked serious about using it, even if her aim might not be the best right now.

"Silly," Reef said.

"Silly? Silly? You're my mortal enemy, buster!"

"No," Reef said, "enemy behind us. We are team. Team with missing pieces." It seemed to become real as he said it. They were a team. Part of the team was missing. His heart beat a little faster thinking of Archavie and Kaeda, out there somewhere, possibly in danger. It was the same sort of concern he would have felt for Khirians in his shoal. "Must find them," he went on. "Should move quickly."

"Frils," the Cat swore. "You're not wrong. Okay, I solemnly swear, this one time I will not stab you. Bend down, I'll get up on your shoulder."

She hardly weighed anything. In a few moments they were on the move again, and sometime toward midnight, they reached the tree line.

If Reef's experience held true, the worms wouldn't come into the forest. The deep root structures would make traversing the soil too difficult. He ran into the trees, the grating of the stone and the smells of smoke and dust fading very suddenly as the trunks and leaves closed around them. The nearest sound now was the rush of wind at the edge of the forest, but even that mellowed as the forest became denser. At last Reef slowed his pace and caught his breath. The thrashing fear had faded. Whatever inside him sensed the UMP, it had calmed as they left the plain.

"Archie! Kaeda!" Gamalielle hollered.

Reef carried her along the edge of the forest, as close to the plain of worms as he dared, but they saw no sign of Archavie or Kaeda.

"Frils. I don't know what do to," the Cat complained. "I can see in the dark but I'm no wilderness tracker. I'm a city girl. I don't know how to find a couple of missing humans. Besides the trees are kinda wavy-like. I might be tripping just a little bit. Or the pain's making me woozy. Or both."

Reef didn't know how to find them either. If they had been in the ocean, it would be no problem.

The sudden rush of sadness took him by surprise. How long had it been now, since he was in the ocean? He had not thought to count the days. He wished wholeheartedly that he could be surrounded by water, water where he could feel Archavie's and Kaeda's heartbeats, where he could sense enemies at a distance, where the water would tell him what was going on.

He thought again of water in the wind, or in the clouds overhead, but it did not comfort him. It would not help him. He had to swallow his sick sad feeling and try make a plan.

He was beginning to suggest that they sit still and wait for Archavie and Kaeda to find them instead, when Gamalielle shushed him. Reef turned his head to look at her and then winced as her huge ear, flicking this way and that, batted against his eye.

"Someone is coming," the Cat whispered.

"Archavie?" Reef whispered back.

"No, too many. Can you climb us into that tree?" She pointed to a huge oak.

"Yes, but—"

"Just do it. If they find us, let me do the talking."

Reef hauled them up and found a sturdy crook that would hold his weight. The tree still had most of its leaves, but Reef didn't doubt that any half-decent tracker would be able to find them.

He waited. He did not hear the footsteps that Gamalielle had heard, but he did see the strangers as they arrived. There were several of them, nearly invisible beneath the cover of the forest and with the moon covered by clouds. Reef could just barely see the glint of armor and weapons on the five or six figures that came to stand beneath the oak, and he thought he saw more, shadows between the trees, further out in the forest.

"It's up there, I'm sure of it," A young male voice said.

"Khirian!" A female voice called, and Reef had to focus to make out her words. They were Molvan, but the accent was strange, deep, as if each word was pulled from some mysterious depths. "You are surrounded. Come down now, or we'll come up after you."

Still clinging to his shoulder, Gamalielle cleared her throat and spoke in a hoarse, screechy voice, "As I'm sure you can see, this is no Khirian, but an extremely beautiful young man."

The armored group just stared up at her in confusion.

"Frils," Gamalielle swore. "Of course, you don't speak Gemmic."

Since his position was revealed anyway, Reef inched his way around to better make out the speakers below. He saw a burly woman with a thick braid of hair over one shoulder. To her left stood a similarly burly young man, and to her right, a patch of shadow darker than the rest of the forest. The look of him put Reef on edge, reminding him of the magician who had just attacked them. But that person had worn heavy, almost bell-shaped robes, and this person dressed in something with a softer drape and… what was that on his face? It looked almost as if he had a beak, a metal beak, sticking out of his hood.

One hand extended from the shadow, holding a staff crowned by a swirl of steel that held a shimmery silver orb. Magical storage, Reef assumed. If Gamalielle could get ahold of that, then they stood a chance of escape.

Gamalielle must have felt him tensing for action because she said, "Don't do anything stupid. We can still talk our way out of this."

The burly woman muttered something to the patch of darkness, which produced another hand, holding two glinting curls of metal. When the two figures in armor had each curled one around their ears, the woman spoke again.

"We have much experience hunting Khirians, and we know there is a Khirian hiding with you. I tell you again, come down."

"Well… well this is my Khirian," Gamalielle bluffed. "I mean, my prisoner. Which I'm pretty sure I can collect a bounty on somewhere. So… go find your own Khirian."

"Why is a Gemmic Cat hunting Khirians in Molva?"

"It's none of your business."

"It is my business. I represent the Torgovyy Channel Monster Hunter's Guild. If you are traveling with a Khirian prisoner, I need to make sure you can take the appropriate precautions. Otherwise, for everyone's safety, I will take custody of it."

Gamalielle paused. "Torgovyy Channel?"

At this the woman pulled a chain up from her collar and displayed it. Reef saw a badge, lit by a fine glowing order. It showed a shield, split down the middle by a branching river, with pine trees on the left and a pair of crossed arrows on the right. "Captain Nadezhda Rozhkov, Team Maelstrom, Torgovyy Channel Monster Hunter's Guild. My lieutenant, Yury Rozhkov, and our magical support, Tsakhia Rozhkov." The young man and the patch of shadow displayed their badges as well.

Gamalielle took all of this in, then spoke in a wheedling tone. "Hypothetically, if I were from the Molvan Magical Crisis Commission and this no-good lizard was the Gemmic Council's misguided attempt to pacify the Khirian hoard… would you help us get safely to the Gemmic Sea? Or anywhere really. But first, our other friends have gone missing."

"The Gemmic Council invited a Khirian?" The lieutenant exclaimed.

"It's kind of a long story."

Captain Rozhkov conferred with the other two beneath the tree. Reef heard the lieutenant say, "It would make sense. I did smell a man and a woman, and olive oil and seawater and imported nip."

The patch of shadow countered in a rustling, dead-leaf voice, "They were meant to land in Vodastad."

"We crashed," Gamalielle hollered down. "General Straton was lost at sea and the rest of us were running away from some giant worms when Archavie and Kaeda both disappeared, and Reef and I don't know how to find them."

"If it is the Commission," the lieutenant said, "then Voda will probably pay us a bundle for bringing them to Vodaniya in one piece."

The dry, rustling voice countered again, "Escorting them would distract us from our hunt."

But Captain Rozhkov lifted a hand thoughtfully to her chin. "How did you crash?" she asked. "The winter storms have not yet come."

"This crazy magic-wrecking whatever-it-was tore the magic out of our ship. We barely made it to shore."

The humans standing beneath Reef's tree looked at one another. Reef heard the shadow murmur, "they hit a phage."

"How could it be out so far?" the captain murmured back.

"If it was taken to Gem City. If *he* was bringing it back."

"We hit a what?" Gamalielle asked, but Team Maelstrom ignored her and continued their discussion.

"They have come to help Molva," Captain Rozhkov said. "We should help them if we can."

"Helping them could bring us into the public eye," the shadow countered.

Just then something came running towards the group. Reef saw the glint of armor but… the shape ran on all fours, definitely not human. Captain Rozhkov noticed it but did not move to attack. Instead, she heaved a sigh.

The armored creature reared up and shifted easily into human form as it reached the captain.

"You're werebears?!" Gamalielle shrieked.

Captain Rozhkov addressed her newly returned scout sharply, "Pasternak, did you smell the strangers in the forest?"

"Yes sir. I'm so sorry sir." He stammered as he glanced up at the tree. "I didn't think –."

"Don't shift unless you know it is safe."

"Yes sir."

"Now give me your report."

Captain Rozhkov listened to the hunter's muttered report while Gamalielle called down comments ranging from, "You know I've always thought bears were really majestic," to "If you need a snack, Reef's got more meat on him, just saying."

"Miss Aisop," Captain Rozhkov called up at last, "if you will stop talking for a moment, I will tell you that Pasternack has found your friends."

"Oh, thank the archons! Are they okay?"

"They are alive, and we will take you to them, and aid the Commission, on the condition that you will not reveal to anyone that some of Team Maelstrom are ursinthropes. Agreed?"

"Absolutely. Totally fine."

"And you Khirian?"

"Yes," Reef answered.

"Then come down, and we will be on our way."

"You heard the lady," Gamalielle said.

Well, he supposed he had no other options. Gripping the trunk Reef climbed down while Gamalielle continued chattering. "Boy are we glad to have some help. The whole trip has been a nightmare so far, you have no idea."

Reef leapt down the last yard or so, landing in time to hear Lieutenant Yury say, "nightmares are our business." He had his pair of short swords drawn now. In fact, all the hunters did as they stood around Reef. Their armor, now that he saw it up close, was not like any armor he had seen in Molva before. Mostly black, and patterned almost like wood grain on a tree. But not quite wood grain. More like many, many, miniscule lines of writing, swirling together across the metal surface. The pieces seemed to bend as the hunters moved, not like the stiff plates of Gemmic armor.

"Now, I know this is the most bizarre thing you've probably ever heard," Gamalielle spoke from her perch, "but honestly Reef probably won't cause trouble. I want to kill him too, but we probably shouldn't. Archavie and Kaeda would be mad."

"Should we cuff him?" This from Lieutenant Yury. "I know he looks like a man, but my nose doesn't lie."

Rather than answer, Captain Rozhkov took a step toward Reef. She was shorter than Yury but just as brawny, and something in the intensity of her expression, the brilliance of her eyes beneath her helmet, made Reef take a step back toward the tree he had just descended so that he bumped into the thick trunk. All sound, even the rustle of leaves and chirp of bats, quieted and as Reef stood before the captain, he began to feel quiet too. The starlight seemed to reach down through the clouds, through the leaves just as he had been sure the UMP, or the phage, or whatever it was, was dangerous, so he felt a weird but certain safety and confidence in the presence of Captain Rozhkov. It didn't make any sense, but what made sense anymore?

The captain sniffed the air and seemed to consider him. "No," she said slowly.

"Khirians are dangerous," the lieutenant reminded her.

"So are we. I don't think we need to restrain him. Just watch him. Your name is Reef?" she asked.

Reef almost wanted to say no and give her his full Khirian name. He thought somehow, she might understand. But instead, he said, "yes."

"Follow orders, Reef, and I don't think we'll have a problem."

Then she turned and walked away.

"Tell me you didn't just pray and get a word from the goddess that he's not dangerous," Lieutenant Yury snorted as Captain Rozhkov walked past.

The captain tossed out a frustrated exclamation that Reef didn't understand. "Just keep an eye on him," she said. Then she addressed the group at large. "Well, now we know why the worms were having so much fun. We'll come back in the morning and—"

"Oh, that wasn't us," Gamalielle interrupted. "I don't want you to think that we're utter noobs. We left the worms alone, but Svevolod—"

She stopped as Captain Rozhkov turned sharply towards her again, and then stammered on, "I mean, can't say for sure that it was him, since we didn't see the guy's face, but we met him in Gem City and, well anyway, all I'm saying is someone attacked us, he looked an awful lot like the dov's advisor, and he set the worms off."

"We will discuss this later," the captain said. "Until then, you will say nothing more about it." Then she addressed the group, "we will postpone our harvest of the worms—"

"We can't wait," Yury interrupted. "We need that magic."

"If the dov's advisor is truly out on the plain, it is too dangerous."

"It's going to be dangerous if we remain in Sosna Village without magic," Yury countered. "If Tsakhia's too scared."

"This is not the time to bicker, lieutenant."

"You'll endanger all of them by protecting him."

"I will go."

The shadow of a man, who had retreated before Reef jumped down, now wove his way back through the group. The steel beak of his bird mask and the silvery top of his staff stood out against the darkness, as if floating toward Reef of their own accord. But not smoothly. The magician wasn't just carrying the staff, Reef realized, but leaning on it, like a cane. As he limped toward Reef the comfortable peace brought by Captain Rozhkov's presence faded, and Reef felt an odd stirring. It wasn't the dread he had felt in maybe-Svevolod's presence, but it was uncomfortable, as if this Tsakhia reminded him of something, but he couldn't tell what it was.

"We can wait until morning," Captain Rozhkov said to Tsakhia, but Yury spoke up again, in a biting voice aimed at the magician in the robe.

"You were the one who estimated some of them might snap by dawn."

"That is why I will go," the masked man spoke with equal sharpness. Then he said more gently to the captain, "I will take Pasternak and Chelomny. They know how to use the equipment. But only with your approval."

At length the captain nodded.

"Oh, but before you get going," Gamalielle said, "Could you maybe heal me first? Pretty sure I broke my arm and the pain's kind of chasing me around, ready to get me in a corner when the happy leaves stop doing their job."

"Oh, of course," Captain Rozhkov said, and she nodded to the magician.

The magician lifted his staff and began adjusting the many metal rings that decorated it, twisting and clicking them in place. The diaphanous sleeves of his black robes drifted around him while he worked, as if he were surrounded by water, not air. When he had finished, he held the tip of the staff out toward Gamalielle. "Touch the staff," he instructed, "and the healing magic will flow out."

The Cat extended an arm and set her tawny paw on the orb. "Wow!" she exclaimed, and when the shadow had withdrawn his staff, she leapt down from Reef's shoulder. "Wow, you're as good as Kaeda! What a rush! I feel great!"

Shortly, they all set off, the shadowy Tsakhia with two other hunters, each carrying a leather box on their backs, and the rest of the group, including Reef and Gamalielle, following Captain Rozhkov. Lieutenant Yury kept pace with Reef and Gamalielle, who after a few steps asked Reef if she could ride on his shoulder again.

Reef didn't particularly want her on his shoulder, but without magic to fly the cat had taken to walking in front of him, weaving back and forth in such an erratic manner that Reef had almost stepped on her more than once. He gave his acquiescence and Gamalielle leapt up and resumed her perch and immediately struck up a conversation with Yury.

"So, Captain Rozhkov, is she like, your wife?"

The lieutenant burst out laughing. "No. If Nadia wasn't my sister, I don't think I could put up with her."

"Yeah, the feeling is mutual," the captain said from the front of the group.

"Not like she puts up with Tsakhia," Yury added.

"Be nice, Yury," the captain called back.

"Your magician did a swell job on my arm," Gamalielle commented.

"Oh yeah, Tsakhia's a magical powerhouse. When he's breathing."

"That's enough, lieutenant. Don't forget we're on a mission."

"I should stop talking before Nadia takes my badge."

"Maybe we could talk more later," Gamalielle said lightly, and Reef felt her tail flick behind him.

A bit of a wry smile appeared on the bit of Yury's face that was visible through his helmet. "Sure, Whiskers."

Something was going on, Reef realized, some social mammal thing. But it felt as far beyond him as gulls soaring in the blue sky. He would ask Archavie to explain it all later.

Chapter Twenty-Two

ZILLYA

Kaeda

I had intended to stay put and look out for Reef and Gamalielle, but when the trio of monster-hunting scouts found Archavie and I on the edge of the forest, they assured me that a Khirian and a Cat would be easy for them to track down, and when I explained who I was, I saw their faces brighten.

"A magisophic healer! We could use your help," one said.

Having just dragged Archavie away from a strange magical battle, and with chaos of the worm attacks behind us, I didn't feel like I could be much help to anyone. What had happened? Where was Turus? Had I done enough to stop Svevolod? Why was Svevolod after us, if indeed it was him?

These questions rolled through my mind while one scout ran off to find their captain and the others said something about a flu epidemic and relief efforts. Normally this would have grabbed my attention immediately, but now I kept looking back.

"If I'm going to help you, I think you'll have to help me first," I said. Archavie had collapsed into the curled-up, sometimes-catatonic state that Turu's absence seemed to produce. I couldn't even persuade him to stand anymore. "Can you help me move him?"

The scouts looked at the wizard with uncertainty.

"Is that really Wizard Archavie?" one of them asked.

"Yes," I said, "but he's... well he's different from... nevermind. If I knock him out, can you carry him for me?" I didn't doubt they could. They were easily the most robustly built Molvans I had met so far.

"Yes, we can make a stretcher in a pinch."

"And do you have any magic I can use?"

In answer, one of the scouts handed me a tiny silver vial.

"What's this?" I asked.

"Zillya. A magical concentrate."

Concentrate was right. The liquid inside, resembling mercury, was packed with magic at a higher density than I had ever seen before.

"How do I get it out?" I asked.

The scouts looked at each other, as if each hoping the other could explain.

"How do *you* get it out?" I asked.

More looks. Finally, one said, "You'll have to ask Tsakhia."

Very helpful. I handed the vial back, afraid that if I upset the balance of the enchantment, it might cause a magical explosion. I would have to just explain to Archavie as best I could and hope he would forgive me for whatever extra terror I subjected him to. I took the wizard's face in my hands, got him to look at me, and explained, for whatever good it might do, that these nice people were going to carry him to a safe place.

I didn't think he understood. In fact, I suspected that as the hunters stretched out their makeshift stretcher and I tried to drag Archavie toward it, he simply fainted in sheer terror.

Well, at least we'd be able to move him. Shortly we were trudging through the forest. The chill of the night seemed to creep up through my boots with each step, and the darkness seeped into me from the shadows around. By the time we saw the glow of the fort up ahead, I felt ready to collapse and cry, more from fatigue than anything else.

The log doors of the fort walls surrounding the village opened as we approached, golden light spilling out, and with it a bounding figure.

"Kaeda!"

Gamalielle leapt into my arms, and I found myself sobbing into her fur as she clung to me.

"Healer Straton," a voice said. "I am happy to see you in one piece. And your wizard?" I looked up through my blear of tears and saw a woman, framed by the light from the gate, her helmet under her arm, a frayed braid of chestnut hair over her shoulder.

"We've got him, captain," the scouts reported, carrying the still-unconscious Archavie between them.

"Archie!" Gamalielle exclaimed. She leapt down and bounded over to peer at the wizard. "What happened to him?"

"Turus… I don't know if he stayed to fight or if he was trapped," the details seemed more and more muddled as I tried to explain. As I brushed the tears from my eyes, I spotted Reef, looking less tall than usual between all these huge Molvans. He craned his human neck to look over their heads and check that Archavie and I were okay. Part of me wanted to run and hug him too. But that would seem strange, wouldn't it?

"I am Nadezhda Rozhkov," the woman with the braid introduced herself, "captain of Team Maelstrom. Gamalielle and Reef have already filled us in on many parts of your adventure. I am sure you are tired, but I am afraid I am going to ask you for help."

As she spoke another lady made her way briskly out of the fort. Rather than the wood grain black armor that the rest of Team Maelstrom wore, this woman had on a skirted coat, leggings, and tall boots. Her hair spilled down across her shoulders in a sunset of colors. "Is this Healer Straton? Alta Arahi," she nodded to me. "I'm Team Maelstrom's medic, but I'm much better with a stab wound than a virus."

I left Archavie with Reef and Gamalielle, assured by Team Maelstrom that they would find him a safe place to rest. Then I followed Alta and Captain Rozhkov. They filled me in as we walked through the village of cabins within the fort's walls. They had been enroute to deliver the head of a vodyanoy to complete a contract and had heard word of werebear attacks in the area. They had traveled south to investigate and on the road a messenger from Sosna Village had found them.

"They said they had an epidemic, likely trader's flu, but that is not really the problem," Captain Rozhkov explained. "I am sure your friends will tell you soon enough that most of my team are werebears. Yes, including me. Like many of the creatures of this land, we need magic to stay healthy. My team sometimes travels from village to village, bringing relief, but our stores of magic were low by the time the messenger reached us. We would have gone back to the channel to pick up more magic, but Dov Miro has closed all the channel's ports in his dovniya."

"We can't give away all of the zillya," Alta went on. "The team needs it in case of emergencies. But without magic, the flu is killing these people."

"What do you want me to do?" I asked.

"Anything you can, until our primary magician returns," Captain Rozhkov said. "I have sent him to harvest more magic from the worms that attacked you."

We had reached the lodge at the end of the main road. A pair of guards, not in Maelstrom armor but dressed in leather and furs, stood at the top of the steps. They opened the doors for us and let us in.

It was like Fari after the homecoming. Too many sick crowded into one place, laying in rows, some in beds, some on the floor, some coughing, some moaning, some crying. A couple of wooden chairs, draped with blankets, sat in the central aisle of the room, and an antler chandelier hung overhead, candles burning. Not nearly enough light, not nearly enough magic.

I took off my cloak and began rolling up my sleeves. "Can you give me any magic?" I asked.

"If you use any magic on them when they are so sick their bodies will take it apart," the captain told me. "It is difficult to explain. You will see when Tsakhia gets back."

"What do you have?"

"Some drugs and herbs," Alta said. "I'll show you."

Within minutes I had determined that there wasn't much I could do that they couldn't do themselves, but that didn't matter. They needed extra hands, and they needed someone who could triage with confidence and prioritize and prescribe the team's limited remaining doses of herbal immune boosters and chemical fever reducers.

Captain Rozhkov helped Alta and I, but I could tell she was distracted. She kept looking towards the door of the hospital and Alta kept saying, "He'll be fine. He'll be here any minute."

The hours stretched on. Other hunters brought us tea. Gamalielle checked in to say Archavie was okay, Reef was okay, and she was going to sleep. Captain Rozhkov continued to watch the door. It seemed as if lines were etching themselves onto her face before my very eyes as her concern grew. Finally, the door to the lodge opened and Yury came in, carrying a large, leather-covered box.

"They're back," he said.

The captain ran past him. I saw, in the doorway, a tall shape, not quite solid at the edges, holding a staff. For a moment I remembered Svevolod, and my heart shivered with fear, but this dark figure was different, narrower, and with a glinting mask shaped like a bird skull sticking out of the hood's magical shadow. The captain threw her arms around this strange figure and he returned her embrace.

"Where do you want it?" Yury asked me.

I pulled my attention away from the captain and the person who I assumed must be Tsakhia the magician. "Um, what is it?"

"Zillya," Yury answered. He set the case on the edge of the nearest chair, unbuckled the straps that kept the box shut, and opened it. Inside, carefully secured, were dozens of tiny silver vials.

The smaller bottles had droppers in them, and the amount of magic packed into each drop of the elixir was what I would expect to find in several square feet of diffuse ambient magic. As Yury and Alta and the captain and I began dosing the patients, I found that the captain was right. When the elixir reached their stomachs, it broke down, but rather than exploding in a burst of ambient magic it was… the only word I could use was digested.

If I had not recently discovered that lungs could do magic on their own, I would not have known how to make sense of what I saw with my magical senses. The werebears digested the magic just as human bodies would digest food, breaking down the elixir bit by bit and then carrying the magic throughout the body to where it was needed. Healthy cells began blocking viral proteins, barricading themselves against the virus, while the digested magic swept into infected cells, pruning out viral DNA and restoring the cells to health in a way that I wouldn't have thought possible. I watched as the supplementary magic bathed the tiny tangles of the ursinthropic curse spread throughout the patient's bodies. Suddenly the B cells started making antibodies at an alarming rate.

The virus was utterly defeated. There was nothing else for me to do.

Captain Rozhkov joined me at the bedside of a five-year-old child who minutes ago had been tossing in the delirium of fever. Now she was peacefully sleeping. "You can go get some rest," the captain said. "They will continue to improve."

I nodded numbly. "Archavie. I should check on Archavie."

"Reef is with him," she told me now. "We set up a tent for the two of them to share. They are probably asleep now. You should get some sleep too. The sun is rising, but the village will be quiet a little while yet."

The sun was indeed rising, the clouds breaking, the day fresh with birdsong. Maelstrom's sentries directed me to a tent where Gamalielle was snoring. An empty bedroll was waiting for me, and I collapsed into it.

Chapter Twenty-Three

SACRED

Kaeda

I woke to the green glow of the tent walls, glowing green with morning sunlight. Gamalielle continued to snore. I could have probably gone back to sleep myself – I couldn't have slept more than a couple of hours—but I heard activity outside, and I didn't want to miss anything. When I emerged from the tent, eyes aching with weariness, I found myself shading my eyes, not just against the sun, but against the color. The forest at the edges of the village was not only green, but yellow, orange, and red, as if the fires of the previous night had floated benignly up into the trees and become decorations, instead of dangers. When my eyes had adjusted enough to take in my surroundings, I saw that the main street of the village had been turned into a camp with a row of bonfires cooking breakfast.

It seemed almost like team Maelstrom had brought a holiday to the village. Werebears came out of their cabins bringing food and drink to the fires, and in exchange received rations of zillya. Chairs had been dragged out for the older members of the community, who sat knitting or carving wood. Werebear children were running around and – I thought I recognized one of them from the clinic.

When I went back to check in at the hospital, I found half of the beds empty, and most of the remaining patients sitting up, eating. After checking a few vital signs, I walked out in a daze of disbelief. Well, time to turn my attention to my next patient.

"I'm looking for Archavie and Reef?" I asked the first Maelstromite I saw. "Do you know where they are?"

He pointed me to a tent. "Reef?" I asked, as I drew near. "Archavie?"

The tent flaps parted, Reef looked out at me, and I started in surprise. His pupils had changed shape. They weren't quite the Khirian diamond shape, but not human round either. What made me jump, however, was the change in myself when I saw him. My heart raced and suddenly I felt warm, disoriented, almost feverish.

Words, Kaeda, words. "Your eyes," I stammered. Reef grumbled and held up his other hand, displaying the fingers just barely beginning to grow claws. "The magic must be wearing off," I managed. Hence Reef's slow transformation, and hence my reaction as my feelings for Reef grew back, just as Archavie had said they would. Frils! I had hoped my attraction would only last as long as Archavie's disguise.

And yet why had I thought that? Reef was brave, self-sacrificing, thoughtful, patient. These qualities seemed to shine from him, drawing me nearer, regardless of what he looked like.

But other people might not see that. What was I going to do?

Reef shrugged and grumbled as if to say he didn't know what to do either, though of course he didn't know my extra thoughts. He turned back toward Archavie.

At least I could anchor my attention on a patient. The wizard lay on a bedroll, curled up with his hands over his head. I went in and Reef and I sat down on the other side of the tent, facing Archavie. "Has he been like this all night?" I asked.

Reef grumbled again. "Yes. Sometimes he says things. I don't understand what he says."

"And there's been no sign of Turus?"

"No."

I remembered Svevolod pointing at Archavie, and the warped, wavery voice saying, 'you are mine.' Had he been talking about Archavie? Or Turus? What had he done to him?

"Archavie?" I said, "It's Kaeda."

Archavie just gave a bit of a shrill of terror and hid his face further.

"I don't know what to do." I admitted. "I'll see if Team Maelstrom have any ideas. Maybe the Torgovyy channel have Markish- Gemmic translators. Have you had breakfast?"

Reef shook his head.

"I'll bring you some. Thank you for staying with him."

I brought a plate of toast and sausages to Reef and Archavie and asked another hunter where I could find Captain Rozhkov.

"By that middle fire," she replied, pointing the way.

I was surprised I hadn't noticed them, the captain and Tsakhia, for there was quite a gathering of children around them. Tsakhia had something in his hands. To me it looked like nothing more than a jumble of metal, but when he let it go, it flew up into the air like a silvery hummingbird.

The children jumped up, laughing with delight, and I saw that there were many other little constructs on the ground resembling pill bugs and grasshoppers, springing and rolling about the dirt.

The captain saw me coming and waved them away with a smile. "Why don't you take Tsakhia's toys off where there is more space? We don't want them hopping into the fire."

The children gathered up the metal creatures and departed happily with a chorus of "Thank you Magician Rozhkov!"

The captain smiled after them, and Tsakhia's bird mask watched them go. Then the captain turned her attention to me, "Healer, please sit, let me pour you some tea."

I found a seat nearby and waited while she gathered up a thermos and a steel cup. She had taken off her armor and rolled up the sleeves of her tunic as she sat on a log beside the fire. Her hair, loose and wavy from yesterday's braid, covered her shoulders in long, thick tresses. Seeing her muscular forearms and her mane of hair, it was easier to believe that she could turn into a bear whenever she wanted.

I accepted the cup from her, breathing deeply the smell of ginger and oranges, and I noticed that the tea had a tiny shimmer of magic throughout. "I won't be able to digest this like you can," I said.

The captain shrugged. "It might do you some good anyway. You are from the Gemmic Commonwealth where magic is plentiful. You probably feel the effect of the lack of magic here, even if you don't notice it."

I sipped the tea, and felt the magic as a warm tingle, like the spice of the ginger but livelier. It was comforting, somehow, to have a bit more of that magic within me.

"I'm not from the Gemmic Commonwealth actually," I told her. "I'm from Fari."

"Oh!" She exclaimed, and she straightened up, looking at me more attentively. "I am so sorry!"

This was not the response I expected. Usually if someone expressed surprise at where I was from it was because they didn't expect an educated single woman to be from the island.

Captain Rozhkov didn't seem to know what to do with her surprise, and looked at me, as if so struck by my revelation that she couldn't speak.

Tsakhia seemed to notice her distress and at last turned from watching the children. Owl, or raven, which did his mask most resemble? I tried not to stare but the tones of black and steel were intriguing, like Maelstrom's armor, and heavily enchanted, though at a glance I couldn't tell what it was supposed to do. The beak of the magician's mask tilted towards Naida, then towards me and he said, "Nadia's home also suffered great destruction."

"Where are you from?" I asked.

"The Sacred Forest. You may have heard it named Petrified Forest. Since the first magical cascade no one can get in. The trees are like a wall." At my incredulous look she added, "It sounds like a dream, doesn't it? It is like a dream in my memory. There was screaming. Neighbors turning to stone. My mother put her axe on my back and Yury in my arms and told me to run. And you?"

She looked at me earnestly, asking for my story and I felt, not for the first time, like an imposter. "I wasn't there," I admitted. "I was at school when the charges went off. I only felt the most distant tremors, and I only saw the island later."

The captain nodded, her eyes suddenly shining with tears. "You are cut off from the truth of the suffering, as I am. You can never reach the past, as I can never break through that wall."

The magician sitting beside her set a black-gloved hand on her arm. A tear ran down the captain's face, and she brushed it away. "I'm sorry."

"No, don't be, captain," I said. "That's exactly how I feel." I said it, though I wasn't sure. I didn't feel the immediacy as she did, the emotion that made her cry, but part of me said yes, you are cut off from the truth of the suffering, and that is the problem.

"Please, call me Nadia," the captain said.

"Nadia," I agreed.

"And I don't think I have properly introduced you to my husband, Tsakhia."

I nodded to Tsakhia, and he inclined his hood in my direction. Then I asked Nadia, "why do you call the forest sacred?"

"It was the home of our goddess, the goddess of the werebears."

There was a great deal to consider here. I had seen a fanciful illustration of a temple in the Molvan book of fearytales, though the book did not explain the werebears religion. Since Bog sometimes appeared to be female, it would not be impossible that the werebears religiously served the archon. That would fit with Lady Batbayar's description of them as the archon's messengers.

It *was* the home of our goddess, she had said. Past tense. "Was?" I asked.

"Perhaps it is still," Nadia said. "But if she remains there, why would she not let me in? I bear the axe."

She said this as if to herself, or perhaps to Tsakhia. The axe, which she had previously worn on her back, now leaned against the log, secure in its leather sling. I hadn't looked at it properly before, now I did and gasped in spite of myself.

"What is it?" Nadia asked.

"I've seen it before."

Nadia gave a grim smile. "And you will see it again. It is the Axe of Marat, a thing of legend. Many copies have been made to hang on walls, to inspire warriors."

She pulled the axe from its sling to show to me. I didn't know much about weapons, and the blade of the axe looked unremarkable to me: sharp, shiny, decorated with a motif of fire, interrupted in one place by a scuff across the steel. It carried a very dense enchantment, something my father would probably know more about. But the handle…

"Are those bones?"

I hoped it wasn't an inappropriate question. As I looked at the axe handle my healer's mind interpreted the shape of it as a humerus, radius, and ulna. As I looked a little longer, I could see that the axe handle was made of wood, not bone, but Nadia said, "Yes. Ages ago, the fearies spread darkness and death through Molva, and the goddess regretted that she had made them. She told my people to hunt them down and gave this blade to our cleric, Marat, to help him lead them to their final rest. But, in a battle the handle was broken. So, Marat picked up the blade. As he did, his hand and arm turned to medreva."

"Bear stone," Tsakhia supplied. "We assume there is some connection between that phenomenon and the freezing of the forest. A defense mechanism of sorts, but deadly."

"Since then, no one has been able to pry the blade from his grip," Nadia concluded. "The axe has been passed from cleric to cleric."

The double-bladed head of the axe did indeed appear to be gripped by a set of non-human phalanges, though I was far from ready to accept that they were anything than well-carved, magically-reinforced wood with a long history. I remembered the pictures, though, from the book of fearytales, a bear, who was almost a man, picking the axehead up off the ground, faced by a winged creature with pointed ears, clawed feet, and a poisonous expression on its face

"They say it can cut through anything," Nadia went on, as if to herself. "Perhaps if I could find the forest, I could break through the walls, but even in my dreams I cannot find it."

"And the cascade," I said, "the freezing of the forest, you don't know what caused it?"

"My mother gave me the axe and my baby brother and told me to run. That is all I know." She fixed me with a piercing look. "You may be Farian, but you wear the mark of a magisophic degree. A Gemmic magisoph will assume our goddess is the archon of Molva."

"Yes," I admitted.

"And you may be right," Nadia said. "I never learned her name. The bears of clan Bozhe did not speak it aloud. When the forest closed, I was too young to learn it. Perhaps the loss of Molva's archon and the loss of my goddess are the same."

I was puzzling over this and thinking I really ought to make a chart to sort it all out, when Alta ran over, stopping just short of the logs circling the fire.

"Captain, you should come," she said. "You too, healer."

She led us back to the hospital, where a few of the villagers were gathered around a bed, holding down one of my patients. It was an older man, thrashing, biting at the air, and shifting erratically, fur springing up across his face and arms, teeth and claws lengthening and shortening unpredictably.

"What happened?" I asked. I hurried forward, intending to check the man's vital signs, but Nadia held me back. I found myself standing in the doorway with Tsakhia, who seemed to know better than to go in.

"How long has he been like this?" Nadia asked.

"He just woke up a few minutes ago," one of the other hunters answered.

"And he was treated with zillya overnight?"

"Yes."

Nadia walked over to the man's bedside and carefully settled her hand on his forehead. He stilled a little at her touch and she stood there for several moments, eyes shut, before looking up at us, an expression of frozen sadness on her face. "It is magical starvation. The body goes so long without magic that when it receives magic again it responds ravenously. What is his name?"

"Osip."

"Osip," Nadia spoke to the sick man. "The magic in you is broken. There is nothing we can do."

"Wait!" I stepped in, not about to let someone else give the 'there's nothing we can do,' line without my say so. "Give me a chance to study his condition – I may be able to help."

"You have seen the state of him," Nadia said, "If he bites you, you will never be able to work magic again."

"I'll sedate him."

"Magic might not work, not at this stage."

"I'll chemically sedate him. I'll wear protective enchantments. I'll be as cautious as I can."

"I can't let you risk your magical abilities."

"For his life?"

"I have seen were creatures in this condition ravage towns. I have put them down for their own sake," Nadia said sharply. "You may be our best chance to solve the magic problem in Molva. We need your skills. One life to keep you safe is a small price to pay."

"You want me to solve Molva's magic problem?" I replied with equal intensity, "This *is* Molva's magic problem. I intend to start my problem solving now."

For a moment Nadia and I stared at one another. I saw a fierce sadness in her eyes. I felt it. That fierce sadness was my fierce sadness at every unnecessary death I had ever seen.

"Alright," Nadia said, "You have until sunset."

Chapter Twenty-Four

WHAT I SEE

Kaeda

IT took that long. After sedating Osip I took a blood sample. Having spent hours treating sick werebears I was familiar with the ursinthropic enchantment. It was a tumbling tangle of magic, tiny enough to fit inside its host cells, all of them, creating a whole-body shimmer of magic. To try to discover why a lack of magic would make Osip sick, I had to go deeper, look at the structure of the enchantment, and see how it behaved.

Most Gemmic enchantments were static, or with basic linear instructions, but I did know a bit about the sort of active, tangling and untangling sort of stetsals that formed ursinthropy. Letting my mind focus on the magic I could see the tangles, miniscule and intricate, linking to the DNA inside of each cell, and… it was hard to describe. It reminded me of Farians dancing, a circle of people going in and out and around each other in a way that I had never quite been able to master. I watched as the enchantment changed Osip's genome. The change rippled through the surrounding stetsals, and I knew that if I were watching with my eyes, rather than my magical senses, I would see that part of his body shifting from one sort of creature to another.

If I had had the time, I would have sat back in disbelief, and then watched again, making sure I hadn't imagined this phenomenon. Since I didn't have time, I just accepted it.

Besides erratic shifting though, the enchantment seemed to be behaving normally. I compared Osip's shifting tumble to that of a healthy werebear and didn't see a – no wait.

"I need to make a magical stasis field," I said, gripping the arms of my chair to steady myself as I let my awareness rush back to the visible world.

I looked around the room for something I could use to anchor my field and saw Tsakhia's beaked face looking in at the door as it had many times throughout the day. I assumed Nadia had barred him from the ward, not wanting him near my dangerous patient, but he was clearly interested in my work, and now, hearing my comment he said, "We have a stasis chamber, will that work?"

"Yes, that would be great."

Tsakhia vanished and returned a few minutes later with Yury and Nadia who carried a large glass box with steel edges and corners. It looked like an armored fishtank, but I could sense the stasis enchantments built into the steel, both to freeze magic and to preserve whatever was inside.

"What's this?" I asked, as the werebears set it on the empty bed behind me.

"Noggin box," Yury answered.

"Deceased Specimen Preservation Crate," Tsakhia corrected.

Yury shrugged. "We mostly use them to carry heads. Keeps them fresh and keeps any relevant magic intact."

"Put it on its side," Tsakhia instructed.

Nadia and Yury did, and Tsakhia opened the lid, giving me a perfect chamber for teasing apart magic.

An hour later the shadows of autumn afternoon had stretched long, the smell of roasting venison had reached the hospital, and I had mapped out a stretch of Osip's ursinthropy. As I mapped healthy ursinthropy from a donor, I could see the gaps. Osip's enchantment had degraded. No wonder he couldn't process magic properly.

It should be no problem to repair the enchantment, at least not in this static form. Whether I could create a reparative therapy to reverse the damage across his entire body, I couldn't be sure. But first things first.

I created filaments of magic based on healthy ursinthropy. It should have been no problem to anchor them to the gaps in Osip's enchantments.

But the filaments wouldn't stick. They wouldn't even move into place. It was as if they were blocked. I tried and tried but the new pieces just bounced off.

"There's nothing in the way," I said to myself. "There's nothing there."

I needed a break. I sat back and let myself return to the room, and as I did, I saw Tsakhia again, watching me.

"May I take a look?" he asked.

"Of course," I sighed. I moved my chair, and he dragged over a second one and settled himself into it. I had noticed that he often moved slowly and carefully like an old man and I wondered what afflicted him, for his voice certainly didn't sound that old. I heard him breathe deeply and guessed that he was doing as I had just done, sinking into his magical senses to inspect the enchantment. He let his gloved hands rest in his lap, and I noticed that the right hand was larger and more angular. Perhaps when I had built a little more rapport with either him or Nadia, I would ask about his condition.

He spoke so suddenly that I jumped. "Let me show you what I see."

He gripped his staff, lay it across his knees, and began to rearrange the many rings of steel that decorated it. I had thought they were purely aesthetic. Now I noticed that the different rings, each intricately etched, carried different bits of magical instruction, and could be loosened and anchored together in different configurations. I guessed that they drew magic from the globe of zillya anchored to the top, and produced magical effects. This was all fascinating. Technomancy was a fairly shallow field in Gemmic magical practice. Gemmic magical devices usually did one thing, and relied more on magic than on the physical construction. Tsakhia's staff, though, could be adjusted to produce many effects, and now as I watched, he anchored the rings so that they bordered two handholds.

"The staff will create a psychic connection. It will allow me to show you what I can see."

For some reason this seemed clandestine to me. I looked around the hospital. All the other patients had gone home by now, and most of the hunters and villagers were preparing for dinner.

"And I just… grip the handle?"

"Yes, in a moment. Let me focus on the enchantment again." He took hold of the staff and after a brief silence he said, "Alright."

I wrapped my fingers around the other handhold. I saw the enchantment again, complete, the gaps filled by… magic, but magic of a different quality. If trying to describe standard magic in sensory terms I would have said that it was warm, golden. This magic, however, was cold, blue.

"What is it?" I asked.

Tsakhia didn't answer my question. "If I remove it, will you be able to repair the enchantment?"

"The gaps exist in every stetsal in Osip's body. It would be impossible to do manually. I would have to create a targeted SMaRT enchantment – that is a Selective Magic Replacement Therapy. How can you see that?" I asked, focusing my attention on the blue filaments shared from Tsakhia's awareness.

A rush of fear came across the staff. I felt, for the briefest moment, the discomfort Tsakhia felt sitting in the chair, the tightness of his chest, and a pain in his side. It ended as quickly as it had begun, as Tsakhia pulled his hand away from the staff, and since I didn't think Tsakhia had shared this on purpose I decided to pretend I hadn't noticed anything.

"Make your SMaRT enchantment," he said. "I will fill in what you can't."

I worked it up. A tumbling enchantment that would gather up rejected bits of magic and replace them with new pieces freshly constructed. It would need fuel, but the zillya would provide that. All I needed was the final bit of instruction: what magic to remove.

"It's all yours," I said.

"How much will we need?" Tsakhia asked.

"Not much, though the more we have the faster it will work. I've crafted enough for about one koutali at standard concentration. I'm planning to mix it half and half with zillya and put it in an IV bag."

Tsakhia nodded his understanding. He had remained beside me, watching, while I made the SMaRT enchantment and now, he settled himself back again, relaxing to focus. I focused too, trying to see what he was doing, but the pieces he added to the SMaRT... some of them I could sense, some looked fuzzy, dappled, as if half-visible, and some remained invisible, mere gaps to my magical senses.

While I was watching and trying to make sense of this, I heard a shout.

"Tsakhia! What are you doing?" I returned to the room and saw Nadia hurrying over in alarm. "Stop!" she cried.

"I'm almost done."

"That's an order," she said, but it didn't sound like an order. It sounded like a plea.

"It will save his life Nadia," Tsakhia replied.

"What about your life?"

"What about my life? What good is it if I can't help. There. It is done." He shifted, releasing his magical focus. I saw fear on Nadia's face, but I didn't understand why. We might have just made a significant breakthrough in the treatment of a previously fatal condition.

Then Tsakhia reached a hand toward Nadia. She helped him out of his chair, he leaned on her, and I realized that working the magic had taken a toll on him that I was not aware of. Why? Wasn't he the team's primary magician? Didn't everyone say what skills he had?

And yet I realized I had hardly seen him do any magic himself. Even the psychic connection had been pre-enchanted into the rings of his staff.

"Can I help?" I asked.

Nadia looked to Tsakhia, who shook his hooded head.

"No," Nadia answered. "Thank you. Just take care of Osip."

They left, Nadia supporting Tsakhia as he staggered beside her.

I took a deep breath. It's not your fault, I told myself. Tsakhia offered his assistance. You didn't know what would happen. If they allow you to treat Tsakhia later, maybe you'll be able to help him.

I turned my attention back to Osip, hooking up the IV and watching as the SMaRT enchantment began to do its work. The ursinthropy within him was refreshed. I had to add a bit more zillya, but I guessed he would make a full recovery.

And Tsakhia? Did he have asthma? Some other lung condition? A wound? Some variety of allodynia? A bone growth condition like Osto's Monstrositor? I kept replaying the flash of psychic connection again and again, mentally examining his mismatched hands, and finally told myself to stop, stop already and go check on Archavie.

Dinner was in full swing on the main street of the Sosna village, fires burning brightly, smoke drifting up toward a clear sky full of stars. I glanced at the biggest tent, which I knew by now to be shared by Nadia and Tsakhia. A pair of Maelstromites stood outside the door on guard. They hadn't done that before.

Should I go ask after Tsakhia? Or should I leave them alone?

I had decided to go ask the guards if Tsakhia was alright, when I heard Gamalielle's voice. "Hey Kay!" the cat shrilled. "I hear you've cured magical starvation!"

She hovered by Reef and Archavie's tent, a steaming plate in her hands. I saw Yury standing behind her. He caught my eye, glanced at Nadia and Tsakhia's tent, and shook his head as if to say don't bother them.

With a sigh, I walked over to them.

"Tsakhia and I did it together," I told Gamalielle. "It seemed to take a lot out of him. I was hoping to check on him."

"Yeah, we saw him hobble across the camp," Gamalielle said, narrowing her eyes at Yury. "Yury won't tell me anything about it."

"I'm not allowed to," Yury explained. He drew out the word "allowed," in an irritable way. "But I can tell you, you won't see Tsakhia again tonight. Probably not Nadia either."

The tent flaps parted, and Reef crawled out. He looked almost as uncomfortable as Tsakhia as he rose, slowly unfolding his joints. His arms were a little too long for his human clothes now, and shiny and white in places, as if the skin was turning to scale. His feet were still more or less human-shaped but clawed and too large for his boots. He looked downright bizarre, but still my heart beat faster and a flutter in my stomach made me jump back a little as he emerged from the tent.

"Decided to take us up on our offer?" Gamalielle asked, waving the plate in front of him.

Reef nodded.

"Great! Yury and I will wizard-sit for you while you eat some dinner."

Reef took the plate from her and Gamalielle passed him, zipping into the tent.

"Enjoy," Yury said, and he followed her.

I looked in after them and saw Archavie still curled up on the bedroll Nadia had provided. "Just do your best not to upset him," I said.

"We'll just be playing some Bytva Bytva," Gamalielle assured me.

I noticed then that Yury had a leather case with him. He opened it up to display a game board and a host of glowing pieces. "I have all the expansions back home," he told Gamalielle, "but this is my travel set."

We left them to it and went to find dinner for me. Venison, carrots, and cabbage. The Maelstromite who dished it out added a thick slice of grainy bread to the top and the mingled smells made my mouth water. I hadn't realized until that moment how hungry I was.

"I don't think I can bring myself to sit down," I told Reef. "I've been sitting for hours."

Reef grumbled his agreement.

"How about over there?"

We found a spot beside one of the cabins where we could lean against a wall and eat standing up. With everyone walking, packing, and pausing to eat, we didn't look out of place.

I knew that Reef probably wasn't the best person to process my recent experience with – he didn't know much about magic, after all – but I needed to process it all and I at least could trust that he would keep what I said to himself.

"I saw something," I told him, "And I don't know what to make of it."

"What?" Reef asked, as he struggled to spear carrots with his fork.

"A different sort of magic. Or maybe not different. I don't know. I couldn't see it, but Tsakhia could." I related to him what had happened, trying to keep the magical details as simple as I could.

Reef listened and kept eating. He did not seem at all alarmed by what was, in my opinion, a very alarming circumstance. By the time I had finished, I could tell by the furrow of his brow that he was thinking.

"What do you think about it?" I asked.

"I think… we have not been able to talk to Archavie, but maybe with Tsakhia's staff, we could."

"Oh, yes, that's an excellent idea," I said, surprised that I had not thought of it myself. "But what do you think about the invisible magic?"

Reef shrugged. "I can't sense magic. You can. It doesn't bother me," then he turned towards me, brow furrowed again, for I had gasped. "What is it?"

Reef had now twice pointed out the obvious, and it turned out to be exactly what I needed. "What if Tsakhia is a different species!" I exclaimed, keeping my voice low. "And that's why he can sense a different spectrum of magic."

Reef blinked. "What kind of species?"

"I don't know. Something undiscovered. Or," I had to pause, for the ideas were exploding in my mind too quickly for me to get ahold of them and shape them into words. "Or maybe whatever condition he has, has changed his genome. Like ursinthropy. The enchantment reconstructs the host's DNA. Maybe it's changing him. Or has changed him already."

Reef blinked again. "Can we still use his staff?"

I didn't see why not, but of course we wouldn't be able to ask until he or Nadia emerged from their tent, and as Yury had predicted, that wouldn't happen tonight. Instead, after Reef and I had eaten and stretched our legs with a walk around the camp, Reef returned to keeping Archavie company, and Gamalielle came to sit by me, as I watched the fire and thought.

The cat sat in silence for a few minutes, tossing bits of twig and leaf into the fire, then she said, "So, what do you think about Yury?"

"What do you mean what do I think about him?" I asked.

"I mean, he's pretty cute, right?"

The visions of dancing DNA vanished from my mind. I looked at Gamalielle and… was it just the firelight or were the insides of her ears a pinker pink than usual?

"And he's, you know, responsible-ish, which is probably more important to you than what he looks like."

"Are you asking if you should try to set the two of us up?" I asked in confusion.

"No!" Gamalielle exclaimed. "Frils, no. No offense Kaeda, but he thinks you're about as interesting as his cloaked and cursed brother-in-law. But," she stripped a few more twigs off the branch she was holding, tossing them into the fire, and looking a little sheepish, "but we've been having a good time together, you know, hunting, foraging for mushrooms, playing Bytva-Bytva. You know about human feelings, right? Do you think he could, you know, like me?"

Trying not to gape, I looked around the camp until I spotted Yury talking to some other Maelstromites. I hadn't really considered Yury's appearance before. Now I studied his long nose, thin lips, dark hair and sharp grey eyes. I wouldn't have used the words "pretty cute," to describe him, but that hardly mattered. "As a healer, I have to remind you that Yury carries ursinthropy, and that if you contracted it, you would permanently lose your ability to work magic."

"Oh, don't worry about that. Cats are immune. It only attaches to humans, according to Nadia. I asked real casual like."

"I would still want to test it myself."

"Okay but stop being a healer and tell me as a friend, do you think he likes me?"

Stop being a healer? Not so simple, but I did my best. "He… seems to prefer your company to the company of others." And of course, as I said it, I began to analyze Reef's behavior. He seemed to prefer my company. But perhaps that was just because I was one of the humans he knew better. Could Khirians get the fluttery, heart-rushing feelings of attraction humans did? Did Khirians form lasting romantic relationships? Even if he could, even if they did, based on the body print I had built for Reef I doubted that human and Khirian anatomy would be compatible in a –

Kaeda this is not something you need to be thinking about, I interrupted myself.

I set my teacup between my feet and put my hands over my eyes.

"You okay?" Gamalielle asked.

Should I tell her, I wondered? But I remembered that Gamalielle had fought in the Gemmic navy, seen Khirians slaughter her fellow sailors.

"I'm just worried about Archavie," I said.

"Yeah. I'm glad I don't have a crush on *him.*"

Chapter Twenty-Five

NOT ALONE

Reef

REEF didn't know what genomes or DNA were, but whatever Tsakhia's affliction, the magician was on his feet the next morning, though Reef noticed he leaned a little more heavily on his staff as he walked.

When Kaeda proposed Reef's idea to use Tsakhia's staff, the magician nodded, and his dead-leaf voice began to drift from his hood. "There's no reason it wouldn't work with your wizard, but the psychic connection of the staff is not as precise as communicating through a Magic. Without practice the content of your minds will simply flow across. If one mind is louder, it may drown the other out."

Judging by the almost unceasing terror Archavie had dwelt in for the last couple of days, Reef guessed the wizard's mind was quite loud. But that didn't worry Reef.

"I think it's our best chance right now," Kaeda said.

"I believe the lodge has been returned to its original state. We can meet there."

Attempts to coax Archavie to his feet failed. Eventually Kaeda gave Reef permission to simply haul the wizard off his bedroll and sling him over his shoulder, sobbing and gibbering.

Reef wanted to tell the wizard to stop being such a pathetic wreck. He felt embarrassed just carrying him. Normally Reef would avoid anyone who caused him such embarrassment. He couldn't risk the threat to his reputation. But now? Well, he didn't fully understand why he bore it. Maybe he owed Archavie for all his help? Or perhaps he believed that the wizard still had strength and power within him? Something had broken him. Maybe if they could fix it, he would come back. Reef wasn't sure.

"Have you been able to get him to eat anything?" Kaeda asked.

"No," Reef replied.

"How about drink?"

"A little."

"If we can't get him out of this… I don't know. I'll have to do something to make sure he gets some nutrition. I don't know whether to try a calming enchantment or what. Usually, I would ask his next of kin or at least have some treatment preferences to consult but—"

The healer went on and on while they walked to lodge. Reef had noticed that she had started rambling more and more around him. Maybe it was the nerves of being in this strange situation. He had noticed that she didn't seem to be able to look at him for very long. She did look at him, quite often, but then looked away, with a vague upsetness about her.

But that's no surprise, he told himself. You probably look hideous. He had felt an itchiness in his cheeks and found that his bone structure was changing, his facial ridges returning, as Archavie's magic wore off.

They stomped up the wide wooden steps of the huge log-built structure. Reef knew that it had very lately been a hospital and the site of Kaeda's recent medical advances. He felt proud of her, which surprised him a little. But it made sense, didn't it? She was part of his shoal, and she had discovered and achieved things that impressed the other mammals, which added to the prestige of the group, so he was glad to walk beside her, even if she rambled.

The lodge was a hospital no longer. Inside, Reef did not smell blood or sickness, but instead the dusty aroma of cedar and fur. Heads of elk and indrik decorated the walls, and the sprawling white pelt of a yeti lay on the floor. Nadia and Tsakhia were already there.

"Here, please have a seat," Nadia said. A group of chairs, crafted of wood and antlers, were already arranged in a circle.

Reef deposited Archavie in a chair, where the wizard did his best to hide himself in his arms and legs. Then Reef looked around at the rest of the chairs. He didn't know if he would be able to manage to sit. Not with pants on, not with his budding tail. But he didn't want to deal with that, not until after they had taken care of Archavie.

He sat down as best he could in the chair to Archavie's right, and Kaeda sat on the other side. Nadia and Tsakhia sat across from them. Tsakhia held his staff across his lap. Reef saw that the magician had cleared two spaces on the staff, moving the rings of steel out of the way.

"Archavie," Kaeda reached out toward the wizard. "Archavie." As she touched his shoulder the wizard jumped and yelped, but he did at least look around at the room and seem to see them.

"This staff," Kaeda said, pointing, "will connect my mind," the touched her temple, "to your mind," she pointed to Archavie's head.

Kaeda repeated this a few times, while Archavie stared at her. All of a sudden, the wizard seemed to comprehend her explanation and he burst out with what Reef, after many hours with Archavie, had come to understand as a Markish no: "Nil, nil!"

"But Archavie," Kaeda began, but Archavie interrupted her, saying something emphatically and pointing at Reef.

Oh, it was his name. His name in Khirian. Almost. A human voice couldn't quite speak Khirian. But close enough.

"I think he is asking for me to do it," Reef said.

The humans exchanged glances.

"Archavie has read my mind many times," Reef went on. "We are... familiar with each other."

"It's okay with me," Kaeda agreed.

"Alright," Tsakhia said. "I have set up two handles, here, and here." He indicated two smooth stretches of wood. "If one of you holds one, and one of you holds the other, the psychic flow will begin."

He handed the staff to Reef. Reef gripped one of the smooth handles.

If at any point in his life someone had asked Reef if he would willingly share a psychic connection with a human, he would have thought the question too absurd to respond. Now... well, Archavie already knew all of Reef's secrets. If Reef ended up with some of Archavie's... they would only be even.

Archavie reached out. His palm settled onto the smooth wood of the handle. And...

Reef expected to feel Archavie's mental presence as he had before, as a sort of sunshiny glow sitting beside his own mind, ready to talk. Instead, with a jolt he found himself running through a dark forest where the shadows moved behind the trees, chasing him. "Turus! Turus!" he screamed.

But it was not his voice, but Archavie's. The heart he felt raced, the feet stumbled desperately across the gnarled roots and clots of leaves. Those were Archavie's, too. He and Turus had quarreled, Reef remembered with Archavie's mind, and the Magic had left him, saying "just try to live without me."

A shadow slipped into Archavie's path. Another leapt on him from behind. Their soft, gaping mouths burned like acid as they clamped onto the wizard. The terror that overwhelmed him was such that Reef could barely separate himself from Archavie, and eventually so intense that the memory broke, became like palm branches in a strong wind, hard to grip.

Another memory fell into its place. The wizard was tied to a stake, aching from head to foot. The blue-painted Markish wildmen had smeared the shadow bites with a salve to stop Archavie's skin dissolving, then tied him up in the center of their village, not far from a roaring fire. Laughter as an overripe plum struck his head. Rotten fruits and vegetables pelted the wizard, followed by fish guts and the blood of a recent kill.

Well, Reef understood now why Archavie felt so panicked in the middle of the firelit werebear village.

"Archavie," he said. "Archavie!"

It took a few tries, but finally the filthy, sobbing young wizard looked up at him. "I begged him to come back," he said to Reef. "I promised to do whatever he said. But when he did, he killed them all."

"You aren't here," Reef told him. "You are safe. You are with allies."

Archavie shut his eyes, shuddering. "I'm never safe without him."

Reef rumbled, and happily found that in Archavie's imagining he was fully Khirian-shaped. He let his tail smack against the ground in frustration. "You were not safe *with* him if he abandons you."

"I'm so pathetic and weak and useless. The rest of you, you're so smart and strong."

Reef felt a little guilty. Hadn't he thought the same thing about Archavie? And yet he didn't really think the wizard was weak. "To have survived this," he said, "is not pathetic. Your mind must be strong to go on living after all of this. You are like the unrelenting waves. No matter how far the tide goes out, it always comes back in, bringing the voice of the ocean. You have kept going. That is what I would name you. Resilient Tide."

"Really?"

"Yes. You faced this alone, but you are not alone now. We are your shoal," he went on, finding it easy now to explain. "We will fill up your weakness. And we need your resilience. We need the tide to come in again."

The wizard blinked. His eyes brightened. The chaos of the wildmen's village faded, replaced by the lodge. Reef saw Archavie taking a deep breath and he took one himself. The other humans looked at them.

"I think he will be alright," Reef said.

"What did you say to him?" Kaeda asked.

"I told Archavie that we are his shoal," Reef said, not sure what else to say. What had seemed so easy to communicate through the staff was difficult now to put into words.

As the humans continued to sit in surprised silence Reef wondered whether he should say more, but it was Archavie who broke the silence. The wizard cleared his throat and said with something a little more like his old tone, "Reef, tall?" he lifted his hands in the air to emphasize the question.

"Tall?" Kaeda asked.

"Tall. Tall," Archavie repeated.

"Reef is tall," Kaeda agreed.

Archavie stood up and gestured to his backside. "Tall!"

"Oh, tail!" Kaeda exclaimed.

Now Reef felt embarrassed for himself. "I am growing a tail," he admitted. "It is not comfortable."

At this, Nadia burst out laughing. "I can relate to that. Not many clothes are made to shift to bear shape and back again."

"In time the wizard's magic will wear off completely," Tsakhia said more thoughtfully. "Do we want to maintain Reef's disguise?"

"How could he even change Reef's shape to begin with?" Nadia asked. "Magic like that shouldn't work on a Khirian."

"It's complicated," Kaeda said.

"If it works, I think I can fix it." Tsakhia's went on. "I see what the wizard did. Once the transformation is properly in place again, I think it could be maintained within the bubble of warmth he wears. The zillya could fuel it."

But Nadia shook her head. "We are monster hunters; it would not be unbelievable for us to have a Khirian in our custody."

"Miro might not let us keep him," Tsakhia countered.

"Miro won't mess with the guilds."

"Hasn't he already closed the entrances to the trade corridor within his dovniya?"

Nadia couldn't refute that, but Reef could see that she was hesitant to maintain his disguise, or at least hesitant to allow Tsakhia to do the magic. She turned to Reef. "What do you think, Reef? Would you prefer the safety of a disguise? Or would you rather return to your Khirian form?"

Of course, Reef would always rather have his tail, his fins. "I would rather be Khirian."

"Then it's decided," Nadia said. "I'm sure we can find you something more comfortable to wear until you get your scales back."

"We should also talk about the SMaRT enchantment," Kaeda piped up. "It successfully treated Osip, but I think it would need to be tailored to each patient, depending on the unique degradation of their ursinthropy."

"Tsakhia filled me in, but I don't think we have the magical resources with us. However, when we reach the Torgo, Tsakhia can explain it to our healer's guild and begin working on standardized treatment protocols."

Reef stood up. Since Kaeda had started speaking healer words, he understood his part of the meeting to be over. Kaeda, however, said, "No, wait." As Reef sank back into his seat, she spoke to Tsakhia. "Tsakhia, yesterday you showed me magical structures I couldn't see."

A single sentence, but Reef blinked in surprise at the shift in the atmosphere in the room. It was as if a cloud had covered the sun, bringing dark, cold, shadow. Even Archavie seemed to be aware of it. Reef noticed him sitting up straighter, paying attention though he couldn't understand the conversation.

Tsakhia said nothing, but turned his hooded face toward the captain, who spoke for them both.

"Tsakhia disclosed his magical abilities without discussing it with me first, however, I know he did it to save a life. I do not want to hide our knowledge from you, however if the… details of Tsakhia's abilities came to the wrong people, even the guilds could not protect him."

She looked very uneasy, Reef thought. Strange, for the werepeople so far had seemed very bold, confident. Reef understood that there was some sort of social negotiation going on here. Not a battle exactly, but a contest. Who would disarm who? Who would cause their opponent to surrender?

"But why?" Kaeda asked. "Most of Molva believes that their magic is gone, but Tsakhia's magic sense leads me to believe that the magic may not be gone, but simply invisible. Is that true?" When they didn't answer Kaeda pressed on, "Tsakhia, if I held the staff with you right now would I find that we were surrounded by invisible ambient magic?"

Still, the magician didn't answer, but Reef saw his hands beginning to tremble. Nadia rose to her feet as if to shield him. "It is not easy for him to answer these questions. It is not as simple as what is, and what isn't."

"Reef can sense it too," Kaeda said.

Nadia froze. Tsakhia gripped the arms of his chair. Kaeda had managed to slip past their defenses with a piece of knowledge that proved they were not the experts they thought they were.

"He can't see it," Kaeda went on, "but he can tell us when one of the magic destroying storms, what you call magiphages, is nearby, how close, and where it is."

"How?" Nadia asked.

"We don't know. He just can." When Nadia and Tsakhia remained stunned, Kaeda added, "I don't want to put anyone in danger, and I believe in healer-patient confidentiality, but if I am to help Molva, I need all the information I can get. I don't need to tell you this issue affects more people than just you. I hope you will tell me what you know."

"We will discuss it," Nadia conceded, looking down at Tsakhia. "We believe we can trust you, but it is not easy." Then she turned toward Kaeda again. "And Svevolod, what do you know about him?"

Kaeda breathed deeply and shrugged. "He's Dov Voda's advisor, and he apparently wants to kill us, though I don't know why."

"And that is all?" Nadia asked.

"I'm guessing he also has hidden magical skills," Kaeda said, with a nod to Tsakhia. "At the Gemmic Council Building a dead body exploded." Kaeda told the story, concluding with, "Svevolod pulled the rib from the dead wizard's chest and the spread of the curse stopped. I don't know what he did, and he wouldn't tell me. But you know what he did, don't you? Is he like you?"

This was directed at Tsakhia, who hauled himself up on his staff, saying "No!"

Suddenly the chandeliers rocked and the log walls creaked as if hit by a wind that Reef didn't feel. Archavie and Kaeda leapt up as their chairs lifted from the floor. The fur of the yeti rug stood on end.

"Calm, Tsaka," Nadia exclaimed. She faced him and gripped his trembling shoulders. "Look at me. It is over. Remember. It is over."

It was very much like what Reef had just done for Archavie. These powerful magic users and their feelings, Reef thought with some exasperation. If having magical aptitude meant dealing with overwhelming feelings like this, then Reef was glad he couldn't do a shred of magic.

Tsakhia's shoulders rose and fell. The chairs settled back onto the floor. The creaking stopped.

Kaeda watched them. She was diagnosing, Reef thought, or strategizing. She sat back down and when she spoke her astuteness once again impressed Reef. "Involuntary Magic-Working in Extreme Emotional States is not uncommon in talented magicians, but it tells me that you are indeed surrounded by ambient magic, and that you have personal experience, intense personal experience of Svevolod. I don't want to cause you pain, but you can see he's done something to our wizard. If you know what it is, please tell us."

Still shaking, Tsakhia sank back into his chair, and Nadia sat down beside him, holding his hand, gazing at the impenetrable bird mask. Reef wondered if she could see through it somehow. "It is up to you," she said.

They all waited. Reef wondered how long Kaeda would wait. She didn't seem to be in any hurry. She reminded him of himself when he fought a battle. Better to wait and attack at the right moment. But Kaeda didn't attack. She had no intent to harm. It was fascinating.

At last, Tsakhia said, "tell me what happened."

Kaeda related the end of the worm battle, how she had stalled Svevolod with a spike of magic and helped Archavie to safety. Reef felt his heart race all over again thinking he should have been there to defend them, and also relieved that Kaeda could defend herself, at least against magic.

"He said, 'you are mine,' and I don't know if he was talking to Archavie or Turus," Kaeda said, sounding puzzled even as she told the story.

"He shouldn't have been able to do it so easily," Tsakhia said. "Normally, to wrest a Magic from its wizard takes time, wearing down, torture."

His voice trailed away, but Kaeda had her question ready. "Wresting?"

"To take control of the Magic. It could be done more easily to a wizardless Magic but… for a wizard… there must have been a division between them already if the wrestor could tear them apart so easily."

Well, yes, there was, Reef thought. He had seen how Turus manipulated Archavie, allowing the wizard to believe in his own helplessness so he would rely wholly on Turus's support and protection. Archavie did not trust Turus, though he depended on him, and Turus, well, if he cared about Archavie clearly that care was heavily tainted by vanity.

Reef didn't voice this however, but let Kaeda go on with her questioning. "How can we get Turus back?"

"If the Magic has the strength, he could break free, however, by now Svevolod likely has command of many phages. If he holds your wizard's magic long enough, it will be consumed."

Tsakhia's voice stumbled more and more as he went on, as if these things were difficult for him to say, and as he concluded, Nadia said, "If Svevolod manages to track you, he may come after Archavie again. He may want a piece of him."

"A piece of him?" Kaeda asked.

"A piece of his body, to solidify the command of the Magic. Then he could kill Archavie but maintain his control."

"But why would he do this?"

"Archavie's magic reads minds, does he not? Everyone has read *Wizards at Sea,* everyone knows. Would you want to take a mind-reading magic to a place of secrets?"

"But to chase us down and try to kill us!"

Nadia shrugged, "As far as most of Molva knows, you were lost at sea, crashed, maybe drowned. Even if it is known that Svevolod came to shore, he can say he was looking for you and couldn't find you., Even if you live to tell the tale, no one here will believe your word over his. To most Molvans the Gems are distant and uncaring neighbors who didn't step in when giant lizards were eating us."

Reef saw Kaeda close her eyes and pinch the bridge of her nose. She seemed to have run out of conversational strategy.

"I will hope that since Svevolod has not attacked us yet, he does not know where you have gone," Nadia said. "If we can get you to the Torgovyy Channel we have magical allies there who can protect you. However, Dov Miro has closed all Torgo entrances in Mironiya. We will have to cross the border to Vodaniya first."

"I have more questions," Kaeda said.

"I am sure," Nadia replied, "but perhaps you can leave them for another time. And I trust you can keep everything Tsakhia has said confidential, within the Commission at least?"

When Reef and Kaeda had nodded their agreement, they and Archavie left the cabin.

"I'm sorry," Kaeda said right away. "I shouldn't have revealed your phage sensing abilities without asking you first."

Reef shrugged. "It was a good maneuver." He did his best not to bump into Archavie, who was on his feet, but unsteady, and seemed determined to stay as close to Reef as possible.

"Still, I should have asked," Kaeda said.

She was the acknowledged leader of the commission. As far as Reef was concerned, she didn't have to ask. But humans did things differently. "It is fine," he said.

"So, what do you make of… all that?"

Reef grumbled and considered Tsakhia's reactions. Some things, even strengths or victories, might come from events so awful they didn't bear repeating. He glanced at Archavie and could imagine the wizard's voice telling him to go ahead and say that out loud. "Some things," he said, "even power could come from… something terrible."

Kaeda nodded. "We'll give them some time. They're so focused on helping others that I can't imagine they would keep this a secret unless there was a good reason." She paused and then repeated, "We'll give them some time."

Chapter Twenty-Six

FLOWERS AND FINS

Reef

BY the middle of the day the camp was packed up and ready to go. So far, they had only seen Team Maelstrom travel by foot, but it turned out they had a small wagon to carry the team's noggin boxes. The noggin boxes were currently filled with chunks of rock worm, which, if Reef understood properly, contained fragments of magic, making them valuable cargo. This wagon was to be pulled by indriks. Team Maestrom, Reef learned, had a whole herd of the creatures, stabled at the edge of Sosna Village.

Of all Molva's domesticated animals, indriks were Reef's least favorite. They were one of the few creatures in Molva bigger than Khirians, with huge trampling hooves, protective shaggy coats, and a single curved horn that Reef had seen gore more than one Khirian. When Reef and the others assembled with Team Maelstrom's mounted force, indrik nostrils flared and hooves stomped.

"They smell Reef," Captain Rozhkov explained, "but don't worry. They're used to traveling with a variety of creatures. They won't spook."

Then her voice shifted, the accent deepening until Reef couldn't understand the words of the singsong rhyme she spoke to the indriks. Whatever it was, the shaggy beasts seemed pacified. After supervising the loading up of the noggin boxes onto a wagon, Captain Rozhkov led an especially large and plodding indrik with cherry brown fur over to where Reef and Archavie stood.

"Archavie," she said. "I think you will get along well with Rozovyy Gora. Reef, perhaps you can help the wizard get on and lead it until he figures out the reins?"

Reef did, wary of the indrik as it frequently fixed its eyes on him, eyes as black as ocean depths, glossy as tidepools, and ferocious as the spiked maw of a moray eel. However Rozie felt, she allowed Reef to lead her, and did not try to kill him. By the time they stopped to camp that evening, Archavie was patting the indrik's neck, talking to her, and capably directing her all on his own, and Reef was able to distance himself from the creature's glares.

When Archavie had dismounted, Captain Rozhkov walked over with a bag.

"Archavie, maybe you would like to give Rozie a treat?" She pulled out an apple and coached Archavie on how to feed it to the indrik without getting his fingers caught in her teeth. The wizard laughed as the creature's bristly lips tickled his palm.

"I'll show him how to brush her and tie her up too," the captain said to Reef and to Kaeda who had come to stand next to him. "I think it will help him feel like he can still do something without his magic."

As Captain Rozhkov and Archavie walked away toward the group of hunters taking care of the indriks, Kaeda said, "I'm kind of jealous I didn't think of it."

"What?" Reef asked.

"To give Archavie a therapy animal," she said. "Look at him. He's having a great time. He's anchored by this big, steady presence, and he has a job to do. Nadia's come up with an excellent treatment plan."

Archavie continued to improve as they set up camp. They were in thinner trees now, with space to set up tents in between. A few werebears took the wizard out to gather firewood, and Archavie came back with an armful of sticks, looking pleased with himself. While the group ate dinner, the hunters taught him words and though Archavie's face frequently turned bright red as the hunters laughed at his pronunciation, they all seemed to get along.

Reef was glad that the wizard didn't understand all that had been said and didn't know that the magician Gamalielle referred to as Mr. Evilpants might come after him and try to take a piece of him.

He was also glad that Archavie had someone else to keep him company, because the growth of his tail and the migration of his eyes to the sides of his head left Reef severely disoriented and off balance. He managed to eat dinner and was just deciding to retreat to his tent when Nadia stood up.

"We should reach Mirostad by sundown tomorrow," she began, and a gloomy chorus of groans and grumbles replied. "I know," she said. "Dov Miro, may his tribe decrease." And she spat on the ground.

"May his tribe decrease," Team Maelstrom echoed, followed by a patter and sizzle of saliva on the dirt and in the fire.

"It is on our way," Nadia continued, "and he will pay us for the worm pieces, and I don't need to tell you we could use the money. I also don't need to tell you that if he finds out what you are, he will skin you, and use your hide as a rug."

Silence as the captain looked around at the gathered werebears. "So, be on your best behavior," she concluded. "Don't cause any trouble. The shielding enchantment Tsakhia made for us will cloak our ursinthropy as long as we don't shift. So, no shifting. Understood?"

A chorus of agreement.

"Good. We've been to Mirostad before. We know how it works. Keep calm and we'll be back to the forest again in no time."

The group began cleaning up, Archavie happily helping, and Yury and Gamalielle pulled out the board game they were so obsessed with playing. Reef, afraid he might fall over if he did anything more than walk in a straight line, crept over to his tent, crawled inside, and shut his eyes.

As soon as he did, he felt lonely. Archavie wasn't there to talk to him and being with a group of humans was not like being with a group of Khirians. With Khirians Reef always felt connected. With these humans… Reef heard their chatter outside and felt apart from it.

"You alright?"

Reef opened one eye, saw Kaeda peering into the tent, and closed it again.

Reef grumbled.

"Looks like you're almost there."

Almost, and yet nowhere near it seemed.

"Do you want company?"

Competing waves of yes and no crashed together in Reef's mind, but he certainly didn't want to lay here for hours alone, paying obsessive attention to the slow extension of his spine and the drift of his eyes. "Yes," Reef said.

He heard her come in and sit down. After a while she asked, "Is there anything you want to talk about?"

Reef had, in fact, been thinking about many things on the road. In the past he had usually kept his thoughts to himself, but having grown used to talking to Archavie, he found he now had an overload of ideas waiting for a response.

"Captain Rozhkov," he said. "Is she a usual human leader?"

"Well, she's a werebear."

Reef rumbled and said, "But are human groups like this?"

Kaeda thought about this. "All human leaders are different. I would say Nadia is above average in terms of personability and niceness. The group is almost like… one big happy family."

Reef didn't know much about human families, but he knew what she meant. The camaraderie in Team Maelstrom felt almost like the way Reef felt about the ocean. Many pieces part of a seamless whole.

"What are Khirian leaders like?" Kaeda asked.

"Khirians fight for power and respect and fight to keep it."

"That sounds stressful."

It was, but Reef couldn't quite bring himself to say it. Would it be admitting weakness if he told Kaeda he was tired from that constant fight? Then he remembered her conversational maneuver against Nadia. She would get through his defenses too, Reef thought, and then what would he do?

"I think Nadia has power and respect because the team trusts her," Kaeda says thoughtfully. "They know she cares about them, and they know she'll try to do the right thing."

If I tried to lead like that, the others would kill me, Reef thought. You should say that out loud, he reminded himself. "If I led like that, the others would kill me."

"Really?" Kaeda asked. "But isn't that why you saved Beach Cliffs? Because you cared about your swimmers? Because you wouldn't let fear or prejudice keep you from asking for help?"

Reef wasn't sure. Beach Cliffs was a valuable asset. Other Khirians might not have seen it, but he did. He had taken a risk to preserve that asset. But while he wasn't sure he could say he cared about Beach Cliffs, he definitely cared about his shoal as a group, and the Khirians as a whole, and as he listened to the "one big happy family," outside his tent, he thought that he wanted that for his shoal and for the archipelago. He wondered what he would need to do to make it happen.

By the following evening Reef felt much more like himself, had abandoned the remains of his human clothing, and could see and walk comfortably with his tail swishing behind. They had reached the vicinity of the city of Mirostad at last, and saw the city in the distance, a heap of boxy habitation with birds circling overhead. The birds made it look ominous, Reef thought, like a place of death, but Maelstrom camped at a far distance, this time on the edge of a meadow. In the morning the sun rose in a clear sky, heralding a golden autumn day. As soon as breakfast was over Archavie found some blankets and recruited Reef and Kaeda to help him carry them out into the tall grass.

Usually by the time Reed had gotten a good view of a Molvan meadow it had been trampled beneath a horde of feet. Now as they spread out their blankets, Reef marveled at the tall swaying grasses, the sunbursts of pink and purple, the clouds of little white blooms, and the buttons of bright yellow, dense, and round as mushroom tops.

When he looked up from the flowers, he spotted a patch of black limping back toward camp. A bouquet of fiery blossoms stood out against the pitch darkness of Tsakhia's robe as he made his way through the wildflowers. Nadia met him on the way. Tsakhia stopped, Nadia approached. He held out the flowers. She took them with a smile. Then she reached an arm up around his neck. Tsakhia bent his head, Nadia pushed up his mask, and for a moment Nadia's face disappeared into the shadow of his hood.

Reef watched all this, feeling confused. He felt more confused when he looked back at Archavie and Kaeda and saw them both smiling. Before he could figure out what question to ask, Nadia joined them, still carrying her bouquet.

"We won't be gone long," the captain told them. "Yury has volunteered to stay behind. The rest of us will go into Mirostad and collect our payment."

While the bulk of Team Maelstrom set out for the city, Yury and Gamalielle scoured the meadow for herbs and mushrooms, and Reef, feeling warm and content with the sun above him and the blanket-covered grass below, dozed. In between snatches of sleep, he saw Archavie return with armfuls of blooms, and watched as he twisted them into wreaths. The wizard walked over and set one of these on Kaeda's head.

Kaeda laughed and turned to Reef. "How do I look?"

Reef had never seen such a thing. Her face was like a bird, sitting in a colorful nest. Was that an appropriate thing to say? He wished he could ask Archavie.

The wizard said something in Markish and approached Reef with another crown.

"Well, I think we've found something Archavie is good at besides working magic," Kaeda said. "Clearly he's a talented florist."

"Florist?"

"It's a person who arranges flowers. For decoration."

Arranging flowers for decoration? What a strange idea. That reminded him of what he had witnessed between Nadia and Tsakhia. He decided to ask Kaeda about it. "Why did Tsakhia give the captain flowers?"

"Because it's romantic."

"Romantic? What does it mean?"

"Well… it has to do with human courtship."

All thoughts of flowers fled Reef's mind. Courtship? But it wasn't mating season. Was it? In a panic Reef realized that he didn't know. How blind had he been? What had he missed? He looked at Kaeda, searching for some sign of the sun-soaked madness so familiar to Khirians in the summertime. He did not find any. She sat, still and calm while Archavie fastened a ring of flowers around her wrist.

"What?" Kaeda asked.

"When is human mating season?"

"Human mating season is… year-round I suppose. The look on your face! I'm sorry. I don't mean to scare you. We're used to it. It's normal. Is Khirian mating season not all year?"

Reef shook his head, almost too stunned to speak. "Only summer," he said.

"And I'm guessing you don't give each other flowers."

Reef shook his head again. "We fight," he said, but he couldn't say anything more. He was looking at Kaeda, tall, strong, young, healthy Kaeda. If mating season was year-round, some human male must be courting her. He watched Archavie add flowers to Kaeda's other wrist, wondering for a moment if this could be a courtship ritual, before remembering Turus's demand that Archavie only pair with his counterpart's wizard.

"Human courtship can involve some fighting too," Kaeda said. She looked intently at the pile of daisies Archavie had set in front of her. The wizard seemed to be trying to teach her how to thread them together. "Do you have a… mate back home?" she asked.

"It is not mating season," Reef answered.

"Oh, so, it's not a… continuous sort of relationship?"

Reef couldn't even understand what she was saying.

Kaeda looked up from her flowers to explain. "Nadia and Tsakhia, they're married. They've made a commitment to stay together for life. That's one of the primary purposes of human courtship, to find a mate for life."

Reef lay back on the blanket and looked up at the sky. Trying to comprehend her words was like trying to reach up and grab the clouds. "Why?" he asked. But he already knew the answer, because wasn't that what he wanted? The safety and stability of ties that didn't depend on him fighting, day after day, to keep them? Wasn't that what he was looking for?

"I think humans enjoy the safety and stability of family ties, and marriage is one of the bases for that."

"How?" Reef rolled over to look at her again. "How does it work?"

"What do you mean?"

"How do they decide?"

"Well… I think there are a lot of factors, but most humans found their relationships based on love."

"Love?"

Kaeda gazed out over the field. "Wow, I wish Archavie could talk because I think he could explain this much better than I could."

Reef wouldn't have thought that his mind had room for more astonishment. Something Kaeda couldn't explain? Couldn't she explain everything? Hadn't Archavie told him that she had more education than most sane people?

And yet Reef had to admit to himself that he couldn't explain mating season either. It came, it went, and he did his best to endure it.

"Speaking of mating season," Kaeda said.

Gamalielle and Yury were on their way over. "Okay, flower children," the cat said. "Yury and I are going to take a dash into the city. Yury says there's some great street food. We'll be back soon with lunch."

"Those two are some mating season waiting to happen," Kaeda commented quietly as the cat and werebear walked away.

By the time Gamalielle and Yury returned, more clouds had blown in, casting patches of shadow across the meadow and dimming the fiery colors of the forest. Reef saw a denser flock of clouds on the horizon. Judging by the increasing strength of the wind, he thought they would be facing a storm before nightfall.

"Let's see," the cat said, as she and Yury unloaded armfuls of parcels and folded envelopes. "We got meat pies, various fried items on sticks, lots of pickles and some stuffed baked potatoes."

"Not to mention a few bottles of the local lager," Yury announced, as he set down the box he was carrying.

But Reef's attention had been drawn to what looked like a wide, thin booklet that Gamalielle had dropped with her haul of paper-wrapped food. He had noticed it at first because there was an etched picture of a Khirian on the cover. A dead Khirian, or soon-to-be-dead, with a young Molvan standing on top of it, driving a spear into its chest. But what really caught Reef's attention, what made Reef grab it from the heap, was the cape that the young man wore.

Reef narrowed his eyes, looking intently at the figure. A spiky collar framed the young man's face, and Reef could just barely see more of the same toothy, wave-like texture continuing down the back of the cape, though the angle of the picture didn't show it. As Reef's eyes took it in his heart began to pound louder, and harder, until his whole body seemed to vibrate with the sound and pressure. Fins. Khirian fins. It couldn't be.

"What is this?" he asked, his tongue now dry in his mouth.

Yury looked over his shoulder. "Oh, Dov Miro. That's a drawing of a statue of him. It stands outside the palace."

"These?" Reef asked, pointing to the jagged lines of the cape.

Yury also narrowed his eyes, then he said, "Huh, I guess those are probably Khirian fins. I've never thought about it before. There's kind of a lot of gruesome Khirian decoration in the city. No one else wears the fins, though."

He had to see it for himself. He had to know if this picture showed reality, a strange reality where a human would cut out and wear a Khirian fin. Reef started forward toward the city but found Yury blocking his way.

"Where do you think you're going?"

"I have to see it," Reef said.

"You heard what Nadia said about Miro. I can't let you charge in there. You'll put us all in danger."

Reef knew that, but he couldn't just stay here when this atrocity waited inside. He started forward but Yury grabbed him. Reef found himself locked, arm to arm, in a grapple by a surprisingly strong human-shaped opponent. For just a moment. The werebear freed one arm, wrapped both around one of Reef's as he turned, and jerked.

Yury moved with magic-induced speed and clearly had done this before to pull his opponent to the ground, but Reef suspected he had never done it to a Khirian. Reef simply had too much stability, with his clawed feet in the ground and his heavy tail behind him, for Yury to pull him over.

"Frils," Yury swore, while Reef ducked in, turning his arm and catching Yury's elbow. He did his best not to claw him while he pushed into Yury's middle to throw him down.

Yury met him with what was certainly also a magic-fueled rush of strength. "Zillya!" Yury shouted.

"On it!" Gamalielle hollered back.

Yury's hands were on his head, but again, Yury didn't seem used to trying to grip the aerodynamic scales of a Khirian, nor did he anticipate Reef's tail. As Reef slid through his arms, he whipped his tail up and felt it impact Yury's head.

"Stop it!" Kaeda screamed. "Stop, it, both of you!"

Reef had circled around to see Yury regaining his footing and taking a silver flask from Gamalielle.

"Reef, there's nothing we can do about it," Kaeda said. "We'll only get ourselves in trouble."

Listen to her, Reef told himself. Listen to her. But he couldn't. The image of the severed fins blazed in his mind. I could bite him, he thought, as he readied himself for Yury to lunge at him again. I could bite him, Kaeda could heal him.

Yury looked at the flask in his hand and growled. "I don't want to waste our magic fighting with you. Fine, I'll get Tsakhia's backup robe. It should hide your shape, but you have to promise me you won't break your cover."

Reef stood still, tail swishing through the grass. How could he promise?

"We'll go in," Yury went on, "You'll see that Miro is a jerk. We'll come out; we'll drink it off. Deal?"

Reef heard the grass rustle. Kaeda and Archavie had come to stand beside him. They would want to go with them, and he didn't want to put them in danger. "Deal," he said.

Yury dressed Reef in Tsakhia's extra robe, which floated around Reef like an aura of shadow, and they trekked through the meadow. The birds they had seen from a distance now circled overhead and as they approached the city Reef saw other creatures hiding in the brush or skittering between the low stone walls of long-dead worms.

"They're drawn to the city because of the dov's magic reserves," Yury explained. "Brace yourselves, it's about to get grisly."

They approached a drawbridge into one of the city's gates. The drawbridge crossed a spiked trench, and within it Reef saw foxes, deer, badgers, even a couple of indriks that had fallen to their deaths. The stench of rotting carcasses wafted up from below.

That was strange, Reef thought. In his limited experience of Molvans, they always tried to take care of their animals, both the ones they kept as pets and servants, and the ones that lived around them in the wilderness. But he had never been in a big city in Molva, only rural areas. Perhaps these Molvans did not so highly value the lives of the creatures around them.

"Yury Rozhkov, Torgovyy Channel Monster Hunter's Guild," Yury said, showing his badge at the gatehouse.

"Back so soon?"

"Couldn't get enough of those crispy potatoes."

"And your companion in the cloak?"

"Tsakhia's cousin. Turns out they all dress like that. Why Nadia decided to mix herself up with that family I'll never understand."

The gate guard chuckled as if to say families were weird. "You can come on through."

"Stay close," Yury muttered as they crossed through the gate. "I'll take you to the governmental district, you can feast your eyes on that statue, and then we'll get out of here."

The city closed around them. Reef felt as if he were walking through a narrow canyon, and instinctively looked up, almost expecting an ambush from the tops of the walls. But he didn't see any archers or waiting magicians, just the macabre decoration Yury had mentioned. Long, carved bones decorated windowsills and door frames. Half a ribcage had been turned into a planter. The people of Mirostad carried satchels made of Khirian skin, wore bits of armor decorated with polished Khirian scale.

Reef was familiar with the idea of trophies. He had quite a collection of shark teeth back on the archipelago, and he had seen how Molvans decorated their walls with antlers and heads of elk. But… this didn't seem quite the same. Indeed, the longer he looked, the more Reef got a weird sense that this city was built on a Khirian skeleton. Or perhaps a skeleton of memory. The memory of war.

"Quite a way to rebuild from the rubble, huh?" Reef heard Gamalielle comment behind him. "I think I might buy myself some of those scale boots."

"Don't you dare," Kaeda snapped back.

"Why, because I might offend Reef? His presence is offensive to me and no one's sending him away."

"He is on our team, and he stopped a giant worm from eating us."

Gamalielle grumbled, "yeah I guess that's true."

Yury slowed to walk side by side with Reef and whispered, "You're not the only one. See?"

The werebear looked toward a tavern. Outside a creature stood frozen – its skin looked real, but loose, a shell over a wooden form, trapped forever between human and bear form. Its eyes were empty, arms raised menacingly.

"Nadia says people used to think well of us, but I guess the menace of magical starvation has changed that."

A few knives and one hand axe had been thrown at the werebear and remained there, embedded in the wood. Past the bear man, through the open windows, Reef could see a Khirian skin on the wall.

"So don't lose your cool," Yury reminded Reef. Then he stepped up again to take the lead.

The dirt and cobbled streets at first were quite narrow but broadened as they moved towards the city center. Meanwhile the displays of Khirian trophies increased in elegance. Stones were covered with Khirian scales, lacquered, and used in mosaics on both walls and floor. The mosaics depicted, for the most part, battles where Molvans triumphed, and Khirians died gruesome deaths. Since the Molvans hadn't won any battles, Reef thought these must have been portrayals of the Khirian retreat.

Finally, they reached a second wall with a second guarded gate. "Governmental District," Yury explained. "Let's get this over with."

Again, he approached the guards and explained that they were here to check in with the rest of Team Maelstrom. The guards let them in and they walked through the gate and entered an open square flanked by three tall, official-looking stone buildings. "The palace," Yury said, gesturing to the grandest of the three. "Then over here, the Security Authority.

That's where Nadia and the team will be. We'll head into the memorial garden. I know the statue is in there somewhere."

Short, neat hedges, most turning brown, and low patches of flowers looking cramped and sad as autumn withered them, filled the garden boxes. Reef found himself longing for the foliage of the Khirian islands, the tall stands of palms, the bursts of color of bromeliads and hibiscus flowers, the thick beds of ferns, tall enough and dense enough to hide a Khirian.

Maybe that was what he really wanted, to be able to hide.

"Okay," Yury went on as they passed pieces of statuary. "Here's the late dov and dovetsa. Eaten by Khirians. Well, mostly eaten. I think this one is one of the current dov's sisters and her kids. Also eaten by Khirians. And here we go."

The statue in the next viewing area was in stone,that which Reef had already seen on paper: a young man standing on a Khirian, driving a spear into the Khirian's chest. The young Molvan wore armor, but a crown instead of a helmet. A long cape of stone billowed dramatically behind him, surely supported by magic, and… Reef could be sure of it now. Fins, over a dozen of them, depicted in carefully carved stone.

Reef felt his knees giving out and dropped onto the nearest stone bench. No matter how intently he looked, he couldn't believe it. Surely no one, not even a Molvan, would cut out and wear a Khirian fin. He began to think about how difficult it would be to physically remove an entire fin but stopped himself. If he followed those thoughts, he would cease to function. Yet someone had done it. And the Khirians whom those fins belonged to were now without them. He couldn't imagine it, to be without the connection to the ocean, to be apart from it, forever, severed by… a blade, a human's cruelty.

Kaeda put her hand on his shoulder. He thought she said something. He thought Yury said something. He couldn't listen. His eyes were full of the sight of the stone fins but then Reef thought if Miro was capable of doing this to Khirians, what might he do to team Maelstrom, how might he harm even the Commission if he discovered them, hiding a Khirian?

I shouldn't have brought them here, he thought. I have put Kaeda and Archavie in danger.

The thought cleared his mind, and as it did, another feeling flared to life, sudden and certain. It brought Reef to a halt and forced him to focus.

"Phage," he said, leaping to his feet once more.

"What?" Yury exclaimed.

"Phage. North."

"Frils! All the phage hunting gear is back at the camp. Nadia will be furious!" Yury ran a hand through his hair. "Okay, Gamalielle, you get into the Security Authority, find Nadia, tell her what's up. The rest of us will get back to camp as quickly as we can and fetch the phage perimeter. We'll meet up on the plain outside the city."

"Yessir," Gamalielle exclaimed, and she zipped away through the air.

"Hurry," Yury motioned to Reef and Kaeda. "If we're not prepared, I don't want to think about the consequences."

Chapter Twenty-Seven

AGONY

Kaeda

THE incoming storm whipped my curls about my face and the hooves of the indrik I rode thundered beneath me as we raced back from the camp across the plain. I had only ridden an indrik at our slower travel pace, and as I bent across the creature's back, I expected any moment to go tumbling down onto the grass. I really didn't want to fall, especially since there was a bundle of five-foot stakes, really more like spears, tied onto the creature's back behind me, and falling might involve falling past them and acquiring a wealth of lacerations. So, I held on desperately, and trusted the indrik to follow Yury, since I couldn't possibly hope to steer it.

Reef would no longer fit on an indrik, and had fallen behind as he chased after us. And… was that a scream from the city? Or just my imagination? I couldn't hear much over the sound of hooves on ground. As I glanced over my shoulder toward the city walls, I spotted tiny figures, Team Maelstrom, riding out from the city. Several yards above them, a dark figure hovered in the air.

"We can stop here!" Yury shouted. "We'll spread out and set the pitons."

Yury and I leapt down from our mounts, and Yury caught Archavie, who slid off behind him. "Archie, watch the indriks, okay? Kaeda, with me."

We each took an armful of the spears. They reminded me of Tsakhia's staff, stakes of wood decorated with enchanted rings of steel covered in Tsakhia's minute etching. I could sense the magic within them, complicated and riddled with gaps that were probably filled with the other magic.

"What are these stakes going to do?" I shouted back.

"They'll trap the phage."

"And then?"

"How much has Nadia told you?"

Not much, that was the truthful answer, but, well, maybe Archavie and Gamalielle's social scheming was rubbing off on me. I decided to bluff with my guess, "Tsakhia will wrest the phage," I said.

"Wow, I guess they really do trust you," Yury replied. "Yeah, Tsakhia will get the phage in position, the perimeter of pitons will keep it here, then when we activate them, the enchantment will shred the phage."

"So, they create a magic disassembling field?"

"I don't know the technical terminology, but sure. The pieces of the phage will be too small to cause trouble, at least for a while."

I said nothing else as I continued to place the pitons, but my mind was racing. Tsakhia had said that Svevolod had command of many phages. I had guessed that Tsakhia had similar abilities, but I had used the word 'wrest' without really considering the implications. To wrest, according to Tsakhia, was to take control of a Magic. If he could wrest a phage, did that mean that it was not simply a storm or an unruly magical phenomenon, but a Magic, a magical being? I wanted an answer to this question before I could condone Team Maelstrom shredding one. Disassembling a Magic would be as close to killing one as possible. A Magic couldn't be killed, of course, any more than magic could be truly destroyed, but it could be dispersed in such a way that it would take hundreds of years to gather again. Gemmic law included this as a hypothetical punishment for destructive Magics, but as far as I knew that penalty had never been sentenced.

Reef caught up to us, and staggered to a halt beside me, panting, as the ground began to shiver beneath our feet. When I looked up from my last piton I saw Nadia and the others on approach, their indriks' hooves shaking the ground, and Tsakhia flying behind them, arms in their voluminous cloak spread out like the wings of a giant bird. The crumbling of stone and change in the wind patterns on the grass gave away the phage's presence, but it stayed behind him, doubtless held in check by his control.

"The pitons are set," Yury called, as the team thundered in. Gamalielle leapt down to join Reef and I, and the rest spaced themselves out around the circle. They dismounted, and each found their place at one of the pitons, including the one nearest me. I stepped back to where Nadia was swinging down from her mount. We had left a ten-foot gap in the perimeter on the city side of the circle. This space, Yury had explained, was left for Tsakahia's staff, which Nadia now held in her hands. "Activate the perimeter," the captain called.

Crackles of blue leapt from piton to piton as Team Maelstrom twisted and set the etched rings. A barrier formed like a fence of lightning, except in the gap where Nadia stood.

"Are the phages Magics?" I asked her.

"What?" Nadia turned toward me, shaken for a moment from her task.

"If Svevolod and Tsakhia can wrest them, are they Magics?"

"We will discuss this later."

"If they are Magics, they are people, and if you are about to disassemble one, that's –"

"Self-defense," Nadia interrupted, holding the staff poised to complete the circle. "You have seen what they can do, and you have seen how my people are full of magic. You can imagine what would happen if the magic was ripped from one of our bodies." Then she called, "the perimeter is set. Tsakhia, bring it down!"

The floating form of Tskahia drifted into the center of the ring and sank slowly, hands grasping the air as if he were dragging the phage down with him. His feet touched down in the grass and we waited.

"Tsakhia, come on," Nadia shouted. "Get out of there."

Another gust blew across the meadow. Tsakhia didn't move. "You are mine," I heard him say, "Obey me."

For a moment my heart felt chilled by his voice. He sounded just like Svevolod, his tone flat, heartless, cold. But then he jerked, as if hit by the wind, and his knees buckled.

With a short scream, Nadia plunged his staff into the ground. The crackle of blue sprang to life just in time. The lightning flashed as the phage bombarded the perimeter. When my view through the barrier cleared, I saw Tsakhia on the ground, half hidden in the tossing wildflowers, one gloved hand still lifted toward the phage. "You. Are. Mine."

Nadia twisted a piece of Tsakhia's staff and the door in the perimeter opened again. She was about to run in. I wouldn't have realized it quickly enough to stop her, but Yury did. He had predicted his sister's instinct and run around the perimeter just in time to tackle her, knocking her to the ground just outside the rim of pitons.

"It will kill him!" Nadia roared, half shifting to wrestle with her brother.

"It will kill you!" Yury argued, shifting in kind, and pinning her to the ground. The rest of Team Maelstrom watched, uncertainly. Apparently, this was a complication they had not experienced before.

"Archavie, get Rozie," I said. The moral quandary remained, but I wasn't going to let Tsakhia die if I could help it. "We don't have magic in our bodies," I told Nadia. "We'll go."

"Me too," Gamalielle said, and then she shook her head. "Oh, frils I ate those magic beans."

"It's okay, Archavie and I can handle it, right?"

The wizard didn't understand a word I was saying, but he had heard his name, and Rozie's, and led her over, and hearing the question in my voice he nodded and flashed a smile.

We led Rozie through the perimeter. Inside the pattern of the wind changed. It was silent, and restless, shaken unevenly about by magic. Even though we had taken only a couple of steps, it seemed as if we had entered another world, a world surrounded by crackling blue, where the only inhabitant was Tsakhia, propped up on one elbow, other hand still reaching up.

"You… are mine," he repeated.

"Can you stand?" I asked, as we approached.

"I can't move. I will lose my grip."

"Okay. Archavie will lift your feet, I'll lift your shoulders. Then, Archavie, maybe we can put him on Rozie to carry him out."

"Oh, oh Rozie," Archavie agreed, and he turned to the indrik and said something and patted his hand in the air. This apparently made sense to her. Rozie bent her knees and lowered herself down onto her belly. Yes, that would make it much easier.

Archavie caught on as I indicated Tsakhia's feet and then moved to get my hands beneath his shoulders. It was a strange experience, feeling his robe which looked so diaphanous but turned out to be thick, almost stiff. His shoulders were as broad as they looked, but, well I had brought Rozie along guessing by Tsakhia's visible size that he might be very heavy, but in fact he was so light I felt a little worried. I could feel one very bony shoulder, and one padded, but not by muscles or fat. Perhaps by bandages.

But now was not the time to puzzle over Tsakhia's illness. Archavie got Tsakhia's feet over Rozie's back, and I climbed on behind him and held on to him while Archavie gave the order for her to stand and then led us out.

As soon as we had left the perimeter, Tsakhia released his grip on the phage. He fell against me so suddenly that the two of us tumbled off of Rozie and into Nadia who seemed to expect Tsakhia's collapse.

Yury, poised at Tsakhia's staff, activated the barrier once again.

"Shred it!" Nadia ordered.

While Reef and Gamalielle helped me to my feet the crackling magic in front of us leapt higher, raced inward and upward in a swirl of light, and then collapsed down again. A rush of wind whipped across us. Then it was over. The blooms and grasses within the magical fence had been reduced to a powder of green and yellow and purple.

For a moment we stood stunned in the grey silence of the meadow. Then a cry of pain cut through the air.

Nadia had already gathered Tsakhia into her arms and now swiftly carried him over to her own indrik.

Since I had already witnessed him experiencing involuntary magic-working, I wouldn't be surprised if he was also prone to magician's fatigue after intense magic-working. But it shouldn't cause pain.

"Can I help?" I asked, following her. "You know I'm skilled in treating unusual magical ailments. If there's anything I can do…"

Her indrik had knelt to let her put Tsakhia on more easily, but he hardly seemed capable of sitting upright. His breath moved his whole body, then ceased as he seemed overwhelmed by another wave of pain and barely held back a cry.

"I don't know I… I must get him back to camp. I'm sorry."

Of course, she would be too focused on him to think about me now, or indeed any of us. If she had remained a moment longer, I thought I would have been able to persuade her that letting me in would be a good thing, but she did not remain. She mounted the indrik and galloped away toward camp.

As I stared after them, I felt a tug on my sleeve. Gamalielle whispered in my ear, "look behind you."

I glanced back and saw that Yury and a trio of other hunters had carried one of the noggin boxes into the center of the circle. As I watched, Yury used a long pair of metal tongs to pluck something from the grass. I saw a shimmer of metal and a thrashing, as if the tongs had caught a panicking spider made of steel.

"What is that?" I asked, hurrying back, but the team swept a cover over the box before I could get a look and tied it up deftly.

As I approached, Yury blocked my way. He spoke to Gamalielle more than to me. "I'm sorry, but I'm not allowed to show you, or disclose any information."

"We are here to study these things," I began, but Yury interrupted.

"The Guild has specific confidentiality protections for both proprietary gear and any captured creatures, dead or alive. It's in the handbook, and I'm not big on handbooks, but Nadia is."

"Are you kidding," Gamalielle chirped over my shoulder. "That thing wrecked part of the city and nearly finished off your brother-in-law and you're not going to let my smarty-pants friend even look at it?"

"Believe me, I get sick of the secrets," Yury said. "But if I start spilling details while Tsakhia's sick, Nadia will take my badge."

"It's fine," I said to Gamalielle. "It's not going anywhere. We'll talk to Nadia when we can." I wanted to get back to camp, in case Nadia and Tsakhia needed me, in case they changed their minds.

By the time we reached the camp the clouds had rolled in, turning the flowers brown and the grass blue. I saw Yury taking care of Nadia's indrik. She and Tsakhia must already have retired to their tent, and I could hear them, or him at least, an assortment of groaning, shuddering, and occasionally screaming, that told me he was trying to bear a great deal of pain.

"I suppose you're not allowed to talk about this either?" I asked.

Yury patted the indrik, the corners of his mouth drawn down. "I know this must seem alarming to you, but it's not unusual. Working magic sets it off, and it's worst if he wrests a phage. Tsakhia made some soundproofing drapes. I guess Nadia hasn't had a chance to hang them on the tent. I'll set them up and then I should go report back to Dov Miro. He'll be wondering what happened. Just don't bother Nadia. She gets in a state. One of these days… anyway, just do your best to ignore it."

The rest of the team returned, took care of the indriks, and made sure all the tents were appropriately tied down and prepared for the approaching storm. As the rain began to fall, Reef, Archavie, and I all retreated to my tent. We didn't say anything, but it seemed appropriate to stay together after what had happened, and as we continued listening to the now magically muffled sounds of Tsakhia suffering.

When Gamalielle slipped in to join us, her expression was as grim as the cold patter of the rain. "Well, I snuck a look at the thing in the box."

"And?"

"It's this… knot of metal wires. You know like, models of the solar system? Kind of like that, but like, really tiny and kind of twitching."

I waited, for I could see she had more to say as her frown deepened. "It's got his handwriting all over it. Tsakhia's. You know how his staff and the pitons all have those little, tiny etchings? This thing has them too. Same style."

"Maybe it came out of the pitons," I said. "Maybe it's some sort of phage prison."

"Maybe," Gamalielle admitted, "but did you see anything coming out of those pitons? Did you notice any pieces missing? And aren't we all wondering how Tsakhia knows so much about all this?"

I was thinking the same thing. "We'll have to talk to them."

"Yeah, later," Gamalielle said. "Wouldn't want to interrupt whatever is going on now. It sounds like he's giving birth."

Whatever was happening with Tsakhia went on for hours. As a healer, it was agony, knowing that someone was suffering, probably from a magical ailment, and not being able to help. I did my best to take Yury's advice and ignore it, and focus on Bytva Bytva instead, since Gamalielle was determined to teach me. I couldn't keep track of the rules and kept losing in a few rounds.

After a while, Yury returned and looked in on us, and met a tent full of silent stares. "Miro said thanks and asked our price for the defeat of the phage," he said awkwardly. "I gave him our standard compensation for a big monster that could kill us all and… I figured I might as well ask for this too."

He held out a bundle of deep purple fabric and tossed it to Reef. "I said Nadia had taken a fancy to it. Miro laughed and said she had good taste."

He paused while Reef unfolded the edge of the bundle, then quickly wrapped it up again when he saw the Khirian fins. Yury spoke up again. "If Miro was wearing Nadia's pelt across his shoulders, I'd probably have gotten myself killed trying to get revenge." He paused, and when none of us said anything added, "I also got the dov to throw in a cow and as many potatoes as we could carry so… there's plenty of food out here."

He left, and I saw the end of Gamalielle's tail twitching. Finally with a growl she said, "Ugh, I just can't stay mad at him," and she left.

Reef followed shortly after, leaving Archavie and I behind. Archavie looked at the tent door, tapped his fingers on his knees and finally looked at me and said, "Reef, sad."

"Yeah," I answered. "I think right now, everyone is sad."

Archavie shooed his hand toward the door, then me, then from me toward the door. "Reef."

"You, you want me to go talk to him? The last time I talked to Reef, I ended up explaining to him how mating season was year-round." I felt the blood rush instantly to my face as I remembered that embarrassing discussion.

Archavie made a dismissive noise. So, he must have at least had some idea what I was talking about. "Reef," he repeated, gesturing to the door of the tent.

I sighed. "Alright, alright, I'll go talk to him."

Chapter Twenty-Eight

DEEP THINGS

Kaeda

REEF was not in his tent. After looking around the camp with no success I found the hunter on watch and asked if she had seen Reef.

She nodded. "He asked if there was a river nearby. I said there was, and that he could go if one of our hunters went with him. It isn't far. I'm about to trade off with Chelomny so I can take you if you'd like."

I agreed and followed her through the forest. The trees grew nearly to the river's edge, then gave way to rocks, painted dark grey and brown by the weather. I didn't see Reef anywhere, only a chaos of droplets on the surface of the dark water.

"Reef! Reef!" I shouted, but it was no use. He was probably underwater, and even if he surfaced, I didn't know if he would be able to hear me over the rush of the river and the patter of the rain. I considered wading out. If he was nearby, he would sense my footsteps in the river… but I was cold and damp and miserable enough as it was.

"Would you like me to take you back?" the hunter asked when I turned back toward the trees.

She had been talking with the other hunter who had escorted Reef. I got the impression that the two of them wouldn't mind staying behind together.

"I can find my way," I said, and I began to pick my way back through the dark trunks and hidden roots of the dripping forest.

Of course, I overestimated my ability to find the camp. I knew it wasn't far away, but I wasn't used to navigating the forest. An ocean, sure, but not a maze of trees dropping soaked leaves around me. At least the rain was beginning to let up. I peered between the trunks, growing darker and darker in the early autumn evening, looking for the glow of a campfire.

I didn't see it, but I did, finally hear a voice. I thought it was speaking Molvan, but my translator didn't pick it up. After listening for a moment, I recognized the depth and tone as belonging to Nadia. Relieved, I followed the voice, but I stopped short when I finally found her, kneeling in a clearing on a carpet of glistening red and orange leaves. Her eyes were shut, her hands lifted in the air.

Normally I would assume such a posture to indicate focused magic-working, but werecreatures couldn't work magic. I remembered our conversation about the sacred forest, and wondered if she was praying. Most Gems didn't pray much, occasional petitions to the Creator to remember them after their deaths and not consign their souls to the Oblivion of divine forgetfulness, but that was it. Farians might call out to their ancestors at the Guiding Moon, but didn't *pray* at all, so, I really wasn't familiar with the phenomenon. But if Nadia was praying, she was praying earnestly, with tears streaming down her cheeks, teeth long and sharp, and fur bristling across her neck and the backs of her hands. It didn't seem like something I should interrupt.

I would do the tactful thing and retreat, I told myself. When she had finished, when she had risen to her feet and dried her eyes, then I would step on a stick, make a sound, pretend I had just arrived.

That was my plan, but as soon as I took a step back, I found myself tripping over a slippery tree root, nearly landing in the sodden heaps of autumn leaves. Nadia looked over as I clung to the rough bark of the nearest tree, steadying myself. She brushed away her tears and rose to her feet.

"I'm sorry, I didn't mean to disturb you," I said as she walked over to me.

"It is no problem."

"I went to the river to look for Reef and I got lost on my way back. If you can just point me in the right direction, I'll let you get back to…" I gestured to the clearing.

Nadia smiled sadly. "I will go with you," she said. "Today, there is no answer. Come, this way."

She walked past me, and I followed, stepping more carefully across the treacherous covering of wet leaves, a swath of questions unrolling before me like a scroll. Remember, Kaeda, I told myself, she's just been caring for her sick husband. Be sensitive. "How is Tsakhia?" I asked.

"The worst has passed," Nadia said. "I will return to him now."

I waited to see if she would say anything more, give me any insight into his condition, but she did not. I decided to change the subject, returning to something she had said a few moments ago. "Do you sometimes get an answer? When you… pray?"

"Yes. Sometimes a word. Sometimes a feeling. Sometimes… sometimes I think I hear someone crying, calling to me from a great distance. But I don't know how to follow the voice. I don't know how to help her. Those times are rare. Not like when I lived in the forest. We used to hear her, we used to see her, in her temple, when we lived in the Forest."

"What did she look like?" I asked.

"Like a woman made of sunlight."

Sounded like an archon to me. I slipped and Nadia caught my elbow. I thanked her and as we kept walking Nadia continued. "In the forest, she seemed to be everywhere. We knew how she felt. She could speak to any of us, in our minds. There was a grassy space in front of the temple. It seemed always warm, the grass always soft, and so I and the other cubs would play there often. The goddess would watch us, and I could tell that she was happy, and we were happy too."

I pondered this, thinking that of course a being who shed magic would create a comfortable environment for the werebears who thrived on it, and also wondering about the extent of the goddess's psychic abilities. As I was thinking I began to smell dinner cooking. We were nearing the camp, but before we arrived, there was one more thing I wanted to say. "Nadia," I stopped walking, and she stopped too and turned to face me.

"Yes?"

"I'm no goddess, but I do have an advanced degree in magical pathology. If there is anything I can do to help Tsakhia…"

Nadia did not rebuff me. "I have told Tsakhia that I think he should let you examine him. Maybe there is nothing you can do, but maybe there is something. But I cannot force him. He has agreed to talk to you about the phages, but nothing more. Tonight though, I think he must rest."

"Of course, thank you."

We returned to camp and ate dinner. I went to the river one more time and shouted for Reef, who either didn't hear me, or ignored me completely. Finally, I gave up and did my best to sleep.

In the morning, the weather was clear. Beams of sun streamed down between the remaining autumn leaves, though most of the red and orange of the forest now blanketed the forest floor in brilliant colors.

I woke up early, too much on my mind to sleep once I saw a hint of light. Confident now that I could make it to the river and back by myself, I told Yury where I was going, and set off.

A hunter still waited, posted near the river. The nearer rocks had dried, returning to a paler grey, and this time, out on a rocky island near the center of the river, I spotted the purple bundle of the fin cape.

Relief washed over me. So, Reef must still be here. I had feared he might swim away.

I took off my boots and socks and gathered up my skirts around my knees. The river ran swiftly, but I didn't think I would have to go far. I just needed Reef to notice me.

The icy rush of the water took my breath away, and soon I could barely feel the slippery rocks underfoot. No Reef yet. I waded out a little further, nearly up to my knees, stepping gingerly. I would have to work up some magic to keep my feet warm. How did I want to do it? I thought through the stetsals as I tried to pick my next step and too late felt the rocks starting to shift beneath my weight.

"Healer!" the guard called, but I was already falling toward the river.

Then Reef erupted out of the water. He caught my wrist and held me up like a fish snatched from the current. I didn't feel as if I had been rescued, but as if I had been caught sneaking up on him. The opposite was true, I told myself, and I exclaimed, "Have you been watching me this whole time?"

"Why are you here?" Reef barked back.

Why would he suddenly be so angry at me? "I came to talk to you," I shouted, as the water soaked my skirts and the cold crept up my legs.

"Why?"

"Because I know you're upset about the fins and because Archavie told me to. The water is cold. Can we talk on the shore?"

Reef looked past me to where the watching hunter had already splashed into the water to help. Then he glanced back at the rocky island.

"Or the island is fine too," I said.

Reef grumbled and without warning bent down and slung me over his shoulder.

"It's fine!" I called to Nadia's guard. "Don't worry!"

I hoped I sounded calm, but I didn't feel it. My heart crashed against my ribs. He was completely Khirian-shaped now, that was for sure, I thought as I watched the droplets of river water run down his back. I felt his latissimus, trapezius, and teres muscles move beneath his scales, and thought maybe I understood a little of why people found Khirians so frightening. But also, stunning. Why didn't they see that? I gave up all hope now that any of my feelings for Reef would fade as he returned to Khirian shape. He was Khirian-shaped now, and those feelings seemed alive and well.

As suddenly as he had picked me up, Reef set me down on the rocky island. I found my footing and took a deep, deliberate breath.

"The current," he grumbled in a gentler voice. "Strong."

"The current?"

"Too strong for you to walk."

He was explaining why he had picked me up. But not apologizing. "Next time I would recommend you ask before you pick someone up. It's alarming."

Reef looked across the river. Looked down it. Looked at the rocks. At the cape. My panic calmed. I thought maybe he was having too many feelings to figure out how to interact with a human. I wasn't sure how to interact with him either, but my feeling of awkwardness, of poor footing, began to fade as I realized more and more that we were experiencing that awkwardness together.

I also softened my voice, "I would feel a little better if you apologized."

"I am sorry," Reef rumbled.

"Thank you," I replied, then I watched as Reef climbed over the rocks, gathered the fin cape up in his arms, and carried it back in my direction.

"Want to take them off. Can't."

"Why not?" I asked.

"Hands, claws, not good for it." Then he admitted. "I don't want to touch them."

I held out my arms for the cape, but Reef didn't give it to me.

"I have a steady hand," I assured him. "I've trained as a surgeon. I promise I'll be careful."

"What is… surgeon?"

"It's a kind of healer who knows how to open up a body to fix pieces inside, and how to put it back together."

This was apparently not comforting. Reef held the bundle of fabric a little closer.

Fins. I knew they were special. I had, after all, studied the intricate webs of nerves bordering Reef's fins. Still, I couldn't think of any piece of human anatomy that I would protect in this way, not unless I knew the people the body parts belonged to.

"Were they from… someone you knew?" I asked.

"No. I don't know. Maybe."

"If not that, then… what is it? Why do these fins upset you?"

The angry edge returned to Reef's voice and the ridges above his eyes tilted forward. "If I tell you, then maybe you will do this."

"What?! Cut out a Khirian's fins? Why would I do that?"

"Revenge. Khirians hurt many humans."

"If you know me, you know that I would never do such a thing. And I don't think revenge makes anything better. If you answer torture with torture, you just perpetuate the cycle of violence. To stop fighting someone has to stop fighting."

I could tell from the depth of Reef's glare that he was thinking about this, but he didn't seem convinced. "If I tell you, then you tell me, what is the worst thing to do to a human?"

"So you can do it to Dov Miro?"

"Yes," Reef said.

"I think the worst has been done to Miro already. The worst thing you could do to me would be to hurt my friends and family. You remember the statues of Miro's family, killed by your people? Miro carved his pain in stone, and also his revenge." I cast a pointed look at the cape.

Reef also looked at the fins wrapped in the fabric. Then he sat down heavily on the rocks of the island, head bent and shoulders curled, as if all the fight had flowed out of him. I felt a pang of guilt. Reef had doubtless killed, even eaten, many humans' friends and families. I had just told him that that was as bad as cutting out a Khirian's fins, which he seemed to view as unbearably horrible.

But that was true, wasn't it? And if he didn't know it already, he needed to.

"Why did you attack Molva?" I asked. "Why did you all come here?"

"The world was angry," Reef answered, as if in a daze. "One morning, it was angry, and it was angry at Molva, and we were part of it, and we were angry too."

"And then… it stopped?" I asked.

"It stopped," Reef agreed.

"Does the… world feel anything now?"

Reef shook his head.

I remembered Nadia's words about the goddess: she seemed to be everywhere. I remembered her sense of knowing the goddess's feelings. If the same magical cascade that froze Nadia's home had mobilized the Khirians… what had happened to the archon to cause such a reaction?

I couldn't guess. I returned my attention to the pile of fabric-bound fins now in Reef's lap. "If they aren't from people you knew, then what is so important about those fins?"

Reef took a deep breath and seemed decided to try to explain. "They were… these fins… them… the water. The fins held them together."

"Your fins allow you to sense currents and electric fields in the water," I said, trying to bring my understanding together with his.

"More," he said. He thought for a moment, sitting, and glaring at the water, and I saw again that bright deep look that he had worn the night I met him. My stomach fluttered, but I did not feel as nervous as I had before. Instead, I felt happy, happy that Reef was trying so hard to talk to me, and happy that I got to listen. I hoped I would be able to comprehend what he said.

"If I… took out your eye and put the eye on a rock, would it still be an eye?"

I immediately thought of the eyeball Gamalielle had seen watching her, but Reef seemed to have a different picture in mind. Would an eye on a rock still be an eye? "Yes," I answered.

"No!" Reef countered so vehemently that I jumped. "An eye is to see. In your head, it sees. On a rock, it does nothing. It does not see. It is not an eye."

"Your fins are like eyes?"

"No! I am the eye! In the water, I am an eye. I see for the water. On the land I am… I am… nothing. I can't be an eye for the land."

The fresh, post-rain sun lit his moss-green eyes, which were wider than I had ever seen them, with such a shocked distress that I wondered if Reef had ever thought about this before. Well, then, it was new for both of us.

I made my way across the rocky island and sat down a couple of feet from him. Metaphorically if Reef was the eye, then his fins would be like the optic nerve, connecting him to the metaphorical body, in this case the ocean. Destroying the fins would be like cutting the optic nerve, severing the connection that allowed the eye to fulfill its purpose. That *was* quite a distressing thought. "Do you think of the ocean as one big entity?" I asked.

Reef nodded. Finally, I seemed to have gotten it right. "When I am in it, I am part of it," he said. "If I had no fins, I would not be part of it. I would be separated. They are separated." He looked at the fin bundle. "I will put them back in the ocean. No Khirian should be separate from the ocean. They would not be Khirians. Khirians are Khirians when they are in the ocean."

He was talking about the fins as if they were complete Khirian bodies, but I didn't think I had the mental strength right now to tackle this additional mystery. "So, fins and your connection to the ocean are part of what makes you a Khirian?"

"Yes," Reef said.

"Then… you must miss the ocean very much."

For a moment Reef was very still, then, like the sudden explosion of the body in the council chamber, all at once he shrieked out across the river.

I jumped again and decided to take that as a deep and desperate yes. "You might be separated from the ocean," I told him, "but you're not alone."

Reef turned to look at me, and I continued, feeling unsteady and awkward again. "We're not the same as a Khirian shoal, but we care about you and we're here for you." I glanced at the bundle of fins. "And I don't think any of us are the kind of people who would maim a Khirian for revenge." Well, maybe Gamalielle, I added to myself. Aloud I said, "Not all humans are the same."

Reef thought a little longer, studying the pile of fins in his lap, and finally said, "You will be careful?"

"I will be careful."

We were near enough that he could turn and hand me the cape. I held out my arms to accept it and my hands slid across one smooth-scaled forearm, and one covered by steel. A rush like the thrill of fresh magic or a new dawn raced across my body like a clear wave on sand. I took a deep breath, and another, willing myself to focus before I began to unfold the fabric and inspect the garment.

"You couldn't have gotten these off by yourself anyway," I told Reef. "They've been woven through with enchanted thread to make them stand up straight." I gathered magic into my hand and formed it into a scalpel and heard Reef draw a sharp breath. "It's just a scalpel," I said, letting him look at the translucent purple blade of magic. "The blade is sharp and precise."

When Reef nodded his approval, I made my first cut, carefully severing the threads –almost wires—holding the fin to the cape. After a few cuts he seemed assured that I wouldn't damage the fins, and he looked away.

The fins felt as I expected, bony, velvety, and leathery at the same time, almost like shark skin. They were stiff at first but softened and collapsed as I removed the cape's enchantments. After the first couple of fins had been safely removed Reef was willing to answer my questions about which fins were male and female. The spines of male dorsal fins extended further beyond the webbed part of the fin, having a pointed end like a tooth. Female dorsal fins had smaller, less prominent points. Male ventral fins were shorter, with more flexible spines ending in stiff, but not sharp, points.

"Never touch fins without permission," Reef added, as if realizing this was something I might not know.

"Why?" I asked, "Is it because fins are vulnerable?"

"Vuln-what?"

"Vulnerable. It means easily hurt."

Reef shrugged as if this was not quite right. "Vul – say it again."

"Vulnerable."

"Vul-ner-able," he rumbled. "Yes. So, threatening. Also fins make a Khirian experience the world. If you touch fins, you mean to change the Khirian, its experience."

"Interesting." I couldn't help but glance at the neatly folded seams of Reef's fins. Although I was not happy about the fin cape's existence, I did feel glad that I had a chance to examine these severed fins up close, since touching a live Khirian's fins was such an offense.

As I cut off the fins, I added them to a growing pile. When I was done the pile held enough fins for fifteen Khirians. Reef folded the edges of the cape around them again.

"Thank you," he said.

"You're welcome," I said. "I'm glad I could help. If you need some more time, I can go back to camp alone, but I think Nadia and Tsakhia are ready to let us in on some of their knowledge, and I would like for all of us to be there."

Reef coughed, then at my questioning look coughed again and said, "It means yes."

Chapter Twenty-Nine

MEMORIES

Kaeda

REEF carried me more gently back to the shore and we returned to camp together. There I found Gamalielle and Yury toasting bread over the fire. Gamalielle squealed as her slice caught fire, and the two of them tried to blow it out, the efforts leading to a riot of laughter and one very charred piece of toast.

Yury rose to his feet, still laughing, as Reef and I approached. "Nadia said you'd want to talk when you got back. Here, eat some toast and I'll make sure they're ready for you."

While Yury disappeared into Nadia and Tsakhia's tent, Gamalielle found us some more moderately toasted bread, and brought over a couple of plates of roasted fish with greens and mushrooms.

"Gotta say, after all this land travel, I'm happy to be eating fish again," the Cat commented.

Reef coughed his agreement, and I said, "me too."

"Well, at least that's one thing we all have in common."

After a while Yury returned with Nadia. "Tsakhia will talk to you now," she told us.

Nadia and Tsakhia's tent was larger than the rest, and I was amazed by how much they managed to cram into it. It was like a proper bedroom, with two folding chairs, two cushioned footrests, two trunks, a rug, and a mattress instead of a bedroll, complete with a headboard at the head of the bed.

That part, at least, seemed to be necessary. Tsakhia, dressed as always in his concealing robes and bird mask, lay on the bed, resting against the headboard, propped up with several pillows. If this was his frequent sickroom… well, I guess I understood all the furnishings, and as I walked inside, I felt a tingle of magic around me. Most of this must be enchanted to fold and collapse to travel in Team Maelstrom's noggin box wagon.

"Here, let me," Nadia said. She moved the chairs, one to either side of the bed, and the footrest poofs next to them. "Healer, you sit there."

She motioned to the chair on Tsakhia's left side. She herself went to sit on his right, taking his hand in hers. Gamalielle and Reef settled onto the poofs, and Yury remained standing at the foot of the bed. As I sank into my assigned chair, I saw Tsakhia's staff resting on the bed right in front of me. I remembered the flash of accidental feeling he had already shared with me and felt a shiver of apprehension.

Silence settled in the tent, undisturbed until Tsahkia's voice whispered out from his hood, "The phages. I made them."

No one gasped. We weren't surprised.

"Helped make them," Nadia corrected. "Under duress." She looked across the bed at me, her eyes locked onto mine, as if determined by her earnestness to make me believe what she said.

But I already believed it. "How? What happened?"

"Dov Voda recruited me for a project," Tsakhia said, "It was supposed to help end the magical drought in Molva. I should have known it wasn't right when we couldn't know the location of the lab." The hoarse whisper became strained and faded away. Then his left hand shifted, moving to rest on his staff. "I will show you."

The other handle lay open for me. I almost said no, just do your best to put it into words. But then I remembered what I had already seen through Tskahia's eyes. What other magical mysteries might come unraveled?

I reached out and grasped the smooth wood of the staff and found myself standing behind a stretch of white countertop. No, not myself. Not even Tsakhia. Ivann. His first name. I knew it at once, being in his mind. Ivann Tsakhia Jalair, now Tsakhia Rozhkov. When they married, he had taken Nadia's last name, a simple way to protect his identity. I saw his hands before me, human shaped, a light cinnamon color, like a cup of tea with a bit of milk poured in. He felt excited, confident, the way I did when working on a project. On the counter in front of him I observed a basin of enchantment, with metal fibers stretching across its length and width. These filaments, he hoped, would successfully bind the unruly magic.

Ivann looked up from the basin at the rest of the vast white room. Two figures in hooded robes stood in the center of the floor. Ivann's mind termed them wrestors. Both reached toward the far-right wall. Something was bound against the wall, a giant mass of purple, gelatinous in appearance, trapped by a mesh of enchanted metal. "Purple Madness." That was what they all called it.

As I watched, the figures in robes reached and pulled. I heard them say the same lines Svevolod and Tsakhia had said. "You are mine. You are mine, obey me."

There was a bit of a sound. It reminded me of the high-pitched cry of bats, almost too shrill to hear, but I felt Ivann's relief that the circlet he had made for himself seemed to be working. He had expected a blast of psychic agony, but it had not come.

The wrestors continued to reach toward the mass of purple, and as they pulled, I saw two pieces of the purple madness break away. The bat-like shriek ceased, and the wrestors brought the globs of magic to Ivann and his colleague at their station. Now, time to test if the new harness would hold.

One of the wrestors lowered its piece of magic into the basin, and Ivann, working quickly, connected the ends of the filaments, locking the enchantments and creating a net around the magic. "Okay, you can let go."

Hesitantly the wrestor withdrew its hands. It stepped back. The purple magic swirled and surged within the magical harness and bit by bit it became invisible.

Ivann looked to the wrestor for confirmation. The hooded head nodded. "It has not broken out."

Ivann gave a laugh. "We've done it!"

The memory faded with a swirl, and I found myself back in the tent beside Tsakhia's bed. "The Purple Madness, does Dov Voda believe it to be responsible for the magical drought?"

"The purple what?" Gamalielle piped up.

I took a moment to relate the basics of Tsakhia's memory to the others, then Tsakhia answered me. "Yes. He had captured it but could not contain it. We attempted to do so by breaking it into pieces."

"But it didn't work?" I asked.

A hesitant silence. Tsakhia's hood shifted toward Nadia who said, "When Tsakhia escaped, many of the phages escaped as well."

Clearly, I was missing a large piece of the story. So far, I had seen Tsakhia's past self, working on an exciting project and achieving success. "Escape?" I asked.

"You can tell them," Tsakhia whispered to Nadia, and she took over the story.

"The wrestors you saw, Tsakhia noticed that they were often replaced. He thought something must be happening to them. Perhaps damage from the psychic blasts of the Purple Madness. Eventually he was… recruited to wrest the Purple Madness."

"She was not a mindless aberration," Tsakhia said, "but a Magic, a huge Magic of great power."

"Tsakhia guesses the Purple Madness is what remains of Molva's archon, and what remains of my goddess," Nadia added, "but I cannot believe it. My goddess was nothing like the creature I see in his memory."

"I didn't see it at the time," Tsakhia said. "I thought only of the project, the invention, protecting Molva. I did not see that there was a person, and that we were tearing her apart."

We sat in silence for a while, absorbing this horror and grieving for the torture of this being, until I returned to the history. "So, she was torn in pieces, and the pieces became phages?"

Tsakhia nodded. "We were trying to reduce her power by fragmenting her, but without some sort of binding the pieces would always return to her. Essentially, we created an artificial kentro, an alternative center, creating a pull that would keep the pieces apart."

"An artificial kentro?" In magical theory we thought of a Magic's kentro, the densest part of the Magic, as the seat of its consciousness. A Magic without a kentro wouldn't have a mind, wouldn't have a will.

"We created… monsters," Tsakhia said.

"Children without souls," Nadia said.

"Frils," Gamalielle breathed. "Just when I thought Molva couldn't get any weirder."

I wouldn't go as far as to call them children without souls, but certainly Dov Voda's magiologists had created a dangerous sort of anomaly. Magical reproduction was something Gems only discussed theoretically. So far, no one knew of a Magic that had been created by parent Magics. It was hypothesized, however, that a Magic and its counterpart could mix and create a new Magic. This, however, would require two Magics, not the splitting of one.

"Magics aren't meant to reproduce this way," I said. "The way the phages consume magic… they may be trying to complete themselves, make up for their missing parent. So, you escaped, and during your escape the phages also escaped, and now you're trying to make things right by capturing or destroying them?"

"Yes. It is not safe to set them free. I tried that with the first one we found, hoping it would return to its source, but instead it attacked us."

"It even took a piece off my axe," Nadia said, displaying the axe of Marat. She rubbed the scuffed flat of the blade. "That has never happened before."

"I held it off and did my best to destroy it," Tsakhia continued, "but I suspect it will have pulled itself together now, a phage without even a prison to limit it."

"We'll find it," Nadia assured him.

No one seemed to want to discuss the ramifications of that idea further, and at last I asked a different question, "Sensing and manipulating the phages and this… other magic, is that something that can be learned?"

I hoped he would say, "Yes. I can teach you," but I already suspected the opposite answer.

Tsakhia tilted his shadowed face toward Nadia, and Nadia, lines of worry etched in her expression, said, "It's up to you."

"I will show you," Tsakhia said at last, and he placed his hand back on the staff.

I gripped the other handle and suddenly found myself blinded by a brilliantly lit ceiling. A stabbing pain pierced Ivann's side. A cold so strong it felt like electricity made his entire body shake.

It must be a dream, Ivann told himself. But where was the magical restraint he always wore to keep his somnumancy at bay? He didn't feel it. Instead, he felt ties at his wrists and ankles. In a panic he tried to call ambient magic to himself, but it didn't come. He felt smothered, trapped in a blur of magic-blindness.

"I'm so sorry! You're supposed to be under during the transition!"

Ivann managed to lift his head and look across his body. On his right side, between his ribcage and hip, he saw a stretch of bruised purple flesh, six inches long, six inches wide, bordered by a seam of stitches. Ivann thought he screamed, but it was hard to be sure. The next moment the healer pressed a mask onto his face and forced him back into unconsciousness.

The memory faded and I found my breath shuddering in the aftermath.

"You okay, Kaeda?" Gamalielle said.

I hardly knew how to answer that. I looked to Tsakhia, hoping for some more explanation.

"It was a piece of her wizard," he said. "She told me. She kept telling me, that she had loved him, and Voda had killed him."

The bond between Magic and wizard was much studied in Gemmic theory. Magics mourned a dead wizard, but usually detached peacefully over time. However, if Bog had not been given that time, or if her attachment to her wizard had been a romantic one – a phenomena almost unheard of – and if Voda had killed him, no wonder she had wrought vengeance on the entire continent.

"It is easiest to wrest a magic when you wear a piece of them," Tsakhia went on. "But they did something else to me. When I woke up again, my senses were different. The light hurt my eyes. I did not feel the cold. I could sense the other magic, the bezumnyy magiya, mad magic. I don't know why. Svevolod would not explain what they had done."

"Svevolod? Was he involved?"

"He was in charge. He…"

"He taught Tsakhia to wrest," Nadia supplied. Then she looked at me. "You said Svevolod pulled a rib from a dead councilor after a phage exploded in the Gemmic Council building. He would have been wresting the phage, drawing the kentro out of the dead body, but using the rib to hide it."

I remembered the way the wrestor's fingers had extended toward me on a wiry framework. "Could he have taken the kentro into his body?" I asked.

I explained what I had seen and how Gamalielle described an eyeball watching her in the bushes, while Nadia and Tsakhia looked at one another. I couldn't see Tsakhia's face, but Nadia's look reminded me of how I felt when I suddenly swam out from the shallows into deeper water where I couldn't see the bottom.

When I had finished, Tsakhia, after thinking it over, stammered, "I… can imagine it. It is not impossible."

At the foot of the bed Yury spoke for the first time, sounding rather venomous as he said, "Don't you dare."

I didn't follow his train of thought, but apparently Nadia did. "No, Tsaka, that is not something you are allowed to experiment with."

"The fate of Molva—" Tsakhia began, but Yury interrupted.

"To Oblivion with the fate of Molva. I care about the fate of my sister. She married you and you're going to widow her with your fatalistic resignation to your own suffering."

"Yury!" Nadia exclaimed.

"You don't even have the courage to let the healer look at you!" Yury went on, "If I have to tear that stupid mask off your face."

"Stop!" Nadia roared, and fur bristled across her neck and her cheeks as she shoved her little brother, who had taken a few menacing strides around the bed. "Tsakhia and I will do all we can to reverse the magical plague in Molva, and we will work with the Commission, but whether we seek treatment with Healer Straton is up to us."

With an exclamation of disgust Yury threw up his hands and stormed out of the tent.

"I'll go talk to him," Gamalielle said, and she slipped out after him.

Nadia sank back onto her poof, one hand over her eyes. The other rested on the bed. Tsakhia found it, gripped it with his gloved fingers, and Nadia seemed to find her strength again. "Once we can reach a secure location Tsakhia is hoping to study the phage cores with you," she said to me, "and I am hoping together we can find a way to seek out the Sacred Forest. I feel sure the answer is there, but we need fresh ideas. That is what I felt when I saw you. That there is something fresh. Like the first snowmelt, and that you carry it with you."

She spoke as much to Reef as to me, and I wondered what she meant. Then again, maybe she didn't know.

"In the meantime," Nadia went on, "now that we have captured the kentro of a phage, Tsakhia would like to test Reef's phage sense. Perhaps we can find some clue as to why he can do what he can do."

Chapter Thirty

THE CROSSING

Reef

TO Reef's relief, the only test that Tsakhia and Kaeda could come up with on the road was a sort of phage-sensing quiz, moving the phage's noggin box from place to place and asking Reef to identify its location.

That was easy, once he tried, though he couldn't say why. He just knew, in his gut, where it was. He would tell them, and Kaeda and Tsakhia would stand there and stare at him, and then confer with each other and agree that they hadn't noticed anything and didn't know what was going on.

When they opened the box though, Reef felt completely panicked, and could barely keep himself from running away into the woods.

After that the two smart people seemed to run out of ideas, but Reef noticed the empty eye sockets of Tsakhia's bird mask frequently turned in his direction, as if the magiologist was determined to figure him out.

For some days rain clouds followed them and Reef frequently looked up, wondering when the weight of water would grow too heavy for the sky. Part of him longed for it, for the air to be filled, the ground soaked, as if the ocean had taken to the skies looking for him, and having found him, had crashed down. But he also knew that weather water could be unpredictable and inconvenient, especially when traveling, and that damp gear and muddy roads would hinder their progress.

They had been traveling along the road where Team Maelstrom's wagon could roll smoothly and the group could ride their indriks together, not separated by forest. Reef led Archavie's indrik. The wizard knew how to do it himself now, but he got distracted easily, looking around the bordering trees for opportunities to practice his Molvan vocabulary and frequently exclaiming "Bird! Squirrel! Tree!"

Reef should have been happy that the wizard was in such high spirits. Instead, he felt restless, gloomy, weighed down by the shortening days and the lack of sun. The whoosh of the wind in the trees reminded him of ocean waves, and the fluttering fall of leaves brought to mind schools of fish, but the air was thin and empty, not full and thick with the messages of the ocean, and the clouds that had rolled in outside of Mirostad thickened daily, covering the sun, bathing them in darkness.

It would do no good, wallowing in this heaviness. Reef touched the fin cape bundle, tied in a sling across his chest, and remembered talking to Kaeda.

Terrible circumstances, but the memory stood out like a patch of warmth in the autumnal chill. The warmth came from her. How? It was incredible, and Reef didn't understand it. He felt a flash of it now as he looked at her, riding ahead of him, and saw the curve of her golden-brown cheek, somehow still luminous in the patch of cloud-cast shade that covered them.

Of course, his path forward was obvious. He should talk to her. He should bask more in the warmth of her voice and her gaze and find the strength and energy to move on.

But he hesitated. He had decided, after her pronouncement about mating season, that he shouldn't talk to her too much. He didn't know the rules of mating season, and he didn't want to get into any trouble. Their conversation at the river had been too much already.

And yet… she was part of his shoal now, wasn't she? And very valuable. Too valuable to let some male steal her loyalty. Perhaps, rather than keep his distance, Reef should keep his eyes open for threats?

As they walked on Reef comforted himself with further observations. Male and female humans mingled freely, despite the ongoing mating season. Kaeda and Tsakhia were talking right now, using big words he didn't understand. If this was inappropriate for the mating season, Reef was sure Captain Rozhkov would set her mate straight.

Human courtship, the flower-giving, face-pressing, tent-sharing, hand-holding customs that he witnessed between Nadia and Tsakhia and Gamalielle and Yury must not be like Khirian competition at all.

At last, Reef persuaded himself that talking to Kaeda would not be a fatal disaster. When Tsakhia had moved away, Reef led Archavie's indrik up closer beside Kaeda's, so that he could speak with her.

"What does your name mean?" he asked.

"What does it mean?"

"Kaeda. What does it mean?" Reef repeated.

"It doesn't really mean anything. It's just my name," Kaeda said. Then she added, "It's supposed to be the sound made by one of our island birds, but it doesn't really mean that. What?" She laughed a little at the expression on Reef's face.

"Birdsong?" Reef said with distaste. It wasn't a name he would have chosen for her.

"What does Reef mean?"

"Reef is only half of my Khirian name," Reef told her, and then he said his name in Khirian.

"Say it again?"

Reef did, a few times, and Archavie joined in from behind. He had been in Reef's head so much that Reef supposed the name was familiar to him.

At last Kaeda got it, "FūhrDare?"

"Close enough."

"Is it supposed to be two syllables or three? It sounds like there's an extra something." She attempted a growl in the back of her throat, and this time it was Reef's turn to smile.

"You cannot growl," he said.

"Pardon me for being human," Kaeda replied with a smirk.

"What is… syllables?" Reef asked.

"They're like the steps in a word. Kae-da," she marked each beat of sound with a tap of her hand in the air. "Two syllables. Ga-ma-li-elle, four syllables."

"Ar-cha-vie," Archavie joined in.

Reef considered this. "It depends. Usually two, but that is because the two words are… crushed together. Fūhr and rrrdare."

"Which part means reef?"

"Rrrdare. The rrr means life, that the reef is a living reef, not just rock. Dare without rrr could be any… wall or… something in the way underwater."

"Your word for alive is a growl?"

"Lots of Khirian words are growls, but also not growls. You think a growl is bad. Most of a Khirian's growling sounds are not… not…"

"Aggressive?"

Reef nodded.

"Give me another example."

Reef coughed yes, "That you already know. Yes." He paused, then gave a slow, slapping rumble. "That means no. Then this one," he repeated the sighing grumble that was probably the most often used communication in the Khirian language. "It means… it can mean different things. It is a polite sound."

"You know, I think I already knew that, too."

Reef grumbled his agreement.

"So, what does fūhr mean?"

"It means hidden or not seen. A reef you don't see is the worst kind. If you don't see it, you can run into it. My name means a hidden obstacle."

"That's quite a name," Kaeda said. "Do all Khirian parents give their children names like that?"

Reef glanced over at her in surprise. Had he managed to stumble on a human custom even stranger than year-round mating season? "Your parents gave you this name?" he asked.

"Of course," Kaeda answered slowly. "Most human parents name their children when they are born."

"And no one gave you a better one?"

"I like my name."

Reef couldn't believe it. "Birdsong?"

"That's not what it means to me," Kaeda said. "To me it means that I'm Farian. Kaeda is a Farian name. My middle name, Callista, and my family name, Straton, are both Gemmic, but my first name, Kaeda, is the one I use, the one people call me, and it is Farian."

Reef's eyes were wide with surprise. He had assumed the different languages to just be different shells for the same human words just used by different types of humans. He hadn't realized that the language itself could have so much meaning.

Ideas crashed together in his head. Family. Shoal. Language. Kaeda's name included two. "Is that difficult?" he asked.

"Yes, actually, especially given the history between the Gemmic Commonwealth and Fari."

"I don't know it."

"Well, the island used to be further south, closer to Drakipeiros, but when the Zheng Empire decided to close their borders, they tried to claim the island. The Gemmic Commonwealth protected Fari, and the Gemmic Archons moved the island closer to the peninsula. That was hundreds of years ago, and since then Fari has been… not really part of the commonwealth, but not really independent." She shrugged. "It's complicated, but one of the few things about the relationship that was solid was that the Gemmic military was supposed to continue to protect Fari. So much for that. The Khirians came and the Gems did nothing."

Reef felt something, a stab of sadness. He didn't quite understand why it was there. Why should he feel sad for her or her people? Then he remembered a word that Archavie had used: empathetic. Perhaps he was feeling what she was feeling. Perhaps he had come to understand her enough that he could do that.

"You feel… betrayed?" he guessed.

"Yes."

"Then why do you keep the name Callista Straton?"

"I guess I could change it," Kaeda said, "but I can't stop being Gemmic. My father was Gemmic and, I mean, look at me. You can see I'm not full Farian."

That was true.

"So, I just have to deal with it," Kaeda concluded. Then she glanced at Reef and changed the subject. "So, your parents didn't name you FūhrDare?"

"No," Reef said, willing to follow her lead. "My father gave me a hatch name. Breaking Wave gave me the name Unseen Reef."

"Breaking Wave is…?"

"My pointswimmer. You met him, with Beach Cliffs."

"Ah, yes. Can anyone give a Khirian a name?"

"Any Khirian can give a Khirian a name, but it must fit. Other Khirians must agree to use it."

"So, they agreed that name fit you?"

"I had just killed the leader of our shoal and all his pointswimmers. I was an obstacle they did not expect. And other Khirians can't see what I will do. Often, they are surprised. Like when I got you to help Beach Cliffs."

Kaeda hmm'd thoughtfully as she looked ahead at the trees. "I can see that. The name fits." Then she asked, "Have you given many names?"

Reef nodded. "I give good names."

"Like what?"

"Even Keel, Light Knife, Lionfish." He stopped himself before adding Beach Cliffs to the list. Kaeda might ask about her and Reef didn't want to tell that story now.

Instead, Kaeda said, "Well, if you don't think the name Birdsong suits me, then what would you call me?"

This was exactly what Reef had been thinking about when he approached to ask about her name. He didn't want to change it if it fit, but the thought of calling her Birdsong any longer… he would have to come up with something.

"I am not sure," he answered. "I will think about it."

Name searching gave Reef a happy preoccupation, and the remainder of that day's journey was far more enjoyable than the beginning. They made camp and Reef was returning from a mushroom-gathering excursion with Archavie, when they came upon Nadia and Yury, intently engaged in discussion just outside the cluster of tents.

"Reef," the captain waved him over.

Reef and Archavie joined them. The wizard beamed with a bit of his old cheer and said, "Hello there!" in rather flimsy Molvan.

"Hello Archavie," Yury and Nadia chorused. Then the captain turned to Reef.

"You sensed the phages before, correct? Even at a distance?"

Reef nodded.

"Do you sense one now?" Yury asked.

If he sensed a phage now, he would be telling everyone, fighting the urge to run. "No," he said.

"Yury smelled something strange," Nadia explained.

"Something dead," Yury added. "Dead but moving. It could be a carcass dragged by a larger animal, but the smell of decay isn't progressing as I would expect. It isn't nearby, but we should make our plans now: fight, or flee?"

Kaeda joined them, and Nadia filled her in. "Our priority is getting the Commission to safety," Nadia decided. "We will do our best to outrun the phage. Once we cross Voda's border wall it will have a much harder time coming after us."

"But if it's Voda's wrestors controlling it…" Kaeda said hesitantly.

"The border walls are well-patrolled. I don't think Voda will want to risk revealing his control of the phages by sending it across," Nadia said. "The trickier thing will be persuading the border guard to allow us to take you to the Torgovyy Channel. Still, it will be safer than here. The border should not be far. Less than a day away. Let's get everyone moving."

Camp was only half set, so they reversed unpacking and loaded the indriks again and were on the road soon.

"If it is one of the dead-animating phages," Kaeda asked Tsakhia, as they rode side by side, "how quickly would you expect it to move?"

"Unknown," the magician replied. "I suspect that these phages are also trying to complete themselves. They crave connection to a wizard, and without one, commandeer bodies instead. Once they attach to a creature, they seem bound by the movement of the host body, and this slows them down. However, if it is under the control of a wrestor it may not behave so predictably."

They rode through the night. By morning, the clouds that had been hanging overhead had darkened to a glowering grey. All the forest fell quiet under the oppression of the sky, so the tramp of the indriks seemed loud. Reef hoped that it was only the forest's uneasy silence that made his fins shiver.

No, it wasn't. A pang of fear told him that something was drawing near, and he turned swiftly but saw only Gamalielle, zipping back toward their caravan, gripping her familiar herb tin tightly in her hands. A tinny rattle came from inside.

"I solemnly swear there's a disembodied eyeball in here!" she whispered as she delivered it to Yury. "I spotted it in a stand of mushrooms and nabbed it!"

"Let's get this in a noggin box," Yury said in the same hushed tone.

He called the wagon to halt, dropped the tin into one of the smallest noggin boxes, and shut the lid. The tin sprang open immediately, and just as Gamalielle had described, and eyeball on a stalk of twisted wires burst out and began to scramble around the glass box.

It didn't look like the eye of any creature Reef had ever seen. The pupil was an odd shape. Like a spread-out octopus or perhaps a starfish. Reef only caught a glimpse of it though before Yury drew the wagon's cover back over the noggin box. "We know someone is watching. No point giving them a better view."

"Let's keep moving," Nadia said.

As the morning progressed, rain began to fall in earnest again, heavier, and heavier. No, Reef pleaded with it, wait, wait until we have cleared the wall. But the raindrops were unintelligent, disconnected, and didn't listen. Reef watched the wagon, remembering the weird sight of the scuttling eyeball, until he could no longer see it through the pounding droplets. He was relieved to find that he was not lost when Nadia rode by, shouting over the rain, "We're setting camp. The road is too muddy to pull the wagon. We'll have to wait the storm out."

Something inside Reef said no. No, no, no, no, no.

"No," he said, then shouted louder as Nadia moved away. "No!" The captain came back. Reef was beginning to feel it clearly, danger somewhere out in the grey blur of water, the now-familiar phage-sense. "Go faster."

"You sense it?"

"Yes."

"Where?"

Reef tried to pay attention. The rain confused his senses, running down his fins and sending watery messages that made no sense. He felt that the water was panicked too, trying to tell him something but too frantic to understand. He shut his eyes, trying to block it all out, just for a moment, to focus on the frightened urge to flee. Where did it come from? Where was the source?

He couldn't tell. Even his emotions seemed to be a shambles. "I don't know. Somewhere. Not far."

"Stay here. I'll get Yury."

The captain returned with her brother, both grey blurs in the rain. "You say it's nearby?" Yury shouted.

"Yes," Reef shouted back.

The werebear paused, then said, "Rain this heavy makes chaos of the smellscape. The humidity brings smells up in the air, the rain tears them down. It's a mess. I can't help you."

Reef couldn't see the captain's expression in the rain, but he saw her face turn down as she considered their position. "I don't want to risk facing a phage in this rain," she concluded. "We'll have to leave the wagon. We can come back for it later. I think the indriks will be able to handle the mud. Reef, can you walk in this?"

"Yes." Reef's half-webbed Khirian feet were managing the squelchy road just fine.

"Then we'll keep moving. The gate shouldn't be far now. We should tell everyone to equip the emergency shields, just in case."

The wall, the gate, Reef reminded himself as he trudged on, holding tight to Archavie's reins, and feeling his stomach knot up with fear. The wall, the gate. Nothing to do but keep walking. He kept scanning the opaque air, trying to get a sense of the source of the phage's location, but all he could see was the shaggy fur of the indriks, the endless streaks of raindrops, and glimpses of the road and trees. He thought the phage must be gaining on them, but he couldn't say from where. It seemed to be all around.

All around.

Before Reef could yell that they were surrounded, he heard a hunter up ahead shout, "What's that?"

"Shields!" Yury ordered.

Overlapping panels of blue magic sprang up around and above the group, and just in time. Reef heard no explosion, but he saw blood and trailing intestines mix with the rain running down the magical shielding. The spatter was followed by the baa of a sheep. Then another, and another.

"Circle up!"

Reef found himself in the middle of a crush of shaggy bodies, Archavie and Kaeda's indriks on either side of him, Tsakhia's in front.

"How many?" Nadia called.

"I can't tell," Yury replied.

"Tsakhia can you give us a visual?"

Tsakhia thrust his staff into the air and the rain rose up, as if being lifted by an invisible tent. Beyond the shaggy bodies of the indriks, Reef saw sheep, a flock of them, soaked and glassy eyed, wool dyed pink by gore. With a wavering shriek another sheep popped, sending a spatter of grisly mutton across the group. Reef saw the magic of the phage beginning to eat through the shields. Several hunters exclaimed and threw them down, tossing away the cursed flesh.

"I'm going to wrest it," Tsakahia said, speaking quickly. "The rain will fall. I'll hold them still. Make for the gate."

"But you—" Nadia began, but Tsakhia interrupted.

"Stack the remaining shields around me. Signal when you're through the gate. I'll shred it."

Another shrill of impending death came from the flock, but Tsakhia lifted his hand. "Now," he said.

The rain crashed down on them like a waterfall, and the hunters sprang into action, lifting Tsakhia down from his indrik and beginning to build a cylinder of shields around him. Nadia plunged hers into the mud at his feet, and reached up with both hands, holding his masked face. "I love you," she said. "Don't die."

Then she turned. "Keep your distance from the sheep and move as fast as you can! The sooner we are through the gate, the sooner Tsakhia can shred the phage."

Then she leapt back onto her indrik and rode away. Kaeda and Archavie turned their indriks to follow, and Gamalielle jumped up behind Kaeda. The phage-sense inside of Reef screamed with terror as he ran after them. The indriks barreled through the sheep, knocking many aside. Then a white shape loomed out of the crush of rain, a huge sheep with curling horns. The hunters' mounts were instinctively skirting around it. Its eyes rolled and its head turned toward Reef as he passed, its mouth stretched open as if it would bite him if it could, but it could move no more than that. Reef ran past, hearing Tsakhia's voice obscured by the rain, "You are mine. Obey me. You are mine."

The stretch of mud seemed endless, then suddenly he saw light through the raindrops, a wooden gate opening, a torchlit space inside. "Hurry! Hurry!" Nadia's voice as she rushed them through into a sizeable passage beneath the gate.

"That's everyone," Alta said.

"Close the gate," Nadia told the stunned gatekeepers. "Don't worry about the Khirian! Just close the gate!"

"Stop! He's not dangerous!" This from Kaeda, tumbling off her indrik and letting it continue through the passage as border guards rushed to circle Reef.

"Close the gate!"

A stern voice broke through the chaos. "Why isn't this gate shut already?" Reef saw a Molvan man in a cape, a medallion hanging on his chest, striding through the chaos. "Get the gate shut and get the Khirian in irons."

"He's not dangerous!" Kaeda repeated, and Archavie echoed her tone as he shouted in Markish, also putting himself between Reef and the soldiers.

A decisive thud of wood as the gates shut. Despite the ring of guards, Reef suddenly felt much safer. A whistle sounded. Then the ground shook.

Chapter Thirty-One

BREATHE

Kaeda

THE ground shuddered beneath my feet at the effect of the shredding magic. The rumble passed quickly and as soon as it had I heard Nadia urging the guards to open the gate again.

My brain did a quick triage. As far as I could tell, the guards didn't want to harm Reef, only chain him up. Tsakhia on the other hand, might be in a very real danger of dying. We would need all the help and cooperation we could get.

The dry passage beneath the wall was crowded with soldiers and hunters, but the man wearing the cape and medallion seemed to be in charge. "Listen," I said to him. "I swear to you, this Khirian is not a danger to you or your men, but Reef, will you allow them to restrain you, just until we have time to negotiate?"

Reef looked down at me, grumbled politely, and nodded.

"And you," I looked back at the official Molvan. "Keep in mind that Reef is an official member of a Gemmic Commission, and also in the custody of the Torgovyy Channel Monster Hunter's Guild. If any harm comes to him under your command, I will get a lawyer, and I will destroy you and I suspect Team Malestrom will do the same. Do you understand?"

The official Molvan blinked at me and looked surprised. "Yes ma'am," he said. He gestured sharply to the guards and

Reef allowed them to lead him away toward the other end of the passage, back towards the rain. Archavie gave me an approving nod before following Reef.

"Now Captain Rozhkov's husband is still out there," I continued. "He held the phage back so we could get safely through the wall. I expect you to open that gate and let us out to retrieve him."

The official looked past me, about to speak to the gate guards, but Yury cut in, "Wait," he looked intently at Nadia. "I want you to promise me you're not going to run out there."

"It's Tsakhia, Yury!"

"The shredding magic wasn't contained within a perimeter. There might be pieces of it floating around."

He didn't voice the rest of his thought, but I understood. The shredding magic that tore apart phages could also damage were creatures. "Alta and I will go," I said. I turned to the man in the cape again. "Do you have a stretcher or a gurney? Something that doesn't rely on magic that I can use to transport a person."

The official snapped his fingers and pointed to one of the guards, who ran off. "I can send a couple of men with you to help," he said.

Out of the corner of my eye I saw Nadia, wide eyed, shake her head.

"No," I said. "Team Maelstrom and I will handle this alone. Tsakhia is my patient, and he has a rare magical condition, which will remain confidential. When we return, I expect a room in your clinic, if you have one, and I expect privacy while I treat him."

I thought I saw the hint of a smile on the caped man's face, perhaps due to this foreigner making so many demands, but he fought it down admirably and said, "As you wish, healer."

The guard returned with a gurney on wheels. "Let's go," I said to Alta.

We walked back through the gate, rain drenching us again in seconds. "Let's fold up the wheels and carry it," I said. All we had to do was walk along the road, and we would find him, I told myself, but the road was littered with shards of bone, piles of sheep flesh, heaps of sodden wool, all obscured by the heavy rainfall.

I remembered the explosion at the council building, and the shattering sheep, and the way the flecks of gore seemed to spread death, but Tsakhia's phage-shredding magic seemed to have done its job well enough to render the scattered organic matter harmless. Which was good, since we couldn't possibly avoid all the gore as we staggered through the puddles of mud, blood, rainwater and magic knows what else.

"If he's dead," I began, but I didn't finish the sentence. I wasn't sure what I wanted to say, or what I wanted to know. Thankfully, Alta filled it in.

"The captain knows it's always a danger," she replied. "Just do what you can." Then we saw it through the rain, a heap of black fabric covered by a heap of wrecked shields. "Come on!"

Alta and I hurried together, skirting another pile of sheep remains, and set the stretcher down beside Tsakhia. The steel frames of the shields had fallen around him. As we pulled the wreckage away, I could tell that they had done their job. I sensed magic intact within the magician's cloak. It had not been ripped apart like the surrounding magic. Still, the physical matter of the garments had been torn, and much of the magic destabilized. The magical shadow beneath his hood was gone, but the mask remained, raindrops running in rivers across the sharp beak and carved feathers.

"Tsakhia! Tsakhia," I shouted, as I knelt beside him.

No response. I pushed back his hood, intending to remove the mask, but Alta stopped me.

"Wait! It's enchanted to act as an emergency respirator. If the breathing function has activated, we'll have to take it off carefully." She bent to look under the beak of the mask, and I followed her lead. The bird attributes were not only on his mask. A few wet feathers sprayed out along the edge of his jaw. Yes, the bottom of the beak extended like a spout into his mouth. I could feel his chest just barely rising and falling, and air moving at the nostrils of the mask. I turned Tsakhia's head and felt beneath his jaw for a pulse. "His heart is beating, but slowly. Let's leave the respirator in place for now and get him on the stretcher."

With a one, two, three, we lifted Tsakhia's unconscious, rain-drenched form. We tucked his staff beside him, then struggled back across the muddy road. The gates opened in front of us, and as soon as we had cleared the threshold Yury and Nadia took the handles of the stretcher from us.

"Usenko says they have an infirmary here," Nadia told us.

It was like being back on my ER rotation, I thought, as I found myself running alongside my patient down a stone hallway.

"The mask, what exactly does it do?"

"It activates if he can't breathe."

"Does that happen often?"

"No. Rarely. He has asthma. The mask will measure the oxygen in his breath and dose him with sal'otkryto."

"Sal'otkryto?"

"It is a bronchodilator."

Trailing rainwater behind us, we hurried into the infirmary, a long room with some dozen beds and curtains hanging from the ceiling. It looked as if a bed had been prepared for us.

"I'm Healer Damdin," a man at the door greeted us. "How can I help?"

"If you could please wait outside the curtain, I will let you know," I told him.

"You and Alta take the stretcher," Yury said. Then he counted, "One, two, three," and he and Nadia lifted Tsakhia onto the bed.

"I'm going to set up the arc," I said, searching the head of the bed. Good, there it was, not quite the same as the Gemmic model, but it should still immediately measure his vitals. A halo of blue magic leapt up above Tsakhia's head and began displaying… nonsense, rapidly changing numbers and flashing blanks.

"Magic doesn't always work," Nadia told me. "Not when the curse is active."

"Damdin, is there a pulse oximeter in here?" I called.

"Top drawer," the Molvan healer called back.

"Get his gloves off," I told Alta, while I searched. "And then his hood. Nadia, get the mask off and tell me anything I should know."

"I don't understand," Nadia's voice took on a note of panic as she unfastened the mask. She was looking at a panel on the side, where the mask would have gone over his ear. I saw more of Tsakhia's minute etchings, and three rows of glowing circles. "It has given him four doses of sal'otkryto and one of schastlist. Why isn't he breathing?"

I found the pulse oximeter and turned back to my patient. The right half of his face appeared to have melted, flowing down into a half-formed beak. Blue and green feathers poked out of his hairline. The left side had a more human shape, though the half beak made what lips he had left fit together awkwardly, showing several needle-sharp teeth. Overall, no worse than many other cursed visages I had seen, though rather different.

I clipped the pulse oximeter to Tsakhia's left hand.

"Can you tell me the basics of the curse affecting him?"

Nadia stammered but Yury said easily, "He's turning into a bunch of animals at the same time."

Tsakhia's oxygen saturation was abysmal. "No magical treatment?" I confirmed with Nadia.

While she mutely shook her head, Alta said, "Too risky."

I could think of a dozen reasons his blood oxygen level would be low but knowing that he was affected by a dramatically disfiguring curse, I would start there. "Okay, let's get his clothes off. You can tell me what has changed since you last saw him. Maybe the transformation has affected his airways. Are there scissors? Damdin, get us some scissors."

While Alta watched the oximeter, Nadia, Yury, and I worked together to peel away his black robes. We uncovered his chest, and I searched the patchwork of skin, fur, and scales for anything that might cause him to stop breathing, but it was Nadia who found it. "This! This is new!" When I glanced over and saw the gash on Tsakhia's throat my stomach turned over.

"Water!" I shouted. "We need water. A bathtub, a trough, something clean we can fill with water. Quickly!"

"There's a bathroom for patients at the end of the ward," Damdin said through the curtain.

"Start filling a tub with warm water. Hurry!"

Seconds later we stood in the white and blue tiled room beside a claw-foot tub.

"Lay him down in the tub," I instructed Nadia and Yury, who were already lifting Tsakhia from his stretcher. "We need to get the gills submerged as quickly as we can."

The two of them lowered Tsakhia into the foot of the tub and the gills blossomed, white and grey rather than the red I was used to. I watched the pulse oximeter still clipped to his finger. The number began to rise, Tsakhia's eyes flew open, and what magic remained in the room, whipped to life, spinning into a sudden storm around the tub, nearly knocking me from my feet.

"Shh, I'm here!" Nadia exclaimed. She clasped his human left hand. "I'm here. You're safe." Her voice, which had sounded so panicked a moment before, now sounded soft, perfectly calm as she stroked Tsakhia's arm.

Tsakhia's eyes focused on Nadia, the right eye round and pale golden like the eye of a bird, and the left human-shaped, but with a red iris – if it could be called an iris – shaped like a brittle star, its crimson legs extending from his pupil. As he looked at Nadia the magic settled like a calming wind. His half-beaked mouth gaped. He still seemed to be struggling to breathe, but his vital signs were finally looking normal.

"Blood oxygen is continuing to rise," I reported. "His pulse is going up too."

Then I saw Tsakhia's mismatched features compress in an expression of pain. The lights flickered and the floor trembled. A few of the white tiles cracked.

Nadia spoke in the same calm voice. "I know it hurts, but I swear to you, it will end. It always does. We should get the rest of his clothes off," she said to the rest of us. "He will continue transforming for hours. I usually give him mak'stredstvo for the pain. It was left behind with the wagon."

"Alta, would you please ask Healer Damdin for whatever non-magical pain relievers they have, especially what Nadia mentioned."

With care to keep his gills submerged, Yury and Nadia and I peeled away, and in some cases cut off the black clothing that Tsakhia had worn under his robes. We unwrapped the compression bandages that held down the blue feathers on his right hip and the hedgehog quills on his right shoulder. We unbuckled the braces that supported his mismatched musculature where his right leg, resembling that of a giant bird, connected to his mostly human torso. I saw patches of reddish-brown fur, green scales, and a couple of places where I couldn't identify an animal inspiration, such as his right hand and forearm, where the bones seemed to have simply grown too long and angular, claw-like without claws.

This arm I saw change before my eyes, the bones growing, lengthening, skin tearing, weeping white fluid. It took me a moment to realize that this was blood.

These things at least I was familiar with. Patients with Hesper's Monstrositor had blood that glowed and patients with Osto's Monstrositor often experienced episodes of rapid bone growth, which was intensely painful. Tsakhia looked as if he were trying to scream but couldn't because his lungs refused to work.

"I have it," Alta announced. She returned with a box of vials and syringes.

Without waiting for my instruction, Nadia looked through them and quickly selected a vial. I couldn't read the label, but I recognized it as soon as I swept it with magic. Morphine, or something similar. I watched as she measured a strong, but appropriate dose, and found a vein, as expertly as I could have myself. She didn't seem to notice me watching, but instead focused all her attention on Tsakhia.

"It comes in waves," Nadia told me. She glanced at the clock. "I will give him another dose in four hours."

But the waves of transformation challenged even the pain-relieving power of the opioid as finger-like spikes of bone began to grow from the ulna of his right arm and also burst from his back, clouding the water with more white blood. While Yury and Alta refreshed the water around him, Nadia held Tsakhia's other hand and she and I brainstormed solutions.

"Have you tried putting him in a magical stasis chamber?"

"Yes. It works, but as soon as he comes out the episode begins where it left off."

"What about a magical restraint? If it is his own body doing the magic, perhaps that would hold it off."

"The strain of the magic against the restraint is too great. He shakes and throws up."

"I could put him under anesthesia."

"If he wakes up and his body has changed drastically it is very upsetting."

"I could maybe do a nerve block."

"Like an epidural?" Nadia asked uncertainly. "If there's anything inside his body and his anatomy changes it doesn't go well."

We had had that conversation already when I proposed starting an IV line, but this time I had a different solution. "It seems that currently a great deal of the transformation is taking place in his right arm. If I do a brachial plexus block that will alleviate the pain. All it will take is one injection. The trickiest part will be keeping that shoulder out of the water for the injection while keeping the gills on the opposite side of his neck submerged."

"Okay. Try it."

With Alta's help I gathered the necessary equipment and when the current wave of the curse had relented and I could be sure his arm wouldn't change shape, the others held Tsakhia in position for me. To my relief his anatomy on this side was close enough to human that I could place the needle, and I could tell within minutes that it had worked as Tsakhia visibly relaxed.

At least I had managed to do something. As the night went on, I watched Nadia care for Tsakhia and wracked my brain for other ways to help. I couldn't even properly scan him with magic. Trying to do so was like trying to peer through the heavy rain we had just escaped. I knew something was happening, but I couldn't make sense of what it was.

Sometime after midnight the transformation stopped. We fashioned a sling to hold Tsakhia's head above water so he could rest. Suspended within the cushioning water, finally free from pain, and probably exhausted, he fell asleep.

While Nadia fixed a magical restraint on his forehead as a protection against somnumancy, I surveyed the damage. The gash of gills had crept further down Tsakhia's throat, and the bones growing from his arm turned into what I guessed to be the beginning framework for a bat-like wing. He had lost three human teeth as his half beak took over more of this face, and much of his long, black hair had fallen out, replaced by blue feathers on the right side, and iridescent grey fish scales on the left.

Nadia drew a lock of his hair out of the water of the tub and stared sadly at the dark strands hanging from her fingers. I saw her supporting strength begin to crack.

"Go take a break," Yury said. "I'll stay with him."

"So, will I," I said.

Nadia nodded and rose. Alta put an arm around her and walked with her as she staggered from the room.

Chapter Thirty-Two

MORNING

Kaeda

BY the time I left the infirmary the rain had stopped, and night had fallen. I checked on Reef and found him and Archavie both comfortably asleep in the outpost's dungeon. Archavie and the others must have done some negotiation because the wizard and Reef had quilts, pillows, and a full tea set in their cell. Well, at least I could be sure they would be alright until morning.

Returning to the infirmary, I pulled a cot into the bathroom so I would be nearby in case of emergencies. It turned out to be unnecessary. Tsakhia, exhausted and drugged, slept soundly, and was still sleeping when I woke to the bright clear light of morning streaming through the high, frosted windows of the bathroom.

I saw Alta sitting beside the tub. She raised a finger to her lips. "Nadia," she whispered. She pointed to the door and mimicked eating.

"Thank you," I whispered back.

I found her in the canteen, a rough but friendly stone hall lined with picnic tables and filled with the smell of cinnamon. Nadia was sitting beside Yury and Gamalielle, who, as usual, had a Bytva-Bytva board unfolded on the table in front of them.

"I've got you! I've got you! Oh, you're no match for me! Watch this little guy go zooooom!"

Gamalielle rammed several of Yury's pieces with one of her own, creating a small burst of light.

"This," Yury held up an empty mug. "Was a mistake."

"What is it?" I asked, taking the mug to smell it. I didn't recognize the dark, bitter aroma.

"Whee! Pew pew pew!"

"It's coffee," Yury told me, as he watched Gamalielle continue to wreck his army of little glowing marbles with great enthusiasm. "Apparently Gamalielle has never had it before, but she seems to like it."

"I win! I am the champion!" Gamalielle leapt onto the table, then into the air. The dozen or so guards scattered around the room turned to watch as she crowed, "The Bytva-Bytva champion!"

"Military installations don't usually make it this strong," Nadia murmured, as she sipped her own cup.

Yury leaned back and watched Gamalielle spinning and whooping overhead. "She's great, isn't she?" he remarked. Then to Nadia he said, "Hey, eat that oatmeal. You know your invalid husband always feels better if he knows you've gotten some sleep and eaten some breakfast."

Nadia groaned and spooned another bite of oatmeal into her mouth.

"Kaeda, do you want some oatmeal?" Gamalielle asked, spinning down nose-to-nose with me so suddenly that I jumped in my seat. "No, I know what you want. You want COFFEE!"

She zipped away and returned with a bowl of oatmeal and a mug of a steamy dark liquid. She dropped the bowl onto the table, poured the coffee onto the oatmeal, and then tumbled, cackling, away towards the door.

"I uh, I'll go make sure she doesn't get into any trouble," Yury said, and he followed the buoyant cat.

"I'm going to get a fresh bowl." I said.

When I returned, Nadia was still dutifully putting away oatmeal.

"How are you doing?" I asked, after I sat down.

Nadia sipped her coffee and said, "It's the closest call we've ever had. I'm not glad it happened, but I'm glad we have you involved now. How are you?"

"I have similar feelings," I said.

For a few minutes we both ate in silence, or rather, ate surrounded by the active ambient noise of the canteen around us as the various guards and border employees came and had breakfast, clearly happy that the rain was over. Nadia, pushing around her last few bites of cranberries and oats, said, "When I first met Tsakhia, he looked almost human."

"Wait," I said. I wove a standard confidentiality sound-screen around us.

Nadia glanced at the magic as it settled on our table and then went on. "He had the grey skin, the star eyes, his fingers were a little long and bony, but he looked like a man. We were hunting yetis and we found him in the middle of this maelstrom of magic. The yetis didn't stand a chance," Nadia chuckled. "He told me later that he stumbled into their territory by accident and panicked. As you said in Sosna Village, he is prone to IMWEES. He can really wreck things when he gets upset."

Involuntary Magic-Working in Extreme Emotional States, almost always accompanied by sleep magic-working, or somnumancy, which we were treating Tsakhia for now. Often when those two disorders were present they were accompanied by occasional revma experiences, dream-like magic-working flow states, and then magician's fatigue when the intense magic-working ceased. It would be difficult to manage, both for Tsakhia, and for anyone who cared for him.

I could see the emotional toll on Nadia's face as her smile faded. "That's the hardest part sometimes, just keeping him calm, so he doesn't accidentally melt everything. I think I speak for Tsakhia when I say, we need help."

"I have some ideas," I said, "but I need time and space, a lab ideally, to work on it."

"I was hoping to take you to Tsakhia's workshop in the Torgo, but it sounds like Voda is insisting you come to his capital. The Torgovyy Channel Embassy will suffice, I think. It won't be as good as the lab space Voda could provide, but I would rather keep Tsakhia's condition confidential."

"Of course," I said. I felt uneasy about being taken to Voda's territory, given all we had learned about him, but perhaps our closeness would allow us to learn some of his secrets. Gamalielle would enjoy the challenge. One question though I was sure Nadia could answer, "Can I ask you something now?"

"Of course."

"Is Tsakhia immune to ursinthropy?"

A flush of pink rose in Nadia's cheeks. "Yes," she answered. "We were cautious at first, but now it seems clear he can't catch it. I don't know if it is because of the curse within him or because…"

"Because he isn't human?" I finished.

Nadia nodded as she swirled the remaining coffee in her mug. "Whatever he is, doesn't seem to be able to make a baby with a werebear." She looked up. "You are shocked that we would try when we are both differently cursed."

"Not shocked, but surprised."

"I just… love him. I want to have his babies. Anyway, it doesn't matter. If we could have a baby, we would have by now. I won't let unrequited longing keep me from doing the good that is right in front of me."

Wanting to have someone's babies was not an urge I was familiar with, but fertility issues? Magical manipulation of genomes? Those were things I understood. "When I have the space to work on it, I'll see what I can do."

As I was still speaking, I heard a commotion. Several guards ran by shouting outside. Nadia and I immediately leapt to our feet and ran outside too, but the guards weren't running to the infirmary, as I had feared, but to the brig.

"Reef!" I exclaimed.

But when we had pushed through the armored bodies and made it to the narrow bit of stone hall in front of Reef's cell, we found that the commotion had nothing to do with Reef. Instead, I saw Archavie, standing and shouting in Markish at something I couldn't see. As I watched he shoved a small wad of magic away from himself, as if throwing a ball. The magic tumbled away from him and took a visible form like that of an elongated fox-sized dragon, with the usual shimmery starry eyes of a Magic.

"Turus!"

Archavie burst into laughter. He pointed at Turus and laughed and laughed and laughed until tears streamed down his face. "Tiny," the wizard managed in Molvan. "Very tiny. So tiny."

Turus's form poofed out of visibility, but Archavie scolded, "No, no. See!" He pointed back to the ground where Turus had stood and Turus begrudgingly resumed his visible shape.

"What are you looking at?" The Magic snapped at the guards. "Go away!"

The caped Molvan, who I knew by now as Special Escort Officer Khasar Usenko, had arrived behind us. "It's okay," I assured him. "This is Archavie's Magic, Turus. They have a complicated relationship."

Usenko opened and shut his mouth and seemed to decide not to argue. He jerked his head toward the door and most of the border guards followed him out, leaving only a couple to guard Reef's cell.

Archavie continued to chortle and snort with laughter. "Weasel-lizard."

"Dragon." Turus argued.

"Weasel!"

"Dragon!"

Turus said something else in Markish, but Archavie scolded him again. "Uh-uh. Molvan."

"But *you* don't speak Molvan!"

Archavie gestured to me, and to Reef.

"This should be a private conversation," Turus fumed, but when Archavie folded his arms and turned his back on him the Magic growled, "Fine! Aren't you happy that I'm here? I managed to tear my kentro away from the horrible magic-eating monster, and it was no easy feat."

"Eh," Archavie said, as if he was not impressed.

"I came back to find you," Turus roared, but the sound was small coming from his reduced form.

Archavie fluttered his hand at the Magic. "No need."

"Hah! I'm sure you all have seen what a pathetic twig my wizard is without me." He glanced around at Reef, Nadia, and I for support, but received none.

"No," Reef said. "He doesn't need you."

But Turus remained undaunted. "You won't find her," he snapped at Archavie. "You won't find Evocreda without me, and even if you did, her wizard wouldn't want to marry *you,* not without the power and beauty I give you."

That was such a low blow that I almost intervened, but Archavie blew it off with a dismissive "Pfft. Friends. Happy." He gestured around at the rest of us again, as if to say, "who needs romance with friends like these?"

Turus gaped, speechless, and sat back on his haunches.

When the silence lingered, I soke up. "I think Archavie has proven, to himself and the rest of us, that he can live independently. If you want him to take you back, you might have to try being nice for a change."

Turus pretended not to hear me, but I knew he had.

"And Archavie," I went on, "It would be handy to have Turus's psychic communication available, but I can understand why you wouldn't want to return to leaning on the crutch of Turus's power."

Archavie burst out, saying things in words I didn't understand. I wasn't sure if Reef understood either, but he moved closer to the bars of his cell and said in summary, "Turus is a tyrant. Bully."

Since Reef had communicated with Archavie through Tsakhia's staff, I trusted his assessment. "Well, I'll leave you two to work it out. I have a patient to attend to. Reef, are you doing alright?"

Reef shrugged, "Not bad," he rumbled.

"Have you had breakfast?"

"A mush," he answered with an expression of distaste.

I guessed he meant the oatmeal, and I could imagine it wouldn't be very appealing to a Khirian. "I'll see if the kitchen can send over something suitable for a carnivore," I said. "If you need me, send word to the infirmary. I may be busy for quite a while."

When Nadia and I returned to the infirmary, Tsakhia was beginning to wake up. With his permission I conducted a thorough magical examination. I found that the initial graft of skin from the wizard of the Purple Madness had grown itself into his body in a strange, cancer-like way. It was from this stretch of foreign flesh that the rest of the curse seemed to have spread.

Unfortunately, Nadia told me the graft was impossible to remove. "We tried that at first," she said. "But if you try to sever it, it poisons him somehow."

"What about the transformed parts of his body?" I asked.

"Yes, surgery works, but he doesn't heal well, and the parts can't be regrown by magic."

"I think that may be worth it in this case," I said. "As far as I can tell your diaphragm and other breathing muscles are intact. The growth of the gills, however, has obstructed your trachea. That's why you haven't been able to breathe well. If I surgically remove the gills and reconstruct that portion of your trachea, you should be able to inhale and exhale comfortably again."

Tsakhia glanced up at Nadia again. "It's up to you," she said. Tsakhia mouthed something to her, and Nadia asked me, "what about the bones coming out of his arm and his back? Could you remove those too?"

I inspected the bony fingers. "Yes. In fact, I may be able to use the cartilage from these joints to reconstruct the damaged part of your trachea."

Tsakhia nodded and mouthed the Molvan "da."

"I'll see if the infirmary has surgical capabilities, and if so, we can get you prepped right away."

Soon I had Tsakhia under magical anesthesia. I found surgery refreshingly straightforward, even if the task was unusual. I couldn't heal the surgical wound by magic, at least not as well as I would have liked, and was forced to use stitches and bandages. I was able, however, to place a magical endotracheal tube inside his throat to support the cartilage grafts as they healed. This would be much more comfortable than a physical tube and should allow him to eat and speak as usual. To my relief when the procedure was complete Tsakhia resumed breathing, and when he woke up it seemed that the magical tracheal support fulfilled its purpose.

"Thank you," he whispered as the haze of anesthesia wore off.

"I am glad that I could do something to help," I said. "I hope with more study I will be able to help more. Now, you should rest. Since I can't fully heal the wound, I want you to stay in the hospital where I can monitor you."

Chapter Thirty-Three

VODASTAD

Reef

KAEDA annoyed everyone by demanding that that the group delay their departure. This, Reef understood, was due to the mysterious magician growing gills, among other things.

Tsakhia had risked his life to save them all, and so Reef understood the priority of his treatment and recovery. He trusted Kaeda's judgement and Nadia's. Still, he didn't know how much longer he could stand staying at this border garrison.

SEO Usenko, now vociferously harassed by both Kaeda, and Archavie, had finally allowed Reef to stay in a guest room with Archavie and Yury, and to walk around the cleared land near the gate. But Reef felt the looming presence of the wall and Mironiya to the South, the impending peril of Vodastad to the north, and the menacing eyes of Voda's soldiers all around him. As he took his usual laps of the military installation, he touched the fin cape bundle tied to his chest and felt his trepidation swirl to life.

"I know it's terrifying," Archavie said as he walked beside him, "but I assure you, the dov is more interested in talking to you than skinning you. In fact, there's been a bit of social uproar about him agreeing to host a Khirian at the palace. Usenko isn't just here to keep everyone safe from you, but to keep you safe from them."

The wizard had said something along these lines several times since accepting Turus back, but Reef still found it hard to believe.

"You trust me, don't you?"

Reef glanced at the wizard, strolling through the damp grass. He had once more adopted his brilliant glamour. His hair was flame-red, his eyes blue as reef water at mid-day, and his purple robes had somehow become clean and shiny and grown a bit of a gold edging that Reef didn't remember being there before. But he looked more serious now, no longer the flippant, flamboyant Archavie Reef had met in Gem City. Reef nodded. He took a deep breath and rolled his shoulders, willing himself to relax.

"Yes, relax and watch me destroy Gamalielle at Bytva-Bytva."

They played so much Bytva-Bytva over the next couple of days that Reef got quite sick of it, but with Kaeda holed up in the infirmary obsessing over Tsakhia's curse, Reef didn't have much choice.

Then one day a massive carriage rolled into the garrison's drive. It looked, to Reef, like a room on wheels, and it turned out to be exactly that. Specifically, a mobile hospital which SEO Usenko called an ambulance.

"I think if you look, you will see that you can safely transport your patient in the ambulance," Usenko said to Kaeda, and after a thorough inspection the healer agreed.

"Wow," she said as she stepped down from the back of the vehicle. "This is amazing."

Reef saw the caped official release a relieved sigh. He had been trying for days to persuade her to leave and had finally done it. "Welcome to Vodaniya," he said. "I trust this will not be the last time we impress you."

Wait.

Archavie. Archavie! Reef demanded.

Dear goodness, what?

That man. Is he engaged in some manner of courtship ritual directed at Kaeda?

Reef didn't quite know why he suspected this, but he had a very strong urge to go place himself between Kaeda and Usenko and tell the official Molvan that Kaeda didn't need to be any more impressed.

Reef waited and waited for Archavie's reassurance that he needn't be concerned. But it didn't come. Instead, the wizard thought reticently, *it's really none of my business.*

What?! Reef and the wizard trailed after Kaeda, Usenko, and Nadia, as they headed for the infirmary, discussing the particulars of the journey. Now that Reef was paying attention, he thought that Usenko looked at Kaeda a great deal more than necessary, and that when he looked at her his eyes softened and brightened, no longer the stern commander but the fascinated male.

What should I do? Reef thought to Archavie.

Why do you need to do something?

I can't let him court Kaeda!

Why not?

Reef didn't understand why the wizard was being so obtuse. Usenko was a servant of Voda who, from all Reef had heard, was a lying, scheming ruler whose secrets had hurt Molva.

But Usenko doesn't seem so bad, does he?

Maybe I should fight him, Reef thought.

Reef, look, human mating season is often a drawn-out affair in which two people get to know each other, slowly, erratically, with a lot of awkwardness and misunderstanding, and then come to a mutual agreement that either they want to spend the rest of their lives together or they never want to speak to each other again. The wizard paused, seemed to think better of this, and added, *or that they just want to be friends.*

Reef nearly growled aloud. Why did human customs have to be so infuriating?

What I'm saying is, Kaeda's not going to marry him, or anyone, any time soon. But if you're concerned about it, you can talk to her.

Reef didn't talk to her. He just fumed as they packed and then piled into two more room-on-wheels carriages and departed for Vodastad with Team Maelstrom riding around them. He fumed more as Usenko deigned, often, to ride with the Commission to tell them, but mostly Kaeda, about local history and topography. He fumed most when Usenko played Bytva-Bytva with the group and beat everyone but Yury.

After a few days of travel, they finally neared the capital city.

Reef remembered the city under siege, the surrounding neighborhoods on fire. Now the tall, austere, dark grey stone buildings of the city center rose proudly from an expanse of neatly matching architecture lining neatly positioned roads, and beyond them stretches of manicured parkland.

Usenko went on and on about Voda's genius in city planning and rebuilding after the war. Reef did his best not to listen until the official said, "Most of the buildings in the city center are enchanted to obscure to roar of the falls, but here if we open the windows for a moment, you will hear them."

Reef looked up, watched as Usenko pulled down the window of the carriage, and listened for the sound. Yes, there it was, the distant crash of water. He remembered swimming up the coast, feeling the vibration of the massive falls echoing through the expanse of the ocean. Up close the feeling was almost deafening to his underwater senses, and in that sense, thrilling.

He should have tried to escape, he thought. He should have asked Archavie to spring him from Usenko's forces. He could have been in the ocean by now, feeling the falls, instead of trapped in this rumbling vehicle listening to them. He couldn't imagine that the dov would let him out for a swim in the local waters.

You never know, Archavie said.

They crossed a broad stone bridge and approached the tall smooth walls of the city proper. "Serrinite," Usenko explained, nodding to the marbled grey and black stone. "When polished properly it's impossible to cut or climb without magic, and extremely resistant to erosion by water or weather. Perfect for a coastal city built around a waterfall."

Everything in the city seemed to be built of the stuff, and the residents, Reef noted, seemed dedicated to camouflaging themselves against the walls, wearing black, blue, and grey. Many of them paused to watch the giant carriages rumble by.

"We will arrive at the palace shortly," Usenko told them.

They passed through a gateway and Reef caught a glimpse of an austere courtyard before the carriage drove through another gate and into an indoor hall wide enough to accommodate two carriages side by side. Candelabras glowed on the stone walls, filled with magical tapers, and a thick rug sat before a staircase leading upward.

"I would recommend you don't say anything," Usenko told them, as footmen in neat black livery came to open the carriage doors. "The dov won't want to talk to us until we're in his… I'm not sure of the Gemmic word. Study, perhaps. He sometimes calls it his decision suite."

The ambulance had taken Tsakhia straight to the Torgovyy Channel embassy, where team Maelstrom would be staying, but Captain Rozhkov and Yury had come with the Commission. They handed the reins of their indriks over to the palace attendants as the Commission disembarked and gathered with them, just as Usenko bowed and said, "Your Majesty."

Reef turned his attention to the stairs and saw a man, tall with sharp features and a beard just beginning to grey, silently descending the stairs. His long, black, silver-edged cape billowed slightly behind him and hanging on his chest Reef saw the three-tiered falls of Vodstad, etched onto a silver medallion.

Are we supposed to bow? Reef wondered.

Since we are not subjects of the dov, I don't think we have to, but it would show respect.

Out of the corner of his eye Reef surveyed the group. Nadia, Yury, and Archavie had all bent a little at the waist, but Kaeda and Gamalielle remained upright, watching the dov with curiosity. Reef decided if Kaeda wasn't bowing, he wouldn't either.

"Special Escort Usenko," Voda said. "I am glad to see that you have made it at last."

He didn't sound glad, Reef thought. He sounded as if he were reading words off a script, and he personally detested each one. It didn't show on his face though. His features were as cold and still as the city's polished stone.

"I deeply apologize for the delay," Usenko said, still looking at the floor.

The dov reached the bottom of the steps, cast his eyes across the group, and continued his distasteful script. "I am sorry to say I have had to postpone the ball that I intended to throw in your honor."

"One of our people was injured and needed treatment," Kaeda spoke up.

Voda looked at her with the same hard expression he had shown all of them, but there was something there, finally, Reef thought, some venom in his eyes as if he wished he could say, why don't you all just give up and die?

"So I have heard," the dov said, then to Captain Rozhkov he added, "I hope your magician is faring well, captain?"

"He is stable Your Majesty," Captain Rozhkov replied without looking up.

"I am glad to hear it. Please, raise your heads."

Then, "Kaeda!" a voice exclaimed, and this voice was neither cold nor bitter. General Straton had appeared at the top of the stairs, but he ran down them so quickly that to Reef he seemed almost transported by magic. In a moment he was amongst them, not in Gemmic armor now but Molvan attire, tall boots, embroidered tunic, his arms in their blue quilted fabric thrown around Kaeda, who hugged him back tightly.

Reef blinked. Had the candelabras just flared? For a barely observable moment the carriage hall seemed ablaze with light. He wasn't the only one who noticed. Gamalielle, Yury, and Captain Rozhkov all glanced around, but the illumination was already gone. Kaeda and the General were both crying, Reef observed with interest, really, really crying, but they didn't seem sad.

Mammals cry for a lot of reasons, Archavie supplied. *Sometimes just to deal with an overflow of feeling in general.*

"I was so worried."

"I thought you were dead."

"I couldn't get any information."

"What happened?"

The words tumbled out in a mess of tears. Finally, Straton stepped back, hands still on Kaeda's shoulders, her hands still gripping his elbows. "How did you survive?" she asked.

"When Lady Batbayar heard what had happened, she ordered her ship to turn around. They couldn't get near the shore, but I had managed to shed most of my armor and held on to a piece of our lifeboat. The current pulled me out into the open ocean and the crew retrieved me. And you? What happened?"

"A tale best told upstairs perhaps," the dov interrupted. "If you would all please follow me and say nothing more."

He turned and swept away back up the stairs without another word, leaving them to follow. And follow they did, in the silence the dov required, though Reef could hear, in his mind, Archavie's mental chatter as he filled Straton in on their travels, letting the rest of the group add any details they chose.

Straton, who had dried his eyes, now listened as Kaeda detailed Reef's phage sense, Gamalielle mentioned how they were nearly killed by worms, Archavie filled in that werebears were real and that Svevolod was evil, Gamalielle added that Tsakhia made the phages, and Kaeda clarified that Tsakhia had been a prisoner at the time and was not evil.

But Voda was in charge of the whole thing and is probably evil, Gamalielle summarized.

Yes, my vote is definitely on Voda being evil, Archavie agreed, *but he's wearing robust anti-mindreading magic so I can't say that definitively.*

Oh, and Nadia's people worship a goddess who is probably the lost archon of Molva, Kaeda thought, and the details poured on.

As they walked through an enormous meeting room, filled with leather chairs around an oval table, Archavie called the chatter to a halt. *Now, we know what we know, but Voda doesn't know what we know, and I propose we don't tell him.*

Agreed, General Straton thought.

What's our story? Kaeda asked.

We traveled, we were attacked by giant worms, Team Maelstrom saved us. I suppose it won't hurt to mention the phages, since Voda's people will know we were attacked by one at the border.

A servant had opened a door in the wood-paneled wall. The dov walked through and the Commission, Nadia, and Yury, followed. This smaller office also housed several leather chairs, one of which was occupied by Secretary Essen, holding a clipboard and a pen. There was also a massive desk, which the dov walked around, preparing to also sit down. But none of that mattered. All that mattered was the figure in the black robe.

The Commission's psychic connection collapsed as Archavie panicked and turned to run, but the door had already been shut, and it had no obvious knob. The frantic wizard couldn't find his way out. Reef wasn't sure whether he should help Archavie wrench the door open or catch him and hold onto him until the crisis had been resolved.

"So sorry," Kaeda spoke up. "On our travels we encountered—"

"Another monster hunter," Nadia supplied. "He dressed very much like your advisor, and quite by accident he hurt Archavie a great deal."

"I would be fascinated to learn how anyone could frighten the great Wizard Archavie," the dov said.

Reef bristled at the sarcasm in the dov's tone. He probably knew very well that it had been one of his wrestors, and he didn't care in the least that it had assaulted Archavie and stolen most of his Magic. But Reef remained silent and stood beside Archavie, both of their backs to the wall, the wizard breathing in great gasps.

"Well, we were attacked by worms," Kaeda began, and she began to relate the story of the worm attack, making it sound like the worms had attacked all on their own. "And then this monster hunter showed up," Kaeda said, and she looked to Nadia.

Nadia picked up the story right away. "Based on what the Commission has told me, I am guessing the other monster hunter used a form of magical magnetism to draw the magic out of the worm's bodies. We do something similar, though we usually wait until they are dead, since we view it as inhumane. However, he did not consider that a wizard's Magic nearby might be harmed by this. Understandably it was very traumatic for a wizard and his Magic. The Magic actually fled for some time."

The dov thought this over. He had settled into the tall chair behind his desk, elbows on the polished wood surface, fingers steepled before him. "And the monster hunter?" he asked.

"When I sent my people to harvest the worms for magic they found no sign of him," Nadia said. "But there were heaps of worms in piles. The Commission said they swarmed him, so he may not have made it out."

She sounded reasonably regretful about this, and Dov Voda nodded. "It is a shame," he said, and then to Archavie, added, "I can assure you, wizard, you and your Magic will be safe in my palace."

They all turned to Archavie, who gathered himself and took a step away from the wall.

If anything happens to me, Reef heard in his mind.

I will avenge you, Reef assured him.

And protect Kaeda.

And protect Kaeda.

"How very kind of you, dov," the wizard said aloud, though his voice shook. He put a hand to his chest as if deeply moved by this reassurance. "Turus and I have not had such a scare since we faced the necromancer Olc on Scanrúil Oileán. That was a dark day. The moon hiding her face as if the heavens themselves could not bear to see the dead emerging from the fetid waters of the loch—"

"Is there anything else I should know about your journey here?" the dov interrupted.

The Commission, Nadia, and Yury all exchanged glances, and the responsibility for summarizing their story fell on Kaeda again. "Team Maelstrom escorted us to the border, and the phage attack there you are probably already aware of."

"Yes, beyond our borders the magic is more unruly," Voda said. He seemed to accept their truncated tale. Whether he believed it, or had simply decided to pretend, Reef wasn't sure. Regardless, the ruler changed the subject. "It is fortunate that Maelstrom was able to rescue you." Addressing Captain Rozhkov he said, "You will, of course, be compensated for your protection of the Commission. I am sure it has taken you out of your way."

"We were happy to be of service to Molva," Captain Rozhkov replied, "but I am sure my team will also be happy to be paid."

"And I imagine you will want to return to the Torgo soon."

"My husband will need more time to recover, and Healer Straton is interested in studying his condition. My team also could use some leave after our recent adventures. With your permission, most of them are planning to remain at the Torgovyy Channel Embassy for a while."

He doesn't like that, Archavie thought to Reef. *Can you tell?*

The dov remained still as stone, but yes, Reef thought his eyes looked a little icier, as if he deeply wanted to throw all of these people out of his dovdom but wasn't going to without a reason.

"Of course," the dov said. "I will see to it that you and your officers are invited to the upcoming ball."

"We would be honored."

Voda moved at last, sitting back in his tall chair and resting his hands on the arms of it as he spoke to Kaeda. "I understand that you have been asked to solve the problem of our magical drought, however, the drought is the least of our concerns. The conflict with Dov Miro to the south, and the Lyov family to the north are far more taxing for my people than a simple lack of magic. Our technological advances render magic less necessary than it was in previous generations, and under my rule we have been importing ample magic from the Gemmic Peninsula. Whatever the reason for our archon's disappearance, we continue to thrive without him."

Reef expected Kaeda to argue, but she did not. Instead, she said easily, "I am glad to hear it. In that case, I hope you don't mind if I focus my efforts on helping Tsakhia Rozhkov."

For the first time, Reef saw the dov's expression flicker as surprise caused him to lose his grip on his composure. Clearly, he had not expected her to give in or agree with him, but he recovered quickly, and said, "A worthy pursuit. How propitious that you should be able to lend the Rozhkov's your expertise."

"And, of course, if there is anything else you would like me to work on, perhaps the curse of ursinthropy, which, I have heard from Captain Rozhkov has been endangering Molva's people, I would be more than happy to collaborate with your local experts."

"Molva doesn't need your help." This came from magiologist Svevolod. He had remained silent through the entire meeting so far, and at the sound of his voice the dov's expression went icy again.

"Magiologist Svevolod puts it bluntly, but he is correct. The unrest beyond our borders has caused many attempts at stealing or sabotaging our magical advances and thus we cannot be too careful about who we allow to view our research. However, I will check in with our local hospitals and see if there are any other difficult cases that could benefit from a second opinion."

Definitely not hiding anything, Archavie's comment trickled sarcastically into Reef's mind.

"Sure, I would love that," Kaeda replied.

"Well, I think our conference is at an end," the dov said.

"There is one more thing," Captain Rozhkov spoke up. "Reef is currently in guild custody."

"Ah, yes. How should we proceed?"

"If Reef prefers to be released to you, I can allow that," Nadia said. "But if Reef would prefer to remain with us, I don't think my team will mind that either."

"I must take responsibility for Reef while he is here," Voda said. "The people of the city have put their confidence in my guard. If Reef wants to remain in guild custody, then I will have to send you all back to the Channel."

"I will stay with the Commission," Reef said. "Here."

"Good. My staff have prepared rooms for you in the north wing. I think you will find that you will all be comfortable at the palace." Voda pulled the cord. In a moment the door behind the Commission opened. A sturdy middle-aged Molvan woman stood there, a stiff smile on her face as she looked across the unusual collection of guests.

"Avdotya," Dov Voda said, "please show our guests to their rooms."

Just like that, it was over. The group silently made their way through the larger meeting room, and out into the hall. Reef had the wavering feeling that he had climbed a little too high up a cliff or a tree, and now couldn't quite figure out how to get down.

Yes, Voda and his minions are very opaque. In fact, I'm not convinced Svevolod is his minion.

Reef agreed. As he remembered the wrestor standing to the back and side of Voda's desk Reef had the impression that the magiologist was there to keep an eye on the dov, as Kaeda might have kept on eye on Gamalielle in the woods, to make sure the Cat didn't eat any weird mushrooms.

Indeed. And you can imagine how much that would annoy Gamalielle.

Voda certainly seemed annoyed, Reef thought.

Maybe he wants to eat those mushrooms.

Or maybe he doesn't want to be foraging to begin with, Reef thought, though he was far from sure he understood what this metaphor was supposed to mean.

"We're going to head over to the embassy," Nadia said, as the group walked out into the hall. "It's just down the street. Feel free to come visit once you're settled in. You're sure you'll be okay?" She glanced at the palace guards who had now begun to replace the Maestromites as the Commission's protective perimeter. Reef looked at them too. He really was at the dov's mercy now.

"We'll be alright. We'll see you soon," Kaeda told Nadia.

"And I'll see you tonight?" Yury asked Gamalielle.

A gleeful grin spread across the cat's face. "Definitely," she said.

"Yury's going to take me out," she explained when Nadia and Yury split off from the Commission. "There's a club near the Torgo embassy folks really like. Best place for the three d's: drinking, dancing, and dirt."

"Dirt?" Kaeda asked.

"Gossip. News. The juicy stuff that you're probably not going to hear around here."

"Just don't get into any trouble."

"Pfft! The only trouble I get into is the trouble I want to get into."

They took a few more steps, Reef taking in the patterns on the papered walls and the intricacy of the candelabras. The wallpaper had vertical pastel stripes with flowers between. How strange, Reef thought for a moment, to be surrounded by images of flowers, flat ones, that neither moved, nor smelled. Then Archavie spoke up. "So, General Straton, what have you been up to while we've been gone? Or should I say whom?"

"What?" Gamalielle gasped and turned rapt attention to Straton.

Reef didn't understand. What was so alarming? Whatever it was, Kaeda didn't seem surprised, but Reef thought he saw a bit of color rise on the General's marble-fair Gemmic face. The man replied, as cool as ever, "Lady Batbayar is invested in the success of the Commission."

"I can't believe it," Gamalielle shrieked. "Did you know about this?" she asked Kaeda.

"I... I'm not going to say anything. It's up to General Straton to share whatever he wants to."

What is this about? Reef asked Archavie.

Mating season.

Oh.

The General seemed to decide that it would be pointless to deny the connection. "Lady Batbayar and I met a long time ago, when I visited Molva as a young man. Since her people saved me from the shipwreck we... we have renewed our acquaintance, but now that the Commission has made it here safely I will give my full attention to our assignment, as you all should."

"A lady!" Gamalielle shrieked again.

Straton sighed and kept walking.

Lady Batbayar may be helpful in our efforts at espionage, Archavie psychically suggested. *We should take full advantage of all our resources.*

The dov might frown on us taking full advantage of a Molvan lady, Gamalielle's thoughts heckled in the mental forum.

"Okay, enough, both of you," Kaeda scolded aloud.

"Oh, wow!" This exclamation had come from Gamalielle, now floating over the heads of the group. She looked past them to an open space beyond. Reef saw, to his surprise, a wavering net of light like that cast by a body of water.

Reef hurried forward, feeling almost as if he had entered a dream. The enclosed hallway emptied into the upper floor of a ballroom. Reef saw a banister on the left and went to it, looking down to see not a dance floor, but a crystal-clear swimming pool. Around the pool, white tiles displayed a faint pattern of waterfall waves curling out from the edges of the water. Broad steps descended into the water at the shallow end, and at the deep end a wall of white stone rose in larger steps, forming a miniature version of Vodastad's three-tiered waterfall. The water did not thunder, but flowed calmly into the pool in a shimmering stream. Around the pool, pots and planters held both Molvan and Gemmic plants, including some palm trees that reached almost to the second floor. Looking up, Reef saw that the ceiling overhead was made of geometric panels of glass.

Avdotya, the servant, seemed to expect their astonishment. She paused beside them and said, "The dovetsa, may she rest in peace, suffered during the long, cold winters, so our dov built her this greenhouse to preserve a bit of the summer for her. Now he keeps it in her memory. Guests are welcome to walk there."

Slowly they began moving again, but still peering down often to take in the trellises of roses, wooden benches beneath cherry trees, stands of ferns, and bright hibiscus blooms.

He can't be all bad. Kaeda's thought came through the mental forum.

You're a softie, Gamalielle quipped back.

Reef didn't know what the garden said about Voda, but at that moment he didn't much care, as long as he got to go swimming.

Chapter Thirty-Four

CURSES, CURSES

Kaeda

THE floor. The white expanse between him and the Purple Madness. Ivann staggered forward. The floor did not feel solid beneath his feet. The walls around him did not look quite real. Were there mountains beyond, or stars? Was there really air here? Everything around him felt too thin, as if he might fall right through the air, the floor, the ground, to the center of the earth.

I had experienced this memory a few times now, trying to understand how the curse had taken over Tsakhia's body. I knew his mental and physical state had deteriorated after wresting the Purple Madness so many times, but clearly, he did not yet have the disfiguring curse. In his memory he staggered forward, determined to continue.

He reached out a hand. "You are mine," he said to the Purple Madness.

He tried to brace himself against the psychic onslaught. He had lost track of how long he had been tearing her, and how long she had been battering his mind. At first he had marked the days on the walls of his cell. But eventually it was too difficult to raise his hand, too difficult to remember the passing of time. There was only survival, survival and her loathing, and trying to remember that he had existed before this, that he was more than an atrocity created to commit more atrocities.

But as he gripped the Purple Madness her hatred cut his mind like a knife. *No! That is all you are! A ruin! A weapon! Nothing!*

"You are mine," he said. His magic sense had gripped her, he pulled, but the contact only made it easier for her to access his thoughts and turn them into thorns.

What will they do to you when you can no longer torture me? What will they do when your mind breaks? Will they give you a quick death? Will they take you apart and use the wreckage of your body to make more of you? Will they cut your throat and leave you alone in the snow?

They were his own fears, the fears that drove him to stand here and try to rip another piece from the huge Magic before him. Usually he could fight them down and focus, but this time they seemed to grip his heart. He tried to breathe, but it was as if the air choked him.

Observing this as I had now many times, I could detach a little and pay attention to the periphery of Tsakhia's vision. The other wrestors and magicians, though they were at some distance from Tsakhia, couldn't breathe either. I saw one clutching its throat, another gasping and reaching, as if trying to undo the magic that Tsakhia didn't know he was doing.

The Purple Madness clearly knew, and clearly saw in his involuntary magic working a chance to break free. *Yes,* she shrilled, *you will die alone, you will die in pieces, no one will hold your hand, no one will remember you, even the Creator will cast you into oblivion, you are too horrifying for remembrance!*

"You – you are mine!"

With a rush of terror, he pulled the Purple Madness. She came free, all of her, and crashed upon him.

Now what came next I guessed to be the most important, but unfortunately it was the least clear. Either Tsakhia completely lost his mind, or he was actually taken apart somehow, scattered like weather throughout the unmagic around him, which became a storm. There was stone, screaming, wind, the vengeful cackles of the Purple Madness, her delight at the destruction and death around her. Then eventually there was no stone, no screaming, but instead light, clouds, mountains, crystals of ice. Throughout all of this. Tsakhia felt nothing. Either he was numb with panic or perhaps the Purple Madness had so completely overwhelmed his will that he could not feel.

Then awareness came rushing back, like a shark out of the depths, like the end of a dream. Tsakhia found himself in a snowbank and realized that he was alive.

I repay you. My life, for your life. Your torture, for my torture.

Agony seemed to creep out of Tsakhia's bones until it consumed his awareness. The Purple Madness left him screaming in the snow.

The memory faded. Tsakhia and Nadia and I sat in our usual chairs in their guest quarters in the Torgovyy Channel Embassy. I took a deep breath. Even though I had seen the memory many times it still took a few moments to calm myself.

"And then?"

"I must have drawn the attention of the yetis," Tsakhia said. "I hardly knew what I was doing."

"You wiped them out," Nadia said. "It was a bloodbath. Then he collapsed." She added to me, though she had told me before, and summarized again the attempts at treating him in the Torgo. "But he didn't transform very much because usually he kept a magical restraint on. As you have seen, if he is overwhelmed, he works some overwhelming magic.

Clearly. I hoped we would never face a situation where Tsakhia experienced such intense emotions again. But IMWEES I could treat. Tsakhia's Monstrositor on the other hand… Clearly the Purple Madness, Boginya, the goddess, whatever we wanted to call her, had cursed him, and I was beginning to fear that, being an archon, or at least what remained of one, she could do magic that I simply couldn't comprehend. I could tell that there was magic in Tsakhia's body, but it was oddly diffuse, so fine and fragmented that I couldn't grip it and study it properly.

My unsatisfying, incomplete theory was that the Purple Madness had taken him apart, that was how it felt to Tsakhia, and that each of these parts was cursed to strain toward a different type of transformation.

Despite my lack of understanding, I did have one idea, but it was drastic. I wanted another solution. Something else to propose.

I sighed, searching my mind for anything I might have missed, but couldn't think of anything. While I thought, a knock came at the door and an attendant arrived with a tea cart. Nadia poured the tea and passed out teacups and cookies. We all looked around for places to put them.

Tsakhia and I had taken over most of the Rozhkov's guest rooms at the embassy, turning them into a magical laboratory and workshop. Most surfaces were covered with notes, scrolls, plaques of frozen magical blueprints, and stands of test tubes. When, at first, I asked Nadia if she minded, she laughed and said, "Living with Tsakhia, this is normal."

We cleared some space for our tea, and I picked up one of many genome-displaying scrolls. In keeping with my theory, I had discovered that Tsakhia's body contained many different genomes, each within the boundaries of its associated transformed body part. The curse, whatever it was, likely bound them all together, otherwise Tsakhia would simply fall apart. The scroll I held displayed Tsakhia's primary genome, the one that covered the parts of his body not dramatically transformed.

I had hoped this would give me some idea as to how to treat him but was again hitting a dead end.

"I have looked though the city's menagerie and I can't find any clue as to where this genetic material came from or what it can be related to. I have no leads."

Nadia passed out cups of tea and plates of cookies. "But it is not human?" Nadia asked.

"No," I answered. "At least, not fully. I can't say how Tsakhia's DNA has been altered without a sample of his original genetic material." I already knew they didn't have that. "I do have one idea though," I said.

Both looked up, Nadia's bright eyes and Tsakhia's mismatched features filled with hope. I had to tell them. I couldn't keep it from them. But I had a feeling they wouldn't like it, at least Tsakhia wouldn't.

"I don't have the treatment fully developed yet, and I don't know if it will work, but I know that the ursinthropic enchantment can change a creature at the genetic level. If I can take it apart and put it back together properly, I might be able to create a therapeutic form of ursinthropy, tailored to Tsakhia, that will bring his body back in line with his predominant genome. From what I've learned talking to the healers at the local hospital, it seems that ursinthropy is overruling, that is, it can replace other bodily enchantments. I may be able to create a therapy that will replace the curse on Tsakhia's body with ursinthropy. It might reverse some of your animal transformation. If not, it should at least allow us to remove those parts and regrow them according to the old body print you had shipped over from the Torgo."

This was quite an explanation, but they seemed to follow it, Nadia with mounting excitement. As for Tsakhia, the hope drained from his face and when he spoke, he sounded almost as cold as Dov Voda. "Would it remove my ability to do magic?"

"Even if it did," Nadia began, but Tsakhia interrupted.

"Would it?"

"I can't say for sure," I told them, "But my guess is yes. So far, every form of ursinthropy limits the carrier's ability to work magic. You might gain some of the innate abilities that Nadia has, like increased strength and quicker healing."

As I spoke Tsakhia rose from his chair and walked away to the window, where the curtains were shut against prying eyes.

"You can't work magic now anyway," Nadia said, following him.

"I can."

"But it is killing you."

"I'd rather die."

"Than live with me?" she asked, putting a hand on his arm.

"It's the best idea I have," I said, "but I'll keep brainstorming. In the meantime, is this something you would like me to work on?"

"Yes," Nadia said, then she looked at her husband.

Tsakhia's beaked face turned toward her and they exchanged a long look. Finally, he also said, "Yes."

I took fresh blood samples from each of them and began the painstaking work of setting the lively magical constellations out in static shapes so I could begin to imagine making Nadia's ursinthropy robust and complex enough to overrule Tsakhia's Monstrositor. Tsakhia had made himself a set of clawed gauntlets that he could use to manipulate magic without working it, so at least he was able to help me tease out the ursinthropic enchantment and hold it while I filled in new instructions.

By the time I finally headed back to the palace my brain felt like mush. I hoped to go for a swim, but I didn't know if it would work out. Reef spent almost every waking moment in or around the pool and so far, I hadn't been able to bring myself to swim in front of him. He was a Khirian after all. I had seen him swimming from the edge of the *Deterrance* and now got to see him up close, slipping through the water with the ease of a shark and the slick grace of a sea lion. Despite all my human swimming experience I knew that I would look clumsy by comparison, kicking and splashing.

Archavie told me to get over it so often that I almost wished he didn't have Turus back.

The wizard was waiting for me on the stairs when I returned to Voda's palace and he trotted down the last few steps to offer his arm to me when I exited my carriage. "You've missed all the excitement," he said, in cheerful, conspiratorial tone.

"I think *you've* missed all the excitement," I said.

"Ah, the endless thrill of chronic illness! Still, I'd much rather spy on your father and his duchess. I may not be able to find love, and you may not want to, but at least someone can be happy! However, I won't rhapsodize any further until I've checked how you feel about the whole thing."

Of course, he must have noticed the tumble of feelings that I didn't want to deal with.

Well, I wish he could have been happy with my mother and I, I thought back to the wizard, but I do like Georgina, and my mother has been dead for five years. It's not unreasonable for him to pursue someone else, and I can imagine after him nearly dying in the ocean, Georgina has had to decide how significant he is to her.

"That's a very good analysis," Archavie said, patting my hand, "but how do you feel?"

I sighed. Like I want to scream, I thought. I wasn't sure exactly why I wanted to scream. My father and I had spent some pleasant time together since I arrived back in Vodaniya, mostly him teaching me better combat shield stetsals in case I was ever attacked by worms again. It felt strange, but good. Still, the feeling of wanting to scream remained.

"You know, I've heard that at the bottom of the Vodastad falls you can't hear anything but the roar of the water. I'd be happy to go scream with you."

"I don't want to go scream," I said.

"I thought you just said you did."

"I said that's how I felt. I don't want to do what I feel."

Archavie thought about that for a moment and said, "I think I understand. At times, I've felt like killing myself, but I didn't really want to. What I really wanted was for life to be better. And it is." He smiled at me and added, "but I don't think screaming would be so bad."

When I opened my mouth to ask some very healer questions, the wizard spoke up again. "Don't worry, I currently have neither plan, nor intention, to take my life. And since you don't want to talk feelings, go ahead, and tell me what you *think* instead. Can I gush about General Straton and his lady?"

"I like Georgina," I repeated. "I'm happy for them… although…"

Well, I didn't want to sound judgmental, but hadn't my father said he would turn his full attention to our mission? And while he was wooing Lady Georgina, Gamalielle had been spending all her time either at the Torgo embassy with Yury or out on the town, also with Yury. As for Archavie… well I wasn't sure what he had been doing.

Let me assure you that Gamalielle and Yevgeny have been snooping as hard as they can without getting in trouble, and part of your father's pursuit of Georgina has been a successful cover for us getting an invitation to her estate, near where the cursed body was found. The more convincing their attachment, the more likely it is Voda will let us go. Meanwhile, Turus and I have been keeping an eye on everyone to make sure you're all safe. Don't think we're not working hard.

Thank you for your social sleuthing, I thought, as Archavie and I began to climb a second flight of stairs. Dining at the dov's table and playing information games with his flunkies is tiring enough.

Ah, well then, I won't ask you to ply SEO Usekno for information.

Usenko? I asked in surprise.

Whenever he checks in at the palace he asks about you, Archavie told me. *The ball is tomorrow night, and I bet if you dance with him and smile enough, he'll spill a confidential detail or two by accident.*

The ball. Dancing. Smiling. Ugh. I couldn't think about it. Not now. A swim, that's what I needed.

"In that case," the wizard said aloud. "I'll tell you that you should get over your fear of looking stupid."

I groaned. "Does that mean Reef is swimming right now?"

"Of course he's swimming. He really doesn't have much else to do and he's getting stir-crazy in the palace, but trust me when I say that he would like some company."

"He has your company, and Turus's."

"But we don't swim. I personally don't like being in the water. It feels too crowded."

I sighed. I didn't know if I had the mental energy to be around Reef. My heart would begin to do acrobatics, I knew, and possibly my stomach too.

I don't suppose you could fix that for me again? I thought.

I think at this point it would be silly. You know your admiration for Reef is not based on a handsome human persona, so it's likely here to stay. He added aloud, "Reef knows what it's like to have a full mind and just want to swim. If you tell him, he'll understand."

"I guess I have to deal with it sooner or later. And I would really like to have a swim before dinner."

"Brilliant. Well, don't let me interrupt."

The wizard turned off toward the library and let me walk on my own across the balcony towards the guest rooms. I paused at the railing and looked down and saw Reef, making long figure eights in the water as usual. The pool was large, but it only took him seconds to cross it when he swam quickly, as he was now. He reminded me of the animals in the city's menagerie, restlessly pacing their enclosures.

You need a swim; Reef needs company. The solution is obvious. You're going to do it. You're going to swim.

I repeated this to myself as I returned to my room to change into my wetsuit. No sooner had I opened the door than Gamalielle leapt out of somewhere, making me shriek and jump.

"Don't be mad," the cat said.

"I'm already a little bit mad!" I exclaimed. "What are you doing in my room? And what are you wearing?"

Gamalielle looked like a different cat. She was wearing a brand-new frock coat with a close-fitting bodice and full skirt shorter in the front than the back, as well as a pair of wine-red leggings and tall leather boots with panels of buttons on the outer sides. Her fur, which usually stuck out in unkempt wisps had been brushed smooth.

"Do you like it?" she asked. "It's all Vodaniyan cat fashion. Yury thinks it suits me." She grinned broadly. "But enough about *my clothes*. This is about *your* clothes."

She pointed her eyes toward a set of wrapped paper parcels laying across my bed. They were huge. Dress-sized. Ballgown-sized.

"Where did these come from?"

"Don't be mad," Gamalielle repeated. "Remember how Voda's staff kept asking you about measurements so they can make sure you have something to wear to the ball? And you kept putting them off? Well, Archavie and I finally decided to take matters into our own hands. Shusky and Shapiro make gowns with self-adjusting enchantments in the bodice, so all they needed was a description and our best guess."

As she spoke, I tore the glossy white paper wrapping off the largest package. The gown inside was a monumental creation, a tent's worth of shimmering white fabric covered all over in a mosaic of clear crystals. A geometric pattern of swirls, done in gold and crimson beads, swept down the center of the gown, across the shoulder-baring neckline, and down the long, pointed sleeves, reminding me of the design of a Gemmic column. I could see more red and gold patterns across the hem of the dress.

"Whoa," Gamalielle breathed over my shoulder. "I haven't seen it finished yet. ShuSha really outdid themselves."

"Is this really what Molvan ladies wear to a ball?"

"Yeah, well, more or less. A lot of the upper crust will be wearing ShuSha gowns, but most of them aren't quite this sparkly. The other packages are just basic cold-weather gowns suitable for a guest of the palace."

I folded the paper back over the dress. "I can't think about it right now. I need to go for a swim."

"Don't you want to try it on?"

"Not right now."

"Don't you want to hear about the local secrets I've dug up?"

"Not right now."

"Fine. Have your swim. I'll see you at dinner or whatever."

Chapter Thirty-Five

CIRCLES AND LOOPS

Reef

IN Khirian the wavy web of brightness created by light passing through water was called the lisrek. Literally it meant light net. The lisrek held all ocean life together within itself. To be caught within it, for Reef, was to be at home.

That's how he usually felt, but not here. Not here where he could feel the water bouncing off the hard walls, echoing with strange emptiness. No heartbeats, no hums, so muting of mud, no muffling of grass, just the endless ricochet of the water itself. It turned the lisrek into a prison.

He couldn't build much speed in the pool, and this left him frustrated, swimming for hours and still not feeling tired, only bored, passing the endless white of the walls again and again, occasionally bobbing up to check on the fin cape, which he had left on a nearby pool chair.

Eventually the sun set. The murex shell sconces on the walls began to glow pink-white as they did every evening and the lisrek shone more boldly. When Reef surfaced again, he saw Kaeda coming down the stairs from the balcony. He saw that she was dressed for swimming, wearing a second skin of dark blue and slate grey. He swam to the stairs and climbed out of the water at once. Of course, she wouldn't want to swim with him. No one had so far. Who would want to be in the water with a

Khirian, especially in Molva, with the history of Khirian violence?

"Oh, don't get out on my account," Kaeda said. "I don't want to interrupt." She set down the towels she was carrying on a nearby table and began to tie up her hair. "How's the water?"

She had spoken to him so little lately, always out at the lab, that he felt like he had almost forgotten how to talk to her. He shrugged. "Warm. But there is not enough of it."

They both looked toward the pool. What should he say, Reef wondered? I'm tired, goodnight? While he was thinking, Kaeda said bluntly, "Archavie said you could use some company."

That was true enough, Reef thought, but he also felt sad at the thought of accepting human company yet again. He could really use some Khirian company, someone who could keep pace with him in the water, fill the pool with familiar swimming patterns and the comforting thud of a steady heartbeat.

"The thing is," the healer went on, oblivious to his thoughts, "compared to you, I'll look completely incompetent. In the water I mean. Swimming. I swim a lot but, I can't swim like a Khirian."

Reef blinked in surprise. Was that her reservation? That she was afraid of looking ridiculous? "I would not expect you to swim like a Khirian," he said.

Kaeda didn't look comforted. "I like to be good at what I do. If not the best, then close to it. I guess what I'm saying is, promise you won't laugh."

Reef almost did laugh at this request but managed to merely nod his head. "I promise."

Kaeda took a deep breath. "Okay. I'm going to go dive in then."

She walked away toward the deep end of the pool and Reef followed at a distance, curious to see what she would do. To either side of the waterfall were stairs; they turned the waterfall into a sort of bridge between the pool proper and the little garden pond on the other side. Kaeda climbed halfway up the steps and stopped on one, a few feet above the water. Yes, Reef thought as she bent down and gripped the edge of the stair, yes these would be perfect diving platforms. Why had he not thought of it? Kaeda positioned herself with one foot barely over the edge and the other slightly behind her. Then she dove, cutting a shallow curve through the air, breaking the surface with barely a splash, and gliding through the water for several seconds before she slipped back to the surface and swam to the opposite wall.

And she thought he would laugh! Reef had never seen a human move so beautifully through the water! He found himself feeling uneasy. He was a perfectly adequate swimmer and diver, but after seeing Kaeda swim and dive, adequate did not feel like enough.

"I'm just going to swim laps, if that's okay with you," Kaeda called.

Reef coughed a Khirian yes as he walked to the shallow end and down the steps. There's no reason to be nervous, he told himself. She has decided to swim with you. She is not afraid, and you know you needn't fear her. You wanted company. You have it. Swim with her.

He felt it at once as he walked into the pool: the cadence of her heartbeat in the water. It was quick, quicker than a Khirian's even when swimming strenuously. Reef's instinct again told him that she was afraid, but he reassured himself that

that was not the case. Humans were small and warm; their hearts beat faster.

He swam, at first doing his best to keep pace with her, and then, because the pace was too slow, resuming his figure eight, frequently crossing beneath her. Each time he came near he took comfort in the closeness of another creature in the water, and to his surprise he found himself more and more relieved that she was there.

After a few laps he felt her stop, and as he rounded the deep end, he saw her floating in the water, a shimmer of magic over her face. He could tell from the pulse of her breath in the magic and the cadence of her heart that she was catching her breath, but she was also working some magic, stretches of magic that he could sense, since they disrupted the water. She held one foot crossed over her knee, working the magic outward from her bare toes to create an almost-invisible flipper about a foot long. She repeated this with the other foot, then looked up at him with a grin, as if to say, look what I can do, and began to dolphin kick her way over to him underwater.

When swimming, a Khirian would move in a back-and-forth wave motion. Kaeda moved in an up-and-down wave motion, and underwater she no longer splashed or flailed. She looked as though she belonged in the water.

Reef thought this and felt his own heart jump ahead as if startled. Why? Reef tried to examine the feeling behind his response but didn't understand it. He felt admiration for Kaeda, and trepidation. Was he afraid for her safety? With him? Or was he remembering the number of humans killed by Khirians as they tried to swim away?

He tried not to think about it, only to pay attention as Kaeda reached the end of the pool, paused at the wall, shrugged, and gestured out into the water. An invitation, he thought. To swim together? To race? He wasn't sure, but he nodded and pushed off the wall at the same time as her. With her flippers on Kaeda could reach a leisurely Khirian cruising speed, so he swam alongside her to the other side. As they turned to cross the pool again, he began to make loops around her when the depth allowed.

Of course, Kaeda would not know the Khirian swimming game of circling, which young Khirians practiced to build agility. Nevertheless, when they reached the deep end Kaeda suddenly dove and tried to circle him. Reef turned and circled back, and Kaeda also adjusted course to continue around him. When Kaeda broke away Reef chased her and when Reef broke away Kaeda chased him.

They continued until Reef felt a shaking in the water and looked to see Kaeda laughing into her waterbreathing magic. She pointed upward and the two of them broke the surface together.

"I have to stop," she said, laughing and gasping as she clung to the wall. "I haven't swum that fast for that long in ages."

"You are a very good swimmer," Reef said.

"So are you!"

The compliment shouldn't have meant much coming from a human, but it did, and Reef felt proud.

"We should swim together again," she said.

Was it just him, or had her pulse in the water quickened again? Or perhaps that was his own heart, which seemed now to reverberate through the entire pool, drowning out the tedious echoes of the water. "Yes," he agreed. Then he looked from her beaming smile out toward the surroundings of the pool, and sadness brought stillness back to him. He saw again the fin cape, which he had left bundled up on a chair.

"What do you want to do with it?" Kaeda asked gently.

"I want to release them into the sea."

"I'm sure we could work something out with the dov."

Reef nodded. "Archavie and I have spoken to him. He agreed but… I don't want to go alone."

"Won't Archavie go with you?"

"He will go on a boat, but he does not like to swim. He asked Harol and his people, and they agreed to go too, but I do not know them."

"I'll go!" Kaeda exclaimed. "Why didn't you ask me?"

"You were busy," Reef answered, feeling relieved and foolish at the same time.

"I'm busy, yes, but this is important."

"The Molvan ocean is not like the Gemmic Sea or the Farian reefs," he cautioned her, "It is dark, cold." He paused, remembering, and brightened, "but there are also forests unlike any other."

"Sounds intriguing," she said. "So, when do you want to go?"

Reef had been hoping to go the next day, to get a little reprieve from the endless humanness of the palace, especially before it filled up with guests for the ball tomorrow night. Archavie had gone on and on about the dancing, the music, the decorations, to such an extent that Reef wished it was already over. Any curiosity he had had at witnessing the human spectacle was long worn out.

He realized that he had only thought all of this and remembered that Kaeda could not read his mind. "Maybe tomorrow," he said.

"A break before the dreaded ball," Kaeda replied.

Reef blinked at her, surprised again. Archavie had spoken about the ball with unceasing enthusiasm.

"Unless you're looking forward to it?"

"No," Reef replied.

"Maybe we can get ourselves lost at sea," Kaeda sighed. She turned around, leaning her elbows on the pool's edge and letting her legs float out in the water. "Well, anyway, it will be nice to take a break from civilization. It's so peaceful in the water. You can't hear anyone talking."

Reef nodded, numb with astonishment as she voiced his own thoughts.

"I should probably get cleaned up before dinner. Whew, I'm too tired even to pull myself out of the water. I'll have to swim back to the steps."

"Here," Reef said. Then he remembered he should ask first. "I can lift you out."

"Sure, okay."

He sank into the water, wrapped an arm beneath her hips, and when Kaeda had put her arms around his neck, whipped his tail and lifted her out of the water, setting her on the edge of the pool.

She sat there while Reef sank back into the water. He thought she looked alarmed, her eyes bright, cheeks pink, catching her breath even though she had already caught it. "Are you alright?" he asked.

"Yes. I'm just tired. Give me a minute." At last, with a deep breath, she climbed to her feet. "I'll see you at dinner."

Chapter Thirty-Six

A BURIAL AT SEA

Reef

THE next day, with the dov's permission, Reef and Kaeda rode in carriages down to the harbor. North of the falls the harbor had been built into another notch in the rugged coastline, with tall walls of natural stone rising up on either side of the docks. Breakwaters extended further out to calm the choppiness of the waves, and tunnels, roads, and elevators provided access, "no matter what the weather conditions or cargo."

That was what Escort Adjuct Usenko said anyway. Apparently as guests of the dov Reef, Kaeda, Archavie, and Straton were entitled to use the elevator, which lowered their entire carriage slowly down the face of the stone, giving them a sweeping view of the ships at harbor and of the ocean, brilliantly lit by midday sun.

Seeing the ocean, anticipating the greeting of the water, Reef didn't even mind having Usenko along for the ride.

One of Voda's ships took them out, a ship called the *Katerina* which was large enough that the carriage could roll right onto it. Usenko had already cautioned them not to exit until they were out at sea. The people of the city might officially know that there was a Khirian at the palace, but few of them had seen him, and Voda wanted to keep it that way.

The carriage rocked gently as the ship set sail, and finally Usenko came to let them out.

"We are near the coast," he told them, "But a little north. Most merchant vessels will sail south, so hopefully you will not be disturbed."

"Thank you," Kaeda said.

"Are you sure you want to do this, healer? There's no need for you to go. We can send divers with him."

Reef bristled at Usenko's words, but he let Kaeda do the talking. "Of course I want to go. Reef is my friend. Besides, I miss being in the ocean."

When they were ready, Reef, Kaeda, and the divers Voda insisted on sending stood at the edge of the ship while Archavie, Straton, and Usenko stepped back. "We'll see you soon," the wizard said, and Reef and the others leapt from the side.

In a glorious instant the familiar chilly pressure of the ocean had wrapped around him. He shut his eyes as the invisible fingers of the ocean reached in through his fins and spread across his body like the fine filaments of a jellyfish. They filled him with the thousands of tiny stories of the aquatic plants and animals, knitting together into a mesh of constantly changing energy. The water felt thick, thick with the drag of weeds and boulders. The withdrawal of water from the rocky shore felt like a burbling rumble, ticklish in its tumbling. Around and above the rocks Reef felt the stolid hum of sea stars and limpets, and a gentle ruffling in the water told him a skate was swimming nearby. Far to the south he could sense the rumble of the falls, and… was that? No, it couldn't be.

He focused, trying to discern whether the distant chorus of beats and swishes could possibly belong to a shoal of Khirians, but the interference of the falls was too strong. They wouldn't be here. Not in the chill of the Molvan autumn. Not so close to a major city.

He shook the idea away, focusing instead on the comforting rhythm of Kaeda's heartbeat beside him.

When he opened his eyes there she was, waiting for him. He nodded his head toward the coast and began to swim, and she swam down after him.

They had come at midday, hoping for good light, but Molvan waters always seemed to be dark. Reef would try to choose a shallow location, where he could see Kaeda's face and where she wouldn't have to use her headlamp. He located the thick murky tugging of the willows and swam toward them. Soon he and Kaeda were navigating a rich swath of submarine forest. The willows looked much like their terrestrial counterparts, but with flexible trunks swaying in the tide. Their slightly curling branches tended to float, leaving open passage beneath the silver-green canopy.

Reef slowed to swim beside Kaeda. She rolled to the side to look at him, mouthing "wow!"

"Look," Reef mouthed back. He swam over to one of the trees and pointed out the tufts of red, pink, purple, and white decorating the trunk and branches. These belonged to creeping spirobranchus worms, whose residence in the forest made the willows appear to be constantly flowering. The soft drifting of their fluffy tops in the water created a sort of touchable fragrance that floated against Reef's fins with unmatched gentleness.

Of course, Kaeda couldn't feel that, but she smiled delightedly as she swam over to join him. She floated, holding onto a branch as an anchor, and studied the blooming worms. Her curly hair, shaken loose by their swim, drifted out around her face like a blossom of the finest sea grass, decorated by the dancing dappled light filtering through the willows.

Reef had thought before that these underwater forests were the most beautiful part of Molva, and maybe some of the most beautiful places in the world. Now he thought that he had never seen them complete before. He had never seen the ocean complete before, for he had never swum there with Kaeda. Her heartbeat, which he had felt first as a distant mystery, now seemed essential. If he visited these forests again without her, he would know, wouldn't he, that there was something missing?

As he thought it, as he considered the way Kaeda seemed to glow with warmth, not just visibly, but in his mind somehow, he had an idea, and idea for her name.

He would think about it later. Later when he could be alone and think clearly. As it was, he got Kaeda's attention and pointed ahead. He had spotted an especially large willow. He thought that it would be a good place to put the fins.

They swam over and Reef unfolded the fin cape bundle and handed it to Kaeda. Then, one by one he took the fins out and wrapped them around the tree's branches. Despite what the humans might say, Reef could not believe the fins were completely dead. Death, he thought, was just when all parts of a body stopped functioning together. That didn't mean they wouldn't function separately. Khirians assumed most of their organs and tissues took on new life in the ocean, but Reef suspected fins were different. He thought some part of a Khirian must go on being that Khirian, and since fins were the most Khirian part of a Khirian, they were most likely to carry on a Khirian's existence.

When the fins were all drifting gently in the water and the spirobranchus were beginning to crawl across them, Reef felt content. He watched them for a few minutes, then nodded back out to sea and began to swim again. Kaeda swam after him, and he could sense Voda's divers maintaining their distant patrol. As they exited the willow forest though, Reef sensed something else. Boats had arrived. Reef sensed three, not close, but close enough for him to feel uneasy. Hadn't Usenko said that not many ships sailed this direction?

Reef took a moment to identify the ship they had arrived on, resting solidly in the water. His instinct was to swim back to it as quickly as he could, but Kaeda and the other divers could not swim that fast, so he surfaced to breathe and then continued cruising slowly. The humans' heartbeats had not changed. They were not alarmed by the boats. But then, they probably didn't know they were there.

They were about halfway back to the ship when Reef felt a smack against the water. Something had been tossed in, and Reef recognized from the wavery way that it sank across his perception that it was a net and judging by the heavy slap of it, a weighted net.

So, fishermen, though he would have expected Molvan fishermen to use a midwater trawl. Calm, he told himself, and he reminded himself that he was not alone and reminded himself to swim slowly so he wouldn't leave Kaeda behind.

The boat that had dropped the net tilted and righted itself, as if it had not been prepared for the net's hurried descent. But the net did not continue to descend. Instead, it began to race horizontally toward Reef.

If the net moved like this it must be magical, and if magical, and if headed his way, probably made to catch Khirians.

Calm, calm, he told himself. You've been caught in a net before. You didn't die. You have better friends with you this time. Friends who won't let it end as it did before.

Still, he would see if he could make it to the ship. He could at least distance himself from Kaeda, so she would not be entangled with him.

He shot out west toward the ship. The net rushed in from the north. He would have to swim past the point where their paths collided before the net could reach it.

But he could have sworn that the net was gathering speed, changing shape, the center pulled forward and the rest of it extending behind like the legs of a huge, fibrous squid. There was a jerk as it broke its connection to its boat.

He would round the ship from the south, Reef thought, give the net as far to travel as possible. He swam faster. Water and fish flew thickly past him. A school of anchovies scattered in a shower of silver as Reef plunged through. When he emerged from them, he could see it, glinting silver in the blue of the ocean.

A thrill of fear ran down Reef's spine. He felt his heart pounding and his lungs beginning to burn, gauged the distance he had left to swim to the *Katerina,* and knew that he wouldn't make it, and knew that he needed to breathe before he became entangled in a weighted net.

He changed direction, making for the surface instead, and put all his energy into building up speed. He broke the surface in a rush, arcing into the air. "Archavie!" he shouted. At the same time, he felt something sharp bite into the end of his tail.

Time seemed to slow as he turned in the air and saw the net spreading itself beneath him, brilliant and ominous as a dew-clad spiderweb in the noon sun.

Reef gasped in as much air as he could, twisted to land on his back, stretching out his arms to keep the net from pinning his limbs to his body, and fell with a splash.

The net shrank around him as he plummeted down. The strange, weighted cables bit through his scales and backfin like a huge crisscrossing blade. Suddenly the water stabbed him. Currents dug into the cut and exposed nerves of his backfin in lightning bolts of pain.

Some part of Reef knew he shouldn't thrash and scream. Some part of him knew the net was tearing off his skin as he moved, and that his lungs were quickly emptying and that he was sinking farther and farther from the air he needed, but the agony was too intense for him to think or act rationally. Blood filled the water. Water filled his lungs.

Chapter Thirty-Seven

THE BITING NET

Kaeda

BLOOD blossomed in the water around Reef. Within moments I had lost sight of him in the cloud of it. I could swim no faster than I was already, screaming Turus's name into my mask of water breathing magic.

Either the Magic couldn't hear me, or he was busy. I was still too far out to place a mask of water breathing over Reef's face. All I could do was continue to kick my flippered feet, feeling hopelessly slow as the cloud of blood spread.

I watched as the *Katerina* closed in, as well as the hull of another, smaller boat, soon joined by several others. The center of the red blossom began to rise. Then it jerked and began to move in a different direction. As I broke the surface, I saw that a fishing boat had hooked the net and was trying to pull it up onto its boom, while Archavie, Straton, and Escort Adjuct Usenko shouted from the deck of the Katerina. Usenko, Archavie, and my father all reached toward the net. It seemed that they had begun to draw it up by magic, and were now in a tug of war with the other ship.

"This Khirian is a guest of the dov," Usenko called. "Release him at once!"

"Capturing Khirians off the coast is still legal," called a fisherman from his boat. "I think you'll find I have all the necessary permits for catching just about anything."

Reef's head broke the surface, and I heard a sound I had heard once before: the keening cry of a Khirian afraid and in pain. I dove again to continue swimming but bobbed up again at once.

"Khirians!" My warning came just as the first Khirian leapt from the water onto the side of the fishing boat. Within seconds ten or fifteen more had jumped aboard or scaled the sides.

For a moment I floated paralyzed in the water, as skirmishes erupted on the fishing boats and human bodies were thrown into the water, then I saw the rope from the lead boat go slack, and Reef fall back into the water. He would drown without my help.

I ducked back into the water, only to see a Khirian swimming straight at me. I shrieked into my water breathing magic, but the Khirian didn't attack. I recognized her: Beach Cliffs, the huge Khirian whose eggs I had delivered. She whipped forward, grabbed me around the waist, and swam so fast that the water nearly tore my hair from my head.

She carried me straight to Reef. When we surfaced, I saw other Khirians, glazed pink by Reef's blood, gathered around the net, trying unsuccessfully to pull it off. Each who tried cried out in dismay as the net cut their hands.

"It's enchanted," I shouted. "The teeth in the net are enchanted to cut Khirians. Frils!" I had woven an extra-large wrapping of waterbreathing magic, but I couldn't get it through the enchanted net.

The Khirians argued around me, probably about why I was here, and I shouted again to be heard over their voices. "We have to get him out of the water. Listen to me! The net is magic. Only humans will be able to get it off. We have to get him up on a boat."

"Call off your forces!" Usenko shouted down. "Call off your forces now or we'll leave him in the water."

"Please!" I said to Beach Cliffs. "Tell them to stop! If we don't get Reef out of this, he will die!"

For a second that felt like an age she held my gaze, then she barked an order. The attacking Khirians retreated, leaping back into the water, but Beach Cliffs and one other remained, watching.

"I think we can manage to levitate him into a lifeboat," Usenko called.

They hauled two lifeboats up, one with Reef and I aboard, and one carrying Beach Cliffs and her swimmer. As my boat inched its way up the side, I crouched by Reef and tried to find the edges of the net and pull it away. "You're going to be alright," I said, "just hold on." By the time we had reached the deck though this had turned to, "Reef? Reef! Stay with me."

He wasn't moving. Where could I find a pulse? Why didn't his chest rise? I managed to uncover his face, and found one eye destroyed, the other closed, his jaw limp. Until now I had acted with a healer's steadiness in crisis, but now I found myself shaking. Why? He was just a patient. Wasn't he?

"Reef? Reef?"

"Get him on the deck," Straton's voice said, followed by Usenko's order to get the net off.

"No," I cried, for as they tried to pull the net off it tore pieces of Reef's skin off with it.

"Healer?" Usenko asked.

"Kaeda, what should we do?" asked Straton.

Blood, blood in lines across his face, blood creeping across the deck, and every beat of my heart reverberating through me as if I had been struck. I could feel nothing but its dread thunder. I could see nothing but Reef's blood. He would die. It would be my fault. The beat of my heart had become so strong I could swear I could feel it in the boards beneath my feet and shivering in the air around me.

It wasn't just me. The sailors, even Usenko, staggered as if the ship had rocked, and shaded their eyes as the sun on the water turned into a blinding blaze. I thought maybe this had to do with my panic, but I couldn't stop it. I felt lost, terrified. Then I felt my father's hands settled onto my shoulders. He said one word, "Calm." Magic flowed from his palms, flooding my nervous system, and I relaxed so quickly that I nearly fell, and found myself leaning back against my father.

Everyone was looking at me, I realized, but Archavie refocused their attention as he asked briskly, "do you have another medic on board?"

"Yes, but to treat a Khirian –"

"Don't worry about that."

A warm gust of wind and magic swept across the deck and swirled around us. Feeling dazed, I watched as the net, Reef, and a red mist of blood, lifted into the air. The shape in the net changed, shrinking and shifting. Then all at once the net fell away. Beach Cliffs shrieked as she saw the hulking human form Archavie had once again used to disguise Reef.

As Reef settled back onto the deck two Molvans ran over, saying words I should have been saying myself. "I'm going to set an erythropoietic enchantment in his larger bones."

"I'll start the IV with a crystalloid solution," the other replied.

"I'll knit the wounds," I stammered. That, at least, I was sure I could do.

I knelt at Reef's side, took apart my water breathing magic, and made it into a wound-knitting tangle instead. Meanwhile Beach Cliffs shrilled Khirian words. I had seen the other swimmer try to hold her back, but it was a group of Voda's soldiers with lightning-crackling spears that stopped her from advancing on us.

"It's a temporary measure," Straton assured her.

"What?" she screamed in response. "What done?!"

"We've saved his life," Usenko answered coldly.

As if to prove his words, Reef's intact eyelid drifted open. A mossy green iris looked up at me and I found myself laughing and crying at the same time as I held his half-healed face in my hands. "You're okay," I said, in a shivering voice that was utterly unlike myself. "You're going to be okay."

The negotiations that followed were a blurry backdrop as we sailed to the harbor. All I knew was that Usenko persuaded Beach Cliffs and the others to leave, with a promise that they would be in touch, and would be allowed to see Reef again at some point.

"I don't know what we'll do about the fishermen," I heard Usenko say to my father. "It's a nightmare, but the public relations team will deal with it."

The nightmare had preceded us to the harbor, and it seemed that the entire city had turned out to witness our return. Probably they had come to see a Khirian, or Khirians in custody. What they saw was a stunningly beautiful young man crisscrossed by a frightening web of scars, being rushed into an ambulance as quickly as possible.

"Whoa, so it's man-time again, huh?" asked Gamalielle, leaping out of the crowd as we hurried toward Voda's waiting carriage. "Not quite as gorgeous as I remember."

"You don't need to come with us," I said as the medics and I settled Reef onto the bed in the ambulance and anchored a vital-monitoring halo over his head.

"Sure, I do. I need to hear the story before its corrupted by the masses."

"I'll tell you later." I felt almost empty of emotion now, and I didn't want to risk feeling again if I relieved the events.

"Fine," the cat grumbled. She left and my father checked, as he had many times, to make sure we were all alright. Then the doors of the carriage closed, shutting Archavie, Reef, and I inside. The wheels began to turn, the ambulance gently wobbled as it moved along the harbor's crowded street. I watched Reef's vital signs continue to improve. The wizard looked at the ceiling of the ambulance and said nothing.

Archavie saying nothing. That was strange. I looked up across at the wizard where he sat in one of the ambulances folding seats. He had sat there the whole time, not moving at all. There was a hard glint in his blue eyes as he stared back at me, a disdaining anger that I didn't recognize.

"Archavie, are you alright?"

"Oh, now you ask," he replied in a bitter tone. "My wizard only saved your miserable lizard friend's life. Again. Some gratitude."

"Turus!" I exclaimed.

"In the flesh."

"You've taken over Archavie's body?"

The wizard's eyes flicked back and forth irritably, though the rest of his body didn't move.

"Where's Archavie?" I asked.

"As far as I can tell he's resting, though I can hardly be sure. There wasn't much of me here, so my wizard bore more of the magic-working strain. Plague of a reptile," he snarled at Reef. "Always falling apart in bloody pieces!"

"That's hardly Reef's fault," I said, and then added. "Severe mag'kourasi – that is, magician's fatigue. It can lead to a magic-work-induced coma, but Archavie can't work magic."

"No, but he can be awfully convincing, can't he? He wanted me to do this, I did, but I had to rely on him, and of course he burned out. I suppose you can't tell me how long it will last?"

I had never heard of a Magic animating his wizard's body while the wizard was in a coma. I supposed Turus could only do it because of his mind-control abilities. "No, I'm sorry, I don't know."

Turus rolled Archavie's eyes. "I need the rest of myself back. This would never have happened if I were at full power."

We hadn't made any progress on finding out who had Turus, and whether there was any chance of recovering him, and I could hardly think about it now.

"I'll never be a priority, none of you like me anyway. Not that I care."

"Maybe this will give you a greater appreciation for Archavie. Everyone likes him."

Turus made no response to this. We rode to the palace in uneasy silence and settled Reef into his bed in a similar uneasy silence before heading to the decision suite where Dov Voda paced behind his desk.

"The ball will have to be postponed. Again," he said to Secretary Essen, who looked like the calmest person in the room. The secretary took notes assiduously while the dov said, "Send the necessary notes of apology. Reschedule everything for two weeks from today. By then the chatter should have died down. Come in. Sit down."

This last was aimed at us. Most of us did as he asked, but Archavie's body merely staggered across the carpet, dragging its feet, and leaned against the wall. This seemed to be all Turus could manage to make it do.

When we had all taken our places the dov sat down behind his desk. "We have an important decision to make, which is whether to change Reef back to his Khirian form or pretend Reef has been a human all along, cursed into Khirian form by some…"

"Jealous enchantress," Essen supplied.

"Yes, excellent."

"I don't think Reef would want to stay in human disguise," I said.

"Do you think he would prefer further attempts on his life?" the dov asked, and while I deliberated this with myself, he went on. "Yes, a young soldier spurns the affections of an enchantress who then curses him to live the rest of his life as a Khirian until…"

"Until he experiences as much pain as she felt when she refused him?" the secretary suggested, and the dov gave a sharp nod.

"Perfect."

"It's not perfect," I said. "It's a lie."

"It's a lie that will make the people love him," Essen countered, pen poised in the air, "And that will keep him safe."

"And also calm those who opposed you welcoming a Khirian in the first place," I said.

"A pleasing side effect," the dov agreed. "We could even say that the other Khirians were not Khirians at all, but minions of the enchantress. That way we can avoid reigniting Khiri-Molvan hostilities."

"Brilliant," Essen agreed.

I couldn't believe it. "Turus, are you really not going to stand up for Reef?"

Archavie's eyes flicked towards me. "The social bickering of mortals is pointless and beneath me. I care only for finding my counterpart and whether Reef has a tail or not hardly makes a difference."

"General?" I appealed to my father next.

General Straton answered reluctantly, "he would be safer in human form."

While I gaped in disbelief Gamalielle said, "I don't know why you're so upset, Kaeda. Now he's the right shape to get cozy with a human lady. Isn't that what you want?" The blood rushed to my face. As I faced Gamalielle, she threw up her hands and went on. "I saw you two swimming together. I think it's gross, but who am I to judge?"

Frils?! Now everyone would know! My father too! I couldn't bring myself to look at any of them but felt the embarrassment covering my skin like a fresh sunburn.

For a long moment no one said anything, then the secretary murmured, "Rescued by his true love."

"Put it in the story," the dov agreed.

"No," I exclaimed.

"The people will love it," Essen said.

"No. I refuse to let you make me a part of this charade."

"Healer Straton, if you don't want to be a part of it, then feel free to go home." The dov's sharp brown eyes leveled a testing look at me, as if he just dared me to do it.

You'd like that, wouldn't you, I thought. You would like me to go, give up on my research. I folded my arms. "I can't control what rumors you spread, but don't expect me to play a part."

Gamalielle guffawed with scornful laughter. "Yeah, like that's going to be a problem, lizard-lover."

We walked back towards our guest quarters. Gamalielle had a grand time levitating Archavie, since Turus didn't seem to be able to manage the wizard's legs very well. As the two of them lagged behind, my father walked beside me and asked, "Is it true?"

"Is it true what Gamalielle and Archavie say about you and Lady Batbayar?" I didn't know why I said it. I knew they had formed a romantic attachment and I had already decided I didn't mind.

"That is hardly a fair comparison," my father said easily. "But yes, it is true, and I would be happy to talk about it if it bothers you."

"It doesn't," I said, brushing my hand across my eyes. Suddenly I felt very tired. "But I'm sorry if it bothers you that I like Reef."

"I didn't say it did. I only asked."

"Does it not bother you?" I turned toward him, noticing that he really didn't look angry or alarmed, only attentive and concerned and calm as always.

He answered in keeping with his expression, sounding very much like a general giving an analysis. "In my interactions with Reef he has seemed responsible, brave, self-controlled, much like many of the soldiers I have commanded in the past. But he is a man-eating war lizard."

I opened my mouth to object, but my father held up a hand. "He is a man-eating war lizard, and I am one of those responsible for Project Shatter. Which of us is responsible for more deaths, I cannot say, but I do know what it is like to hope people can look beyond the past."

He had stopped walking, and I stopped beside him. Archavie and Gamalielle did not catch up to us. We were passing the pool ballroom and Gamalielle had gotten the idea to levitate Archavie's body out over the water, cackling as Turus protested.

"How could you do it?" I asked in a whisper.

"I was hoping to save lives, the lives of my soldiers. I gave guidelines, required distance for safe detonation." He shook his head and for the first time looked sad and angry, but only in his eyes. "I was so used to being in charge, it didn't occur to me that they wouldn't listen, that destroying the enemy would be more important than preserving the safety of civilians."

Now I really wanted to scream, for the misunderstanding and the years of pain. All this time I had been blaming him, but if I had known his side of the story, I would have mourned with him. "Why didn't you tell me?"

"Because I hold myself responsible. I helped develop the weapons. I did not want an excuse, I wanted…"

"Forgiveness."

He nodded.

I wouldn't have thought before that moment that I could have given it to him, but now… well, I wavered. "And leaving us?" I asked.

Turus had righted Archavie in the air now and seemed to be engaged in a magical push-and-pull competition with Gamalielle as he tried to reach the balcony and she tried to keep him dangling in the air. I wondered if I should intervene, but at least no one was getting hurt. I watched a moment while I waited for my father to answer.

"I have no excuse for that either," he said at last. "It seemed… it seemed as if you had moved on. As far as I could see, you were doing well. Your mother and I were the only turmoil remaining. I thought if I were gone… you might have more peace."

As far as he could see? Well, yes, I had found the appearance of wellness in constant business, and even now that was where I found the most peace. But that wasn't enough anymore.

While I considered this, Turus began to pull himself in, hauling on the air as if climbing a rope. My father spoke again. "I also left Georgina, a long time ago, before I met your mother.

I also thought she would be better off without the complication of having me in her life. I was a young soldier, and she was a lady. I have learned, once again, that I was wrong. I can't fix as many things as I would like. I can't put the island back together. I can't apologize to your mother. But what I can repair…"

Turus made it back to the balcony. Gamalielle gave a little shriek and ran. It looked as if Turus would send Archavie's body chasing after her, but instead the wizard tumbled to the floor. "Frils!" he said.

"I like fixing things," I said quickly. "Forgiveness is not an easy treatment but if that's what the break requires…" I looked at my father. "I can do it."

Frils, that sounded so medical, yet I wasn't sure I could bring myself to say, "I forgive you."

He seemed to accept my words though, a shine in his eyes made them less steel and more ocean as we began walking again, Gamalielle leaping ahead and Turus staggering behind.

"What did you do to me on the boat?" I asked. Now that we had gotten the romantic complications out of the way I was remembering my panic, and my father's calming magic.

"You don't remember?" he asked, surprise softening his face.

"Remember what?"

"I used to calm you when you were a child. But perhaps this is a conversation best had another time," he added, as Turus shuffled past us.

"Don't mind me," the magic muttered with Archavie's voice. "Have your moment. I'll just go on wrestling with this mortal flesh. Ugh, now I understand why humans spend eight hours laying down each day."

A buzz of electricity seemed to have settled around me at my father's words. The hum of energy told me that I did remember, yet I couldn't remember, not clearly. I only remembered that most of my hugs when I was young came from my father, and that they were good hugs.

He gestured back towards the stairs that would take us down to the greenhouse and we walked down them and across the stone floor until we reached a wicker bench with golden cushions, bordered on either side by stands of lilacs. A long planter of impatiens separated us from the pool, but I could see the water, vacillating with its usual shimmer.

When we had settled ourselves on the bench, my father took a deep breath and said, "When you were little, if you got upset, magic reacted to you. It didn't start until you were three, and if there was no magic on the island, it didn't matter, but if there was magic... well, your mother didn't want to put a magical restraint on you. She said you wouldn't be able to learn magic-working properly if you wore one. She said you might grow out of IMWEES, or you might learn how to manage your emotions. She wanted as few interventions as possible."

I could tell from the tone in my father's voice that he didn't agree, and I saw his brow furrow as he looked out toward the water. It was a very Reef-like expression. Or maybe Reef's thinking expression was very like my father's.

"Maybe I should have let you wrestle with it, but you were a child, and I had learned in the Dunamis how to calm a frightened civilian or a panicking soldier. I used those skills to calm you, so the IMWEES wouldn't get out of control. And it seemed that you did grow out of it. By the time I left, I was sure you would be alright."

"When?" I asked, "When did it stop?"

I knew the answer before he said it, "Soon after Gil died. It seemed that when the grief faded, the IMWEES had burned out with it."

I remembered that day, when Gil had gone from silly little brother to blood-coughing patient to lifeless shell, all over the course of twenty-four hours. And I remembered my father's arms around me.

"Is that why you held me?" I stammered. Now that I began to consciously recall the events, I remembered my father holding me many times after Gil's death, and a couple of times carrying me back to my bedroom, where a magic-filtering net had been hung up around my bed. They said it was to protect me from the overflow of frils from the continent, but now I wondered if it was to protect everyone else from the effects of childhood somnumancy.

"I would have held you anyway," my father said. "Your brother had just died. But yes, I calmed you, and your mother and I fought about whether to make a magical restraint for you. She said you would learn to manage yourself as you got older. I said it wasn't fair to not treat the IMWEES for you. But it seems she was right. You've managed your emotions and your magical capabilities just fine."

A strange thing had happened. As he talked, the electrical buzz of revelation faded to nothing. I sat and I listened, and I felt nothing. Yes, I thought, I have managed my emotional and magical capabilities just fine, I thought to myself.

And I didn't believe myself at all.

I hadn't managed my emotions. I had simply stopped them when they became uncomfortable, as my father had stopped them when I was a child. The IMWEES hadn't burned out with the grief. The grief hadn't been able to burn. I hadn't felt it all the way, so it had lingered, gone cold. It was still there. I could feel it, the weight that never left.

Another emotional swell rose at this revelation, but I shut it down without even trying. I remembered Tsakhia shaking the room, and Nadia saying she tried to keep him calm so he wouldn't melt anything. I wasn't like that. I didn't melt things. And I didn't want to melt things. Even if it meant carrying cold grief.

I remembered the deck shivering beneath my feet as I watched Reef bleed. Good thing I didn't feel strong emotions that often. Reef was fine now, and next time someone was in peril, I would be prepared. I felt, now, completely justified in not feeling my feelings.

My father was scrutinizing me, and now I nodded. "Thank you for telling me," I said.

"Are you alright?" he asked.

"Better than ever," I said.

Chapter Thirty-Eight

WHEN I WAS YOUNG

Reef

REEF kept waiting for his mind to settle. He felt that he was caught in waves of thought and feeling. Everything was okay, he told himself. He was in the bed that he had slept in for some days in Vodastad. It was fine. Everything was fine.

Then the net, the stabbing water, the chaos of light and sensation and sound, the fishermen, the Khirians, and her, Kaeda. In his mind her familiar face and her gentle voice changed to a different face with the same brown skin but a very different panicked, screaming voice.

He couldn't make it stop. Whenever he thought he had anchored himself well enough to sit up, another wave of panic and terror would paralyze him again.

He was still laying there when Kaeda came to check on him again. He couldn't bring himself to look at her, but he heard her say, "how are you feeling?"

How was he feeling? He hoped she couldn't see. He hoped the human face he wore wouldn't give it away, wouldn't spill his secrets as the net had spilled his blood.

"Are you in any pain?"

He shook his head.

"You're basically back together in one piece now. Of course, I'm not sure what the effects will be when you are Khirian shaped again." She paused. "The dov wants you to remain in disguise for now," and she told him the story of a young soldier cursed to be Khirian.

No, no, Reef thought. That's not right. I have been Khirian since I hatched.

Then he remembered that it was just a story.

"The dov says he'll bring Beach Cliffs and some of the others in to visit secretly when you're ready."

No, no, they couldn't see him like this. "Not yet," he said.

Eventually Kaeda left, and then eventually returned bringing a tray of dinner. Straton came as well, bringing two more trays. The general sat one on Reef's bed and took the other to the small table nearby. He and Kaeda sat and ate, Kaeda commenting that the pelmeni were very good and the general occasionally remarking to Reef that eating might help him feel better.

Reef couldn't bring himself to say anything.

They left. Night fell. Exhausted, Reef slept, but the uncertainty persisted in his dreams.

He was trapped. The net wrapped him like a spider web. He wriggled like a bug trapped inside. He couldn't swim. He couldn't breathe. The blaze of the sun. Something struck him. Something else. The blows kept falling. His bones would break, he thought. He would shatter. He would be useless. They would leave him behind.

Something passed by. In the dream Reef couldn't see it, but he knew it was there. He lashed out. He caught it in his jaws. Water rushed around him again. No, blood. The blood gushed from his mouth in thick pulses, surrounding him.

"Let go! Reef, let go!"

He heard Kaeda's voice, but he couldn't let go. His arms and legs felt limp and broken, aching. If he let go he would be swept away in the flood.

"Reef! Reef!"

Finally, his heavy eyelids blinked open. He saw a lamp and Kaeda lit by its yellow glow. Still, he tasted blood. Straton's arm was around his chest, holding him still, and with his currently human-shaped teeth Reef had bitten that arm hard enough to break the skin. He yelled in alarm.

"General Straton is working some mild sedating magic," Kaeda said. "Hopefully it will help you calm down. You were having a nightmare. We came to help."

He didn't think the magic was working. He felt weighted and slow, but not calm. His thoughts, the images in his mind, only fuzzed together, but carried on, turning the lamp into a golden blaze of sun, the twisted sheets into a net. Kaeda's face shifted forms, young and old, male and female. His human throat kept making strange screeching noises. He didn't seem to be able to stop.

"Is he awake?" Straton's voice sounded in his ear.

"I think he is. You can let go. I don't think he'll hurt himself now. Reef, Reef, listen to my voice. Look around you. Whatever you dreamed, it is over. You're here now."

Reef did his best to follow her instructions as Straton let him go. He lay back on the rug beside his bed and looked, seeing the papered walls, the coffered ceiling, the stupidly ornate little table, knocked over, a broken pitcher on the ground beside it.

This was all well and good, until his scan of the room reached Kaeda. At the sight of her face the memory stabbed him, and Reef found himself shrieking again, the blood, water, and sun blinding him again. It wasn't just in him. It was in her. He couldn't look at her. He couldn't be near her.

"Let me try," General Straton said. Reef didn't know if the general moved to block his sight of Kaeda on purpose, but he did. Then he said, "Place your palm on the floor like this."

Reef did.

"What does it feel like?"

Reef felt the rug and hauled words from the recesses of his mind to describe it. "Rough. Soft. Warm."

"Run your hand along it. How does it feel?"

"Flat. Solid."

While Straton gave him one sensory task after another, Kaeda slowly rose to her feet and just as slowly inched toward the door.

Eventually, the room was all Reef saw. The terror had seeped away, like water sinking into sand. Straton helped him back into his bed, then fetched a book on Molvan flora and fauna and read to Reef until he fell asleep.

When morning came, Reef was surprised to see the general still there, asleep in his chair. When Reef shifted in his bed, sitting up, Straton stirred and rubbed his eyes.

"How are you feeling?" the general asked.

"Better," Reef answered. The morning light bathed his room in cool calm. Reef could hardly believe it was the same room he had looked around the night before.

They sat in silence for some minutes, then Straton said, "I've spent most of my life with soldiers. I expected certain things from them. Then, the war." He paused. "Healers can take the shrapnel out of your body, but not out of your mind. Sometimes it takes another person to do that."

Reef had never heard the general say so many words in a row, and he couldn't quite believe them. Was Straton offering himself as a support and ally? Why? The general had been reasonable and civil when Reef first joined the Commission, but Reef couldn't quite believe Straton was on his side. Then again, last night Reef had bitten him, and yet here he was.

Perhaps it was the disguise, the story, perhaps Straton believed it. "Do you say this because of my human face?" Reef asked.

"It is easier to talk to this face," Straton admitted. "But I say it because you are a soldier. If you're anything like the human soldiers I have known… to many of them war seemed like a nightmare. Hard to make sense of."

One had no say over what happened in a nightmare. Maybe that was why Reef could dismiss so many of his memories from the war. They felt inevitable, hazy with fear and the flow of necessity. This memory though… it was not like a nightmare. It was too sharp, too real, and too fraught with responsibility.

A knock at the door. Reef glanced over, realizing too late that it would be Kaeda, coming to check on him. She looked around the door and Reef bent his head and hid his eyes at the sight of her face. The room screamed. The light was too bright. Reef tried to shut out the sound of her voice as she asked how he was doing. He heard Kaeda and Straton carry out a whispered conversation, meanwhile his memories of Kaeda flashed through his mind. Her dappled face beneath the ocean willows. Circling each other in the dov's pool. Sitting on the island in the river, talking over the fin cape. Her body pressed against his when he snatched her from the waves when their lifeboat had crashed. And then all the way back to her face, her shocked and frightened face, when he climbed over the edge of Harol's boat, finding a healer for Beach Cliffs.

If he told her, he would go back, all the way back to her shocked, wide eyes. Further. To some point he hadn't even seen yet where Kaeda would revile him, speak of him with disgust as most humans did.

Reef found his human body doing another strange thing, shaking, and heaving, tears pouring from his eyes. "What? What is happening?" he managed.

"You're crying," Kaeda answered. "What is it? What has upset you?"

Reef heard a shifting of furniture, and a hand rested on his shoulder. It was Kaeda's, he could tell by the lightness of it, and her touch made him tense from head to toe.

She removed her hand. "Did he say anything to you?" she asked.

"No," Straton answered. "Not yet."

"It might help to put it into words," Kaeda said. "You can tell us."

He would have to tell her, Reef thought, or all their rapport would mean nothing, wouldn't it? But he remembered what she had said: that the worst thing he could do to a human was hurt their family and friends. It would be the end. She would hate him as he hated Miro. Straton would leave, no longer sit beside his bed, and treat him as a fellow soldier.

But would it take the shrapnel out of his mind? Would it allow him to think clearly and stop these strange reactions?

It didn't matter. He couldn't do it.

"Perhaps it would be easier for Reef to talk to me," Straton said.

A long moment of silence passed, then Kaeda said, "I'll be in the library if you need me."

Reef heard her footsteps, the door opening and closing. When he knew she was gone he relaxed right away, but left his face hidden in his hands. He didn't want to look up until he knew what to do.

The shifting of a chair. Straton moved closer. "Healer Straton's presence disturbs you," the general commented.

There was no denying it. "Yes," Reef said.

"Can you tell me why?"

To get the shrapnel out of my mind, thought Reef. To make this panic end. "They caught me." He had never said it aloud to anyone, at least not anyone who didn't already know. "Farians." He had to pause to breathe, for the memory swelled again and set his human form trembling. Holding on to his sanity and presence in the room was very much like holding on to an anchoring rock while the surf rolled. He tried to relate what he remembered.

"Some of the older hatchlings said something about hunting humans. I had never hunted humans. I had never seen one. We neared a boat, and I was caught in a net. It took me from the others. It pulled me from the water."

The sun overhead. The blinding reflection of the water. The sudden barrage of strange voices. His thrashing, their bludgeoning as they tried to subdue the strange creature they had hauled from the water.

"You were taken from your place of safety," General Straton said, in the same calm voice as always. "From the protection of your group."

"They came to help," Reef said, remembering the sudden screams, flashes of white scale, red blood through the tangle of the net. The blood shone like the water. The boards of the deck became a plane of glossy blood and dazzling seawater. "They started killing the humans."

The other hatchlings freed him from the net, but Reef had felt no relief, no safety. He was bruised all over. It hurt to breathe. It hurt to stand. "I had to prove I was not too hurt to fight," he said. "They might leave me behind. I looked for a human to fight. There was a small one. I expected him to fight me. All Khirians fight, even the newly hatched Khirians fight. The human didn't. His throat. The blood. I can't let go. I can't let go."

The other hatchlings had thought it impressive and funny, the way Reef clung to the boy while the adult humans screamed and tried to free their offspring. Reef simply hadn't known what to do. His decision-making powers had reached their limit and left him paralyzed, clinging to the child with his jaws.

"You can let go now," Straton said. It was his hand on Reef's shoulder this time, and for whatever reason, Reef removed one tear-glazed hand from his face and put it over the general's hand. It was as if he hoped he could hold onto that instead, and let go the memory, let go the child.

"I wanted to escape to the water," Reef said, as he clung to Straton's hand, which was nearly as large as his own, "but someone said, 'it tastes like sea lion.' Then we all had to do it. I don't like eating mammals. I felt sick for days."

Straton was silent. He remained there while Reef breathed, and the pain of the memory slipped away in a way it never had before. It wasn't gone, and it wasn't all better, but it did not seem so unbearable now. At last Reef let go of Straton and the general settled back in his chair.

Feeling calmer, tired and empty as if he had been for a long, hard swim, Reef brushed away his tears. He might as well explain the rest of the problem. General Straton seemed to understand other humans well enough that he would be able to tell Reef what he should do. "Kaeda says the worst thing you can do to a human is harm their family or friends. I killed them. I ate them. I have done the worst thing."

"So have I," Straton put in, before Reef could continue. When Reef turned his head to regard the general, Straton went on. "I helped design the explosives that decimated Fari. I am sure I am responsible for the loss of more Farian lives than you are, yet Kaeda… she has forgiven me, at least partly."

Reef did not fully understand what had happened to Fari. He had been stationed in Molva at the time, but he understood that the weapons that had hurt the island had been deployed at a distance. "You did not mean to kill them, did you?"

"Did you?" Straton asked.

Reef felt as though his mind were tying itself in knots trying to understand all of this. "I… I wanted to survive. I wanted to… do what they wanted me to do."

"And you said you were a hatchling?"

"I was small." Smaller than many in the group, Reef added to himself. That was part of the problem. If only he had been a little bigger, he wouldn't have needed to prove himself so much.

"How big were you?"

Reef didn't know why it mattered, but he assumed the general would not be one to ask idle questions. "My eyes were not above the human's elbows," he said, which was the best answer he could give.

"You were a child," Straton said.

Reef didn't see what that had to do with anything. He stared intently at the general's face, waiting for him to explain, and he did.

"Humans usually recognize that children need extra protection, and extra guidance in making decisions. We don't hold children responsible in the same way we do adults. I understand that it may be different for you. Young reptiles are often like... miniature adults. But Khirians are sentient. It is possible that Khirians have a childhood."

More mind knots. Reef had always thought the relationships between human parents and offspring, to the extent that he had witnessed them, strange indeed. Human parents took care of their children. No one had ever treated him that way. He had never thought of himself as different when he was younger, besides that he was smaller and more pathetic and had to fight more to survive. But he also remembered the terror of his early life, and the fierce and frightened competition between young Khirians and he wondered.

"Was there a time when you recognized that you became an adult?" Straton asked.

"At the end of the war," Reef said. "I took control of my shoal. I said that eating humans had made Khirians crazy, wanting to stay and fight through the cold weather. I took them back through the rivers to the sea."

"If you can recognize that you became an adult, doesn't it stand to reason that you were something other than that before?"

While Reef frowned over this, Straton added, "And you didn't eat people after that?"

"None of us did."

"Eating humans in the war doesn't seem to bother you like eating the Farians did."

"It became… routine," Reef said, hoping that didn't sound too heartless. "It scared the humans."

"It certainly did."

"I needed to. I needed to do what everyone else did, for my reputation, for my safety, so that I could have a chance to get the others to listen to me."

He *had* gotten them to listen to him. He remembered the journey home, the harrowing trek through Molva, the joy of being in the sea, the peril of the political bloodshed on the archipelago. Reef had focused on keeping his shoal out of it and keeping them together. Eventually the navarch had risen to the top of the fighting and things had settled into the shape they were.

"And would you eat people again?" Straton asked.

A terrible question. Reef's fists clenched. His stomach knotted. He remembered easily the taste of human flesh, especially having recently bitten Straton's arm.

While he hesitated, Straton said, "You think you need to do this for respect or safety, but your soldiers, the ones in your shoal, came all the way to Molva to make sure you were safe. They seem to care about your wellbeing a great deal."

Perhaps that was true, Reef thought. He always thought about what he needed to do for them, to preserve his leadership and ensure his shoal's health. Maybe they were thinking about him too.

"If you want more for the Khirians than a fight for survival, you may have to lead them to it by showing them how."

Reef couldn't help but think that this was a very dangerous idea. He didn't want to go too far and end up getting himself killed.

"I will think about it," he said.

To his surprise, Straton nodded. "Think about it when you are calm and have eaten some breakfast. I am sure breakfast is ready by now. I am also sure that Kaeda is waiting in suspense to know what is on your mind. If you have the energy to explain it to her now, I will go and find her."

Yes, Reef thought, he felt spent but he would much rather explain now before he could talk himself out of it. He nodded and Straton went and fetched Kaeda. When they returned Reef was sitting up, feeling far more settled even in his human skin. Kaeda sat down, and Reef told her the story. It was not as difficult as he thought it would be, especially now that he had General Straton sitting nearby. Even if Kaeda was horrified, even if she refused to ever speak to him again, at least he knew General Straton would remain his ally.

She did seem horrified. She listened to most of the story with a hand over her mouth and tears streaming down her cheeks. Then she said, "Oh, Reef, I'm so sorry that happened to you."

Reef could hardly believe it. He repeated what he had said to Straton, that he had killed and at times eaten many humans since then, in the war.

Kaeda wept a little more and asked, "Do you think it was right?"

Right? "It was necessary," Reef answered. "What is right and what it necessary…" he frowned, his mind was getting tangled in knots again. Surely what was right was always the most necessary? And yet it didn't seem that way.

"Would you do it again?" she asked.

How had she and Straton arrived at the same question? He didn't think they had planned it, but perhaps they simply wanted to secure their people against further attack.

"If it would help the Khirians," Reef began, but Kaeda interrupted.

"Would it help them? Would it help them to have another leader perpetuate the atrocities of war?"

Without perpetuating those atrocities, a Khirian might never become a leader, Reef thought. But then he remembered what Straton had said, that his shoal seemed to really value him, when most of Reef's decisions had been to keep them out of fighting, lead them away from violence.

"I don't know," Reef said. "I have to think about it."

Kaeda nodded, taking a deep sniffling breath as she sat up straight in her chair once more. She brushed her tears away and said, "let me know when you've made a decision."

"And now, perhaps we can find Reef some breakfast?" Straton suggested.

"Yes," Kaeda nodded. "You should eat before you meet with your shoal."

For a moment his heart leapt, thrilled that he would get to see them soon. Then he saw the human hands resting on the bedspread in front of him. Would they recognize him, he wondered? Would they believe he was Reef?

Chapter Thirty-Nine

MISSING

Reef

FOR the sake of his blood sugar, whatever that was, Kaeda insisted he eat. Then, dressed in the stiff Vodaniyan clothes that Straton had found in his closet, and still feeling tumbled inside from their conversations, Reef, Straton, and Kaeda went to the dov's decision suite. Turus excused himself, saying he didn't care to be near Reef's mind, and he was sure Reef could act as translator. As for Gamalielle… she was nowhere to be found.

General Straton filled him in on the way, telling Reef that Voda had negotiated with the Khirians, smuggling a few into the palace during the night so that they could check on Reef once he had recovered enough to see them. It was that or risk further skirmishes and bloodshed.

When they arrived Voda was sitting at his desk, the black shape of Svevolod rising behind him like a menacing shadow. He motioned for them to sit, and Reef sank into one of the chairs opposite the dov's desk, but found himself fidgeting, wishing he had a tail to swish to release the nervous energy. At least he didn't have to wait long. A bookshelf slid to the side, opening a hidden door, and several guards stepped through, and then Beach Cliffs and two other swimmers.

Reef leapt to his feet, his entire body thrumming with the pounding of his heart. The Khirians lined up against the wall to the left of the dov's desk and stood looking at Reef. Silence settled on the room so thickly that when Beach Cliff's spoke her voice sounded almost muffled.

"Really Reef?" she asked in Molvan.

Reef coughed a Khirian yes.

Beach Cliffs spoke in Khirian next, her eyes flicking warily from Kaeda to Straton to Voda to Svevolod. "Why don't they change you back?"

"Archavie is worn out," Reef began. He tried to speak his own language, but it hurt the human throat the wizard had built for him. He swallowed gave up, speaking Molvan instead, "Archavie, the wizard, is exhausted. The healer says it will take time for him to recover, but I will change back slowly without his help."

Reef saw Beach Cliffs shift on her feet and her tail thump on the floor behind her. She doubted him. Of course. Who had ever seen a Khirian in human disguise? Yet the humans seemed to recognize him, whichever shape he wore. Would Beach Cliffs not?

He took a step towards her, hoping that she would see it was him. She widened her stance, ready for a fight. "What can I do so you will know it is me?" Reef asked.

"Say something only Reef would say. Tell me something only Reef would know."

Reef knew what to say, but he didn't want to say it in Molvan. He swallowed again, then hacked out each word carefully in Khirian. "At the tall rocks, we cast Wasteland into the chasm." Of course, Archavie would know that story too by now, but it didn't matter. Beach Cliffs hadn't experienced Turus's mind-reading power.

Reef waited in trepidation while Beach Cliffs considered this, and while she stalked forward and peered into his eyes again and again, as if she expected to see something there. Then she asked another question, "What do you do during mating season?"

Reef blinked. An astute question to test his identity. "I hunt sharks," he answered in Molvan.

Beach Cliffs nodded. She looked perplexed, but also decided. "It is Reef," she said to the swimmers at her right and left. The tone in her voice seemed to add, "strange as always." Then to Reef she said, "We are not the first to come to shore looking for you. Breaking Wave and his section already approached Vodastad. We haven't seen them in weeks."

A chill ran down Reef's spine. He spun at once to face the dov. "She says some of my people already came here. What happened to them?"

Voda, as usual, had been sitting with his elbows on his desk, his fingers steepled at his chin. Now he spread his hands in a gesture of ignorance. "I haven't seen them, but you have witnessed the animosity many Molvans have toward Khirians. It wouldn't surprise me if they never made it to shore."

Beach Cliffs shook her head and continued to speak to Reef. "They climbed the falls. They would have at least made it into the city."

Reef relayed this to Voda, who leaned back in his chair and said, "I will make a full inquiry of course, but I can't imagine a group of Khirians could have entered the city without my knowing."

He spoke in that stiff, cold tone that told Reef he wasn't telling the whole truth. Reef found himself looking up from the dov at the equally impassive shadowed hood of Svevolod.

"He is lying," Beach Cliffs told Reef, apparently quite confident that no one would be able to understand their Khirian conversation. "There was blood in the falls. We all smelled it. They must have been in a fight. Wave ordered us not to follow. If they didn't come back, we were to swim back to the archipelago."

If Reef had had his fins, they would have shivered. As it was, goosebumps prickled across his human skin. But he wouldn't confront Voda now. He would take the matter to the Commission. Ask the other humans what they thought. He didn't want the rest of his shoal to end up as casualties of the dov's hidden schemes.

"Why didn't you go back?" Reef asked Beach Cliffs.

"I sent Redwater and his section back, but the rest of us wanted to stay in case you needed us. And good thing we did."

"We will find Wave and the others," he assured Beach Cliffs. "But you should take the shoal back to the archipelago. The weather soon will be too cold for Khirians. It will not be safe for you."

He hoped she would also be able to see that it would not be safe for them to remain near Dov Voda.

Beach Cliff's tail swished, hitting the bookshelf, and sending a few volumes thudding to the floor. "I don't know if I can keep the shoal, not without you, not without Wave."

"You can," Reef told her. "You are Beach Cliffs. The waves crash and the winds batter—"

"But the Cliffs stand strong," Beach Cliffs finished. She grumbled politely. "Alright, we will go."

Reef wished that he didn't have to ask them to leave. He wished it more as the day went on and Kaeda disappeared to the Embassy again. For a while Reef sparred with Straton. The general taught him how to use weapons without a tail to balance him, but Reef couldn't focus, and he kept stumbling. He needed to swim, he thought, to steady his mind.

But this, suddenly, had become a challenge.

When he had walked across the pool ballroom's balcony toward the dov's decision suite and had seen the lisrek decorating the walls he had felt his heart squeeze with fear and the memory of pain flash across his mind. When he came back later, hoping for a swim, he felt it again. Terror. He kept imagining the lisrek would grab him, as the other net had, and pull him into the water where the sharp currents would stab him to death.

He understood that the sharp net had broken his mind. It had torn open his mind as it had torn open much of his body. His memories and feelings had spilled out to Kaeda and Straton. That had not been all bad, but he could not go on like this. He needed to be put back together and he thought that only the water could do this.

Yet he could not bring himself to go near it. He spent most of the day sitting on the balcony, growing stiff and sore from sitting on the stone, looking at the lisrek trying to figure out how to get himself into the water.

Kaeda came back from the lab, checked on him on her way to her room, and passed by again, this time dressed in her wetsuit and ready for a swim. She asked him if he wanted to join her.

Reef just grumbled and shook his head.

"I'd ask you again later, but Gamalielle is dragging me out to a cat club this evening," Kaeda said. She waited for Reef to respond, but Reef's thoughts were too jumbled to say anything.

"Are you alright?" Kaeda asked.

"No."

She sat down beside him. "Are you thinking about the Khirians? I've talked to Nadia, and she said they might be able to get someone from the Guild of Secrets to work on it, but it's difficult in Vodaniya because Voda has his own spy network and lots of red tape. He's probably got someone listening to us right now."

Reef shook his head. He had been thinking a little bit about Breaking Wave, but that was not at the front of his mind. To think about *that* properly, he would first have to resolve his issue with the water. He looked out at the lisrek. "The water," he said.

Kaeda followed his gaze. "Being caught in that net was traumatic," she said. "I'm not surprised it's hard to get back in the water after that. I'll go with you though, if you want to try."

It wasn't so simple. Reef found himself touching the back of his neck, where his backfin would have been if he was Khirian-shaped. He noticed Kaeda watching and stopped.

"Your backfin was shredded," she said.

Reef nodded. He almost couldn't remember what it felt like. The agony of the assault defied memory. He mostly just felt afraid of it happening again.

"You think of the ocean like an entity, right?" Kaeda asked.

Reef nodded again.

"So… you probably feel like it attacked you?"

Attacked. Betrayed. He felt like the one thing that truly knew and understood him had chosen to take that knowing and understanding and use it to hurt him. How deftly it had tortured him in those few minutes he had remained in the net. If it had gone on and on…

Reef felt his heart racing and forced himself to stop thinking. He looked at the banister of the balcony, felt the stone and carpet beneath him, and remembered that it was not happening now.

"Well, let me tell you this then. You can hear me talking, and even if I yelled, it wouldn't hurt, because your ears are working. If your ears were broken, it might hurt even to hear me whisper. The sound might seem too loud or too sharp. But it wouldn't be because I was trying to hurt you. The ocean was trying to talk to you, like it always does, but because your fin was broken, the talking was too loud and too sharp. It didn't mean to hurt you. It didn't know how you would feel."

Reef believed her, but he also didn't.

Kaeda went on to hold up her arm and compare her arm and hand to a neuron and explain to him about nerves and skin and how the nerves in his fins had been exposed to the ocean. Reef didn't really understand all this, but he liked to hear her voice.

Eventually, she went for her swim. Reef watched her go, watched her come back, had dinner with the party and then watched Kaeda and Gamalielle leave, dressed in shiny tunics with sparkly things in their hair and fur. Then he resumed his post on the balcony.

The sun had already set, leaving the skylights overhead jet black, and intensifying the glow of the lisrek. Silence settled in the corridors of the palace. Reef waited until he thought most people would be going to sleep, or at least staying in their rooms, then he began to inch his way along the wall toward the stairs. At last, he came to the point where he sat across from the stairs down to the pool. Now he would have to leave the safety of the wall protecting his back and crawl out into the middle of the floor.

He rocked forward and tucked his feet beneath him, moving into a crouch. He thought he would try to stand, but as he straightened up, he saw the water, and suddenly he was back on his hands and knees again with his eyes shut.

He thought about what Kaeda had said. It didn't mean to hurt you. It didn't know how you would feel.

He kept moving, crawling blindly forward, feeling with his fingers for the stairs, and then crept down them backward, eyes still shut, listening with trepidation to the lapping of the water. At any moment the lisrek would ensnare him, drag him in. The water would attack him.

That's not how it works, he reminded himself. Your fin was broken. It didn't mean to hurt you.

When he reached the bottom, he held onto the stair rail. You must look, he told himself. You must look.

He opened his eyes. The sight of the water struck him with terror as it had before, but he remained still. The water did not rush up towards him. The lisrek did not ensnare him. The glowing liquid remained within its rectangular bed, lapping gently, waiting for him. Reef scooted forward a bit more and glanced around, checking for a human audience, but he saw only the pink-white glow of the murex shell sconces surrounding the pool.

Clearing his throat Reef did his best to speak Khirian. "You probably can't tell I'm Khirian," he said to the water. No response. Of course, the water didn't talk like that, but he felt that he had to say something. "When I was caught in the net, you hurt me. I don't know if you remember. I don't know if you remember things in that way. The healer says you didn't mean it. You didn't know. Please… don't attack me again."

He felt too ridiculous to go on, but a little comforted after having made his appeal to the water. He inched a little closer, surveyed the waves and rotated his feet out in front of him, ready to dip his feet in the water, then remembered that he was wearing boots and socks.

He imagined the water flowing into his boot and making his sock mushy and soggy. He had no experience with soggy socks but thought this would be uncomfortable. He decided to take the boots and socks off. After placing them behind him, Reef again slowly lowered one heel toward the water.

The moments when that foot hovered above the surface seemed to stretch on for hours, but finally the small waves of the pool licked across his skin. Reef's breath caught in his chest, but the water did not hurt him.

It did not hurt him. It did not talk to him. It did not care. Probably it thought he was human. And in the quiet night, with no sun, no company, his mind remained calm.

Reef laughed with relief. He put both feet into the pool. The clear cool water flowed harmlessly between his short, clawless toes. Reef had never really paid attention to human feet. Now he wondered how they, and how he, managed to walk on them.

The hems of his Molvan pants had fallen into the water. The water made them dark and made the fabric stick to his shins. They would not be good for swimming, Reef thought. The fabric would drag against the water, weigh him down. Did he have a wetsuit in his wardrobe? He didn't want to make the trip back to his room to look, not after the effort it had taken him to get here. But what did it matter? He had Kaeda's bubble of warmth around him, and the water was soft and warm anyway.

Reef took off the human clothes, left them on the ground, and splashed happily into the water.

Chapter Forty
JOIN THE CLUB
Kaeda

I had seen galaxies and nebulas through telescopes at school. Now as I followed Gamalielle though Lion Rampant, or Liar for short, I felt that I had walked into one of these, a spinning, flashing galaxy of light and music that somehow people like Gamalielle and Yury found enjoyable. Several stories of dark balconies, laced with glowing décor, circled a central pillar of open air. Bits of light, like radiant raindrops, fell slowly through the central space, and pulsed in time to a drumbeat that made the whole building shiver. Weaving around the drumbeat, I heard several cat voices rising and falling in howls and wavering screeches. Sometimes I could identify the sounds as music, but most of the time it just sounded like noise.

"Isn't it great?!" Gamalielle shouted over the noise.

"It's really something," I shouted back.

Mostly, the entire experience made my head ache. It didn't help when, between spurts of dancing, Gamalielle said over and over how gross she thought it was that I liked Reef so much, and followed it up with, "Who am I to judge? Just look at me and Yury."

Gross was definitely the word I would use for the amount of saliva the two of them exchanged over the course of the evening.

When Gamalielle tugged me away from the dancing to sit at a semi-circular table hidden away in an alcove, I assumed she would want to talk about Yury, Yury, or maybe Yury. She turned a knob in the center of the table, upping the sound-blocking enchantment around it so that the cacophony of Liar faded. I braced myself to hear how gorgeous, how fun, how mischievous and brilliant Nadia's little brother was, probably accompanied by a reminder that he had never eaten anyone. Instead, the cat leaned forward and said, "You wanna hear the rumors I've dug up?"

I let my face fall into my hands. "Maybe later."

"Nah, sorry, this is the best place for the private exchange of information, trust me, especially if I keep sappily smiling and clasping my hands like I'm talking about my super amazing boyfriend."

"Then I'll keep pretending I'm so tired of hearing about him."

"Great, perfect. So, I'll start with the former Dov Voda, Kirill, who apparently used to drive people crazy with his accidental psychic overflows. Apparently the dovdom was in shambles, enemies everywhere, and then suddenly the dov's son, Yakov, our current dov, showed up with a posse of weirdos in black robes."

That got me to look up to where Gamalielle sat with her chin dreamily in her hand. "Your shocked expression says you can't just believe I confessed my love for a werebear. Anyway, apparently Svevolod and his kin helped Voda take the throne, killed off most of his family, and whipped Vodaniya into shape."

"But where did they come from?" I asked.

"Remember, we're supposed to be having a lighthearted conversation about Yury and I?"

"No, I'm deeply concerned about you and Yury. I'm afraid you're going to get yourselves into trouble."

"Yeah, but only the right sort of trouble," the cat said, brushing away my concern. "But no one knows where they came from, or what they really look like. Some people don't think they're people, you know, 'cause they're always in those robes with shadow hoods. But there were only a dozen or so to start and there have been fewer of them since the cascade. Probably got killed off trying to wrest the Purple Madness."

"And they've been trying to make more of them," I said, frowning as I remembered Tsakhia's memories.

"Yeah, but I don't think people see those. The ones that have been out and about in the palace are the originals, but there were only a handful left from what I've heard, and now people mostly see Svevolod and sometimes his second, Matvei. And I want you to know Yury's really pretty responsible and mature. I mean, Nadia basically raised him, so you know he's gotta have some hoity-toity principles. Not that I care about that, but you might."

"So, who is in charge? Voda, or Svevolod?" I said, talking partially to myself. "And why would Svevolod help Voda? Or why would Voda give in to Svevolod?"

"And you're probably worried that I'm gonna like, corrupt Yury, by giving him shrooms or something, but he's really not into that. He likes to keep his senses sharp. Besides which, with the ursinthropy in his body he doesn't really get intoxicated. The magic just kind of filters stuff out."

I shook my head. "I can't anticipate what is going to happen with you and Yury, I just have a feeling it's not going to be good. But why? Vodaniya is better organized than most of Molva and the people seem to be thriving compared to Miro's people at least. Why would Voda be involved in something that has so clearly damaged his land?"

"Maybe he couldn't anticipate what was going to happen." Gamalielle said, sounding a little prickly. "I can tell you, no matter what you say to caution me, I'm not going to give Yury up. And I can tell you I think one of these days Reef will turn on you and see you as a snack instead of a sweetheart, but you're not going to listen to me either. Maybe Voda got in bed with Svevolod without counting the cost and couldn't get back out."

There was so much in that brief rant that my head spun trying to think of which part to respond to. But I was too late. Gamalielle perked up as she saw Yury on his way over to us.

"You got the fried squids!" she squealed happily as Yury set down a tray with a basket of crispy breaded mollusks as well as three small tumblers, each containing an inch of swirled black and shimmery white liquid. "Ooo what are those?" Gamalielle added.

"House special," Yury said, "Polyphonies."

"Here's to phony ponies," Gamalielle said, lifting her glass in the air.

I couldn't handle it. The alcohol-blurred flavors of lime, licorice, and coconut were just too much for me. I excused myself, blaming my very-real headache, took one of Voda's carriages home and staggered back toward the guest wing, trying every tangle of magic I could think of to get rid of my headache. As I entered the pool ballroom the sound of a splash caught my attention and brightened my mood. Reef must have made it into the water! I ran to the steps, delighted, and then stopped short when I saw the pile of clothes at the pool's edge and Reef's not unfamiliar muscular form, completely naked, showcased in the glowing water.

I must have made a sound - probably a yelp of alarm – because Reef turned to look.

"Stay right there!" I cried, and I ran as fast as I could to his room and began rifling through his wardrobe. There it was. A wetsuit. I grabbed that, and a couple of towels and ran back, taking care on the steps with my arms full.

"I've brought you a wetsuit," I announced, keeping my eyes decisively on the surrounding chairs and tables.

"Why?" Reef asked.

"Because it's polite to wear clothes, even when swimming. I'll just leave it here and I'll go change while you change."

I hurried back to my room and changed into my own wetsuit, thinking how I would explain to Reef if he asked more questions. My cat club nebula headache got worse.

Maybe he wouldn't ask questions, I told myself. Maybe I would just show him some swimming strokes and then we would say goodnight.

But when I returned to the pool, I found Reef still in the water and still naked, the wetsuit in a glistening heap on one of the chairs.

"What happened?" I asked.

Reef walked his way to the edge of the pool and sank down so only his head was above the water. "It is too difficult," he said. "And the water is warm."

The wetsuits Voda had made for us were quality. I thought they slid on and off quite easily. But it wasn't beginner clothing for sure. I wanted to swim. I wanted to swim with Reef. But I absolutely did not want to swim with naked Reef.

"Okay, climb out, I'll help you get it on."

He's a patient, I told myself. Pretend you're putting a bandage on a patient. A great big, neck-to-ankles, form-fitting bandage.

I found myself spouting wetsuit trivia and tips, discussing the quality and usefulness of various wetsuit makes I had tried. Reef accepted these remarks with many polite grumbles until at last I helped him adjust the fit across his shoulders. "It's a little bit small, but I think the clasps will come together here." I began to fasten the clasps and then made the mistake of looking up at his face.

Wow, he did have lips, didn't he? The kind of perfect bowed lips that could only be created by a flamboyant wizard like Archavie. And then his eyes, green just like his Khirian eyes, with flecks of deeper green and flecks of gold. If he was really a human man, he would kiss me now, wouldn't he? Or I would kiss him. This seemed like a good moment.

I took a step back. "You can probably fasten those yourself."

He did, and then we stood there, looking at each other. "Well, shall I show you some human swimming strokes?" I asked.

Reef glanced at the pool, glanced back at me, and said, "I will look stupid."

"Maybe," I said wryly. "Maybe I'll be able to swim better than you for once."

Reef grumbled his agreement, and I spent the next half hour or so instructing him in basic surface strokes, successfully banishing my embarrassment. It was very different from Khirian swimming, which involved a whole-body motion. By the end of the lesson, I could tell that Reef was very frustrated and I had to hold back a laugh at the glowering of his human eyebrows.

"Let's try something else," I said, doing my best not to smile. "Here." I wove together a bit of water breathing magic and tossed it onto Reef's face. Then I made one for myself and pulled myself down underwater. Reef sank down in front of me, and I saw the magic pulse on his face as he tried breathing. I held up a finger for him to wait, swam down a little further, and crafted some magic flippers for him. When I had flippers on my feet as well, I gestured for him to follow, and began a dolphin kick to the other side.

That was an easier motion for a Khirian. Reef flew past me, reached the wall, kicked off, and sped back in the other direction. I didn't have much energy left after the long day, but I put what energy I had into chasing him back. Then, remembering our last swim together, I kicked a little deeper, and did my best to circle around him.

Reef took my cue and dove and circled me. I kicked away. Reef chased. I circled him again and he circled back.

The thing was, without the long arc of Reef's Khirian spine, and the precision of his Khirian swimming, we couldn't maintain the graceful distance we had the last time. Before I knew it, I brushed against him. Then he brushed against me. The circles became one close spiral, and I felt glad that Reef didn't have fins now and couldn't sense the racing of my heart.

I couldn't take it. I decided to break the spiral, but as I kicked away, Reef deftly followed, swam in close, and wrapped his arms around me. For a moment he held me against him, then, just as suddenly he let go and swam away.

I hung in midwater, catching my breath as the buoyancy of my lungs slowly carried me upward. Frils! What had happened? My gut told me that, impossible as it seemed, Reef had made a physical advance. The rest of me, however, urged caution. Maybe this was just the usual end to what I had guessed to be a Khirian swimming game.

I could imagine Archavie laughing at me, asking why I was so afraid of my feelings.

Because he's a man-eating lizard, I told myself, but I knew that wasn't the reason.

Because I don't understand him, I tried next. That was at least partially true.

Because if I let those feelings run free, I don't know what will happen. I remembered standing on the deck of the *Katerina,* feeling terrified and paralyzed at the sight of Reef's half-skinned body. I hated that feeling, of being overwhelmed by my emotions. I didn't want that to happen again.

Finally, an accurate diagnosis, and a solution. I didn't have to feel that way again. I could control myself. And if I wanted more information, I could ask for it. I took a deep breath and calmed my emotions piece by piece. Then I swam to the edge of the pool where Reef waited, sitting on the edge. I pulled myself out and sat a few feet from him. Neither of us looked at each other. Instead, we watched the water.

"What happened?" I asked at last.

Silence. Not even a grumble. I glanced sideways at Reef and saw him glaring intently into the pool, and I thought again how young he looked. When I had first done his physical exam when he was Khirian-shaped, I had asked how old he was. He couldn't tell me. Khirians, Archavie had explained, did not track age in years. Based on the authority he had and the way he communicated, I had guessed him to be thirty-something in human years.

Now I remembered what he had told Straton and I, and I wondered if Archavie's human depiction of Reef was more accurate than I thought.

"You said you became an adult at the end of the war," I said, swishing my feet in the water. "What does that mean to Khirians? How did you know you were an adult?"

"I took command of my shoal, and no one took it back," Reef answered. "Breaking Wave gave me a new name. I was expected to fight for a mate in the summer."

"And did you?" I asked without thinking.

"No," Reef stammered.

"Why not?"

"I did not want offspring. Being a hatchling… I did not want to put more hatchlings through what I had been through. I did not think I could protect them."

Frils, could I just stop feeling things? Did I have to be so impressed by him? "Wow," I said, and when Reef looked my way I added, "I think that's very noble. Having offspring would probably add to your reputation, wouldn't it?"

"Yes," Reef agreed. "And you?"

"Me?"

"Do you have offspring?"

"Oh, no. I haven't had a, a mate I guess you would say. I dated a little bit at university, but…"

I let the explanation trail away, but to my surprise, Reef followed up.

"But what?"

"Well, it never worked out. I guess I was more interested in my education and my career than in nurturing a relationship."

Reef grumbled as if that made sense to him. "And now?" he asked.

Keep it together Kaeda, I told myself. He's not asking because he's into you. He's probably just asking reciprocal questions because Archavie told him it's polite. "I don't know. Most humans want love. I guess I do too."

Archons, that was the worst, most vague wish-washy answer I could have given! I kicked my feet in the pool, feeling my face turning red and hoping that Reef wasn't looking at me too closely. I heard a swish and patter of water as Reef rose to his feet. Then he said, "I will not eat your people."

"What?" He had changed topic so completely that I could hardly process his words.

"Farians, I promise not to eat them again."

"Oh, thank you."

"Good night, Kaeda."

"Good night, Reef."

Chapter Forty-One

TEMNOBRE

Reef

REEF reached his room and tore off his wetsuit. He felt smothered inside of it. He felt smothered inside this human body. The wildfire of self-consciousness raged from his curly hair to his weird human toes, and he felt that at any moment it would cause him to explode.

"Turus!" he shouted. "Turus! Turus!"

Calm thyself, foul beast, Turus's mental voice answered irritably.

"Does she know?" Reef demanded.

Know that you were a few more turns from making the first human-Khirian babies ever to garnish the sphere of Verrum with their utter weirdness? She's not stupid.

Reef gave a roar of embarrassment as he stalked back and forth across his room, and Turus went on, *but she is cautious and inhibited, which, in this case, is dulling her judgement. So no, she doesn't know. She only wonders.*

Reef gave another roar, this time of frustration. At least if Kaeda had been completely ignorant or completely sure his path forward would have been clearer. "What should I do?"

You should take a bath. I'm sure you smell like pool water. And go to sleep. I've learned that sleep is very important for mortals.

I can't take Kaeda as my mate, Reef thought, as he continued his desperate pacing. She's the wrong size, the wrong shape. Yet she is perfect, another part of him said. But the Khirians, he argued back, they wouldn't understand. He stopped, clenched his fists, and roared a third time.

Well, fascinating as this all is, I really ought to go back to my wizard, who, you will remember, currently can't run his own body.

They would call him Human's Mate, Human's Pet. They would say Reef was afraid to pair with a Khirian, that he couldn't satisfy a Khirian mate. He had no proof to the contrary. He had only paired with Glasswater those first two summers, and that hardly counted.

But a mate for life? And this mysterious love idea that even Kaeda could not explain? Wouldn't that be worth the name calling?

But not worth his shoal. Not worth his place with his people.

You mortals act like your temporary connections are so important, Turus said dismissively. *They don't even last a hundred years. Creda and I have shared our bond for thousands, but do you hear me griping about how I can't find her in this lifetime? Whatever you decide to do, it's not that important.*

"How is this happening?" Reef asked. "It is not summer. Is it this human form?"

Perhaps. Or perhaps the bubble of warmth combined with the artificial sunlight in the greenhouse is throwing off your annual Khirian rhythms.

"So, it will go away if I take off the warming enchantment? Or don't swim?"

The pair of you, Turus remarked, his tone turning like a great rolling of the eyes. *So deep and so dense all at once. Yes, those measures may dim the physical urges, but honestly can you say you didn't have unusual feelings for Kaeda before? What were you thinking of naming her? Sunshine?"*

The embarrassment boiled up again with such molten fury that Reef thought it might kill him. Khirians did not use the words for sun, or ocean, or sky in their naming. These words were too big, too important for any Khirian. But what Turus said was true. Secretly, Reef had decided on the name Lirelis, Sunshine, for warm, glowing, comforting, healing Kaeda.

Look, I like you more than most flesh-and-blood creatures, so even though I don't care about your petty little mortal relationships, I'm going to give you some advice. Don't try to deny your feelings. Just decide what you're going to do about them.

The Magic waited for a moment and then added, *now, if you're done spewing romantic angst at me, I will tell you my news.*

What news Turus could possibly have that Reef could care about –

About that Broken Wave fellow.

Breaking Wave? Reef stopped pacing. "Tell me."

Well, keep it to yourself. When I've been able to leave Archavie napping or sleeping for a while I've gone and hijacked the minds of some of the dovniya's fish and turtles. Turns out, yes, they've made it up the falls, yes, Voda attacked them, but he didn't manage to catch them. They haven't been able to swim back through the city, however. It's too dangerous. I found them and advised them to meet us upriver, at the lake at Temnobre.

Temnobre? Reef didn't know the name.

You will tomorrow. And tomorrow will come faster if you sleep. But please take a bath first. I have to manage my wizard's nose and I don't want to bear your reek.

By the next morning Reef had decided only that he would stay near Kaeda if he could, to be sure no other male moved in. He walked into the breakfast room, scanning the bay windows, coffee tables, and steaming buffet for SEO Usenko, ready to tell him, flatly, to leave. But instead of Usenko, Reef saw Lady Batbayar, her hair twisted into a soft knot, her deep purple gown decorated by black lace. She sat on the edge of one of the embroidered chairs, perched, Reef thought, like an elegant bird.

Archavie had told Reef that General Straton was courting the lady, and though the wizard seemed to view the courtship as ongoing or unresolved, Reef thought it was clear that Straton had won. The general seemed to have no concern that another male would usurp him, and interacted with Lady Batbayar in the calmer, more understanding sort of way that Reef had witnessed between Captain Rozhkov and her mate. That was encouraging, to think that the stress and strain he felt could eventually lead to a harmonious understanding.

The lady was surrounded by the rest of the Commission, all gathered around their favorite coffee table. Most of them had tiny porcelain cups in their hands. Straton, sitting in the chair next to Lady Batbayar, indicated a chair for Reef, but Reef, after fetching a plate of smoked fish from the buffet, walked decidedly around to sit on the sofa beside Kaeda. He wouldn't want that seat to be open if Usenko decided to show his face.

"Unfortunately, I think I've hit a dead end," Kaeda was saying. "I think our time in Molva may be drawing to a close."

What? A close? What had he missed? Reef looked up from his plate of smoked fish and caught General Straton's eyes.

The general gave the barest shake of his head. Something else was up.

"Well, I can't let you all leave without visiting Temnobre!" Lady Batbayar exclaimed. "The first frosts will be here soon, and the pine forests are absolutely magnificent in the ice and snow. Lysander," she turned to General Straton, "do you think the dov would allow the Commission to visit my estate, purely for country recreation and a bit of a rest before they travel home?"

"I can certainly ask him again," Straton answered.

Turus, Reef thought urgently, what is going on?

Archavie's body had been sitting stiffly in a chair at the far end of the coffee table, opposite Georgina. Now it scoffed, "Ugh! Managing this mortal coil is so inane. I'm sending my wizard off for a nap."

As Archavie's body suddenly slumped in its chair, Turus's voice leapt into Reef's mind. *I can't animate him and talk to you at the same time, but just so you don't spoil things I'll let you know, the Stratons have decided to act like we're giving up, hoping that we can vacation at Georgina's. She's convinced there's something to be found in the woods north of her castle at Temnobre forest. Little does she know she may soon have Khirians in her lake too.*

If it meant finding the rest of his shoal, then Reef supported the idea, even if he grimaced a little at the thought of being surrounded by dark forests at the start of the Molvan winter. Still, Reef doubted the dov would let them out of his sight.

So, he was surprised when Dov Voda agreed to the country trip. The dov imposed only two conditions: first, that Reef remained human-shaped for the duration, to avoid any further incidents. Second, that they all return in time for the twice-postponed ball, which the dov did not want to have to delay a third time. Reef thought the ruler seemed a bit relieved. Perhaps he really did think they were simply planning on an outing in the country. Once the trip was agreed upon, Lady Batbayar extended her invitation to Team Maelstrom and plans were made to depart the next day.

Reef seemed to be the only one not looking forward to it. He reminded himself that the trip might take him nearer to his missing shoal members, but the sky that he so often saw through the palace windows was increasingly grey and overcast. He didn't want to leave the safe, warm water. He also felt concerned that he would leave his surprising affection for Kaeda behind with them.

But then, if he stopped feeling these weird feelings towards her it would make his life easier, wouldn't it? Perhaps this was all for the best.

The next morning, they began their travel to Temnobre, rolling along beneath endless grey skies, passing dying field after dying field until they were swallowed by darkening trees. The humans in the group marveled over the dense forest of pines as their carriage drove into it, but not Reef. Reef hated pine trees. He hated the smell of them. He hated their needles. He hated the dryness and stiffness of them, so different from the lush ferns and palms of the Khirian archipelago.

At last, the trees cleared, and Reef saw the mirror-still surface of a lake, and, rising out of it, a brown lawn and an ominous castle made of rough stone. They drove around the lake to the front of the castle, where the long geometric garden displayed empty fountains, bare flowerbeds, spiky evergreens, and the skeletons of shrubs.

The humans seemed oblivious to the horror of the botanical graveyard. Instead, they remarked on the intricacy of the stonework and the impressive evergreen topiaries as they disembarked and walked past an assembly of servants, mostly cats dressed in black, all lined up in the chilly weather to greet their mistress's return. Once through the doors, pine wreaths, flickering yellow light, burgundy drapes and heavy wood furnishings made the castle just as miserably autumnal inside as it was outside.

Romantic, the humans commented, sounding universally delighted. Charming. Delightful. Elegant and cozy at the same time.

Reef had never felt so completely uncomprehending of human language.

He liked the place less and less as Kaeda and Tsakhia disappeared and left him alone most of that day, and the next, and the next, with only stiff and snarky Turus for company. When Reef asked after his shoal Turus said irritably that he had given Wave directions, and Reef would just have to wait. When Reef peeked into the library where Kaeda and Tsakhia were working he saw huge maps of magical constellations spread out in the air, tubes and frames and noggin boxes spread upon the tables. Stacks of notes and trays of equipment.

It didn't make any sense to him. Sky of Stars, he thought. Amazing, but unreachable. Maybe he should give Kaeda that name instead.

Wrapped in his bubble of warmth he sat beside the lake, waiting for Wave, wondering what kind of sluggish fishes might lurk in the still cold water, and watching the horrible flat covering of clouds turn darker and darker grey as the sun faded. Then, as he looked down at the water again, he saw something strange. A star. Then another. He looked up. The clouds were gone. Stars filled the sky, far more than he remembered ever seeing… when he was awake.

Had he fallen asleep, Reef wondered? He glanced around in alarm, seeing himself still sitting on the shore of the lake, and then started, and scrambled away as he saw that a piece of the sky was sitting next to him.

It was there, as if solid. A piece of sky about the size and shape of an adolescent Khirian, looking like a crisp black shadow, filled with flickering points of light.

"What? What are you?" Reef asked.

The piece of sky didn't answer, but said, "I don't want to be here."

It sounded as scared as Reef felt. "I don't want to be here, either," Reef told it. Is it me, Reef wondered? If this is a dream, am I talking to myself?

"No," the piece of sky said. Then it added, pleadingly, "take us away from here."

Reef felt more confused and terrified than ever. "Who are you?" he asked.

But the piece of sky turned its attention away from him, looking toward the castle. The next thing Reef knew he was lying on the ground. When he opened his eyes, the clouds seemed to be falling on him in little bits of ash.

"Reef! Reef! Are you alright?!" Kaeda's voice. She came running and knelt beside him as Reef slowly pulled himself up.

"I think I must have fallen asleep," Reef grumbled, but Kaeda interrupted him.

"What is that?!"

"What?"

"In your chest!"

She pointed approximately at his sternum, and Reef noticed now that she was wearing something on her eyes, like a pair of goggles.

"It's – it's – now it's gone?!" She peered closer, then pulled his shoulder forward and scrambled around to look at his back. "Where did it go?"

"What?" Reef demanded again.

"There was this… curl of magic. I saw it. I'm sure I saw it." She sat back on the ground with a frustrated huff. "Tsakhia made me these magic-viewing goggles so I could see the unmagic. I don't know, maybe I'm still getting used to them, but I really thought I saw something like… have you ever seen a shark's egg?"

Of course, Reef had seen a shark's egg. He coughed a yes.

"It reminded me of that, of the squiggly baby shark stuck inside and sort of swimming and twisting." She scrutinized him again, and Reef found himself feeling annoyed. That wasn't the way he wanted her to look at him, like he was a problem to solve.

He climbed to his feet with a shrug. "I think I fell asleep."

Kaeda nodded as she rose to her feet too. "You're probably reacting to the darkness of winter. It's never dark this long down south. I'm sure Georgina won't mind if we set up some sunlight lamps inside. And Tsakhia and I should check you out just in case there is some sort of magical something-or-other stuck in you that we haven't noticed."

Reef gave a noncommittal grumble.

"Anyway, I came out to let you know that dinner is ready. Perfect timing since it's starting to snow."

Chapter Forty-Two

LEGENDS

Reef

THEY walked into the castle and to the dining room, a spacious but dense place full of dark wood and heavy tapestries, where candlelight blazed confusedly through the facets of crystal chandeliers. The rest of the party was already gathered around the duchess's table, and already embroiled in a lively discussion of magical theory, punctuated by laughter as Gamalielle levitated the platters of food out of the hands of Lady Batbayar's servants and floated them across the table.

The duchess waved the staff away with a smile. "We will fend for ourselves tonight it seems." She sat back, looking happily entertained as Gamalielle drifted the trays along the table and joined in with the rest of them doing their best to snatch food off as they floated past.

"Tsakhia, will you take a look at Reef?" Kaeda asked.

Tsakhia rose from his seat and moved toward them as Reef and Kaeda came into the dining room. "What is it?" he asked.

Kaeda described what she had seen and Tsakhia took his turn intently looking at Reef's chest. "I don't see anything."

"Neither do I anymore," Kaeda sighed. "But if there is something, it may have to do with his phage-sense ability. We should do a magic-strainer on him tomorrow."

Tsakhia nodded his agreement, and they all took their seats. Reef wondered if he should mention the dream, the starry figure, but it seemed so unreal that he didn't want to try to put it into words.

"How is the research going?" Yury asked, snatching a roll of bread from a passing basket, and the conversation turned to Kaeda and Tsakhia's recent work.

"I'll leave it at Tsakhia's discretion to share whatever he is comfortable with," Kaeda said. She took another sip from her glass of wine before catching the dish of pelmeni as it drifted by.

"Kaeda has been combing through every bit of my DNA and trying to figure out how it could connect to the difference between regular magic and unmagic," Tsakhia answered. He paused before adding, "She concludes I may not be alive."

Yury and Gamalielle snorted with laughter.

"Differently alive," Nadia corrected.

"Perhaps dead," Tsakhia said.

"A little bit dead," Kaeda said, and then she shut her eyes and put a hand to her forehead. "I can't believe I'm saying that. It's so imprecise. But cells and DNA go through certain changes when an organism dies and… it's like Tsakhia's body started to do that, then used those changes to… achieve a different state of life and also harness the unmagic. I think. I don't know. It doesn't make sense."

"It might make sense," Lady Batbayar said, pausing with fork and knife in hand. "Some of the old tales say that the fearies were not deathless, but that when they died they came back. But Tsakhia is human."

Reef saw Kaeda's eyebrows lift and her shoulders raise in a sigh, but she left the disclosure to Tsakhia.

"No," he said. "I was human once. Whatever I am now, it is something else."

Lady Batbayar set her fork and knife down. "But you do not have wings."

Nadia and Tsakhia looked at one another, while Kaeda sat suddenly back in her chair. "I do not," Tsakhia said haltingly, "because Kaeda removed the extra bones and joints." He held up his right arm, where the fingers were noticeably longer.

The atmosphere of the room had shifted. The cheer was gone. Reef felt almost as if the stars had appeared again, an impossible reality settling around them. Reef didn't fully understand what that reality was, but he could feel it shining, like the still surface of the lake.

"Frils," Kaeda's voice broke the stillness. "If Voda's aim was to turn Tsakhia into a feary, then perhaps that is what Svevolod and the wrestors have been this whole time. Their huge robes would certainly conceal wings. Come to think of it, I've never seen Svevolod's hands."

"The fearies have always wanted control," Lady Batbayar said. "It would make sense for them to take advantage of the dov's weakness, promise him help, and then manipulate him. But if they have returned, I fear it will take more than our innovation to defeat them. If only my people were not estranged from Bogdan's bears."

At this, Nadia's eyes met Yury's across the table. Then Nadia rose to her feet. "Not so estranged as you think."

It was the first time Reef had actually seen a werebear shift clearly, and in the light. Nadia grew, her arms lengthened, her nose and mouth became a muzzle. The usual grey tunic that she wore when she wasn't in armor must have been enchanted to shift, because it grew with her until she was a huge, russet-furred bear, standing upright at the duchess's dining table.

Normally Reef might have put this in the category of "things that will make Molvan ladies scream," but Lady Batbayar did not scream. In fact, Reef had seen enough happy tears by now that when he looked at the duchess's face, he recognized her expression as one of overwhelming joy and relief.

Yury, grinning a little as if happy to show off, also stood and shifted, becoming a sleek, almost-black bear, and the mélange of tears and laughter and explanations that followed left Reef quite at a loss. It was like a reunion, though Lady Batbayar had never met the Rozhkovs. She kept saying things like "I have read of you! All my life I have hoped!" as she clasped Nadia's clawed paw, and then her human hand. When Nadia showed the lady her axe Reef thought the duchess might collapse in utter delight.

Reef didn't know what to make of most of it and went on eating.

When the mammals had finally resumed their seats, their cheeks were all round and shining from smiling and crying. Lady Batbayar reminded them to please eat, and they did, all still brilliantly happy.

"We should search the forest again," Nadia said, in much better spirits than she had been before.

"We have searched it," Yury reminded her, "even with Tsakhia's crazy goggles." He didn't sound as bitter as usual.

"We haven't gone past the streambed."

"That is not my land," Lady Batbayar told them. "The land there belongs to the Vysokaya estate. The family line has ended; the land has returned to the throne."

"Traipsing through Voda's territory without an invitation sounds like a good way to disappear and never be heard from again," Yury joked.

Lady Batbayar raised her hand. "We will not speak of that tonight. Tonight, we will pray and thank the archon."

"Yes," Nadia agreed.

Yury laughed, but Lady Batbayar spoke over his laughter, "And there is something else we should do to mark the occasion."

She cast a pointed look at General Straton, who rose to his feet and cleared his throat. "It has come to her ladyship's attention that most of you have no experience with Molvan ballroom dance."

Gamalielle shrilled with delight. Reef saw Yury chuckling, Turus rolling Archavie's eyes, and Kaeda's cheeks turning pink, though she was still smiling, as they all were.

"We don't really need to know how to dance," Kaeda said.

"You'll be opening the dov's ball," Lady Batbayar said from her seat. "Everyone will be watching. Besides, what better way to celebrate?"

Straton added. "Georgina has agreed to teach you all the basics."

"What about you?" Gamalielle crowed.

"Lysander can dance," Lady Georgina put in, smiling yet wider. "If memory serves."

Gamalielle released another peal of happy amusement.

"So, it's settled," Straton said. "After dinner, we dance."

Chapter Forty-Three

WALTZ

Reef

LADY Batbayar led them to a room larger than any they had yet visited in the castle, a room with a vaulted ceiling and a row of mirrors along one side. On the other side a row of windows looked out toward a terrace and the mirror surface of the lake, now obscured by falling snow. Crystal chandeliers cast their light down on a floor covered with a tile pattern of interlocking circles.

A wheezing ringing suddenly sounded in the air. Reef jumped and looked around and noticed a Cat, one of the duchess's servants, holding a wand in his hand. He swished the wand in the air and with it seemed to command the assortment of objects before him.

What were they? A small, gourd-like object, flat on one side, floating in midair while a stick swayed back and forth across it. Other things, similar, in varying sizes, all shiny, blending perfectly into the ornate, gilded background of the ballroom. As the Cat waved his wand in the air these objects began to whine together, creating a sound like a strange cross between whale song and a hive of bees.

At a signal from Lady Batbayar, the sounds stopped as suddenly as they had begun.

"We will start with the steps of a waltz," she announced. "Find a partner."

A partner? Reef turned, planning to claim Kaeda or Archavie, whoever was closer, but found Straton extending a hand to Kaeda, and Archavie sitting with Nadia and Tsakhia, who clearly intended to watch. As he glanced around, mildly panicked, Lady Batbayar approached with unmistakable intention.

She was still glowing from her recent introduction to Nadia, and clearly in the mood to be friendly to non-human people. "Reef," she said, "you have probably never done a human dance before."

"No," Reef said.

"Then I will show you how."

She took a step forward and Reef took a step back, maintaining the distance between them. A smile touched the duchess's lips. "You will need to hold your partner. Come. I am not afraid of you."

She waved him toward her. Reef glanced at Kaeda again and saw her facing her father, who was showing her where to place her hands. There was no escape then.

"Put your right hand on my waist. Your left hand holds mine. There. Now, see how Lysander moves his feet? Watch him for a moment."

Reef did, observing the general's easy and graceful movement, and the more hesitant swish of Kaeda's Molvan skirt.

"Now," Lady Georgina said, "You step forward with your left foot while I step back. Now step up with your right but keep them apart. Good. Then bring your left foot together with your right."

She talked him through the steps several times, seeming always to move perfectly in time with him, regardless of how well he followed her instructions, and soon began to count along to their steps, one, two, three, one, two, three. "You might notice we are making a box. Just keep stepping along the box, and you can turn the box any way you like. Shall we try some music?" She let go his hand to wave to the Cat commanding the wheezy gourds. "Play the First Snow."

As the musicians began to play, the sounds they made linked arms and went swimming along, like a school of silver fish, flashing and sparkling on a peaceful ocean day. Suddenly it made sense. The music was the water. The dance was the swimming. The count was the waves. Move with the waves in the water.

"Ready?" Lady Georgina held up her hand.

It really was not difficult. In fact, it was easier than walking which had no mesh to give it direction. The music, Reef found, would carry him if he let it. He only had to keep stepping.

"You're a natural," the duchess laughed. "Now you lead. You can turn the box, move it around the dance floor."

Reef did this, and felt that they were drifting in a current, easily spinning across the room.

"Lysander is right," the lady said, still smiling. "You are very much like any other soldier. You remind me of Lysander when he was young. We met at a ball. I danced with many young soldiers that night, but Lysander impressed me with his waltz. And his poise. I couldn't tell what he thought of me, and I wanted to know, so I kept dancing with him, over and over."

Then she looked at Reef a bit more intently. "I know you have probably killed many of my countrymen, but I also know that after a war many people wonder what happened, and how they could have done the things they did. Perhaps you want to live a new life. I will not stop you by assuming the worst."

Reef didn't know what to say to that. He had not yet fully processed her words when Straton appeared beside them.

"May I?" he asked.

They had completely circled the room, ending back near the row of embroidered chairs with gilded legs that hosted Archavie, Nadia, and Tsakhia. Reef saw Yury and Gamalielle still out on the dance floor, Gamalielle levitating herself up to the werebear's shoulder height so that he could spin her out into the air and pull her back over and over in dizzying whirls.

Kaeda came to stand beside him as Straton put an arm around Lady Georgina and the two of them drifted away across the room. "Well, Turus," Kaeda said to the stiff figure of Archavie seated behind them. "I think you can see now that you need Archavie at least as much as he needs you."

"How so?"

"You want to find your counterpart, right? And you want to woo her wizard? Which of you is good at making friends? Which of you would be charming everyone on the dance floor right now if he were here?"

Turus's silence was as good as an agreement.

"I have an idea," Kaeda said, and she grabbed Archavie's hand. "Come on, dance with me."

"Why?"

"Because even though you say you want Archavie to come back and fully inhabit his body again, I think you're accidentally keeping him away with your desire to control him."

"What? That's ridiculous."

"You've often tried to control his life, now you really are. I think some part of you doesn't want to let go and let him back in."

Archavie's face glowered. "Even if you were right, I don't see how dancing will change anything."

"You can't make him dance," Kaeda said, now hauling Archavie up. "Only Archavie can do that. So let go. Pay attention to the music and make space for Archavie to do something only he can do. Otherwise you're just going to look stupid."

While Turus contorted Archavie's face into a variety of appalled, offended, and generally vexed expressions, Kaeda dragged him away from the chairs, smacked one of his hands onto her waist, and grabbed the other tightly. She began to attempt the dance steps, with Turus grumbling and snarling as Kaeda pushed him this way and that.

Reef sat down to watch, wondering if she would be successful in bringing Archavie back. As he sat, he heard Nadia, a few chairs down, say "Come on, let's try it," she said.

"You go without me," Tsakhia replied.

"When was the last time we danced together?"

"Three years ago."

"This is the perfect time. Come on," Nadia said, and a moment later they brushed past Reef, Nadia tugging Tsakhia behind her. They took their places on the dance floor, but rather than making a box they simply stood and swayed together. Nadia reached her hands into Tsakhia's hood to put her arms around his neck and he wrapped his arms around her waist.

Three couples were out on the dance floor now. Three examples of the ongoing mating season. Reef watched them intently. It was like the circles in the water, he thought, as he saw Gamalielle laughing and twirling, Georgina and Straton intently gazing into one another's eyes as they breezed across the floor, and Nadia now resting her head on Tsakhia's shoulder.

And then there was Kaeda and Turus. Turus who Reef knew for sure would not be competition. If he had been… well, Kaeda was right, Turus wasn't going to be able to woo anyone. He might as well have been a very grumpy tree, with Kaeda dancing around him. Kaeda seemed to think it was pretty hilarious. Turus didn't spin her, so she spun herself, out and in, and out and in. She didn't quite step at the right time, but Reef found himself smiling at her smile, his heart brightening at her happiness. Then, as she twirled out once more, Archavie's too-blue eyes gave a massive eyeroll, and when Kaeda spun back in, the wizard's freckled face broke into a grin, and he caught her.

"Archavie!" Kaeda shouted.

The light in the room turned to sunshine. The music to the smell of flowers. That's what it felt like at least, as Archavie's joy filled the room. The tapestries sparkled and the floor of the ballroom seemed suddenly covered in shimmering dust that rose in swirls and spirals as Archavie now pulled Kaeda around the room and dipped her low toward the ground as the music reached a final crescendo.

The rest of the mammals applauded. Reef put his hands together a couple of times, but he felt just a little concerned.

Oh, don't worry. Archavie's sparkly mental voice assured him. The wizard led Kaeda back toward the chairs, both of them out of breath and still laughing as Straton, Georgina, Yury, Gamalielle, Nadia, and Tsakhia all gathered to greet the recently returned wizard.

"I can't believe that worked," Kaeda said, cheeks pink, eyes bright with a smile.

"You said it would," Archavie replied.

"It was just a guess."

"You're a good guesser."

They had reached Reef now. Reef had risen to his feet, but he wasn't sure what to say.

"Don't worry, you don't have to say anything. I know you're glad to see me," Archavie said. "And I also know, that Kaeda would much rather dance with you than with me."

He stepped back away from Kaeda, as if presenting her for Reef's consideration, and Kaeda's cheeks turned pinker, the corners of her mouth bending into a more embarrassed smile.

"Oh no, no!" Archavie exclaimed. "Wait a moment." He flourished his hands.

Reef was getting pretty used to it by now, this whole shape changing thing, and it was a relief to feel his tail behind him again, and his Khirian feet planted firmly on the ground. The mammals applauded again, and Kaeda kept smiling and Reef felt a little bit ridiculous as he realized that Archavie had left the human clothes on him, adjusting them to fit his shape. He probably looked absurd, but that wouldn't stop him from trying out dancing as a Khirian. He really wanted to, to try that musical swimming with his body.But not with Kaeda. No, he couldn't dance with her. If he danced with her, he would have to make a decision. If he danced with her, he *would be* making a decision, wouldn't he? He couldn't do it, not right now. He couldn't risk the overwhelming feelings that came when circling her in the water, not here in front of all these people.

"No, I… not now," Reef said gruffly, guilt stabbing his chest as Kaeda's happy embarrassment collapsed into confusion.

"Oh, come on," Archavie pressed.

"I am sure the ball will also include many structured group dances," Lady Georgina interrupted, in a tone meant to draw their attention. "Come, I will tell you all where to stand."

Chapter Forty-Four

THE FOREST

Kaeda

I stayed up later than I should have, eating piles of biscuits with Archavie. He wanted to reminisce about all the things he had missed. He remembered them now, but it helped to have another person talk through it.

I did my best. I was honestly delighted to have him back, but also distracted.

"Because Reef wouldn't dance with you?" the wizard asked, as he took another piece of chocolate-dipped shortbread from the silver tray that sat on the ottoman between us. We were holed up in one of Georgina's smaller sitting rooms, a cozy fire to our right and the smell of peppermint tea everywhere.

"Yes," I admitted.

"Give him time. You know how Reef likes to think about things."

I liked to think about things too. Up to a point. And we had definitely reached that point.

When Archavie and I parted ways, I decided I would confront Reef in the morning. No, confront was too strong a word. I would… well, I would talk to him. Frankly.

With my brain working on what I would say to Reef, I knew I wouldn't be able to sleep, so I went back to the library to work on Tskahia's Monstrositor until I wore myself out.

I was close to having a therapeutic ursinthropy ready for him. I just needed to test it on a few more tissue samples and make sure it wouldn't damage him. I had taken some samples, ranging from blood to skin to fish scales earlier in the day, set them to grow with a bit of magic meticulously removed from my remaining genesis cuffs, and attached them to an artificial circulatory system, so that now I had sizeable pieces to observe. I prepped a dose of the latest and most conservative version of Nadia's ursinthropy, tailored to Tsakhia's primary genome, and released it into the magical circulation.

It should start to work instantly, and sure enough, I saw the scales turning to skin, and the damaged tissue I had taken from Tsakhia's neck turning soft and healthy again.

Now the challenge would be to find a way to test if he would still be able to use magic.

As I was brainstorming, I heard a shuffling in the darkness, a snuffling, and the hair rose on my arms.

"Hello?" I asked. When no one answered I picked up the lamp and walked cautiously toward the hall. "Hello? Is someone awake?" Then I exhaled in relief. It was only Nadia in her bear form. I wondered though why she was wearing her armor in the middle of the night.

"Nadia, you surprised me. You can't sleep either?"

Nadia didn't answer. She shuffled by on all fours, lumbering toward the kitchen. "Nadia? Nadia?"

I walked quickly around to get a look at her face. Her eyelids flickered low, the whites of her eyes just showing between them. Strange. If she were sleepwalking, I would expect her eyes to be open. I sent a bit of magic to examine her brain and found my magic sense completely blocked, not with the usual interference of ursinthropy, but with something more opaque.

"Frils," I muttered as Nadia shuffled past me. What should I do? Follow her and make sure nothing happened? Go wake Tsakhia? Go wake Yury? Nadia had never mentioned a sleepwalking problem to me.

I decided that I would have to wake someone. I hurried to the stairs leading up to the guest rooms and was halfway up when I nearly ran into Yury, also in full armor. "Yury, thank goodness you're awake. Nadia, she—"

"Yeah, I know."

"You know?" I chased after him while he sniffed the air, easily following Nadia's trail.

"I smelled her hyped-on-adrenaline smell. It woke me up."

We found Nadia at the back door leading out of the kitchen. As we watched she stood on her hind legs, magic surged in her body and with one push she broke down the back door. Frigid night air rushed in around us.

"Sir, Madam, should I wake the house?" Lady Georgina's Cat butler, Guasparre Vico had appeared in the air near us, wrapped in a dressing gown.

"Or shall I?" Archavie asked, as he walked briskly into the kitchen, also in a dressing gown. "Turus noticed a surge of alarm," he said to me.

"No need," Yury said as he hastily grabbed a spare cloak from a hook by the door. "I've seen her like this before. I'll keep an eye on her until she snaps out of it."

"I'll go with them," I said.

"So will I," Archavie said, and with a flourish of his hand he turned his pajamas and dressing gown into a quilted, floor-length coat. "Not going to let you run into danger alone. Guasparre, If we're not back in a couple of hours, please let someone know."

"Very good sir," the cat replied. "Please take a set of enchanted wellies from beneath the bench. They will keep your feet warm."

I quickly donned a borrowed cloak and boots, then, with the library lamp in my hand and Archavie at my side I ran out after Nadia and Yury, both in bear form. The thin crust of snow crunched beneath our feet as we raced across the lawn. Nadia was making steadily for the woods at a lumbering gallop.

"What's going on?" I asked when we caught up with Yury.

Yury shifted up to human form to speak with us more easily. "She's in a trance. That's what she would say, anyway."

"And you've seen her like this before?"

"Yeah, a couple of times. When she carried me away from the petrified forest, and when we were looking for yetis and found Tsakhia. She just knew where to go. Frils, though, Nadia, this is not a good time."

"Archavie, do you notice anything?"

"Her mind is more than usually impenetrable, but that's all I can say. Turus says he doesn't even want to go near it. He says she feels prickly, which of course is a very insightful, very helpful analysis."

It was actually. It suggested to me that whatever was causing the effect, it was meant not only to move Nadia, but also to stop interference.

"What should we do?" I asked Yury.

"I don't think there's anything we can do," Yury said. "I'll stay with her if you want to go back."

If Nadia was in a magic-induced trance, or affected by yet another new magical phenomena, I wanted to observe it, but

I couldn't help but think that we ought to let her husband know. "We should send Turus back to wake Tskahia."

"This isn't about him," Yury said, an edge in his voice. "This is a werebear thing."

"He's her husband."

"Imagine this," Yury said as we jogged on, "Tsakhia comes with us, he gets concerned about Nadia, he doesn't have any magic prepared for a circumstance like this because he's never faced it before, so he does some fresh. Then he collapses in a curse-induced fit, and becomes, at best, a useless wailing heap, and at worst a frilsed-up danger to everyone around him. Nadia won't be able to help because she's… whatever she is. Even if he survives, she'll blame herself for whatever happened."

An icy gust found its way through the trees, tossing the pine boughs like weeds in the tide. I turned my face down against it thinking Yury was right. I knew how precarious Tskahia's health was. Yet I couldn't help thinking Tsakhia would be equally distraught if something happened to Nadia without his knowledge.

What do you think? I asked Archavie.

Honestly, I don't care a great deal about them. I'm mostly concerned about you *being out here.*

I gave Archavie the best smile I could manage in the cold, and he returned it. *I do think Tsakhia's a bit of a loose cannon, though. I don't mind not having him around.*

I remained undecided as we followed Nadia. The forest grew thicker and thicker, and the ground became less and less even. Yury ran ahead and kept talking to Nadia as if hoping to draw her out. "Yeah, we've been here. Same badger trails. Same heaps of owl pellets. Nothing new."

Eventually his comments turned to objections. "Yeah, no, Nadia, this is the old streambed. Beyond this, that's Voda's land, remember. Bad idea."

But Nadia didn't listen. She made her way down the frosted slope to the pebbly bottom of the dry riverbed and began to clamber up the other side. "Frils," Yury swore. "I guess that's where we're going. You can go back if you want."

I shook my head and Archavie said, "Perhaps I should send a bit of Turus back to tell people where we've gone."

"You don't have much of him though, do you?" Yury asked, as we all scrambled down the pebbles together.

"No, but—"

"Best keep him around just in case. They'll be able to figure out where we've gone. Nadia's talked about it enough."

Even with the cloak and boots, and even with our quick pace, I was feeling the chill. The cold stung my eyes and burned my nose as I drew breath. I hadn't brought much magic with me, just the handful I had been toying with in the library and a bit in the lamp I carried. I didn't want to use it on a warming enchantment, not if I might need it later.

I couldn't say how far we had gone, or how long we had been weaving between trees, scrambling over fallen logs, and stumbling on needle and moss coated rocks and roots, hidden in the darkness, when finally, Nadia slowed, sniffing the air.

Yury sniffed too, and then threw his arms around Nadia's neck, trying to stop her. "We'll come back Nadia. Not now."

"What is it?" I asked, hurrying to catch up.

"Medreva," Yury spoke through clenched teeth, as he hauled on Nadia. "Bear stone. It smells like her axe. It shouldn't be out here. We didn't smell it before. Stop, Nadia. Stop. We'll come back."

I turned and looked ahead. The forest so far had all looked the same to me. Brown stripes of tree trunks, some thinner, some thicker, lit wherever I shone my lantern. The dropping temperatures had cooled the last of the water in the air into a freezing fog, and the moonlight turned the fog to a grey haze. Now, as I peered ahead, it looked as if the haze had solidified.

"Do you see that?" I asked.

"I see it," Archavie said.

My heart beat in my throat as I remembered Nadia's account of the petrification of the sacred forest. I scrambled past Yury, who had braced his shoulder against Nadia's. I had to see for myself if this place really existed.

The grey wall became clearer as I neared it. It was not made of fog at all, but stone, columns and columns of it, rough like tree trunks, but many bearing the patterns of fabric or the contours of armor. I saw bark textured like tassels that might edge a scarf, and what looked like a breastplate, but elongated upward. I saw no face above it but based on Nadia's account I suspected I was facing a wall of petrified bears. The wall stretched as far as I could see in either direction, straight and endless.

"Frils," Archavie breathed, as he approached behind me. "Turus has nothing to say. He's never seen anything like it."

"Help me stop her!" Yury urged.

His efforts seemed to have made no difference. Nadia pushed him forward, his boots, then claws as he shifted, tearing furrows in the frozen earth. She was now only a few yards from the wall.

I moved myself into her path. "Nadia, you've led us here, now let's stop and talk about what to do."

"She can't hear you," Yury growled.

"Turus will try," Archavie said, but a moment later he exclaimed and stumbled backward clutching his head. "It's not Nadia, that I can tell you."

We knew Nadia's goddess had psychic abilities, that werebears in the sacred forest used to feel her feelings, and that as the Purple Madness she had hit the wrestors with psychic blasts. We also knew that Nadia had announced she would pray, that very night, for guidance in finding whatever was hidden in the forest.

"Goddess," I said, "Or Boginya, or Purple Madness, or whoever you are now, you have brought us here. You've showed us what you want us to see. Let Nadia go, and we'll make a plan to… help, or whatever you need us to do."

Nadia pushed on, as if she hadn't heard a word I said, and drew her axe. I leapt aside as she swung it at the wall. The blade bit deep into the medreva. Nadia tugged it out and swung again.

"Have you lost your mind?" This exclamation came from Archavie, looking in horror at Yury who had drawn his pair of swords.

"If I cut her down, Kaeda can bring her back. Maybe it will drive the parasite away!" Yury lunged forward and doubtless could have executed an expert strike between the familiar plates of his sister's armor, had not Turus caught him. Yury growled as he fought the air, and he might have won had not Archavie narrowed his eyes and cast a pointed look at Yury's swords. The weapons suddenly glowed red hot and Yury dropped them with an angry cry.

"Listen!" I exclaimed, putting myself between them before Yury could turn on Archavie. "Listen!" Both paused. "This is what Nadia has wanted her entire life, isn't it? To return to the forest? It's not a convenient time, but even if she was in her right mind, do you think she would turn around?"

Yury shook his head, and I agreed. "No," I said. "She'd be afraid it would disappear again. And maybe… maybe there's something in there that can help us somehow."

Yury looked back at Nadia and I followed his gaze. Nadia was well on her way to hacking a narrow doorway in the stone. The stone didn't crack or spark as her axe struck. In fact, the impact made a soft sound. It was almost as if, under her blade the medreva turned back, for just a moment, to the flesh of the bears who had formed the wall. The pieces that now lay on the forest floor around her looked like sharp rocks, but had smooth contours, not jagged or crumbling, as if what Nadia had cut out was not stone at all.

Yury watched too, and I heard him whisper something, as if he were trying to speak, but couldn't quite say the words aloud.

"What is it?" I asked.

"I can't go in." He swallowed and blinked wide eyes. He didn't look like Yury the brash hunter now, and I remembered that Nadia said she had carried him out, her baby brother. How much of a baby, I wondered? Clearly, he remembered something, and the something was too much for him to bear facing his home again.

"I will go in with her," I said decisively. "Archavie will go back to Temnobre and tell everyone what has happened. Yury, stay here and guard the entrance and help the others to find it. Alright?"

Yury drew a deep breath and nodded. He picked up his cooled swords and stood ready near the doorway, now deep enough to be a tunnel.

Archavie gave me a sharp nod. *Don't do anything recklessly compassionate,* he thought to me. *My friends are few and far enough between as it is.*

I gave him a wry smile. I'll do my best.

That's what I'm afraid of.

I felt the wizard's gaze lingering on Nadia and I as I followed her through the stone.

Chapter Forty-Five

THE PETRIFIED FOREST

Kaeda

I didn't have much of an expectation of what we would find beyond the wall, but I would have guessed it to be all stone, a place frozen in time, even colder and more still than the regular forest outside.

Instead, as Nadia's axe bit through the last of the medreva, a rush of humid warmth flooded the tunnel. One cut at a time, the wall fell away ahead of us, and as it did, we felt the summery heat, heard the chorus frogs and insects in the darkness, breathed the smell of honeysuckle and ripe pears in the thickness of the air. Nadia stepped ahead, over a small ridge of stone, and I followed her, onto a dense carpet of soft, moist grass.

Beside me, Nadia laughed. She was human shaped again, on her hands and knees, smoothing the grass and moss with her palms. "Oh yes," she said, as one of the crickets, translucent and golden, crawled onto her hand and hummed with an almost human voice. "You are still alive here. You have all died outside without magic." Then all at once her eyes filled with tears and she began to weep.

I looked back, wondering if Yury could hear any of this, but the tunnel, though it remained behind us, looked impenetrably black and still. Was it just me, or was it a little narrower? I thought about going back, telling Yury he wouldn't want to miss this, but I didn't want to get shut out if the not-quite-stone closed like a knitting wound. Instead I put a hand on Nadia's shoulder. "Nadia, do you know where to go next?"

Nadia looked at me, completely bewildered. "I can't think why you would be in this dream, Kaeda."

"It's not a dream. You were in a trance." As I described to her what had happened, Nadia's expression turned from the sublime relief of fulfilled mourning to the harrowed look of one who has suddenly realized how lost they are.

She also looked back, toward the crevice that was all that remained of her hacked entrance. So much for the others coming in after us. At least this place didn't seem to be dangerous. So far.

Nadia rose to her feet. The little cricket crawled up onto her shoulder and sat there as if waiting to see where we would go. "Maybe later I will be able to bring Yury," Nadia said. "But now, yes, we must go. Come; I will show you."

We walked through the meadow clearing where we had landed, picked our way through a grove of pear trees where bees and butterflies drank the juice of the fallen fruits. Nadia plucked a fresh pear from the tree, then picked another and handed it to me. "I would eat so many pears in the summer that my fur would stick to me all down my front," she said. She took a bite and remarked through a mouthful of pear. "They taste the same. Go on, try it."

This didn't seem like the time to be picking fruit, but before I could object Nadia went on: "Oh! Cherries!" She picked an enormous cherry, popped it in her mouth, and pocketed more. "I can never eat the cherries humans grow. They are so small and sour." She spat out a pit. "Tsakhia does not understand. He loves those awful human cherries. I will bring some of these back for him."

"Nadia, you were taking me somewhere," I reminded her.

"I know, I know," Nadia answered, looking around at the treetops, thrilling and late-night birdsong and the happy chirps of bats. "But Kaeda, can you imagine if your island was put back exactly as you remember? You would tell me all about it, wouldn't you?"

I couldn't answer that aloud, my throat suddenly tight, but I nodded.

When we exited the grove though, Nadia's cheerfulness evaporated. Having returned to a home I didn't recognize, I knew exactly how she felt. A cabin rose out of the tall grass. The roof was covered with moss. Ivy grew up the walls and across the windows and doors. In some places the humidity and the prolific climbing of the plants had caused the wood to crumble.

"The Egorovs used to live here," Nadia told me. "Inessa made the best pear preserves." She walked on, coming to what I took to be an old tree trunk, grey and green with lichen, bent toward the grove. "There she is," Nadia whispered.

It was not an old tree trunk, but a woman, stretched upward and petrified. I could see the ripples of her skirt, and the contour of the purse hanging down from her belt, but all elongated. I looked upward but couldn't see an end to her, though I did notice one branch-like arm extended in the direction we had come, as if she had been running, or at least reaching. I wondered if there was a ceiling somewhere above us, and if she was a pillar.

"Come," Nadia said. "The temple is in the center of the village. It is not far."

She narrated as we walked, a murmur of commentary, telling me who had lived in each green cabin, identifying more petrified werebears. I could see them more and more clearly. In fact, I began to wonder if it was not night here, but actually early morning. There was light coming from somewhere, slanting like dawn but oddly soft and diffused. It added golden highlights to the clouds of ferns we walked through, left distinct shadows on the southern sides of the bear pillars and the cabins, and seemed to hold the cricket songs in the air around us. I could almost swear I could see them floating like little motes of—

"Magic!" I exclaimed to Nadia. I had been so caught up in the sights around us that I hadn't noticed. Part of the warmth, part of the summery thickness of the air was caused by an increasing density of fresh ambient magic.

"Yes," Nadia agreed, breathing deeply. "It was always like this. Come."

Soon we reached the last cabin and came to the lawn that she had described playing in. The grass was to our knees now and filled with spikes of purple sage, snowy sprinkles of quinine blooms and bursts of fiery lilies. In the middle of the meadow, stood the temple.

It was an ornate pavilion, sitting above the glass on a platform. Unlike the rest of the village, the wood of the pavilion had remained new, a rich honey brown rising to the two tiers of a pitched roof. Roses had grown along the supporting posts, but in a gentle fashion, not overwhelming the structure. Between the posts, sheer curtains hung, still in the breezeless air, and just as fresh and new as the wood. The sunny glow filtered through them, coming from a point within.

Nadia and I waded through the grass and flowers. They were so thick it felt almost like wading through mud. Stepping out of them onto the lustrous steps of the temple reminded me of stepping out of the ocean, and onto the land. Nadia led the way up and parted the sheer curtains.

The space within reminded me of Nadia and Tsakhia's tent. There was a bed, a very large bed with a chest at the foot of it. A rug covered most of the rest of the floor. On the rug sat a set of chairs and a small table, and on one of the chairs sat…

Well, it didn't look like much except a concentration of light about as big as a human heart, but magic drifted out from it, and I sensed an incredible concentration of magic within. It was the magical equivalent of a heart, I guessed. The kentro of a Magic. Likely the kentro of Molva's deceased archon.

Very good, healer, a bright, intense voice said in my mind. *Yes, I am what remains of Bogrealis, Magic of Daniil. Together we were Bogdan, or Boginya, Archon of Molva.*

Her voice was like the hum of the crickets and the crackle of ice and the rush of a wind all wrapped together. It was almost too much to listen to. Like staring at the sun. I found myself holding on to one of the posts of the pavilion, gasping as if I had leapt into cold water.

Nadia however, didn't seem to mind. She stumbled forward. "You are here," she said, her voice breaking as she fell onto her knees.

Yes.

"But Tsakhia said – the Purple Madness."

The light of the kentro flickered. Images flashed in my mind, Tsakhia's memories that I had witnessed. I guessed the Magic was reading my mind. When she spoke again, there was pain in her voice. *The rest of me.*

"The… the rest?"

Yes, she admitted, and the scalding brightness of her voice increased, the ice cracking further. *They caught my wizard, but my heart was not with him. If only I had gone out with him. If only I had not allowed fear to rule me. I left a piece of myself behind, the most important piece, and without it, he was not as strong.*

That made sense, I thought. The magic's kentro was the seat of its consciousness, the center of its will. I remembered Tsakhia saying that it was not easy to wrest a magic from its wizard, but the halves of Molva's archon, wizard and Magic, had been easily split in two. Easily, because the Magic was never fully there.

Yes, healer. I doomed us, and doomed Molva, by living in fear. When the cascade came, I knew what had happened. I knew Daniil would no longer be able to protect me. So, I sealed the forest, to keep myself safe.

This set Nadia sobbing. She bowed to the floor, and with her forehead against the rug said, "I could have been here with you! I could have been here."

You should have been, the Magic said, and the concentration of magic in the chair flowed out into a shape, a rounded figure of a petite human woman, wearing a fur cloak. A massive pair of antlers crowned her head, her nose was a bit like a cow's nose, and her eyes were huge as a flying squirrels' eyes and starry as a Magic's eyes usually were. She lifted Nadia's face with two clawed hands. *I meant for you all to die. I meant for that axe you carry, that magical blade, to become my anchor. I meant to gather magic and stone to myself until I created a new form, something armored and impenetrable. Perhaps I would have become a creature to rival that Purple Madness, that malicious feary, that controlling Dov.*

"Take it, take it now," Nadia said, holding the weapon out to the Magic, but the antlered woman pressed it back towards her.

Instead, your mother had the presence of mind to send you and that axe away. She gave me time to think, time to grieve. As I caught glimpses of your mind and your world in prayer, I have decided that I no longer want to live in fear, and I no longer want to fight. I only want to heal the land, if I can.

I was beginning to feel impatient, and uneasy, though I couldn't exactly say why. Perhaps it was because when she mentioned using the axe as her anchor I began to wonder what magic exactly it carried. Perhaps it was because I thought I had heard a raindrop on the roof, and that didn't strike me as a thing that should happen in this contained environment. Regardless, I found myself looking back, scanning the illuminated pillars and abandoned cabins behind us. It was quiet. Quieter than it had been.

Yes, Bogrealis agreed. *Yes, they have come.* She rose up, the kentro pulsing gently in the center of her ghostly form.

I couldn't be sure if she glanced up, or whether it was the sound of another slight tap that drew my eyes upward. Another impossible raindrop. Then another. Nadia and I both ran to the steps where we had come in and pushed aside the curtain.

A drop fell onto the steps in front of us. Not clear, but red.

Tap, tap. Across the steps, and across the meadow, drops of blood were falling.

Behind us, Bogrealis spoke, her voice softer now. *I have stopped hiding and they have reversed my magic, melting the stone back to flesh. I should not be surprised. She is me after all. The purple madness. She would know what to do.*

We were about to be caught in the middle of a downpour of werebear blood, and possibly other remains, which were, if my magical senses were correct, rife with both intact ursinthropy as well as tumbling broken bits, combining into who knew what dangerous magical corruptions.

"We should get out of here," I said. Like ice stuck by warm water, the petrified werebears outside had begun to melt, stone turning to fur, skin, muscle, and blood as it slipped away, slowly flattening the meadow grasses beneath a layer of gore. Could I sustain a magical shield against this long enough to make it to the exit, I wondered? I doubted it, especially as the patter of blood overhead thickened with squelching thuds.

It is too late to escape, Bogrealis said.

I'm going to die, I thought. I am going to die in a mythic forest, with a religious werebear, without saying goodbye to my father, or Archavie, or Reef. No, no there had to be a way.

"We have to leave," I said, turning toward Nadia and her goddess. "I can shield us, but we need to go before it gets worse."

It is worse. Bogrealis said calmly. *Even now they raise the dead.*

I flung the curtain aside again. A shape began to grow out of the swamp of blood, reaching up with an arm like a red tree branch, fingers of bone and tendrils of flesh twisting together as it pushed itself off the ground.

Swallowing a scream, I staggered back.

I confess, I am afraid.

"I am not," Nadia said, striding back to the glowing image of Bogrealis. "Tell me what to do, and I will do it.

I cannot defeat them, the Magic said, speaking quickly, *but there is one who can. With your help, bear daughter, I will withstand the onslaught until he arrives.*

"One? Who? What?" I asked, hurrying back to join them.

I can make you something new, Bogrealis went on. *Something they cannot break, but you must give yourself to me.*

Bogrealis extended her hand, as the arm of a bloody creature slapped onto the polished wood of the temple's floor, pulling a body, a body vaguely reminiscent of a bear's, up the steps. It had no skin, eyes on its shoulders, and jaws both on its face and along its ribs, as if the pieces of melted flesh had gathered and stuck wherever they found a place.

I felt my heart pounding in my throat. Something. Anything. I fumbled through the satchel on my hip with shaking hands. A magic disassembler. Maybe I could magnify it quickly enough to—

"I have always been yours," Nadia said, "but the healer."

"Yes, bring her here. Give her the axe. They must not take it."

Nadia's strong grip pulled me a few steps backward, though my eyes remained glued to the blood-seeping creature that now opened the one properly-placed mouth it had and gave a roar.

"Kaeda. Kaeda, Hold this."

Nadia had given me her axe. Her axe and the pouch full of cherries. My brain seemed to have stopped working. I stared at her numbly, asking "Nadia, what are we doing?"

"The only thing we can," she said. Then she wrapped her arms around me and shut her eyes.

Past her armored shoulder I caught a glimpse of a tall, black-robed figure gliding through the blood rain. Then a flash-like lightning, and a rumble of thunder in the roar that came from Nadia's chest. The roar went on in a deep crackling, as of trees falling as Nadia's body seemed to bend and stretch.

I might have screamed, but I was so deep in a surreal state of numb disbelief that it was difficult to tell. Svevolod's furious cry of, "You are mine!" faded as glowing golden veins and chestnut brown wood swept around me.

Chapter Forty-Six

DANGER

Reef

THE warm ocean and the starry sky had melded together. Reef swam through the stars in a glorious expanse of dark humming water. Or perhaps air? Reef wasn't sure. All he knew was that it was warm, thick, mesmerizing. Too mesmerizing to pay attention to whoever was calling his name.

"Reef! Unseen Reef! FūhrDare!"

No, it doesn't matter, stay here. The words came from inside him. But Reef wasn't talking to himself. It was someone else. He remembered the shape of the night sky sitting beside him on the shore of the lake.

We're safe here, it said, sounding anxious. Reef felt its presence all around him. *We're safe here. Let's stay.*

"Reef!" and then *Wake up you idiot.*

Archavie, Reef thought, looking around at the stars and understanding that he was in a dream. Turus. They are calling me. It sounds important I must wake up.

No, no, don't. Sleep. Let them go without you.

Out of the depths of the night sky came the sound of Archavie's voice, closer and closer with each moment, shouting, "Reef! It's Kaeda! Wake up! Turus go wake them all up!"

Kaeda!

Reef rolled out of bed, nearly knocking the wizard from his feet. Where were his weapons? There.

"Turus has gone to get the others. Hurry."

"What's happened?" Reef asked as he made for the door, ignoring the tiny voice that said, no, no, don't go.

Archavie leapt over Reef's thrashing tail and shook his head. "Nadia found the petrified forest, and Turus thinks the wrestors are nearby. I'll tell you on the way. Come on."

A panic of preparation. Gamalielle screeching on and on about how could Archavie have left them all asleep and how she was going to kill Yury when she found him. General Straton coldly demanding details, and Reef and Tsakhia, silent, though if Tsakhia's feelings were anything like Reef's it was the silence of contained fury and concealed terror as they listened to the bizarre tale. A trance. A fog. A forest made of stone.

Of course, it was no good now telling Archavie that he and Yury should have notified the rest of the commission.

Lady Batbayar met them in the entryway of the castle, she and the cat butler helping the humans layer on enchanted cloaks.

"Oh and we may want to take a few more of those," Archavie added, "since Turus says Reef's Khirian friends are also out in the forest, a little bit lost, and freezing to death."

"What?" Reef exclaimed.

"Yes, he noticed them on the way back, and I'm sending him now to tell them to meet us. They have fire at least. I think they will make it."

There were entirely too many feelings now for Reef to sort them out. Later. For now, he looked to the lady of the house who said, "Yes, of course, Guasparre?"

Within minutes Reef and Straton had bundles of enchanted cloaks, scarves, muffs, and hats to carry, spilling warmth out across their arms as they ran across the snow and to the forest.

The fog Archavie had described had spread, and they soon found themselves running through it, calling to one another to make sure no one got lost, straining their eyes to keep track of Archavie ahead, Gamalielle above.

Then, somewhere between the trees, Reef heard another sound.

"Stop!" he called.

They did, the Commission finding their way through the mist to reform around him.

"What is it? A phage?" Straton asked.

Reef shook his head. For just a moment concern about Kaeda had left him. He listened with all his focus. He was sure he had heard it.

"We can't delay," the general went on, but then Reef heard it again. The call to surface. A short Khirian sound meant to carry over distances.

Reef called back, and a reply shortly followed.

"Yes," Archavie agreed, "Yes, Turus has found them again. He'll bring them to us. From the west. Look for torches."

Soon they came through the fog, a dim orange glow. Reef ran to meet them. Two dozen Khirians, shuffling in chilled misery through the forest.

"Reef!" Wave shouted when he saw him. "Stop," he called to the rest of his section. "We can stop now, light fires."

"I have better," Reef said, and he dropped the bundles of clothes at Wave's feet. "The magic will keep them warm. Help me get them dressed."

Some of the Khirians were too cold to lift their arms. They swayed where they stood, eyes drifting closed, about to collapse and surrender to the winter, but after being wrapped in scarves or having cloaks tied around their necks, they began to warm and recover.

"If I was not worried out of my mind this would be the most hilarious thing I've ever seen," Gamalielle remarked, as the Commission witnessed the final touches, hats torn open on the top slid onto Khirian tails, furred muffs slipped onto ankles. Reef didn't know if it looked hilarious or not, but he could tell that the swimmers felt much better.

"What is happening?" Wave asked Reef in Khirian. "They would not come out here for us." He scanned the group. "Where is the healer?"

Reef had felt bright with joy when he saw them, wishing he could leap like a hatchling, wanting to nose Wave back and forth with relief, but he had contained himself. Now the joy faded, and he remembered why they were out in the forest.

"Come with us and I will explain," Reef said.

As they walked through the forest, now a much larger party, Reef did his best to convey the situation. "There is a place," he attempted. "A place like a fortress made of werebears that have been turned to stone. The mammals think that what remains of the Molvan archon may be inside, and Nadia – she is a bear warrior – and Kaeda, the healer, have gone in to find it. But Dov Voda's wrestors want it as well, and they have attacked us before."

"What are wrestors?"

"They are… people who… can take control of a Magic."

"Like a wizard?"

"No, the wrestors command Magics that do not belong to them."

Wave frowned at that. Of course, it was difficult to comprehend. Neither he nor Reef could see or feel or sense magic or Magics.

Reef thought that and then thought… was it true? He noticed that there seemed to be a haze of warmth around Archavie, drifting and swirling a little like a slow-moving flame, with bits drifting off, looking around, and then coming back. Was it just a trick of the fog? How had he never noticed it before?

"Most of the Magics that Voda's wrestors command are phages," Reef went on. "They are monster Magics. They eat other magic, maybe Magics too. Werecreatures cannot be near them. They have magic all throughout their bodies. If a phage tears it out, they will die."

That probably didn't make sense to Wave either, but it suddenly made much more sense to Reef as Yury came bursting out of the fog. Reef could almost see a shimmer within him. It reminded Reef of the telltale ripples of feeding fishes on the surface of the water, but it wasn't on the surface, and he couldn't see it. It was more like he could feel it. Like the reverberations of the magic at work in Yury had reached him through the air.

While Gamalielle exclaimed, "Yury!" and leapt forward to throw her arms around him, the voice inside Reef said, *Go back! Go back!*

"What's happened?" Archavie asked.

"The wrestors," Yury gasped, somewhere between panting and sobbing, "It's melting. Hurry."

They ran on, Yury now leading the way, and soon reached the streambed. Yury scrambled down the rocks. The rest of them followed, but as Reef reached the center of the streambed, the voice inside him gave a firm, *no,* and Reef's feet stopped moving. He fell heavily to the frozen stones, and the Khirian behind him had to leap to avoid tripping on him.

Reef gave a great growl of frustration and addressed the voice: what are you doing?

We can't go. They will see me. They will get me, or you!

"What's going on?" General Straton asked. He had been all the way up the opposite bank but slid back down to check on Reef.

"There is something," Reef growled in confusion. "It will not let me move."

Then Reef heard an exclamation of alarm from Tsakhia. The magician leapt, soaring down to Reef in a great rushing of black fabric, and as he landed a few feet away he immediately flung out his hand. "You are mine."

If Reef had fallen into another blood net, it could not have hurt so much, though the pain did not seem to be in his body anywhere, so much as his mind.

Then Wave tackled Tsakhia, knocking his bird mask askew, and the magician's grip was broken. Tsakhia threw Wave back with a blast of magic from his staff, Wave called the rest of the Khirians to action, and it all could have gone very badly if Straton hadn't magically amplified his voice and boomed, "Stop!"

They did, the Khirians poised to attack though Tsakhia had flown twenty feet up into the air.

"What is going on?" the general demanded. "Magiologist Rozhkov, what did you do to him?"

"I attempted to wrest the phage that is apparently attached to him somehow."

"Phage?" Straton asked. "But I can see it."

"I can see it, too," Gamalielle said.

This gave Tsakhia pause. He drifted down and towards Reef, who had climbed to his feet, feeling shaky and nauseous in the aftermath of Tsakhia's wresting. Wave and the other cozily dressed Khirians positioned themselves protectively around him, eyeing the magician.

"You're right," Tsakhia's voice came whispery from his hood. "It is made of both magics. I don't understand." His voice became strained toward the end, and he sank to the ground, leaning heavily on his staff as his feet touched the rocks.

"Well, it's not killing anybody," Gamalielle said, hands on her hips on the opposite bank. "So, can it wait? We've had enough delays already."

"It won't let me go," Reef told Straton again. "It does not want to go."

"If it truly will not let you move, we will come back for you."

Straton started off back toward the slope of the opposite bank. Yury persuaded Tsakhia to ride on his back so the magician could rest.

They would leave him behind, but somewhere out there Kaeda was in trouble. He could not remain here, stuck helplessly in the middle of this streambed.

"Pull me," Reef said. He held out his arms to Wave and to UrchinSting who was on his other side.

They each tugged his arms while Reef strained forward.

"How are you stuck?" Wave grunted.

"I don't know. A Magic won't let me go."

"Why should a Magic care what you do?"

"I don't know!"

Wave and his section all pulled and pushed Reef, trying to move him forward. Something hurt. It was hard to tell where. It was as if he were playing a game of tug of war with his entire body. I don't have time for this, Reef thought furiously as he saw the mammals disappearing into the trees on the other side. "If you don't want to go then stay!"

The growl of his voice shook snow from the trees. Reef felt a spear of pain in his back, small but sharp, near his right shoulder blade, and suddenly he found himself falling forward.

Exclamations came from Wave and the others. Reef reached over his shoulder and felt blood, but the wound seemed small. "Come on," he urged, and he ran forward, climbing the rugged slope of the northern bank. He didn't bother to look back and see if a Khirian made of stars was standing in the streambed, or if it was holding onto a tiny piece of his shoulder.

Don't leave me! The voice pleaded, but still Reef did not look back. He made for the trees. Wave and his section followed without further comment. Whatever had happened, Reef would deal with it later, when Kaeda was safe.

They ran through a stretch of forest where everything felt confused and dark. He could see the movement of Gamalielle in the trees ahead, and the lumbering bulk of Tsakhia riding on Yury. He followed them, as the pines extended so far overhead that they seemed to form tunnels and caverns of trees.

And was it just him, or was the forest warmer now?

Everyone seemed to have felt the change in the air. Straton held up a hand for them to stop and Gamalielle said, "Do you smell that?"

"I smell it," Yury replied. He sat back, letting Tsakhia slide off his back as Yury shifted back to human form.

"Blood," Gamalielle said. "Lots of it."

Reef could smell it too, though his sense of smell was not nearly as sharp on land as it was underwater. Now that they had stopped, he was sure the forest was warmer. The ground felt softer underfoot, and ahead of them the fog rose, thick and lively, as if the earth had exhaled a great steaming breath.

"I don't smell any human blood," Yury told the group. "Only Ursine."

"How?" General Straton asked. "Lady Batbayar has never seen werebears out in these woods."

Then Yury jumped, looking down as if startled by the ground. Straton did the same and called out, "Blood!"

It reached Reef and Wave a moment later, seeping around Reef's toes in a thick, viscous layer of red.

"Ugh, gross," Gamalielle wailed, from her perch in midair.

"The blood does not appear to carry any malignant magic," Straton said. "Nevertheless, Yury, it might be best if we leave you here. We don't know what is ahead."

"But I do," Yury replied, his voice thick with emotion. "I know where we are. The pines are thicker ahead. Then the orchards begin. The pears, can't you smell them? Oh Nadia."

The bear man seemed to choke on his words and Gamalielle zipped down to hug his shoulders.

"Yes, she told me," Tsakhia added. "The orchards at the southern border of the village."

"Lead on then," Straton said.

They trudged through the muck of blood and dirt and pine needles. Reef kept expecting it to freeze into slush, but it did not, only dried and congealed, crusting their feet in brown.

"We soaked some fields in blood," Wave murmured, "but never like this."

They reached the place Yury had spoken of, where the trees still seemed almost to be a wall, growing thickly together. These pines stood distinct from the rest of the forest, not only in their thickness, but also in their decoration. Not snow, but gore, as if blood and bones and haphazard bits and pieces had rained down on them. It dripped, still, as if the forest had thawed for the spring and the thaw had revealed all of winter's deaths.

"On the other side," Yury said, his eyes staring as if he saw something the rest of them could not, an echo of memory perhaps. "Beyond the pines, the groves. Then the paths. The houses."

There was more beyond the pines than just paths and houses, Reef thought. He could hear sounds, growls he thought, and an occasional squelch, though muffled by the thickness of the flesh-clad branches.

"Miss Aisop," Straton spoke quietly, "can you get up above the trees, scout the landscape for us?"

"Really, with all we've been through, you gotta call me Gamalielle." The cat glanced at Yury, still holding his hand in both of her own. "But yeah, I can." Then she flew quickly up and out of sight.

They waited. The forest continued to breathe, a mist drifting up from the ground and out from the trees ahead. Wave whispered to Reef, "Does any of this make sense to you?"

Reef replied that it didn't. "But be ready," he said.

They were, weapons in their hands, tails swishing evenly, watching the still forest. With his swimmers around him, Reef had to remind himself every moment not to charge through the trees. They weren't facing Molvan peasants, but strange magic. Without planning, this fight, the fight for Kaeda, and for Nadia, could end in disaster. He could not bear that. He could not even consider it. He would wait.

When Gamalielle dropped back down through the trees, her eyes were as wide as Yury's. "Okay, so, find me a stick and I'll draw this nonsense for you. Thanks. Frils there's nowhere to draw in this muck."

"Here," Archavie said. He waved a hand and a flat plane of glowing magic appeared before Gamalielle. "Turus will borrow the memories from your mind as you recall them and populate the battle map."

"So, what we've got is the village," She drew a circle that took up most of the magical surface. "And we're here." She stabbed her finger into the magic outside the surface and little figures leapt up, tiny versions of Reef and the others less than an inch high. "There's the orchards Yury mentioned, kinda groups of trees, and then cabin things, basically just mounds of goo and entrails at this point." As she poked the magic they appeared, overgrown houses, trees, all obscured by gore.

"So far so good, right," the cat said, taking a deep breath, "but this frils that's all over the trees and whatnot, it's alive in there." She stabbed her finger into the map again and other figures appeared, indistinct shapes, but most including a head and four limbs. They were bigger than Khirians, but without tails. "I don't know how many," Gamalielle went on. "They're wandering around, patrolling probably, for these guys." She stabbed the map again, and wrestors appeared. "I counted five, but who knows? I'm pretty sure our old friend Svevvy is here," her voice rose in pitch as she said it, as if she really wished it wasn't the case. "And I'm pretty sure he's also got a piece of Tsakhia's old friend the PM with him."

A purple patch materialized on the map, near one of the wrestors. It looked like little more than a shadow, but Reef could sense the increased tension in the air as it appeared.

"The rest of Turus is in there too," Archavie told them. "I don't know where, but I can feel it."

"If we can figure out which wrestor has a grip on him, maybe we can give him a chance to escape," Gamalielle said.

"They seem to be gathered near the center," Straton observed, returning their attention to the map.

Gamalielle had left the center of the circle empty, and now she said with some difficulty, "Yeah, so, there's something there. It mostly looks like a pile of wreckage," she drew a smaller circle in the middle of the village and a heap of what looked like broken wood appeared. "And there's like… I don't know, I guess it's a tree? I didn't get a good look because I didn't want the wrestors to spot me."

She had dragged a finger up from the center of the pile of wreckage, and a shape had appeared. It looked like a tree to Reef. It was an up-and-down shape that splayed out toward the top.

"I think they're trying to do something to the tree," Gamalielle said, "and I think we probably should stop them because it looks to me like the tree is making magic, which doesn't make any sense, but what does?"

"No sign of Kaeda or Nadia?" Straton asked.

"None," Gamalielle said, but the trees creaked around them, and as one the mammals turned toward Tsakhia.

"Take a deep breath," Yury said. "We'll find them."

"The tree," Tsakhia rasped. "Look at the tree."

They all leaned in, peered closer. Reef wasn't sure what they were looking at. The closer he got, the more it looked like a tree, though maybe a dream tree, with whorls in the patterns of its bark and many small branches crowning it almost like a head of hair.

"We don't know—" Yury began, but Tsakhia bent his head, the wind blew, the mist swirled, and the gore slithered across Reef's feet.

Swiftly, Straton moved to set his hands on Tsakhia's shoulders. "Calm. We don't know what happened to your wife, but this is our opportunity to find out. If we can find Kaeda, perhaps she can tell us more. Can you help us?"

The wind stilled, the trees, the slush, and the mist settled. Tsakhia nodded.

"Do you have a magical restraint with you?" Yury asked. "You might want to put it on."

"I can handle it," Tsakhia said.

Yury didn't look like he believed him, but Straton didn't seem to want to waste time arguing. "Here's my plan. Reef, take your shoal to the west. Make noise, draw the creatures to you. Their magic shouldn't hurt you, or at least less than it would hurt us. Tsakhia has been working on phage-shredding javelins. We'll send half of the javelins with you to use on the phage-golems. Tsakhia and I will go through the eastern side of the village and see how close we can get to the tree. We'll take some of the javelins with us and give some to Gamalielle. Gamalielle, stay aloft and don't reveal yourself except in an emergency."

"The shredding magic… that's pretty dangerous, right?" Gamalielle asked hesitantly.

"These have a self-contained radius of detonation," Tsakhia explained. "About fifteen feet. As long as you stay at range, they won't affect your magic." He paused. "At least, that's how they're supposed to work."

"What about us?" Yury asked, gesturing to himself and Archavie. "You're not just going to leave us here?"

"If the wrestors see either of you, we'll have someone else to rescue. Gamalielle will keep you appraised of our movements."

"But—"

"No buts. Stay here. If we must retreat and we are wounded, we'll need your help. The rest of you, let's go."

With a few of Tsakhia's phage-shredding javelins tucked into the sling for his maul, Reef and his swimmers formed up a little east of the Commission's position. The Khirians looked uneasy, fascinated and confused, eyeing the bloody trees, and Reef knew he should say a few words.

"This does not seem like our fight," he began, "but it is. We think we feel no magic, but you remember the rage that called us to war? That rage was not our own, but came from the purple thing the mammals call the Purple Madness."

Reef had explained this to some extent already as they walked, so none of the Khirians were surprised, but he wanted them to remember. "Until it is dealt with, until the magic in Molva is healthy, we will not know if our thoughts and feelings are our own."

He looked across the row of Khirians, who, one by one, coughed a yes of assent. He wanted to add another reason, that though they didn't know them, the people in the commission were worth fighting for, that Kaeda especially was worth fighting for. But he didn't think they would understand, so he just said, "We will protect the magic-users while they figure out what to do. A blood swamp and flesh monsters doesn't even sound as bad as mating season."

Gravelly laughter. The thwack of a few tails on the ground. Honestly, when Reef put it that way, it sounded pretty true.

Chapter Forty-Seven

BLOOD AND WIND

Reef

WITH Reef and Wave in the lead they pushed through the trees. Apparently, the orchards extended this far east. When they left the pines behind Reef found the smell of blood sweetened by the aroma of crushed pears. The fruit hung around the shoal, glossy and red like kidneys or hearts dangling from the trees. Fallen pears hid in the muck underfoot, making the ground uneven so that Reef and his swimmers had to tread carefully. When they reached the edge of the grove Reef called a halt.

There was a light somewhere ahead, somewhat like lanternlight and somewhat like dawn. It cast shadows back toward the treeline, long, dark, slanting shadows. Reef saw a shape moving ahead, a silhouette against the glow. At first it was barely distinguishable from the gore-drenched cabin some three or four yards away. Then it stepped out, a creature with a long face, teeth arranged above, below, and all around where its mouth might have been, and eyes above that. It was a patchwork of bone and muscle, bloody fur and fat and it gleamed all over with blood and moisture from the mist. One limb plunged toward the earth, then another, but Reef couldn't tell whether it lifted its feet or just extended and retracted parts of itself.

Possibly more intimidating than mating season, Reef thought, as his heart beat faster. But not by much.

Reef pulled out a javelin and took aim just as the thing fixed its eyes on him. A cacophony of grumbly voices rose from it, but only for a moment before the javelin plunged into its trunk and exploded with a metallic "ting". The shards of javelin flew out like a school of tiny silver fish fleeing from a predator, and the magic followed, a sizzle and flash of lightning from fish to fish forming a sphere that enveloped most of the golem. The monster collapsed to the ground in a heap.

"On!" Reef barked the command to advance, and they ran.

Growl, ting, sizzle. Growl, ting, sizzle. The swimmers behind Reef hurled Tsakhia's handiwork as other fleshy constructs, alerted to the Khirians' presence, began closing in. Reef and Wave kept running through the red landscape, warm and languid as a swamp in a summer night and striped with patches of golden light and shadow. Reef wanted to get them deep enough into the village to view the tree so they could witness what happened when Tsakhia and Straton reached it.

But they didn't quite make it that far. The ground ahead of Reef bulged and blossomed and formed itself into a new creature with a gnarl of teeth on its face and arms all around, part bear, part vicious octopus that began to stab down with the bone-covered tips of its tentacles.

Reef rolled to the side as one arm stabbed down at him, and Wave did the same, dodging in the other direction. Teeth of Sharks didn't make it in time. A third tentacle plunged into the Khirian's chest and then burst out in red fingers through his back and sides.

"Shred it at the base!" Reef shouted, hefting his maul from his back. He swung it in great sweeps, knocking aside one spearing finger and then another. They broke easily, like fountains, but like fountains kept coming. A shard of bone sliced across his shoulder while he looked for an opening and noted uneasily that two more monsters were on approach from the direction of the glow.

Then as Wave and Reef and Sting fought the limbs, Lightning dashed in, quick as his name, dove and slid across the gore, and stabbed two javelins into the base of the anemone. Ting. Flash. Sizzle. A splatter and a wriggle as the creature's arms fell to the ground. Lightning stood, coated in the slime and carnage that had burst around him, and surveyed his scales with disgust.

"The ocean will wash it off," Wave laughed as they ran past him. "Come on."

As Wave and the others engaged the next two blood bears in a mess of thuds and splashes and roars, Gamalielle dropped down beside Reef.

"So, here's the deal. Straton and Tsakhia have gone in from the other side. Tsakhia wrested a couple of these golems to use as a meat shield, but a wrestor noticed. He and Tsakhia had a little bit of a mind-power contest and Tsakhia won but Straton got a little bit eaten by one of the monsters. Not a *lot* eaten, he finished off the wrestor, but he's pretty hurt."

On the other side of the village, Reef hadn't heard any of it, but if Tsakhia and Straton had drawn the wrestors' attention and were getting mobbed by monsters, they would need help. "We will make our way to them," Reef said, and he hurled another javelin at a monster that had come galloping in from the west.

But a vague look had come into the cat's eyes. "Actually, Turus says he has a plan, if you can just get him free. He's nearby and—" The cat squeaked, thrashed in the air, and plummeted to the ground. Reef saw one of the robe-clad figures, a wrestor, drift into the path between the houses. It had a hand outstretched and must have stolen the magic Gamalielle was using.

"Hope you don't mind if I ride on your back," she yelped, as she scrambled up onto Reef's shoulders. "I'm not staying down in that goo!"

Turus nearby? And a wrestor nearby? Possibly a coincidence, or possibly this person, human or feary or whatever he was, held Turus in his magical grip. With his maul in his hands, Reef gave a roar and charged straight at the wrestor.

The wrestor had been hovering in the air. Now he flew straight upwards. No, Reef wouldn't let him escape. He leapt.

"I gotcha!" Gamalielle shrieked. "I think!"

Reef soared through the air as if in a dream. He caught the hem of the wrestor's robe. He bit and felt blood and bones that definitely did not taste human.

The wrestor screamed and suddenly Turus's voice burst into Reef's mind.

It took you long enough.

"You are mine," the wrestor said, as he tried to keep a grip on the Magic, but then he rocked in the air as Lightning, springing from Boulder's shoulder, also collided with the wrestor. Lightning sank his teeth into some part of the cloak-shrouded figure and the wrestor began to sink beneath their combined weight.

The magician gathered magic. Reef saw it bursting out in a blue shimmer. Gamalielle leapt from his back to stay out of the way, but of course the Khirians didn't mind the magic one bit. As the wrestor sank lower, Wave leapt onto it from behind and within a few minutes the robed figure had been crushed into the mush of gore around them.

Wave and Lightning each gave a short roar of triumph. The flesh monsters nearest them stopped, suddenly confused as the wrestor died, and for a few moments Reef's group pushed towards the tree with ease.

Then another bloody bear rose up and wrapped its arms around Lionfish and stuck him full of shards of bone. Another monster lumbering around a cabin cut Lightning with its long claws and left him staggering, and a misshapen maw latched onto Wave's shoulder long enough to wear away the flesh to the bone before Sting stabbed the golem with one of their last stakes.

Did Turus really have a plan, or had he just wanted to motivate Reef to help him? If he does not do something soon, I will need to call a retreat, Reef thought. I cannot ask them all to die.

For Kaeda, though? But they do not know her.

The tree had come into view at last, a radiant pillar some fifteen or twenty feet tall in the center of a pile of wreckage. Now Reef saw what Gamalielle meant, that it looked like a tree, but also not like a tree at all. The trunk had arms, not arms like limbs, but arms wrapped around itself, head bent down, hair fanning out into the branches overhead.

Reef didn't know what to make of this, nor how they would reach the tree. Four wrestors stood around the tree. Reef recognized one, taller than the others, his still posture and the black-on-black embroidery of his sleeves now unfortunately familiar. Svevolod had his back to Reef, facing the tree with his arms lifted. Reef saw, as Gamalielle had described, the mass of the Purple Madness, gathered in the branches, and at times swirling across the trunk as if looking for a way in. The other wrestors though, faced away from the tree, watching for threats, and now raising new monsters from the swamp of gore.

"How can they have any phages left to golemize?" Gamalielle shrilled in Reef's ear. "You've shredded so many!"

But more golems rose, and Wave and the others stood watching the flesh blossom into fresh shapes and waiting for Reef's orders.

Was it worth speaking to Svevolod? Negotiating, in case he had Kaeda somewhere? But then, he had told his shoal that they must defeat the Purple Madness. Perhaps they should run in, attack the wrestors, hope that Straton and Tsakhia would reinforce them with some robust magic.

He was about to give the order when, at last, he heard Archavie's voice. It had no words in it, just delight, and suddenly, in a rush of splashing thunder, there was the wizard, on the back of a caribou, leading a whole herd of the animals. They had the rest of Tsakhia's pitons tied to their antlers and as they charged through, they gored the golems as well as two wrestors who didn't manage to levitate in time. The wrestors fell into the blood swamp and were shortly trampled by the stampede.

Svevolod turned his attention from the tree to the red-haired wizard and said those words that were now, to Reef, very terrible: "You are mine."

The color left Archavie. Reef saw the wizard flatten himself against the caribou's neck and cling to its fur. Even without Turus's control the deer did not fling him off, it merely snorted and continued its charge across the clearing and back into the trees.

Memories, Archavie without Turus, Tsakhia gripping the star creature at the streambed, crashed together in Reef's mind and he roared, "On!" He would not let this magician harm his friend, not again.

Gamalielle leapt off her perch on his back as the Khirians ran into the trampled wake of the caribou. Svevolod and the other remaining wrestors were high in the air now, and the only way to reach them would be to scale the tree, but the trunk was not smooth. Easier than climbing a giant worm. Reef reached it and began to climb. The others of his shoal were around him. Reef could tell by the shimmer and shudder of the air that the wrestors were tossing magic at them, but of course that didn't matter. Reef reached the branching part of the tree and ran out. He knew the tree wouldn't support his weight, but what he knew about trees proved not to be true. He found himself easily dashing out on a splay of small limbs, saw briefly Svevolod's dark hood tilted up, the shift of the magician's robes as he made to fly away, then Reef threw himself down.

It felt rather like hitting a palm branch resting on the water's surface. There was resistance, due to the water, but then Reef and the fluttering branch both went down. Turus's voice said in Reef's mind. *I shall not forget this. And now I shall return to my wizard.*

Then he had the wrestor pinned to the ground. Reef opened his mouth. He would grip the hooded face in his jaws, jerk it, break the man's – or feary's –neck. He would have done it, but suddenly the clearing turned purple, and in the purple Reef's mind and body suddenly hummed and would not obey him.

Break this tree, a voice said, a seething, furious voice. *Break it!*

Reef fought it, but he slowly lifted his hands from the wrestor. Svevolod began to writhe, trying to free himself from his robe, which Reef was still standing on. At last he unclasped his cloak, turned, and scrambled out. A pair of horns, a long plait of white hair, and finally two massive, carefully folded, grey wings. The feary took one look back at the tree and the purple with his red-star eyes, and fled into the woods.

No, Reef thought! But the rage sweeping over him from the Purple Madness was too strong to ignore. He turned, slowly, and saw the others of his shoal already lifting weapons to attack the tree.

As he staggered towards them, another voice cut through the fury ringing in his ears. "Nadia!"

Tsakhia's cry shook the ground, and shook the Khirians from their rage. The magician staggered across the clearing, pushing aside General Straton, who had been supporting him.

"Retreat!" Reef called, suddenly certain that whatever happened, it was going to be dangerous. "Away! To me!"

Wave's section listened and stumbled back, gathering around Reef as the shadows cast by the tree stretched longer, then rose and spun, taking their darkness into the air. The shadows tore away the haze of the Purple Madness in great pieces, caught in a rushing wind that pulled the gore from the trees in a rush of bloody rain. The thickness, the purple haze, the fury, all were torn away as Tsakhia clambered across the rubble, reaching for the tree trunk. "No! Nadia! No!"

"Reef!" Gamalielle's voice screeched. "Help!"

She was so tiny that the wind had knocked her down and sent her tumbling across the bloody ground. Reef gathered her up and she wrapped her arms around his neck and her legs around his chest, trying to not be torn away by the wind. "I take back every unkind thing I've ever said about you," she muttered.

Meanwhile Wave asked, "Leader, what should we do?"

It was very like a hurricane, and in a hurricane Reef would have told them to seek shelter, but they had not found Kaeda yet, and Straton beckoned him back towards the tree.

"Wave, Sting, with me," Reef shouted over the wind. "The rest of you, meet us outside the forest." When they hesitated Reef roared, "Now! Go!"

The others left, and Reef, Wave, and Sting bowed their heads and pressed on against the wind. They reached the pile of broken wood and tangled bloody roses and ivy. Reef scrambled to the top and Wave and Sting followed.

Tsakhia had reached the trunk and wrapped his arms around it. His shoulders heaved and Reef thought he made a sound, but Reef had to focus to try to hear it, as if the sound was beyond sound. Straton meanwhile shouted to be heard over the wind.

"Here!"

Reef saw it. A tiny change. A gap in the glow. Then in the gap a flash of steel. The blade of Nadia's axe again bit into the trunk from the inside.

"Wave, Sting!" Reef called.

Meanwhile Straton drew as near to the gap as he dared and shouted, "Kaeda, hold the axe. We're going to get you out."

While Wave and Sting anchored their claws, Reef watched Tsakhia. Would he mind if they tore the tree open? But he didn't seem to be paying attention. Indeed, Reef wasn't sure he was aware of them at all. The magician embraced the wood, with arms that seemed longer with each passing moment, bony white fingers bursting through the tips of his gloves and extending across the bark as the sound-beyond-sound went on and on.

"Ready, pull," Straton ordered.

The swimmers pulled. The wood split. Reef and the general lent their strength to widening the rent in the warm, glowing wood, then caught Kaeda as she tumbled out.

Reef knew right away that something wasn't right. She felt too warm, and though she looked up at them her eyes were glassy.

"She's burning up," General Straton said quickly. "The concentration of magic within the tree – Farians are prone to magic-induced hemorrhagic fevers. We need to get her back to the house. Reef, can you carry her?"

Reef already had Kaeda in his arms, terrified by the heat flowing off of her. He barked a command to the shoal and soon they were running back through the wreckage of cabins, the rising hurricane of blood and bones and crushed pears, back into the chilly stillness of the pine forest.

Every step felt like ten, every foot of ground seemed endless, then suddenly they were sliding down the stones into the streambed. Reef felt Kaeda cough, an uncomfortable tingle across his ventral fin, and when he looked down, he saw a splash of red across his scales.

He might have made a sound. He couldn't tell. The world around him seemed to have vanished. All he saw was Kaeda, broken veins on her cheeks, blood on her lips, as he lay her on the frozen rocks.

"The magic in her won't come out," Straton said. His voice seemed to come from a great distance, though Reef saw the man's knees at his daughter's side. "I hoped it would disperse when we left the wreckage, but it is stuck to her. I can't heal her. The magic is too thick."

Then Reef felt something else. A presence at his back. The starry being who refused to go into the forest. With it near him Reef saw Kaeda differently, not just her physical form, but also the dense brilliance of the magic within her. It hummed with intense energy. Reef knew what the energy of a human body should feel like. He was familiar with the heartbeat and surrounding resonance of Kaeda's body in the water. This was too much. He could imagine that it was tearing her apart.

And he felt a groan, a groan of hunger, from the creature behind him. It wanted that magic. It wanted to eat it.

Fear thrilled through Reef. No, to tear the magic from a creature, that would kill it. Reef didn't understand how it worked, but he had heard Kaeda and the werecreatures say it often enough.

The starry being hesitated. *You know how she should be, don't you? Can't we leave her that way? Just take out what doesn't belong there?*

Reef felt the creature's craving. It made his own mouth water.

Meanwhile Straton bent over his daughter. "I can't," the man stammered. "I can't get it out."

"What can we do?" Gamalielle asked. "There's got to be something we can do. Something in her bag? To bring the fever down."

"At this stage it won't make a difference," the general said. Tears ran from his eyes, crystal lines shimmering in the moonlight.

"I can," Reef said, and before he could change his mind he added to the starry being, do it.

The Magic rushed upon Kaeda. Straton, Gamalielle, and Yury all screamed for him to stop. In their voices Reef recognized his own terror, that Kaeda might die, and that now if she did it would be his fault. But now that he had set it loose he couldn't stop the Magic, nor ignore its flare of delight as it drank the magic from her body.

Reef thought with all his might of Kaeda, the Kaeda he knew, the Kaeda he felt in the water, the Kaeda he had held, only for a moment, in the pool, and he willed for her not to be torn apart.

Then it was over. The Magic withdrew and rolled across the stones, looking for any traces of magic dragged from the forest, and Reef saw that Kaeda still breathed.

Chapter Forty-Eight

REPAIR

Kaeda

WHEN I woke up, everything hurt. I tried to open my eyes, found my eyelids too heavy, and gave up. Instead, I gave my attention to the soft cushioning of the mattress and pillow beneath me. It felt like my bed at Temnobre. The dried rose potpourri scent smelled like my room at Temnobre, mixed with the stale sweat and saliva scent I associated with sickness.

I was not surprised to find myself sick. I sort of expected it, though I couldn't remember why. In fact, I felt relieved to find myself in one piece, and in bed.

As my awareness returned, I began to seek out a bit of magic, something I could use to scan myself. As I did, I heard a shriek, and a weight on the edge of my bed shifted. "You're alive!" Gamalielle's voice cried.

She must have launched herself onto me. I felt her weight on my chest as she hugged my shoulders.

"They said you would live but you were asleep for so long I thought it might go on forever."

"How long?" I asked. I struggled to draw breath or to even lift a hand to hug her back, but I did manage to open my eyes to see her unkempt fur and tearstained face.

"It's been a day and a night and most of this morning. Lady Georgina said she thought if you made it through the night, you'd be fine. She did some nursing in the war apparently, and your dad knew all about the hemmy-whatsit-fevering. Between the two of them they got your immune system to calm the frils down while Turus and I shooed any extra magic out of the room."

I remembered now. The density of magic in the tree, so thick that after a while it felt like trying to breathe water. I had started feeling dizzy and feverish, but the magic was packed around me so densely that it was difficult to grip with my mind. I had finally concluded, with what remained of my sanity, that if I wanted to live, I had better try to hack my way out.

So, I had finally experienced a magic-induced hemorrhagic fever. I felt strangely relieved. So many Farians survived them as children, but I had never had a problem. It was as if I had finally endured the right of passage so many of my family and neighbors had lived through.

But that was the smallest piece of what was happening now. "Nadia?" I asked.

"Yeah, Nadia is a tree," Gamalielle said, as if she didn't really believe this, but couldn't deny it. "But that's not the weirdest thing. The weirdest thing – and I know you're not going to believe it because it's not possible, but I swear it's true – the weirdest thing is Reef is a wizard."

If I had had the strength, I would have smacked my forehead. "Of course!" I exclaimed.

"Of course?! Not 'of course.' He's a Khirian!"

It may have sounded absurd to her, but for me many things were falling into place. "He had a magical something inside of him and I couldn't figure out what it was. It was the kentro of a Magic! The phage sense, the selective magical susceptibility, it all makes sense."

"Well, I'm glad it makes sense to you, because it doesn't make sense to anyone else, and Reef won't talk to anyone about it. Since we got back to the estate, he just swims and swims and sulks and trails muddy ice through the castle coming to check on you."

I felt that I was missing many pieces of the story. "Tell me everything," I said, and Gamalielle began a tale of journeying through the forest to fight flesh monsters and wrestors and concluding with Reef summoning his phage to eat the magic out of me.

At this point I gasped, and Gamalielle paused. "What?"

"No wonder Reef is so upset," I said.

"Because his Magic is as monstrous as he is?"

I did not rebuke her, but thought, yes, exactly, that's how Reef will see it. It must be horrifying to him that he should end up having special magical powers that, of all things, included a Magic that ate other magic. Now he was waiting to see if I would die. If I did, he would blame himself and carry a weight of fresh guilt.

Meanwhile Gamalielle went on, telling me that Tsakhia's maelstrom had expanded beyond the original borders of the Petrified Forest, but at least it seemed to have trapped the Purple Madness and phage fragments there. "But now Yury won't talk to me, either. He's all 'this is my fault' and went to camp in the woods as close to the maelstrom as he can, but we had to drag him back because Voda sent the army and he's all, 'you've done enough' and your dad's trying to talk sense into him and get him to let us help, not that we know how, but Georgina's contacts say Voda's seized the Torgo embassy and taken Tsakhia's technology and he's working on adapting his phage-shredding perimeter to set off a magical disassembler that will take apart Tsakhia's maelstrom—"

"But that will kill him!" I exclaimed, managing to sit up a little in my alarm. "And it could destroy the tree, too!"

"I don't think Voda cares at this point, he just doesn't want his entire northern forest enveloped in a raging frils-frost storm."

"I have to talk to him," I said, throwing off my quilt before remembering that I couldn't hope to get out of bed on my own. Not yet.

"Well, we'll try to get him in here, but like I said, he seems to view us as enemies of the peace."

"Turus told me he sensed your mind!" Archavie had appeared in my doorway, bright and cheerful as ever. He held a tray with legs. The bowls and basket on top produced a cloud of steam.

"Oh, are the garlic rolls done?" Gamalielle squealed, bouncing up into the air and zipping over to Archavie.

"And the chocolate brioche is proving."

Gamalielle groaned in anticipation. "Archavie and I made a pact to bake and eat as much bread as we could until things are resolved. It gives us something to do and makes our brains happy."

"It has truly been a delight, and I am happy to say that we have seafood chowder, a traditional Markish comfort food, to accompany our rolls."

"I've never been so happy to know foreigners," Gamalielle commented, as she plucked a roll from the basket and continued to float through the air, tearing open the shiny brown shell of the bread and sinking her teeth into the steaming insides.

Meanwhile, Archavie set the tray down across my lap before taking one of the chowder bowls in his hands.

"This isn't the time for bread and chowder," I stammered, but the smell of garlic and clams made my mouth water.

"This is exactly the time for bread and chowder," the wizard said. "You need to recover your strength." He lifted an eyebrow at me. "You're wondering why I'm so happy? We've accomplished our mission. We figured out what was going wrong with Molvan magic, and since we've defeated Svevolod and his minions, we've essentially solved the problem. In addition, Reef attacked the wrestor that was holding on to Turus, so I've got most of him back now. The worst thing that can happen now is that Voda shreds Tsakhia and the magic tree, but even then Molva will be in a better state than it was before. And I don't think Voda will have us killed. That would be too much of an international kerfuffle. So, we're safe, and we're successful."

"Tsakhia isn't safe," I said, "and Reef..." How would his being a wizard affect his social standing with the other Khirians? I could see it going either way.

"I know you'll do the best you can to help them," Archavie said, "as will I, of course, but right now you need to take care of yourself. Now, do you have the strength to hold a spoon, or should I feed this chowder to you?"

"If anyone is going to feed Kaeda chowder it's going to be me," Gamalielle said through a mouthful of bread.

I fed myself, at times tasting the thick richness of the cream and clams and lobster, and at times tasting nothing when the depth of Tsakhia's grief or the tangle of Reef's confusion rose in my mind again. At times I remembered Nadia, her arms around me in those final moments, and felt my throat too tight to eat anything.

By the time my father and Lady Georgina came to check on me, I was feeling much stronger, and trying to persuade Archavie and Gamalielle that I wanted to get out of bed and get dressed.

My father rushed in and took my arm as I rose to my feet. He said nothing, but I could see the relief in his eyes. Georgina meanwhile came and checked my vital signs. "You've pulled through," she said with a smile.

I could have told her that, but it was reassuring to have a second opinion. "I need to talk to Voda," I said.

My father looked at Georgina who looked back at him, and then at me. "Ordinarily I would say no, you need to rest, and I am sure you would say the same to your patients, but" she added, as she saw me about to object, "you may be the only one who can dissuade the dov from his course of action. Lysander has tried, Archavie tried."

"Yes, the only reason I'm not in jail is that Voda knows I'm best friends with the most influential merchant in Qawah," the wizard paused and explained. "Turus and I started to mess with their heads, and frankly I think we would have been successful if the dov hadn't had a magical shock built into his mind protection. I have, however, been officially exiled from Molva. Not that I especially care." He sighed. "I'm up for trying to get the dov's mind again, though. A more forceful approach, and then a progression from one guard to the next and I think we could—"

Georgina cut him off, "I would rather do this properly if we can."

"Suit yourself. I think we could probably take the dov out," Archavie said.

"Set up our own government," Gamalielle added.

"You want to be in charge?" Archavie asked.

"Frils, yeah," the cat said. "Yury can be my king."

While Georgina watched with increasing alarm as the two bantered, my father said to me, "Before we speak to Voda again, we should have a plan."

"I have a plan," I said. "It would break healer-patient confidentiality to explain it, but I am confident that I can end the maelstrom."

"If you could tell us," my father said, "perhaps we could move forward."

I shook my head. "What I do will change Tsakhia's life. I want to speak to him first, which means I have to persuade Voda to allow me into the maelstrom."

"We have decided that a coup is definitely the way to go," Archavie said lightly. "Gamalielle has always wanted to rule her own country."

"Absolute dream come true," Gamalielle agreed. "Of course, I'll have to cull the more irritating peasants."

"Oh dear, I don't think I can support that."

And off they went again while my father said, "And the Purple Madness?"

"What about it?"

"When we left the tree, it had been swept into Tsakhia's magic storm, and now it seems to be creeping toward the tree again. Even if you end the maelstrom, we will still have the Purple Madness to contend with." He paused, and I could tell by the way his lips pressed together that he was hesitant to say whatever came next. "I think we should consider Reef—"

"No," I said.

"It may be the only way to end the threat."

"She was captured and tortured; we can't simply condemn her to death!"

"But if we let her go free—"

"We have no idea what she might do."

"During the recent battle she tried to incite the Khirians to attack the tree."

"She wanted the tree because it holds her kentro!" But this made me pause. The kentro had not seemed eager to reunite with the rest of herself. In fact, the forest, the tree, had protected the kentro from the purple aberration. Even if the Purple Madness and the goddess had once been the same person, were they any longer? And how could I possibly know?

While I considered this my father said, "We need to at least consider the abilities of Reef's Magic. If it can consume the Purple Madness--"

"We can't ask him to do that."

"The tree is making fresh magic but the fragments of the Purple Madness are absorbing it. If we want to restore magical health to Molva, we may need to remove her from the situation. Even if she is shredded, she will re-form. Our limited surveillance suggests that she has already gathered most pieces of the shredded phages caught in the maelstrom. She's bigger than ever."

"I need to talk to Reef," I said, but the effort of standing, and trying to wrap my mind around the complexities of our dilemma had spent the rest of my strength. My head felt foggy, my throat swollen, my eyelids heavy. I felt my knees giving out and my father, Georgina, and Archavie, all helped settle me back in my bed.

"I can't rest," I protested. "I need to help."

"If the maelstrom begins to destabilize, we'll wake you," my father said in a gentler voice. "Until then we can be sure Tsakhia is alive and the Madness is contained."

"But Reef."

"We'll tell him you're awake," Gamalielle said. "Maybe that will get him out of the lake. If he comes in here, you'll smell him. They all smell like a swamp."

Chapter Forty-Nine

REUNION

Reef

THE water sat, still and cold, the slow heartbeats of the chilled fish, the muffled hum of the hibernating turtles, gave Reef the feeling that the entire lake was slowly dying. He swam through that death, between the still surface, feeling unusually rigid as ice crept across it like lichen on a log, and the schools of resting fish, clustered in the warmer water near the bottom. So close to death on one side, so close to death on the other.

As Kaeda had been.

Archavie and Straton had shouted updates or sent Wave with messages. Reef had listened. He knew that Kaeda had not died. He knew that he had somehow saved her life. But it felt wrong. He knew that his Magic had consumed the magic inside of her. That couldn't be okay. Could it?

He didn't know what to do but keep swimming and telling the Magic, *his* Magic, to stay within the boundaries of the lake. It swirled and fed, consuming the unmagic that filled the area. Reef saw it. Or didn't exactly see it. It was like fin sense, but not exactly the same, the awareness of the magic around him, most of it deep and dark and cold like the open ocean, occasionally a little sparkling and bright. No matter how much his Magic ate, more poured in. The Magic ate that too. Now that it had started eating, nothing seemed to fill its endless hunger.

Hunger, that is what he would name it.

Reef couldn't say how long it had been when Hunger finally stilled, satiated, or perhaps merely fatigued. He felt it rest, heavy and contented, as it settled down to digest the magic it had consumed.

Did that mean he also could rest? While Kaeda had hovered between life and death Reef had slept only briefly, draped across the dormant fountain that rose in the center of the lake. Could he risk sleeping on the shore?

As he considered it, he felt a tremor in the water, a footstep, cracking the ice at the lake's shore.

Reef surfaced immediately and, looking toward the water's edge, saw Wave, white scales pearly and brilliant in the moonlight.

Many times, Wave had visited him over the last couple of days. Many times, Wave had tried to persuade Reef to come warm himself with the rest of them in Georgina's stable. Reef would not. He was afraid Hunger would break something. He was afraid the rest of the Khirians would see that he had changed somehow. He was afraid that he wouldn't be able to talk to them, lead them, and keep track of the strange sensations of magic around him. He had asked Wave to keep the rest of them away, and Wave had reluctantly agreed.

Now the swimmer walked in and dove. Reef waited, and Wave shortly surfaced a few feet from him in the center of the lake.

"The Healer is awake," Wave told him.

Reef's heart swelled to bursting with relief, but then Hunger rolled sluggishly over. Wave was wearing a bubble of warmth now, created by General Straton and Gamalielle. Hunger wanted to nibble the magic that fueled it.

No! Reef thought. Not that magic.

Hunger turned grumpily away.

Wave watched Reef, and glanced around at the air, blind to what was happening. "Will you come talk to her?" he asked. "They want you to come talk to her."

Reef felt Wave's heartbeat in the water, quick. He felt the uneasy twitch of Wave's tail. Wave didn't like any of this, but so far he was keeping it to himself, trying to follow Reef's lead though Reef wasn't leading.

But Reef didn't know how to lead right now. He considered the magical radiance of the house, the enchantments like vibrating spiderwebs in so many of the items within. He could feel them from here, as he felt the delicious lure of the Khirians' magical warmth bubbles. Reef longed to stay with them, but he was afraid he would not be able to control Hunger. Hunger would break the magical warmth, and who knew what other enchantments he would find to destabilize. Reef couldn't keep track of it all, couldn't keep up with this creature, couldn't be sure he wouldn't wreck something.

Reef shook his head. "It's not safe."

Wave's tail whipped impatiently. "Then let's leave."

"Leave?"

"The shoal and I have talked. It seems like you are trapped. We will take you away."

"The Magic—"

Wave's composure snapped. "The Magic, the Magic, you speak of the Magic, but we can't see it. We only see you, swimming yourself to death in this frigid excuse for a body of water. The rest have kept their distance out of respect, but they don't understand why you have separated yourself."

Of course, they couldn't understand. They didn't know what it felt like to have a Magic attached to them, to have it always there, knowing his thoughts and speaking into them, to sense the tingle of ambient magic and the chill of unmagic. And Reef knew they never would.

"You lead them," Reef said.

Reef expected Wave to be surprised, expected him to exclaim, expected his tail to thrash in the water again. Instead, the pointswimmer said, "I thought you would say that. Always ready to give yourself up for the shoal. You think we'd be better off without you?"

"Yes," Reef argued. "I have led you here, to this cold place. Some of you have died. Now, I cannot come near you."

"Not cannot, won't," Wave growled. "We don't understand what the humans say you are, but you seem the same to us, and you haven't harmed me. As for the rest of it, you did not lead us here. We came here to find you, because we decided to, because we knew you would do the same for us. We followed you into battle because you always keep us out of a fight unless it is absolutely necessary. If some of us died, well, we've already lived longer than we would have without you."

For a few moments they silently tread water together, Reef trying to think despite his fatigue, and Wave waiting. At last, the pointswimmer spoke again. "The first time I stood by your side, do you remember? You decided to take on the old leader and his pointswimmers."

Reef remembered. There had been a stolid Molvan pond, quite a bit smaller than this one, but no less depressing. The old leader and his pointswimmers had been tossing the family of the house into the water, swimming after them and slaughtering them. There had been something in the water, some chemical or enchantment. The Khirians were all becoming unfocused and hazy. Hiding in the hedges nearby, Reef had seen his chance to kill them all and take leadership of the shoal.

Of course, it had been too much for him to take on alone. Wave had made the last kill, but he gave Reef all the credit.

"You were small," Wave reminded him, as Reef recalled the memory. "Whatever was in that puddle hit you hard. You probably would have drowned if I didn't help you out, but I thought, even then, there was something different about you. And I was right. You think after all that effort, I'm going to let you give us up?"

While Wave's tail beat a steady back and forth in the water, Reef thought. He had often thought that the way he differed from other Khirians was a hazard. He had said to Kaeda that he would do what he needed to win their respect, which he thought meant conceding to usual Khirian customs when he could. It had not occurred to him that the others might recognize his difference and view it as beneficial.

Could it be beneficial? He had saved Kaeda's life. He knew that, yet he felt only guilt. He wasn't sure how to turn that feeling around, how to be glad about the good he had done. But thinking of Straton and Archavie coming out to try to talk to him, and seeing Wave still steadily treading water while he waited for Reef's response, Reef thought that if he kept running away from them, he would be lost in guilt forever.

"We cannot leave," Reef said. "If the Purple Madness still lives then this fight belongs not only to the humans, but to us."

The water shivered with Wave's grumble of exasperation. "I should have known you would say something like that, but you are Unseen Reef, an obstacle no one expects."

"You named me well."

"So, what do you want to do?"

"I don't know. I must talk to the humans." But as Reef looked up at the castle his heart seemed to shiver and thrash. The lit windows, brilliantly golden, contrasted with the blue twilight, and Reef knew that behind one of those windows was Kaeda. He wanted more than anything to go to her, but he also feared a fresh scream, this time a scream at remembering her near death, and how impossible it seemed that he would be able to go on living without her. He wasn't ready. He didn't think he could face it.

Wave of course would feel the change in his heartbeat, and Reef couldn't guess what he thought about it, but the pointswimmer said, "It is almost dinner time. Come back to the stable with me. The others would be glad to see you."

"The Magic," Reef began.

"The Magic is barely moving. They say it eats magic?"

"Yes."

"Then perhaps it is full. Like a swollen snake. Leave it here."

Still Reef hesitated.

Wave tried again. "They say it is young, like a hatchling. I have many offspring. They also need to rest after they have eaten. Just tell it where you are going and what you expect from it and promise it a reward if it obeys you."

Reef hadn't thought of it like that, like the Magic was a hatchling. It seemed so huge. Yet considering it this way made a great deal of sense, especially as the Magic rolled again and gave what Reef could only describe as a burp, releasing a puff of sparkly warm magic above it.

Hunger, Reef thought, and he felt the Magic pay attention. I am going to go with Wave. I will be back in the morning. I expect you to stay over the lake and only eat whatever unmagic flows into the lake. Do you understand?

The Magic gave him a begrudging yes.

If you do what I ask, tomorrow I will take you into the forest to find more magic.

At this the Magic brightened, and Reef could tell that it agreed to his terms.

"It worked," Reef said.

"Hatchlings love promises," Wave said. "Just make sure to keep it. Now, ready?"

Reef followed him, retracing Wave's footsteps through the snow back to the stable. When the servant stationed at the stable opened the door, Reef heard a chorus of greetings.

"Reef!"

"Leader!"

A steaming trough in the center of the stable seemed to be full of stewed fish. What remained of Wave's section of the shoal had been sitting down around it but they rose and gathered around Reef as he came in. To Reef's surprise no one recoiled from him, instead they all had questions. Reef found himself recounting much of his adventure with the Commission, to a very willing audience who seemed determined that he eat and talk at the same time.

"And now… we can go back to the archipelago?" UrchinSting asked, as Reef's story caught up to their current time.

"Not until the Purple Madness has been defeated," Reef said, and he repeated to them what he had said to Wave. The other gathered Khirians considered this, and one by one coughed their assent.

"What do you need us to do?" Lightning asked.

"Tonight, I will speak to the humans," Reef told them. "I will find out their plan."

At this the gathered Khirians exchanged looks which settled on Wave. If Reef and Wave had been alone, Wave probably would have blurted out some blunt admonition, but in front of the shoal, Wave grumbled deferentially and said, "Their plans can wait until you get some rest."

Reef looked back out at the group, all doing their best now to not look at him, probably so he wouldn't be offended by their concern. They didn't want him to think that they thought he was weak. Why hadn't he seen it before? He was glad they felt concerned for him! He felt terrible!

Reef barked a laugh, "You are right," he said. "Their plans can wait."

They formed their sleeping circle not long after. No one wanted to stay awake in the cold darkness. For the first time in a long time, Reef slept contentedly in the center of a swirl of Khirians.

When Reef woke the stable was still dark. He lay there for a while, listening to the breaths of his shoal around him. Khirians' breaths tended to synchronize as they slept, creating a tidal rise and fall of inhalations and exhalations that called others to deeper sleep, but Reef couldn't rejoin them.

Kaeda, he thought. He needed to talk to her, but he would like to see her first, to get the swell of emotion over with. Perhaps he could go into the castle, look into her room, and just see her. The servants would understand if he said that he wanted to make sure she was alright. That was the kind of thing that the mammals would do, check on their sick or wounded. Then the initial swell of feelings would be over, and he could feel calmer when they spoke.

Carefully, he began to nudge his way through the sleeping Khirians. When he had made his way out, he met Sting, who was on guard, at the door.

"I am going to the castle. I will be back soon," he said, and he walked out into the snow.

Chapter Fifty

NIGHT

Kaeda

SOMETHING woke me in the wee hours of the morning. At first, I thought maybe it was how cold my nose felt. Then I noticed a smell in the air, something like pondwater, and I heard, barely, the swish of the door on the thick rug. I started awake just in time to see a white-scaled hand pulling the door shut.

My heart leapt. "Reef?" I whispered into the darkness.

The door and the hand froze in place, then vanished.

No, I couldn't let him go. I couldn't spend another day thinking about everything I wanted to do and couldn't. I couldn't spend another day separate from him and not knowing what he was thinking.

Lady Georgina had found a walking stick for me to use if I needed to get out of bed, a cane with a great knobby head. I gripped this now as I rolled out of bed, pulled a blanket around my shoulders, and staggered to the door.

"Don't go. Wait."

I feared I might be too late, but when I pushed the door open and braced myself in the doorframe I saw him there, a little further down the hall. He looked smaller than I remembered, or maybe simply more bent, as he stared down at my feet. The hall was dimly lit with the soft warm radiance of the night-light sconces, but a smearing of dry mud and algae dulled the shine of Reef's scales.

I wanted to run forward and throw my arms around him and tell him everything would be okay, but Reef and I hadn't had that sort of exchange so far. I didn't know what he would think about it. What if I scared him off? Besides, I wasn't sure I could walk much further, let alone run.

Suddenly I had no idea what to say. All my plans and speeches seemed to have evaporated.

"I saw your magic from my window," I stammered. "Over the lake. It's huge."

Apparently, this was not a good thing to say. Reef flinched and took a step backward, then another.

"No, wait," I said. I started forward. Not a good idea. My legs wouldn't have it, and I wasn't used to walking with a cane. I stumbled against the wall and might have ended up a heap on the carpet if Reef had not come back and caught me.

The pondwater smell wasn't so bad when Reef's arms were around me. It reminded me of swimming, and that, combined with his nearness sent a rush of happy warmth throughout my entire body. The hall suddenly seemed brighter, the carpet softer, and I didn't feel nearly as sick as I had before.

I was ready for an honest-to-goodness hug, but rather than hold me as a human might, Reef fell to his knees and shoved his nose into my stomach with so much force that it pushed me back against the wall and almost knocked the air from my lungs.

"I thought you would die," he said, in a quiet, screechy voice.

The pressure of his nose beneath my ribs made it difficult for me to respond. "I didn't," I said, trying to figure out what manner of embrace this was meant to be. I couldn't quite reach around his shoulders, so I held his face instead, as I had seen Archavie hold Rozie the indrik's face. "From what I hear, you saved my life."

"It wanted the magic. I didn't know what to do."

"What you did worked."

"It eats magic!"

"That's not your fault."

Another screech and Reef's nose pressed harder into my stomach. "I need to breathe," I said. "No, no, you can stay. Just don't push so hard."

He settled his nose a little more gently against my stomach, the top of his head leaning into my chest, and I went on. "If it is a phage like the others, it already knew how to eat other magic. You didn't teach it. I know you probably think it chose you because you're alike somehow but Magics usually choose a wizard to complement them. You've met Archavie and Turus; are they at all alike?"

"No," Reef admitted.

"No," Kaeda agreed. "They need each other, and this… weird new Magic, it needs you."

"How? I know nothing about magic."

"None of us know much about this magic, but you know what it's like for people to think of you as a monster, and you know how not to be one."

While Reef silently considered this, I considered my position. Some animals nuzzled each other. Perhaps Khirians did the same. I was hardly going to nuzzle him back. Instead, I ran my hands along either side of his neck, brushing away the traces of lake grime.

"Even if your magic isn't a monster, I can imagine it's very uncomfortable for you to be with."

"Now that it is awake, it is always hungry," Reef said, seeming less upset than before. "Wave has told me to think of it like a hatchling. Do you think that is right?"

"It is a young Magic, so perhaps. Has it spoken to you? Has it told you its name?"

Reef turned his head a little to glance up at me, and then turned it back down. "I have named it," he said hesitantly. "I have named it Hunger."

Tears sprang to my eyes. "You didn't name it monster," I said.

"No," Reef agreed, sounding surprised at himself.

"Hunger is just a feeling. You can feel it without feeding it. You can decide what to do."

"Yes," he said, and now he sounded truly relieved. His breath poured out in a long sigh, as two long streams of warmth against my stomach. It seemed to dissolve my strength, as if I would melt into the floor.

Perhaps it was this, or perhaps the way his posture changed as he relaxed. Whatever the reason, as I absently stroked his scales my fingertips slipped into the slight dip on the right side of his backfin.

I jerked my hand away, expecting Reef to growl at me. He didn't. My heart, which had begun to pound in fear, continued loud in my ears as Reef nudged his nose against my stomach. It felt like an invitation. But why? And what if I was wrong?

There was only one way to find out. I settled three fingertips into the seam of Reef's backfin, this time at the back of his head where the fin began. I let the insides of my fingers rest against the folded spines, then, as if nothing had happened, I continued my gentle stroking motion. The fin felt both stiff and soft beneath my fingers, and more flexible and alive than the fins that had adorned Miro's cape. I could feel Reef's heartbeat beneath the leathery skin and a warmth that didn't come through his scales.

"The winter probably makes it all worse," I whispered, just for the sake of saying something. "Khirian winters are probably nothing like this. You're used to warm days, open water, sunshine. You're probably more affected by the weather than humans are."

I felt the fin relax beneath my fingers, and then lift a little like an opening wing. I took this to mean that Reef felt safe and at ease with me, and I was glad. I could feel each spine separately now, slim flexible bones wrapped in the fin's ocean sensing skin. I set my fingertips at the base of one spine, tracing them toward its sharp pointed end. "And in the midst of all of this you've been thrown into human politics, and everyone has been talking about magical theory and then suddenly you find out you're a wizard. It must be overwhelming." I chose another spine and began to repeat the motion.

Just then a growl rumbled up from Reef's chest. He threw himself backward and I, no longer held up by his arms and nose, almost fell. "I'm sorry," I stammered. "I didn't ask."

Reef had recovered his poise almost instantly. In fact, he suddenly looked far more composed than he had yet that night. "It is fine," he said.

"Did I hurt you?"

"No."

"Are you angry?"

"No."

"Are you sure?"

"Yes."

"I didn't ask for permission."

"It is fine."

Should I ask more, I wondered, as Reef and I faced one another across the hall, and I leaned heavily against the wall. Should I ask what it all means? Or would that just make him think, no, I can't be close to this human.

I had just decided that I better ask, even if it was awkward, when Reef said, "Can I take you down to the lake in the morning?"

"Sure. Why?"

"At dawn."

"Sure but—"

"You should rest," Reef said, and he came to my side and held out an elbow as if he were providing a formal escort.

I gave the elbow a wry smile before threading my arm through his. "A little bit of Archavie rubbing off on you?"

Reef coughed yes and walked me back to my bed.

Chapter Fifty-One

DAWN

Reef

IF he had still been wearing a human body, Reef was sure that he would have been sweating. The wildfire of self-consciousness that filled him from nose to tail was almost unbearable.

He had gone to the lake to cool down and swim off the adrenaline. She hadn't understood him, had she? No, of course not. She thought that he had growled at her, and no one else had been awake to say otherwise. Not that anyone else would have understood anyway. That sound wasn't translatable into any human words Reef knew.

But you know. You've heard that sound before. You've made that sound before. Only during the summer.

His fins snapped shut and open again, trying to shake away a fresh rush of embarrassment and his tail thrashed behind him, giving him a burst of speed. Why was this happening now? Why here, away from Voda's artificial sunlight? Why at the beginning of a cold dark Molvan winter?

It was the touch of her fingers, the bright bursts of warmth on his back that seemed to spread through his entire body like… well, he had already thought it, hadn't he? Hadn't he decided what he would name her?

But it was more than that, more than just sunshine. She lit up his darkest thoughts. She warmed him inside and out.

Even if his shoal hadn't shown up, her presence might have been enough.

But what would they think, Reef asked himself, as he flipped in the water to change the direction of his figure eight. He had never had a real Khirian mate. The others would ask why, why would he choose this human over a Khirian?

He couldn't stand it. He flipped again and spiraled and twirled in the thick, chilly darkness, willing the water to wash away the tension. He was a wizard now, apparently. His shoal had accepted that, but would a female Khirian? What if he produced magical offspring? Would that be good or bad? Would a female Khirian want to risk it? Would he? Perhaps courting Kaeda would be his best chance of having a mate of any species.

But then he thought about Kaeda, soft and warm as a summer beach, and much smaller than a Khirian, and he thought of his experience of Khirian mating season, and he thought that putting Kaeda and mating season together was a terrible idea.

She might not even feel the same way, he reminded himself, and he knew Turus wouldn't venture out near Hunger to enlighten him. As much as Reef had observed and puzzled over the idea of human mating season, this year-round thing that led to lifelong commitments, he still didn't understand it.

So, he took a mental step back. He would take her out to the lake. He would tell her, if he could, how important she was to him. He would see if she comprehended it. That was all.

Accordingly, just before dawn, Reef checked in with the Khirian sentry, and then returned to Kaeda's room. She was ready, dressed, a fraying braid of curls hanging over one shoulder.

"I should get a parka."

"I have brought you one," Reef said, and he also threw one of Lady Georgina's blankets over his shoulder.

"Oh, thank you."

She held Reef's arm as they walked across the snow, now marked by many trails of footprints. There were a few benches set at a distance from the water. Reef led her toward one that he had already cleared of snow. They were just in time. A haze of magenta crept up from the east, warming the sky's deep blue. Between the earth and the sky, clouds had already begun to catch the light of the sun, their edges gleaming yellow, and the lake, where it was still liquid, reflected the clouds in turn, in wavering patches.

"So, what are we doing?" Kaeda asked as she cocooned herself in the blanket Reef had brought.

"Watch," Reef said. He nodded to the east where the forest of pines rose, sharp and black, a toothy barrier between the vibrant lake and the vibrant sky. The suggestion of a brighter light began to glow on the horizon. The gold-edged brilliance of the clouds increased as pink began to infuse the indigo of the sky. Then, all at once, the tip of the sun burst through the trees. Its light crashed upon the lake, making the slight waves flicker as if with fire and turning the crust of frost and ice into a blaze of dazzling colors.

Reef looked at Kaeda. She had shielded her eyes against the brightness. "Wow," she said. "I didn't know a sunrise could be so beautiful without an ocean."

"You asked me what I would name you," he said. "This is what I would name you. Ahfa, Dawn."

"And what does it mean?"

Reef looked back out at the lake, glittering with a rainbow's worth of color, and scoured the scene for some way to explain. "The rising of the sun changes everything. You see, even the deadwater comes to life in the dawn."

Reef counted his heartbeats, one, two, three, four, five, waiting for her to say something. Would she like it? Would she understand? He had given her a piece of himself now, hadn't he? What would she do with it?

All these things ran through Reef's mind until Kaeda said quietly, "I'm honored."

Relief flooded Reef, then astonishment as Kaeda scooted closer to him. She leaned against him. In a flash Reef remembered Yury's arm draped around Gamalielle as the two of them lounged together. Reef put his arm around Kaeda. She snuggled closer. Reef searched his memories again and saw Nadia's face disappearing into Tsakhia's hood. Reef bent down and nuzzled the top of Kaeda's head. She smelled like roses and lake water, but Reef only smelled her for a moment before she looked up, took his face in her hands, and touched her nose to his.

That was enough, wasn't it? Enough to tell him that she felt the same way?

Then Kaeda looked past him at the road that exited the woods and wound into the castle's gardens and her eyes widened. "Sweet magic," she exclaimed. "Is that the dov's carriage?"

The light of morning illuminated a string of carriages, and the crackle of their wheels on the ice told Reef the moment had passed. He walked with Kaeda as they hurried back to the castle, and left her on the step, but not before she had gripped his hand and squeezed it. He met her eyes, the deep brown sparkling like something hidden from the dawn, something only he knew, something to remind him. He squeezed her hand back, and said, "I will tell the shoal the dov has arrived."

But he didn't make it all the way back to the stable. Wave was on guard outside, pacing and when Wave noticed him, he barked an order toward the stable and then strode out to meet Reef.

"What is it?" Reef asked, when Wave reached him. He could tell that something had alarmed the pointswimmer.

"You tell me," Wave said. He continued walking and Reef turned and kept pace with him as the pointswimmer continued toward the lake. "We should make sure we are out of earshot before I tell you that I followed you to the castle last night."

"What?" Reef roared, but the anger was to cover his embarrassment.

Wave was not deterred. "You've been stranger than usual. I wanted to make sure nothing happened to you. I kept my distance, but I still heard it."

He didn't have to say what "it," was. Reef knew it must be the surprise mating call.

"When you explained your reasons for staying to help, was it true? Or do you only want to stay for her?"

"It was true," Reef said. "But to leave her, it would be difficult."

Wave rumbled. They had reached the edge of the lake, certainly out of earshot of everyone. Reef waited for his pointswimmer to say something, some harsh judgement or frank advice, but Wave was quiet for a long time. Then he said, "Is that why you never wanted to take a mate? You wanted a female human?"

"No!" Reef exclaimed, for he had certainly wanted a Khirian mate. "I only did not want offspring."

"Well, you certainly won't have them with her."

A knot of sadness twisted in Reef's gut. Wave didn't have to advise him. He knew he was doing something wrong. Or maybe not wrong but… unwise. Something that would wreck his reputation, everything he had tried to build.

He spotted a colorful figure emerging from the castle. Archavie, wearing a blue greatcoat and a fluffy red hat. He began walking towards them, likely to summon Reef to their official meeting.

"Just think about it," Wave said. "Think about what you really want, and whether this will get you there."

Chapter Fifty-Two

MAELSTROM

Kaeda

KNOWING Dov Voda, I was not surprised that he wouldn't speak a word to us until we were all arranged in Georgina's dining room, with the dov at the head of the table, Secretary Essen at his right hand, and the rest of us along either side. Yury and Gamalielle did not join us. Gamalielle had said that she was afraid Yury would try to kill the dov if he knew he was here, and I thought she was probably right. She volunteered to stay with him while the rest of us negotiated.

Reef and my father helped tuck my blankets around me, and Archavie kept giving me looks and waggling his eyebrows as if to remind me that he knew things.

I just think it's marvelous that you and Reef have finally had a defining moment, as it were.

Well stop thinking about it, I thought back. You're making me blush.

As well one should when one has nose-pressed a giant lizard.

I rolled my eyes, feeling yet warmer as I remembered Reef's arm around me and his nose against mine. But a little tiny piece of me ached and said, it would have been nice to kiss him. If he were human, or at least a creature with lips.

Lips shmips. If Turus's wizard was a lizard I'd marry her tomorrow, Archavie thought back to me. Then he paused. *Or maybe I wouldn't. You know, I might actually think about it first. I'm growing as a person!*

I congratulated Archavie, then did my best to drag my mind away from complicated romantic entanglements and focus on the meeting ahead. When we were all settled the dov, eyes blazing above dark circles of sleeplessness, fingers fiercely steepled, said, "I could shred everything in that forest right now—"

"You would kill Tsakhia," I interrupted, "and Nadia and the tree."

The dov raised a hand for silence, and his words bit the air. "I am perfectly aware, and that is why it has not happened. Much as I would like to eliminate this wreckage, I do understand that the tree is making magic."

He hadn't agreed to the value of Nadia or Tsakhia's lives, and I bristled at the omission.

"Molva needs that magic," Voda went on, and his eyes fell on me. "It is my understanding that you have a solution. Since I believed you confined to your bed by a dire illness, I have traveled here to hear it."

I ignored the sarcasm in his last sentence, and said, "Yes, I do have a solution. As I am sure you know by now, Tsakhia was in my care for a severe magical malady. I have a treatment ready which should both remedy his condition, and also end the maelstrom."

Voda waited for a moment. Then his eyes widened in impatience, and he waved a hand for me to continue.

"To say more would violate healer-patient confidentiality."

"Lives are at stake and as I am the sovereign here—"

"I don't care who you are, and lives are only at stake because *you* have endangered them with your reckless disregard for the lives of Magics and biological creatures alike." I felt myself trembling with adrenaline. The lights in the room flickered and I reminded myself that I needed to stay calm. If this kept happening to me, I would need to start wearing a magical restraint as Tsakhia often did. I took a deep breath and concluded more evenly. "Nadia's goddess is gone because of you. Tsakhia has suffered because of you."

The dov did not answer fury with fury, but seemed to retreat, his voice more and more cold and measured. "I could tell you of the state of Molva before I took the throne. Of the chaos and madness and death. I could tell you of the promises of fearies, and the prices they exact. You would not understand. For the moment I find myself free of them, and in that moment I must act, for they may return and if they do I must be ready. I must prepare my land. I would prefer to do it with the magic of the tree, but if not, I will at least do it without the interference of the Purple Madness."

"Then let me go in," I said. "Tsakhia and I had already discussed the treatment, so I suspect he will accept it, and if he does, it will end the Maelstrom. Then we can take whatever action is necessary to deal with the Purple Madness."

I did not tell him that I also hoped to converse with the Purple Madness and see if there was some way to bring peace between her and the rest of Molva.

"I will allow you in," Voda agreed. "It would be a relief for someone else to manage some of this nonsense. However, you will not go anywhere until you have signed the agreement that my secretary has drawn up."

Secretary Essen cleared his throat and brought out a sheaf of pages, which he passed to Georgina, who was nearest.

"A non-disclosure agreement?" she commented, as she flipped through.

"And exile," my father added, looking at Georgina with concern.

They passed the sheaf of papers to Archavie who barely glanced at it before handing it to me. "I'm already exiled," the wizard said flippantly. "As for all that's happened, I'd love to tell it over a campfire, but I'll follow the wishes of the rest of the party."

I took the contract in turn and skimmed the pages. Non-disclosure of a specified list of items, exile from Molva for the duration of our lives, medals of honor and titles and compensation appropriate for a group of heroes of the realm. Most of that I didn't care about, but to hide the truth…

"And if we refuse?" I asked.

"Then Tsakhia and the tree will be annihilated," the dov said calmly, "and I cannot guarantee your safety through the rest of the winter. As you know, Molva can be a dangerous place, especially once the snows fall."

I took a deep breath. "I'll sign it," I said, holding out my hand for the pen Essen had ready. "We'll go back to the Gemmic Commonwealth, we'll put this behind us, and Molva's magic will be restored."

I found the place for signatures and signed my name, then passed it to Archavie who did the same. Essen had brought an ink bottle so Reef could ink his thumb and press it to the page. Then we handed the document to my father and Georgina.

"You would be welcome in the Gemmic Commonwealth," my father said to the lady.

"Yes," I agreed. "Very welcome."

"But I know it won't be home," my father added.

Georgina looked sadly at the paper. "Perhaps it will be," she said. "And my staff?" she asked the dov.

"Depending on their knowledge of what has transpired, they may be allowed to remain, or to go with you wherever you choose to go."

Georgina sighed and nodded. She signed the paper and then handed it to my father who signed as well.

"We will have to discuss this with Gamalielle and Yury," my father said, as he handed the document back to Secretary Essen.

"Yes," the dov agreed, "but since I have healer Straton's signature I will allow her to gather her necessary equipment and meet us at the sledges. My staff will escort you to the edge of the Maelstrom at the old Vysokaya Estate."

Accordingly, I gathered what tools I thought I would need, and dressed as warmly as I could. No one wanted to be left behind, even Yury. Gamalielle's description made it sound as if he had gone completely wild, but he showed up, trudging out of the woods with Gamalielle holding his hand.

Fortunately, Voda's sleighs had room for all, even Reef, who rode beside me as we piled in. The other Khirians watched us from a distance. Dov Voda had said, in no uncertain terms, that he didn't want to bring a group of Khirians into a military encampment, and Reef's shoal seemed to have accepted this, though I saw many tails swishing in a concerned way as Reef climbed into the sleigh.

Part of me wanted to keep Reef out of it too. I didn't want Hunger to accidentally be put in a situation where it broke something or harmed someone. But I also hoped Hunger might be able to help me get through the Maelstrom. It slid along behind us now, a bizarre amalgamation of magic and unmagic. I couldn't see or sense the unmagic of course, but I could guess where it was based on the gaps in Hunger's form. The mass of the Magic filled the road and rose nearly to the treetops as it followed us, rather like a giant invisible slug.

I knew about the experience of losing someone I loved. If Tsakhia's emotions were anything like mine… I wouldn't trust any physical or magical insulation to protect me from the maelstrom. Hunger though, was alive, and large and strange. Large and strange as grief. If it could absorb the magic, perhaps it could protect me.

"How could we not see it?" I murmured as we rode. "Even if it was purely unmagic before, Tsakhia should have sensed it inside you."

Reef shrugged. "Hiding," he said. "Hiding well."

Of course, Nadia's goddess had done that too, hadn't she? Hidden a part of herself so well that we couldn't find it until she chose to reveal herself. And Hunger was her child. Perhaps it had inherited… whatever skill that was. Still, it must have been small, at least as small as the goddess's kentro, yet now it was larger than any Magic I had ever seen.

"And it speaks to you?" I asked. I spoke low, but I knew that my father, riding in the sleigh with us, was listening.

"Yes," Reef said.

"So it isn't like the other phages," I mused. It must have found some other fragment of magic, something to add to the piece of Purple Madness to allow it to become a new, complete Magic. Theoretically this would need to be a piece of Bog's counterpart, but… how and where had Hunger found that?

I thought about asking Reef to ask Hunger if it knew but decided against it. I didn't want to distract myself by puzzling through another mystery. Not until everyone was safe.

We drove along the road, now nothing but a river of white between the trees, until we came to a different portion of the streambed. Here the sleigh carried us over a stone bridge, and into a road more thickly bordered by pines. Eventually I saw crumbled stones between the trees. Not boulders, but ruins of walls.

We paused briefly as troops in the road called us to a halt, and then drove on toward a commotion. Where the trees opened up, tents filled the ground, huge, black tents, with Voda's curling waterfall motif decorating their enchanted canvas. The tents made a small village around what remained of a castle. It might have once been grand and was certainly larger than the castle at Temnobre in a rambling sort of way, but it looked a bit like a child's construction that had been shaken, stones laying here and there in heaps.

The camp was alive with soldiers, and I saw many of them carrying familiar steel-ringed stakes as they hurried out of the camp or taking report from others returning.

Special Escort Officer Usenko met us as our sleighs slid to a stop. The dov disembarked and disappeared into a tent, seeming to want nothing more to do with us, and Usenko took over.

"I will lead you to the edge of the maelstrom," he said.

We trudged through the snow. I was feeling stronger, but our meeting with the dov seemed to have exhausted me again, perhaps because of the rush of anger and ensuing adrenaline. My father supported me on one side, Reef on the other, as we walked through the camp, and into the trees. We could already see it a few yards ahead, a place where the calm forest stopped and a grey wind began. Snow, mud, droplets of blood, bits of trees, magic, unmagic, blew toward the north, the outskirts of a clockwise rotation.

"Tsakhia Rozkhov is at the center of the maelstrom," Usenko told us. "There is a calm space around him – the eye of a storm. Do you have a plan to reach him?"

"I believe Reef's Magic will be able to absorb the magical effects of the storm," I replied.

"What about the rest of it?" Usenko asked.

I looked at the chaos ahead. I hadn't quite anticipated such a large amount of physical matter in the maelstrom. I turned to Reef. "What do you think?"

Reef grumbled, and we all jumped and moved out of the way as Hunger slumped forward. It moved itself around toward the edge of the storm, and, like a child testing the water, poked a bit of itself toward the wind.

The dirt and gore splattered against it but didn't seem to bother it. It pushed in a little further and spread itself out, forming a tunnel we could walk through.

"Nice work," I said to Reef. "See, you're getting the hang of it already."

Escort Usenko's bearded jaw had dropped. "But we've attempted magical absorption shields against the maelstrom and—"

"Hunger is both magic and unmagic, I think that makes it more flexible. It also seems to be empowered by absorption, rather than worn out, as an enchantment might be over time." I didn't want to go so far as to say, "it eats the magic and is nourished by it."

While Usekno continued to gape, I turned to Gamalielle and Yury, "We don't all have to go."

But the words had barely left my mouth before Yury spoke up. "It's my sister. I'm going."

"It's my Yury," Gamalielle added, arms around the werebear's shoulders. "I'm going."

And so, at a nod from Usenko, we started into the tunnel.

It was a strange walk, watching clumps of snow wash away a patch of blood, only to have the snow replaced a moment later by a spatter of dirt mixed with leaves and fur. Eventually the walls seemed to solidify, and though we at times heard the howl of the wind, and at times heard a high-pitched ringing in our ears, the tunnel became more regular, dark except for a golden light ahead.

When Hunger's tunnel spilled into the eye of the storm, I saw that most of the wreckage of the temple had been cleared away. The tree of Nadia looked more tree-like than ever without the broken boards around it, since now we could see the roots splayed out and anchoring the tree into the earth, and all still glowing between the whorls of patterns in the bark.

Sitting on the roots, and reaching up the trunk, was Tsakhia. He had transformed, of course. The bird half of his face was more beak-like. The other half had longer sharper teeth. He had one long pointed ear and two very long arms, which would have been wings except that they lacked webbing between the fingers. These long, spindly fingers reached around the tree. One hand covered the fissure I had come out of, which seemed to have nearly healed.

All that I had expected. What I had not anticipated was the layer of shimmery purple goo draped over Tsakhia like a blanket.

"Oh, frils I think I'm gonna hurl," Gamalielle muttered.

"Save it for later and we can hurl together," Yury replied.

"Deal."

The covering of the Purple Madness slithered and swept like a blobby violet fire across Tsakhia's body, but she made no move to attack us as I inched forward.

"Tsakhia?" I called softly, "Tsakhia?" Tsakhia's eyes remained shut, his cheek pressed against the bark of the tree.

"Can't you just stick him with your remedy?" Gamalielle asked.

"Not with the Purple Madness there," my father said.

I nodded my agreement. "It could contaminate the magic. I would have to find a clear spot and even then, I would rather have his consent."

"This might be an ask questions later kind of scenario," Gamalielle said.

I wasn't quite ready to resort to that. I looked around and saw Tsakhia's staff laying on the ground. I picked it up.

"Are you sure it's safe?" my father asked.

"I need more information," I said. "But if the Purple Madness starts crawling toward me, pull me away."

Reef nodded and my father said, "Be careful."

I cleared the two necessary handholds, and moved forward again, looking for a place where I could slide the staff under one of Tsakhia's elongated fingers. Finally I found a dip in the contour of the tree and slid the staff under Tsakhia's almost-wing. His skin touched the handle and…

The storm was gone. I stood in a purple meadow. Purple sky. Purple grass. Purple flowers. Only the tree remained golden, lending a twilit glow to the otherwise dark landscape. At the foot of the tree sat a man, leaning against the glowing bark, his eyes shut, face decorated by the shining lines of recently fallen tears.

I knew it must be Tsakhia, and probably Tsakhia as he had been before the curse changed him, but having never seen him in fully human form, I did not recognize him. Straight black hair fell to his waist, and a smattering of freckles decorated his tan skin. As I walked forward and knelt down I took in the details of his appearance with fascination. The bump in the bridge of his nose. The slight upward curl at the edges of his lips despite his sadness. All features erased by the curse. And I felt sad. Nadia said he had looked mostly human when she met him. This was the Tsakhia Nadia had fallen in love with. And she would never see him again.

"Tsakhia," I said gently.

He did not stir.

"Tsakhia, we need to end the maelstrom. If you and I can't do it, Voda will, and it will kill you."

Only his face twitched, the hint of a grimace.

"It will likely destroy the tree as well."

The shadows around us seemed to expand and tighten as if a giant glowing heart had pulsed at the edges of the light. The meadow no longer appeared twilit. Now it seemed to be night, except for the patch of light where we stood. Finally, the man beside the tree whispered, "It is all that keeps her at bay."

"I don't understand."

"I know I can do this. Detach from reality through intense magic working. You would call it a—"

"A revma state, yes."

Tsakhia nodded, but still did not open his eyes as he went on in a flat, whispery tone. "There was no one here, and she began to land on me. I can only wrest when I am calm, but I was not. I knew I could come here, escape from her. She wants to control my mind. She hopes she can use me to break the tree, because of the bond Nadia and I share. I will not let her, if it means I dream the storm forever."

It was noble, and reasonable in the circumstances in which he had found himself, but now impossible.

"Voda has taken your magic-shredding technology," I told him. "He's making a perimeter around your storm."

The darkness pulsed inward again and Tsakhia's eyes flashed open. *They* were not human. Two red, brittle star irises blazed at me. "I will make the storm bigger."

"No," I interrupted. "The bigger it gets the more afraid people will be, and the more they will try to destroy it. If you want to save Nadia, we need to end the maelstrom."

"I can't. Do you know what waits out there?" He looked out toward the darkness around us. "Sadness so big it erases everything else. Pain so overwhelming I can't think. Here I feel little. There… I have never felt so much pain without Nadia at my side. I am afraid of what might happen."

He said it all without emotion, but I felt a sting in my heart. I knew how he felt, to be afraid of being overwhelmed by pain.

"I don't think it will be worse than what's happening now," I told him, though I didn't quite believe it. "The physical pain at least I can help with. I've brought the therapeutic ursinthropy with me. I'm not sure exactly what shape it will put you in, but transformations associated with ursinthropy are not usually painful, and the enchantment should enhance your body's ability to heal."

"And I will never be able to work magic again."

I looked around at the purple meadow, the glowing tree. "You won't be able to retreat to a magic-work-induced revma state, no."

Tsakhia took this in, looking out at the darkness. "I understand," I stammered. "A little anyway. I recently learned that I used to have IMWEES episodes when I was a child. My father used magic to calm me. Now… I automatically shy away from the heights of emotion. This is the space I prefer to inhabit." I gestured to the glowing bubble where we found ourselves.

Tsakhia gave me a questioning look, as if he doubted I could comprehend the depths of his pain.

"I held my little brother as he died," I said. "Magic-induced hemorrhagic fever. Blood everywhere. Nothing I could do." As I said it, I felt nothing, nothing but the dull sadness of the memory of the event, and my voice was as flat as his.

"Then you understand," he said. "That I can't leave. I can't go out there."

"Not by yourself," I said, and I held out my hand.

I didn't have a distinct plan, and I certainly hadn't considered this ahead of time, but I had an idea. "It occurs to me that it might be difficult for my grief-induced magic and your grief-induced magic to coexist. The resulting magical interference might cause the maelstrom to collapse."

Tsakhia considered this, frowning. "Yes," he said. "It might. But the Purple Madness."

"The whole Commission is here," I said, and in spite of myself, I thought of Hunger. I hoped it wouldn't come to that. "We'll figure something out. You don't have to die."

Tsakhia hesitated a moment longer, then he reached out his hand, skinny, cool, and completely human shaped. I gripped it tightly and remembered my little brother, his round face, his brown curly hair, his brilliant smile. Then I visited the memory. I remembered the frightened pitch of his voice when he told me his stomach hurt. A moment later, he was throwing up blood. It was everywhere. The blur of activity and voices that followed said and did many things but achieved nothing.

"There's nothing we can do."

"No!" My voice, a scream. I grabbed Gil's too-hot, blood-damp body and wouldn't let him go. I felt my father's arms around me, around both of us, as the life left Gil's body and my grief strained toward a peak.

This time, I reached it. Like Tsakhia had said, it was sadness so big it erased everything, pain so overwhelming I couldn't think. It was a storm.

I clung to Tsakhia's hand and wept. I was hardly aware of him putting his other hand on mine, but then I felt the shaking of the ground beneath us, I saw the shadows swelling like flames. With a cry Tsakhia bent down, both of us crouched on the purple ground, as the darkness rushed in.

Chapter Fifty-Three

HUNGER

Reef

REEF didn't know what Kaeda was doing, but he remembered connecting with Archavie's mind through the staff and his tail swept the ground with worry. He watched the blobby miasma of the Purple Madness swarming across Tsakhia, prepared to tear Kaeda away if it began to reach towards her, but moments passed, and nothing happened.

Then a sound came from Kaeda, a shuddery gasp. The eyelashes of her closed eyes shone with tears.

"What does it mean?" Gamalielle yelped. She, Yury, Straton, and Reef all stood poised around the healer, and Reef, though Reef knew from Kaeda's analysis that Khirian bones were very strong, he still felt as if the tension across his body might break him.

Meanwhile, the still air of the storm's eye grew even more calm. Reef heard a splatter, then another, and another, then a crush of sound, the thickness of a muddy waterfall, as blood and gore rained down. The maelstrom had begun to collapse.

Then Kaeda and Tsakhia's eyes flew open at the same time.

"The syringe!" Kaeda shouted, while Tsakhia silently mouthed, you are mine. You. Are. Mine.

The Purple Madness shrieked aloud, so shrilly that Gamalielle and Yury bent and covered their ears. As Tsakhia reached toward Kaeda with a wing-like arm the Purple Madness seemed to be blown back from him, as by a wind. She still clung to his back, but his head and left arm were free.

"Here," the general put the syringe in Kaeda's hand and Kaeda gripped Tsakhia's long, angular limb, pushed up what remained of his sleeve, and plunged the needle through his grey skin.

Immediately, the magician began to transform. The weird half-beak began to shrink back into this face and the porcupine quills fell from his back. As far as Reef understood, that was what was supposed to happen. But as the magician changed, the Purple Madness swelled up, tall as the tree, like a great purple wave about to crash.

"Listen!" Kaeda spoke hurriedly, while Straton dragged Tsakhia away from the purple wave. "We want to help you! We know what has happened to you, and we want to remedy what we can."

Remedy! The voice of the Purple Madness rang out in Reef's mind and struck him with terror. Suddenly everything looked purple. We must leave, he thought, we must run, but he saw Kaeda standing as determined before.

You! You claim to be a healer of wounds and righter of wrongs, yet you will keep me from claiming the core of my being!

"No!" Kaeda said, and Reef seemed to see her words, golden in the purpleness. "I want you to be whole again, but I can't let you destroy Molva. If you want our help, you will have to work with us."

With you! Pawns of Voda! Thieves! Grave-robbers and cradle-robbers!

The wave continued to swell. Reef knew how waves worked. In the ocean. This wasn't water, but still, he saw the motion of the visible magic, and how it was swirling up, drawing bits of dirt and grass and stone into itself. It would become a plunging breaker, he thought, curling with crushing force down onto Kaeda.

Time seemed to slow. Kaeda might have made another appeal, but Reef doubted it would make any difference. He scanned the clearing, seeing Straton drawing his sword with one hand and gathering magic with another, seeing Gamalielle likewise drawing what magic she could from the radiant tree, and Yury taking over the responsibility of hauling the now unconscious Tsakhia away. Everyone but Kaeda seemed to understand that that wave was about to break, but Reef doubted that any of them would be able to stop it.

Then he felt Hunger at the edge of his mind. The Magic was watching the frozen moment, paying attention to Reef's attention, and taking in Reef's thoughts. As it looked at Kaeda, who seemed oblivious to the danger, it felt less afraid. In fact, for the first time it didn't feel afraid at all.

Then the frozen moment ended. The Purple Madness gave a psychic shriek of rage and crashed so quickly that Reef and Straton barely began their desperate lunges toward Kaeda before a red swell rose up from the bloody ground and intercepted the purple wave. Hunger had eaten the dirt and blood like it had eaten everything else, and its brown-red bulk caught the purple shimmer and grappled with it, while Kaeda staggered back and they all gathered, watching with wide eyes.

"What is it doing?" Kaeda asked.

"I don't know," Reef said. "I didn't ask it to do anything."

For a few moments they wrestled, Hunger drawing in more and more of itself, casting one long, red limb after another across the thrashing bulk of the Purple Madness, drawing in more and more of the melted maelstrom gore and catching little bits of the Purple Madness when they flew off. Eventually the shadowy purple was completely enclosed, though still barely visible, in the massive hill of Hunger.

Did this mean Hunger had won? The battle, if it was a battle, seemed to have ended, yet Reef felt uneasy. More than uneasy. Unwell.

"Hunger feels sick," he said, then he fell to his hands and knees as Hunger's wave of nausea struck him.

"Reef!"

Reef felt Kaeda's hand on his shoulder but saw in his mind the memory of the Purple Madness poised over her. Don't let it out, he told Hunger. Take it away from here. Take it far, far away, where it won't hurt anyone.

He felt the Magic assent and begin to drag itself away, and the Purple Madness with it.

"Where is it going?" Yury asked.

"I don't know," Reef answered. "But it will take the Purple Madness far away. Tell the dov not to stop it."

"I'll tell them," Gamalielle said, and she zipped away. The rest of them watched as Hunger lurched and slumped its way across the tree's clearing and out into the ruined remains of the bloody forest.

"Thank you," Kaeda called, as they watched it go.

Hunger was too focused on not vomiting up the Purple Madness to respond. In fact, Reef felt it less and less as it slipped away, and he felt a tightness in his chest as he rose to his feet and watched. He had constantly pushed Hunger down, and when he finally had to acknowledge its existence, he hadn't wanted it.

And yet Hunger had leapt in and protected Kaeda, without Reef even asking it to.

Guilt and confusion bubbled together in Reef's stomach. How far would the Magic go? Would it come back? Should he follow?

He heard Hunger's voice one last time. *No, too dangerous. Not now.* A pause and then. *Goodbye.*

Chapter Fifty-Four

REPAIR

Kaeda

WE stood and watched until the red hill of Hunger was barely visible between the scraggly skeletons of trees. I held Reef's hand and my heart ached. I felt that I had failed, failed to reunite the Madness with her core, failed to protect Reef from his Magic from consuming another sentient Magic. Did Reef's heart ache as well? I couldn't read his face, and his expression became stonier still when we heard footsteps coming through the trees.

"You did it!" Usenko exclaimed.

"Reef did it," my father said.

"Hunger," Reef said.

"Hunger," I said. "Reef's magic." Then I saw pain flash briefly in Reef's eyes and knew that he felt something, something that hurt.

I did my best to explain what had happened, and to emphasize that Hunger must not be bothered, and then to explain it again when Voda received us in his tent. The dov looked spent, resting back in his chair as if the surprising relief of our success had finally finished him. When I finished explaining he only said, "And you believe this Magic of Reef's can contain the Madness?"

I looked at Reef, who nodded.

"Yes," I said. "And we have noticed pockets of fresh ambient magic near Hunger. I have a hypothesis that it may be able to digest unmagic and restore it to a standard magical state. It is possible that in time, the Purple Madness will be—" I didn't want to say digested. "Returned to Molva's magical atmosphere."

This seemed a sufficient explanation for the dov, who waved us wearily away.

As the rest of us turned to leave, Yury said, "I would like to return to the tree."

The dov leaned his forehead into his hand, rubbing his brow.

"It is all that remains of my sister," Yury went on. "If I am to be exiled from my homeland, I would like to say goodbye."

"Yes, fine," the dov nodded. "Usenko will take you."

All I wanted was to talk to Reef about what had happened and how he felt, but this was impossible on the sleigh ride back. I spent most of the time making sure Tsakhia was stable. I had fully expected him to experience Mageia-Ergasia Kourasi, that is, magician's fatigue, after such intense magic working, and was not surprised that he had not regained consciousness.

The therapeutic enchantment had shaped him into an interesting fusion of human and the pictures of fearies that I had seen in Georgina's book. He had the pointed ears, the horns curving back along his skull, and long, angular arms. His thumb and first two fingers were almost human, merely extra-long, but his last two fingers, plus one extra, had grown long enough to look like the structure of a wing. These wing-shaped fingers had no webbing between them, however, and his eyes were not as large, nor his features as sharp as the illustrations of fearies would suggest. Whether his vital signs would have been healthy for a fearie, I couldn't say, but they definitely did not match those of a healthy human. His heart beat regularly, but slowly, and his temperature remained low. I had hoped that the ursinthropy would return him to a more familiar metabolic baseline, but oh well. At least he was breathing.

When I had a spare shred of attention, Gamalielle filled my ear either with raptures about the epic showdown at the tree, or about what she should do to support Yury, who had insisted she return to the castle without him.

"He wants to be alone. Is that okay? Should I let him?"

"Yes," I said, glancing at Reef and my father, who both glared silently out at the snow, each likely deep in thought. "But keep checking in. He'll talk when he's ready."

When we exited the forest near Temnobre we found ourselves driving into a shower of rainbows refracted off of towering sculptures of ice.

"Is that you, Kaeda?" Gamalielle asked, shielding her eyes as she peered at one of the sculptures.

It was me, depicted in ice, standing boldly with a glittering syringe in my hand.

"And there's me!" Gamalielle squealed, "and Yury!"

It appeared someone had bordered the road with ice effigies of all of us, all looking quite heroic. And of course, it was no mystery who. Archavie's herd of reindeer milled about the castle, and the wizard himself came running down the castle steps and met us in the circular drive. Behind him, Georgina picked up her skirts and dashed through the snow, clearly on the verge of tears as she ran into my father's arms.

"What a show, Archie," Gamalielle said, beaming as she leapt out of the sleigh.

"Oh, that's the least of it," the wizard replied, mirroring her delight. "The duchess and I thought you deserved a proper celebration, so once you had everything in hand Turus and I decided to stay at the castle and craft each of your faces in bread."

Gamalielle's screech of joy made me jump."How did you know I've always wanted a bread mask of myself?"

"I just knew," Archavie said. "And there's also a pond of pudding in which you can fish for sweet dumplings."

"You're saying I could take a bath in pudding, Archie? For real?"

"You should probably ask everyone else first," Archavie said, and then watched benignly as Gamalielle ran past him into the castle. "I can always make a second pudding pond," he mused. "Georgina's cook gave Turus permission to read her mind, and it turns out he doesn't mind cooking when he's bored."

I had given directions to Georgina's staff about moving and settling Tsakhia, and now I stepped forward, and accepted a hug from Archavie. It was brief, and bright, a rush of psychic warmth and a smile as the wizard stepped back thinking, *I'd hold onto you quite a bit longer, but then Reef might challenge me to single combat. Still, I am glad to have tangible proof that you are in one piece. Also, don't turn around, unless you want to see Georgina and your father snogging.*

Snogging?

Kissing.

I don't mind, I thought, but I didn't turn around anyway. I had spotted the Khirians jogging over from the stable. Reef strode over to meet them and was soon surrounded by a chorus of growls and grunts and coughs and tail swishes that I assumed constituted a gruff, Khirian congratulations.

I would like to be snogging him, I thought, but I didn't want to feel disappointed about that now.

"No indeed," Archavie said. "Now is a time for feasting. Eclairs! Wellingtons! Biscuits hanging from the ceiling! We have channeled our affection and desperation and joy into baked goods! Please enjoy the edible emotions!"

The ballroom had become a banquet hall large enough to hold two dozen Khirians, and there were indeed cookies hanging down from the ceiling decorated with icing and sugar and bits of gold leaf. Eventually Gamalielle drank too much to recount our harrowing battles any longer. Eventually the Khirians consumed most of the fish soup, and the rest of us most of the meat pies and pastries. Eventually only the pond of pudding and the shiny brown bread faces and a few dangling biscuits remained. Gamalielle excused herself to nap, the Khirians retired to the stable, and we all agreed to leave planning for the next day.

I felt the exhaustion of recent sickness returning and went upstairs and had a bath and fell asleep in the chair by my window, watching the Khirians breaking up the ice at the edges of the lake so they could swim.

When I woke, I found that someone had tucked a pillow between my head and my shoulder and draped a blanket over me. I smelled the familiar smell of pondwater and looked down to see Reef asleep on the rug at my feet.

"Reef," I said.

He blinked and stirred.

"I meant to say goodnight," I went on, "but I must have been more tired than I thought."

Reef stopped me from getting up, and instead moved closer and put his head on my lap. "You have not been well," he said.

I rested my hand on his head and looked out at the lake where the floating pieces of ice looked like scattered fragments of blue glass in the moonlight.

After some time, Reef said, "Do you think it will come back?"

"Hunger?"

"Yes."

"Well, Magic cannot be truly destroyed, and a Magic usually bonds with a wizard for the course of that wizard's life, so I think, probably yes."

Reef rumbled, and I thought it was probably a positive sound. Eventually he spoke again. "When we leave Molva, I will need to return to the Khirian archipelago. I will need to report to the navarch. But I will find a way to come back."

I had not considered this. Of course, eventually the Commission's task would come to an end, and of course Reef had responsibilities at home.

I nearly suggested that I go with him, but of course that was a reckless idea. Instead, I said slowly, "You know, I've heard it's very difficult to travel in Molva during the winter. Banishment or not, we may be stuck here for some time."

Reef tilted his head to look up at me and the ridges above and below his eyes lifted back and up in a smile.

How long we sat there I couldn't estimate. It might have been minutes, it might have been hours, but I was drifting off to sleep again when a mild tremor shook the castle.

Reef leapt to his feet and offered me a hand as I also rose to peer out the window at the estate. I didn't see anything, and at first, I didn't feel anything either. Then it reached me, a subtle wash of magic. Not forceful or overwhelming, but mild, like the outer edge of a ripple.

I turned to Reef, "Do you feel that?"

Reef shook his head.

"It was like… a waft of magic. I wonder if Hunger released it."

"It has done that before. Like a burp."

"Yes," I said, and my heart even lighter. "I think Hunger and Molva will both be just fine."

Chapter Fifty-Five

THE LONG-AWAITED BALL

Kaeda

"OKAY, go ahead and step out the door."

My patient glanced again at her husband, who held her hand. When he nodded back, she did as I asked and stepped forward into the courtyard of the Vodastad City Hospital where the gently falling snow softened the hard lines of the severe architecture. I saw the terror in the tightness of her face, and caution in her shallow breaths. Then her eyes widened in surprise. She breathed deeper. She smiled. Her husband smiled. They embraced, laughing together as she safely breathed the winter air for the first time in years.

I couldn't help smiling too as I stepped forward, sweeping magic across her lungs to examine them. "No ice crystals. I'll want to test the efficacy in our rain chamber as well, but if all goes well, you'll be free to go home and enjoy sledding, ice skating, all that fun winter stuff."

"Thank you!" the woman said. "Thank you so much, healer."

I returned to my section of Vodastad's medical research laboratory to file yet another complete remission into the astoundingly successful clinical trial of my ursinthropy-based immune system therapy. For now, we were calling it UrsRem, though that sounded a bit clunky to me. Of course, the treatment had a high cost: permanent loss of magic-working abilities. But for some patients who didn't work much magic anyway, this was a price worth paying to be able to breathe in any weather or see other stubborn magical maladies disappear.

I heard a knock on the door behind me and turned to see Archavie, all gaudy red and purple against the lab's grey. "Don't tell me you've forgotten the ball," he said.

I rolled my eyes. "The ball isn't for hours."

"Only two hours. That's barely enough time."

"It's enough time to change another life."

"Well, change my life by coming back with me. People keep asking me where you are and why you're not getting dressed yet."

"I need to check on one more patient."

The wizard groaned. "Fine, but be quick about it. I am not leaving this hospital without you."

"He's not in the hospital. You came in a carriage, right? Would you mind driving me to the falls?"

I had expected Tsakhia to be in a coma for a couple of weeks while his mind and body recovered from the intensity of magic-working he had experienced. But that was an expectation based on my experience with non-ursinthropes. Tsakhia woke up after a couple of days, suddenly overwhelmed by the contradictory experience of feeling more physically well than he ever had in his life, but more emotionally wrecked than ever.

I couldn't keep him in the hospital. He wouldn't stay. But I made sure to check up on him from time, and since we had come to the city for Voda's ball, I knew where he would be.

We drove to the edge of town and then I left Archavie behind in the carriage and walked through the snow across the rocks to the edge of the beach cliffs where a figure was waiting by the guardrail. He wore Team Maelstrom's wood-grain armor, and had his sister's legendary axe slung across his back.

"No Gamalielle?" I asked as I joined Yury at the overlook.

"She's getting ready for the ball," he murmured. "She says she'll be so shiny I won't even recognize her."

There was an ironic twist in his voice, as if he knew this should amuse him, but the depths of his grief would not allow him to feel it. He looked from the horizon down to the cliff face, treacherous with stretches of ice and pockets of snow. A wiry, long-armed figure clung to the rock, wearing all that we could convince him to wear, which was essentially a wetsuit with the arms cut off. Tsakhia said the cold didn't bother him, and after so much time separated from everything, now he wanted to feel the air, the wind, the stone.

On top of the modified wetsuit he wore a climbing harness connected to a cable, but only because I told him if he wouldn't wear one, I would keep him at the hospital for a psychological evaluation. He hadn't fallen once. With the UrsRem in his body, and with his innate talent for magic-use, he metabolized magic astonishingly well. I hadn't had a chance to test the limits of his strength, or the heightened senses I suspected he had now as well. He didn't want to be studied. Yet.

Knowing his affinity for discovery and knowledge, I thought he would come around. Right now, as far as I could tell, he just wanted to escape.

"I told him this was the last climb," Yury said, shouting the last couple of words over the edge of the cliff. "I need to get ready too. Gamalielle threatened to paint me with her glitter gels if I show up looking shabby."

"Did you convince Tsakhia to come?"

"No, he won't. I told him he has to come to the palace, and that as soon as it's over we'll sled back to the Tree one more time before leaving."

That was our route. Back to Temnobre to say a final goodbye to Georgina's home and to Molva's Tree of Magic, and then to the nearest branch of the Torgovyy Trade Corridor. The dov was eager to get rid of us and the rivers were safer for travel in the winter. The Torgo's Transport Guild would take us safely to the Gemmic Sea. There the Gemmic Council's ships would pick us up and carry us back to Gem City. After that… well, the dov had paid us off so well, money and titles to be announced at the ball, that we could go anywhere. But most of us didn't know what we would do. I know for me, being in Vodastad with the snow falling, with a ball to attend, I felt like I was in a dream. Maybe when I got back to the Gemmic Peninsula, to the sun and the palm trees, it would all feel more real.

"How are you doing?" I asked Yury.

"You mean grieving Nadia?"

"Yes."

Yury gripped the guardrail a little tighter, his huge shoulders hunched a little more and his eyes sharpened as he looked out at the sea, iron-grey beneath the heavy cloud cover. "I felt sad at first. Maybe I'll feel sad again eventually, but right now… well, she got what she wanted, didn't she? She wanted to hear the goddess's voice. She wanted to be near her. And now she is. Of course, she'd choose her goddess over us."

He sounded bitter, angry. I understood. I knew what it felt like to think someone had left me for something more important, and when it came to Nadia… well, it was true, wasn't it? She had given her life to protect the kentro of Molva's archon, knowing who she would leave behind. I didn't know if there was anything I could say to help, but I could at least be there.

Tsakhia's long, spindly fingers reached the guardrails at the edge of the cliff. He pulled himself up, all long bones and wiry magic-fueled muscles, his black hair pulled back and knotted into an ice-crusted tangle. He climbed over the fence and landed, breathing heavily, on the frozen ground and fixed his star-pupiled eyes on me with a glare, as if daring me to tell him to take care of himself.

This time I didn't say anything. He was in no danger, and I knew he was doing his best to deal with our upcoming departure from Molva. He would have to leave what was left of his wife. We wouldn't have dragged him away from the Tree at all if not for Voda's intention to posthumously honor Nadia with various medals and honors for her surviving kin. Yury would accept these, and Tsakhia would probably watch from a window. I hoped the recognition of Nadia's sacrifice would give him some small amount of closure.

Though I felt sad for Tsakhia, I also felt a well of warmth in my chest as I remembered that Reef was alive, and that he was waiting for me at the castle. I felt thankful that, despite everything, he had lived, and I would be able to see him, touch him, hold him, soon.

"It's almost time for the ball," I said, watching as Tsakhia's gaze raked the edge of the city, as if he were still expecting his wife to suddenly appear. "I've come to collect Yury. He says you're coming back to the castle."

Tsakhia shut his eyes for a long moment and then stalked past us toward the carriage. We followed at a distance and watched as he climbed up the back of the vehicle, unto the top, and curled his first two fingers around the luggage racks, and folded the others back along his sides.

Yury shrugged and shook his head. "That's fine. Sure. Let's go."

"Gargoyle on the roof again?" Archavie asked as Yury and I climbed inside.

"Always," Yury said.

"Ah well, you never know, perhaps it will become the fashion."

When we pulled into the palace's sheltered carriage drop-off a host of staff were waiting. Heads bobbed and hems sank toward the ground as we exited the carriage. Then the maids and footmen erupted into instructions.

"Healer Straton, we've been keeping a bath ready."

"Your gown is laid out in your room."

"I've prepared a selection of jewels."

"My Lord's evening attire just arrived from Shusky and Shapiro."

This last was directed at Yury, who rolled his eyes. "That's got to be a surprise from Lil' G. Can't wait to see how fabulous I look."

His voice said he was pretending to be annoyed, but really amused, but he turned before going up the stairs and his eyes followed Tsakhia who had detached himself from the coterie of servants and was heading back out into the snow.

"You think you should stay with him," I observed, pausing beside Yury at the bottom of the stairs.

"I think Nadia would want me to but… I can't live the rest of my life taking care of her husband."

I touched his shoulder. "He'll be alright for a few hours."

Yury sighed, and the three of us continued up the stairs, letting the servants follow. Meanwhile I felt Archavie's cheerfulness rising like the smell of a rose.

I'm glad we get to have an adventure that involves dressing up, not traipsing through the wilderness, the wizard thought to me. *And as far as I know, Voda has no corpses, cursed or otherwise, hidden anywhere in the palace. No explosions tonight, just music and dancing. We're allowed to feel happy about that.*

For once I did. Dancing, fancy clothes, those weren't things that usually excited me, but Reef and I had by now taken a few lessons with Georgina and my father. Once Reef explained to me about melodies being like currents in the water of music, I found it much easier, and with Reef in Khirian form, somehow it was easy to follow his movement. I couldn't wait to dance with him again. And as for the clothes, well, this time I had seen to it that there would be no drama about what I chose to wear.

Shusha had made me a Molvan-shaped ballgown, but with sand-colored taffeta swished and tucked almost like a Gemmic toga. When I reached my room, it was hanging there waiting for me. In the sandy folds I saw bits of sea glass, pearls, and shells, sewn with care, and I knew, after having two fittings with them, that the dress would fit perfectly.

"The jewels healer," a maid reminded me. She held a tray draped in black velvet displaying diamonds, emeralds, and perfect pearls.

I shook my head and walked over to my bedside table. "This," I said, picking up my knotted pearl necklace and holding it out. "I'll wear this." I had brought it with me to Shusha's studio, so I knew the tea-stained twine would match my taffeta perfectly.

The maid looked at the necklace, then at the tray of jewels, pursed her lips thoughtfully, and said, "Perhaps the plain pearl earrings, then?"

An hour and a half later I had washed away the hospital smell, sat still long enough for my hair to be twisted and pinned onto my head, and been laced into my sea-floor gown. It swished beautifully and I kept feeling it beneath my palms, surprised to be so delighted with a dress. For the finishing touch one of the attendants attached a set of clasps to my shoulders. By the end of the night, they would hold a chain and a medallion, the visual indicator of my rytsarship. Lady Georgina had been preparing me for the last couple of weeks for people to begin bowing to me, calling me Lady Straton, Honorable Hero of the Realm, and a host of other titles, at least until we got back to the Gemmic Commonwealth where no one knew what a rytsar was.

"Ready to go?" Archavie peeked in, dressed as usual, all in red and purple.

He held out his elbow as I came out into the hall. As I laced my arm through his, Gamalielle came soaring toward us, a full skirt of black feathers fluttering around her, a spray of feathers and silver snowflakes pinned in her fur.

"Wait for me," she called, and she settled beside us, lacing her hand through Archavie's other arm. "I hope the medallions aren't too gaudy," she commented. "I'm sure it's not going to go with my gown, regardless. Do you think we have to wear them all night?"

She kept up her questions, and Archavie poured out reassurance as we made our way toward the dov's grand ballroom. My father, Lady Georgina, and Yury were waiting in the anteroom, the general's medals and the duchess's diamonds glimmering in the light from the massive cascades of chandeliers overhead. The rest of the guests had already arrived, we could hear them through the closed doors.

Gamalielle drifted away from Archavie and I to hold Yury's arm instead, and the two of them rubbed noses. Yury was also dressed in black, velvet with snowflakes. Alone he might have looked ridiculous, but with Gamalielle at his side… well, they looked rather like a pair of performers about to go onstage, which was kind of what we all were.

After exchanging ballgown-distanced hugs with my father and Georgina, I glanced around. "Didn't the dov assign you a partner?" I asked Archavie.

"Ah, no, I'm going in alone," he replied. "Since Gamalielle will walk in with Yury, and you with Reef, and Turus wouldn't take kindly to any other ladies walking in with me. It's alright," he added, as I opened my mouth to object. "I like being the center of attention, and I don't mind so much now the idea of being single. Especially if I'm the only one. It makes me rather special, doesn't it?"

I had never thought about it that way, but before I could consider, Archavie lifted his eyebrows and looked over my shoulder. "Speaking of not being single…"

I spun around and my heart skipped in my chest as I saw that Reef had just turned the corner. In the chandelier light his scales looked warm and almost golden, shining like the surface of a pearl.

I thought running in a ballgown might not be the best idea, but I hurried back toward him, feeling unusually light despite the voluminous gown rustling around me. Perhaps it was the magic, surging around me at my delight. "You look nice," I said. This barely expressed a fraction of my delight at his presence, but the ambient magic did that for me, making the lights blaze brighter and the air hum.

By now, Reef was used to the occasional outburst of involuntary magic-working in my presence, so I knew that wasn't what caused him to shift uneasily. He glanced back the way he had come, then across, toward the other direction of the intersecting hallway.

"What is it?" I asked.

Reef frowned and his tail twitched.

"Did you sense magic?"

"No."

I kept checking. Reef's magic-sense ability had faded after Hunger left. I had concluded that he was like Archavie, a wizard, but not a magician.

Reef took a deep breath and rolled his shoulders, as if trying to shrug off whatever worry clung to him. "the… these."

"The epaulettes?"

"Yes. They feel strange."

"They look nice, though," I said.

I stepped beside him, and he tilted his head and seemed to really see me for the first time, and the last of his concern drifted away like clearing clouds. "You have brought the ocean with you," he said. "Like when I first saw you."

"It's where I'm from," I said.

Reef coughed a yes. "I also." He held out his elbow and we walked back to the group, who were lining up, ready to walk in.

"Who knew a lizard could be so shiny," Gamalielle remarked. Then we heard the voice of the announcer.

"Presenting General Lysander Straton of the Gemmic Commonwealth and Her Grace the Duchess of Temnobre."

The footmen pulled back the curtains leading into the ballroom. Lady Georgina took my father's arm and smiled at us one final time before, head held high, she and Straton stepped out. Applause followed.

"We're next," Gamalielle said to Yury, tugging him over.

"Yury Rozhkov of the Torgovyy Channel, and Magisoph Gamalielle Aisop of the Gemmic Commonwealth."

Archavie took up position.

"The Wizard Archavie Johnsbee of Marklund."

Archavie winked at Reef and me before stepping through the curtain. I heard the whiz and crackle of fireworks and gasps and laughs from the gathered guests.

Reef and I took a step forward. I took a deep breath and saw Reef's chest rise and fall as he did the same. I held his arm a little tighter, and just then the announcer spoke again.

"Unseen Reef of the Khirian Islands and Healer Kaeda Straton of the Island of Fari."

The curtains parted, we walked through, and stood on the top of the stairs, a sea of gowns and faces beneath us. The applause swelled, and we held one another's hands and let it wash over us.

THE END

ACKNOWLEDGEMENTS

One day my husband, Elliott, saw a post by a guy named Thomas, saying that his wife, Amanda's publishing company was at a fair and asking if anyone wanted to stop by. We weren't around, but Elliott messaged Thomas right away asking if he could send my book synopsis over for Amanda to look at and Thomas said sure. Well, that publishing company was Line by Lion and you can see what happened. Many thanks to Thomas and Amanda for being out there and being genuinely lovely people who are a joy to work with, and many thanks to Elliott for being my advocate and agent when I didn't have an agent!

I've got to say a few more thanks to Elliott because without him this book might not have any action scenes and probably wouldn't make sense. Elliott is my combat choreographer and plot partner and has patiently listened to my rambles about fictional people and their fictional problems for the eleven years of our marriage. Elliott, you're the one for me.

This book might still not be finished if not for the extraordinary efforts of my in-laws who have not only allowed me to be their writer-in-residence but have watched over my offspring while I absconded to fantasy worlds for hours on end. Sherry and Allen, thank you so, so much for taking care of the girls so I could write this book! And Victoria and Season, thank you for lettingme close my door (sometimes) and write! You're always welcome to open it if you need to.

I have also had the support of some amazing readers and writers. Thank you to Bryan, Matt, and Tim who read my finished manuscript and added their words of praise to the back cover!

And thank you to the earlier readers who read rough versions and tore them apart so could put them back together better. Thank you RaeAnne, Miki, and Moriah for all the brainstorming.

Thank you Sara, Sarah, Liana, Carolyn, and Moriah for reading. Watch out; I'm going to keep sending books your way. Special thanks to Moriah who finally gave me the inspiration I needed to shorten Out of the Gemmic Sea to a manageable length and then leant me her artistic skills and created my incredibly stunning cover! The book would not look or read the same without you!

A few more thanks, first to my sister, Grace. Thank you for leaping into fantasy worlds with me when we were little, whether it be Barbie drama or the worlds of Brian Jaques. Your creativity fed my creativity and I hope mine fed yours!

Next to my parents, Margie and Gerry, who let me fill my room with books and didn't roll their eyes when I said I wanted to be the next C.S. Lewis, J.R.R. Tolkien, or J.K. Rowling. Thank you for paying for my creative writing degree and reading the entirety of the Lord of the Rings out loud as a family!

Speaking of college, thanks are also due to the amazing professors at Wheaton College who expanded my awareness of literature and honed my writing skills. Special shout outs to Alan Jacobs, E. John Walford, David Wright, and especially Nicole Mazzarella. Pretty sure my brain grew like the grinch's heart in your classes. I also want to thank Bradley Dendulk, my boss for many years, who gave me a flexible remote job and nudged me into the world of online marketing. Those years allowed me to have the time to write this book, and that experience made my writing more engaging and concise! Thank you!

The last thanks cannot be big enough. God has been with me since before I could write, and when I didn't know what to do with myself, He said, "Just write your book and don't worry about the rest." Well, I can't say that I didn't worry, but I did write the book. Thank you for having mercyon me and giving me a word when I needed it. I give these words back to you.

Printed in the USA
CPSIA information can be obtained
at www.ICGtesting.com
LVHW011934200424
777776LV00005B/142/J

9 781948 807746